NO MAN'S SON

Simon Phelps

Cover illustration and design by Yasmin Burton-Lawl.

CONTENTS

PLACE NAMES

I have used spellings as close to the time the novel is set as far as possible to create a flavour of the times. My sources are various and spelling at the time varied from writer to writer so accuracy is impossible. Regions and Earldoms, even nations had different boundaries from today so names that are similar to modern ears do not necessarily correspond to present day mapping. Towns usually are where they were a thousand years ago.

Alresford - Allerford, Devon
Aswaldton - Penzance, Cornwall
Brandanreolice - Flat Holm Island, Cardiff
Conor's Dun - Connor's Downs, Cornwall
Belestede - Belstead, Suffolk
Bristou - Bristol
Caer Dydd - Cardiff, Wales
Canterberie - Canterbury, Kent
Cantium - Kent
Deope - River Deben, Suffolk
Dorchecestre - Dorchester, Dorset
Dyflin - Dublin, Leinster, Eire
Fleet Holm - Flat Holm Island, Cardiff
Gipeswic - Ipswich, Suffolk
Grontabricc - Cambridge, Cambridgeshire
Hamptun - Southampton, Hampshire
Lundunburh - The City of London
Lundunwic - London, west of the City
Micklegard - Istanbul, Turkey

Middletone - Milton Regis, Kent
Northwic - Norwich, Norfolk
Pentwithstart - Land's End, Cornwall
Porloc - Porlock Devon
Redehelde - Redhill, Surrey
Sandwice - Sandwich, Kent
Sencliz - Shanklin, Isle of Wight
Sudfulc - Suffolk
Sudwerca - Southwark, Surrey
Sumersaeton - approximately modern Somerset
Suthwalsham - South Walsham, Norfolk
Tanet - Isle of Thanet, Kent
Temese - River Thames
Thorney - Westminster
Waltham - Waltham Abbey, Essex
Wincestre - Winchchester, Hampshire

In 1051 disputes between Edward, King of the English, and Earl Godwin of Wessex ended in the exile of the Earl and all of his sons from their country. In the spring of 1052 they decided to return to regain their power, by force if necessary. The events following their return provide the background to this story.

SIMON PHELPS

PART 1

CHAPTER 1

I was the first to see them as I went out in the dawn, milk bowl in hand. The storm of the night before had cleared completely and the sea heaved gently, sparkling in the morning light. Two boats were drawn up high on the mud, not in our bay of the two rivers as visitors usually did, but on the Safearn side of the spit. Silhouetted black against the muddy sea it was clear they were not fishing boats or coastal traders. Those would never moor there unprotected. These were lean and sleek, with places for many oarsmen. Warships! They could only mean trouble.

Milking forgotten, my mother's commands came to mind, 'If trouble comes, set the goats free.' I pushed aside the hurdle and they rushed bleating out of their pen to scramble up and over the ruins of Caer Dydd.

I yelled 'Wake up! Get out!' while throwing stones down onto the roofs of our village to rouse the people. Looking back to the shore I could see there too few men by the boats to be their whole crew. Where were the others? I bellowed in to my Ma, my beloved twin sister Moira and the other kids. 'Something's wrong! Get out and run!' Panic surged through me and seized with a sudden sick energy I climbed up after the goats only to find them bounding back down towards me. The old Nanny followed them bleating piteously.

'She wants to be milked I thought,' then I realised she too was panicking. 'Hoy, hoy!' I shouted trying to turn her back. As she dithered, not knowing where to go, the other goats scattered and three figures appeared on the crest of the mound.

Lit up by the morning sun their size, their power, their weapons and their magnificence were striking. The central figure was that of a huge mailed man, scars running through his beard. His eyes, reflecting the rising sun through the holed metal each side of his nose-guard, gleamed savage and cruel from under his helmet. In one hand he held a long-poled axe with a wicked shining blade. At each side of him walked spearmen also wearing mail and arm rings. The man with the axe stopped and swung both arms up and forward, his hands arcing across the sky. He was signalling. He roared some command to his men. Terrified I turned to run. Below me on both sides men were running out from behind the ruins. These must be the men missing from the ships. Our village, built on the spit below the ruined Roman fort, was now cut off from escape inland. They were circling around us from behind, crouched low, spears in hand. Then they too raised a terrifying roar. All amongst the ruins and the huts on the shore I could see people running, dragging children, others were hiding, hoping the storm would pass. The circle inexorably tightened. As I scrabbled back down, the rubble was shifting and sliding from the weight of the warrior's feet, falling onto and around me. They descended slowly, unhurriedly, horribly. I rushed towards Moira, who I could see between the huts. Her dark red hair, same as mine, marked her out even amongst the chaos.

'What's happening Sar?' she gasped.

'Raiders!'

I grabbed her hand as a spear butt jabbed painfully into my back. I stumbled, confused and hurting, into a huddle together with the other villagers. Scared for their lives many were pleading for mercy. Not one blade had been used. We'd been herded, like sheep to slaughter, with sticks blows and fear. They laughed and joked as we, humiliated and shivering, clung together. White faces turned here and there to seek kinfolk, friends or missing children. Our Mother and our siblings were nowhere to be seen.

Meurik an elder of the village stepped forward, a whining note in his voice as he pleaded to their leader for our lives, 'Take our beasts, we'll give you all we've got if you leave us be.' His voice shook as he spoke.

'Cease your gibberish Welshman,' their leader growled in English. Then he grabbed his massive axe in both hands, whirled it around and sliced off the top of Meurik's head like some conjuring trick. But it was real. His brains spattered across our faces as his corpse slumped to the ground. There was a strange deep sigh from the crowd around me. I was disgusted and fearful but also awestruck and exalted by this lethal power. That's how I would like to be, not huddled here like some stupid beast. I felt shame as well. Sick with myself, I'd known Meurik all my life. My gentle step-father, my Da, came into mind. He'd not want that I should be a killer though I'd lapped up his tales of the old heroes far more readily than those he told of the Lord Christ. He was away at the moment, no doubt with one of his 'other' families. I was pleased, neither his Celtic faith nor his bog-oak shillelagh would have helped him here.

'You murderous scum, get gone from here.' It was my mother's voice clear and loud also speaking in English. 'Yes you! You pirate with only the courage to prey on the weak!'

The axe wielder slowly turned to face her, his whole body emanating malevolence. 'You bitch, you talk down to me. I am the Shipmaster Eardwulf the Fox and nobody tells me what to do.' As he spoke he took in my mother's fierce defiance and her still handsome appearance.

He was puzzled by her clear English in this Welsh harbour and her lack of fear. He was also aroused by it. 'And I am Inga once of East Saxons and I call you scum,' she retorted standing tall like some queen from the old stories. I was shocked. I'd never seen her like this. Her anger and disgust had taken her beyond reason.

Eardwulf stalked over and grabbed her by the face, 'To me bitch, you are nothing'. She spat in his eyes as he pushed her backwards into our home and out of our sight. I moved to rush over but Moira seized my clothes and pleaded with me, 'Do nothing, stay still, stay still, they will kill you!'

Rough hands pulled us apart as the spearmen divided us into groups. The older girls and younger women in one while young men and boys like me were put into another. The other women and small children were pushed to one side. Before anyone knew what was happening the rest of the men were all killed. Spears thrust into their bodies in brutal and efficient murder. My world spun apart. There was no coming back from this. My gaze flew to Moira and the other girls who were clutching each other and screaming. Then, to the corpses of men I knew well, to the grim faces of the surrounding killers, to the hut into which my mother had disappeared.

Suddenly there was a roar, 'The fucking bitch cut me!'

Eardwulf came out of the house dragging my mother by her hair. His face was bleeding as he pulled her to her knees. As her hands went up to her head he smashed it into the doorpost, three or four times. There was a sickening crunch. I pushed past the distracted guards and threw myself on my mother's body while Eardwulf stared, amazed, at his blood-spattered hand while the other clutched his bleeding face. I turned my mother's head towards me but there was no face to recognise just a bloody mess. I clung to her in a way I'd never have been allowed while she still breathed. Before the tears could spill from my eyes boots thudded into my ribs and stomach. I curled up in shock, winded, writhing on the ground my arms flailing into my mother's body and clothes. My left hand closed on something familiar. 'Our knife, the family knife,' I pulled it against my body as hands grabbed my feet, dragging me back and throwing me into the huddled group of youths, winded and stunned.

I lay curled in misery, sobbing to myself, only vaguely aware as our livestock were slaughtered and our huts searched for any meagre supplies of food and drink they might offer. I stroked the knife, memories flooding through me. This had been the only real knife we had, slowly thinning over the years as we had used it for everything from skinning goats, cutting hides for rope or gutting the fish I could sometimes beg from the fishermen. In my mind I could see my mother's hand as she sharpened the knife against an old stone, an act so regular, so commonplace that I'd never really seen it and now never would again. I hugged it against me, its foot-long length narrow and sharp.

From outside the ring of guards we could hear screams and see groups of men wrestling women to the floor. Their pleading ignored as they were repeatedly raped. I realised we were being kept for another purpose, slavery, the fate my mother had escaped. Large fires were lit, made from the remnants of our homes. Our beasts were quickly dismembered and set to roast. Then they set about feasting, relaxing, eating our food and drinking our ale. They were laughing now secure that we were completely subdued, leaderless and cowed.

A voice shouted from the ruins above, 'Sir Earl Harold's ships are approaching the shore'.

'Not really an Earl at the moment, is he? No better than a rebel now. If he wasn't so rich he'd be nothing, but then he'd not be paying us to have our fun either eh? He's not here just yet anyway. Gives me time for a bit of fun of my own,' shouted Eardwulf to his men's evident amusement as he grabbed his crotch in his hairy blood-stained hand.

Eardwulf, now helmetless but no less fearsome, strode over to the group of younger women and girls. 'Gytha gives a good price for the likes of you, pretty young things to be sold away over-seas.' The girls cowered whimpering as they had sobbed themselves dry. 'She prefers them unmarked but I could use something younger after that sour bitch.' He half crouched, hands on his knees as he leered into their terrified faces. He reached out, 'Yes, you with the red hair.' I heard his words. That could only mean Moira. I looked up to see him starting to pull against her resistance. Without his helmet I could see a clear triangle of skin behind his beard and below his ear as he leant forward. It seemed to fill my whole vision and I found myself moving faster than I had ever moved before. As I lunged with my whole body, knife extended, across the open space, the world seemed to slow. Startled faces turned towards me and arms reached out as the knife point sunk into the pale triangle. I was in a pure blind rage. My left arm swept around his neck. My head butted into his teeth cutting my scalp as he reared back. He seemed not to know whether he was pulling me off or the knife out. In that moment of hesitation I tugged it out and hot blood spurted across the side of my face. My legs wrapped around him and we crashed to the floor. I stabbed again wildly as hands grabbed at me. As I was pulled back violently to my feet I could see Eardwulf choking his last out on the floor, blood pulsing from his neck and spraying, frothy, from his mouth.

'Got you, you bastard!' I screamed at him, beside myself now and beyond caring, 'Kill my mother, you fucker, I've fucking shown you now.' I was practically foaming at the mouth with rage and despair, 'You're dying you fucking turd eating pig, you shit bag.' I spluttered and swore, retching and sobbing as I struggled with the men who held me. A fist smashed into the side of my head stunning me into silence, 'Oh God, what have I done,' I thought. 'They'll kill me now.'

There was a deathly hush as Eardwulf's body twitched grotesquely then stilled. No-one was prepared for this sudden change of events or for a weapon to have appeared, as if from nowhere, and now their leader was dying on the floor. One of my eyes was rapidly closing, my vision blurry, as I frantically tried to gather my senses. A boot crashed into my bollocks and I puked snotty phlegm and bile. Now tightly held I was unable to double up. Involuntarily my knees bent and as my feet came off the floor another fist punched into my throat and my arms felt wrenched from their sockets.

'Hold the little shit still. Hold him still!' I was held fast, the fight knocked out of me I slumped against my captors.

I felt a slow cutting trace the line of my jawbone, my skin tugging against a blade. Through my one good eye I could see a hand holding my knife. I found myself looking into the strangest pale blue eyes, cold and scary, in a young man's face. The face was pale, the hair so blonde as to be almost white. The knife trembled in his hand as he continued to cut along my jaw. I could feel the blood running off my chin, mingling with the slime from my mouth and nose, as it dripped onto my chest.

'That was my father!' His voice raised to a scream, 'My father!' Then it dropped almost to a whisper though clearly audible in the stunned silence that surrounded us. 'I am going to flay you alive.' The knife moved round to behind my ear tracing another warm sore line of blood. 'You are going to die very, very slowly and very, very painfully. You are going to live in Hell and you will beg me to kill you before your soul leaves.'

I pissed myself. It spurted out warm and shameful. I was already scared but now I was sick with terror, trembling before him. A warm, rank smell engulfed us as the piss combined with the sweat of my fear. His face wrinkled with disgust as he stepped back sneering at me, 'You foul little bastard.'

As he stepped back I could see now that he was more finely dressed than his companions, almost elegant. His mail gleamed and his sword and dagger were in finely decorated sheathes. Nothing like his brute of a father to look at but I could feel he was dangerous. I could feel his cruelty. I believed he meant exactly what he threatened.

'Oh Lord Jesus Christ help me now,' I prayed knowing there was no help anywhere, 'Help me die quickly, help me die.' I was crying now, sobbing, snivelling, everything had happened so fast. I was covered in blood, puke, mud and piss. I shuddered, exhausted and gave myself up for death.

'This stops now! Throw that boy down and stand back!' I fell to the ground. There was a new presence in the village. The other ships had beached. 'It is I, Harold, who commands here.'

I peered out through the slits my eyes had become. A tall, very tall, broad shouldered man with long fair hair was striding through the shallow water. He was so richly dressed he seemed to sparkle with gold buckles and jewelled rings. While Eardwulf was powerfully beastlike this man moved with a lithe, supple strength, confident in his authority.

'That little shit has just killed my father.'

'Good Christ! So he has, that's the great Eardwulf!' said Harold standing over the corpse, seemingly more amused than angry. 'You say this boy killed him – how was that?'

One of the guards spoke out nervously. 'He moved so fast Lord. I've never seen anything move so quickly. We'd searched them all but somehow he had a knife.'

'Yes, and you'll pay too as well as this scum,' screeched the man who had cut me.

'Oslaf son of Eardwulf, listen to me and listen well, I decide who lives and who dies here, not you.' Harold spoke with quiet authority, 'What are you doing here anyway?'

'What's that got to do with it? He killed my father. He must die.'

'Your father was a murderous fool, a killer of peasants, a great warrior once, maybe, but not in recent years.'

'He was your brother's friend.'

'Yes, one of Sweyn's stupid companions, like him exiled, a rebel because he has no one who would bother to speak for him.' Harold strode towards Oslaf who flinched, 'I asked you why you are here? Do you know where you are?'

'I don't understand. We're taking slaves and food.'

'This is Wales you idiot! Iestyn ap Gwrgan's homestead is only a short ride from here. We're here to teach Edward a lesson not stir up the Welsh!' retorted Harold. 'Load your captives. Do not burn the village. We don't want to alert those nasty little head hunters. We must be out on the tide or we'll be pushing the ships out over the mud.'

'But this murderer must be dealt with,' Oslaf jabbed our knife in my direction.

Harold looked at me and laughed, 'As for this great warrior tie him up well and throw him in my ship. We will decide his fate tomorrow.'

The sky spun crazily above me as I lay on the boards, my arms bound behind me. I closed my eyes to see visions of blood spurting or my mother's ruined face. I couldn't say we'd been close. She'd named me Sar, meaning pain while my twin's name, Moira, meant bitterness. Sometimes I would come in and she'd look at me and shudder. I knew I looked like the father I'd never known. The man, who had abducted her, had tired of her and had planned to sell her into slavery. He'd not told her but she'd overheard him scheming with the steersman as they sailed toward Bristou. She'd grabbed his seax, slashed at him and thrown herself over the stern to end up washed into the bay at high tide. The seax remained to prove the tale. Its blade whittled down through time to become the slender knife I'd used today.

How she'd survived those first months pregnant and unable to speak Welsh we never knew. I have the vaguest memories of an old woman my mother was devoted to who died when we were young. She was hard with us and we begged for food before we could talk. Things got better when my Da came along. He gentled her into some kind of better place and gave my sister and me the love my mother couldn't. He gave her two more children as well. Many of our village saw him as a saint. He saw himself as a priest saving our ancient heritage. He shaved high above his forehead from ear to ear, wore monk's habit and would disappear for months on end 'ministering' to his flock. 'Carrying the word of God,' so he said, but rumours of other women always followed him. His story telling attracted the people. He would bless them and they would bring food and drink to hear him speak. Behind his back some would say that he was no priest that my mother was a whore, and we children were all misbegotten English bastards. Sometimes, when he drank too much, he would forget his saintliness and remember his Irish forbears. Then he would challenge all comers to fight him as he had the blood of heroes in his veins. This didn't always end well and come the morning we would be wiping up blood and vomit but usually when he was home we ate well and had fun. He could never stay for long. He couldn't really cope with being a father. We would be left to our own devices once again, to scraping a living and to our mother's tough love.

I thought of her and grief came over me. I tried to turn to hide my face. 'Keep still boy,' came a gruff voice from above, grunting with the effort of rowing. I was wedged between the chests upon which the oarsmen sat, my back wet with bilge water. I choked back a sob. My body ached all over and my wrists burned where they were tied. My matted hair was glued to my face by Eardwulf's clotted black blood. It wasn't long before the keel ground on sand and I was pulled to my feet and thrown over the side.

'You stink like a latrine pit and need a wash.' It was the same gruff voice. I spluttered and fought the water, struggling to get to my feet with my hands tied. As I got to my knees I saw a big, burly man, heavily muscled with roughly cropped hair and a large drooping moustache, 'I'm Scalpi and you're a dog,' he said and pushing me back down he pumped me up and down in the muddy swirl around the ship like a woman washing clothes. 'That's got to be better,' he said, dragging me through the shallow surf. He hauled me to my feet and I stumbled along beside him with the rest of the ship's crew.

I could see other ships and hear the voices of many more men than those around me. There was a much larger force here than I had seen so far. There were fires along the beach encircled by groups of men their black shapes stark against the flames. Other well-armed men stood guard by the ships, the setting sun gleaming on spear points and shield bosses.

We marched further inland up steep banks to where more men and tents could be seen as the land levelled out. There was a row of posts at the top. The men marched past them. I went to do the same but Scalpi held me back. There was a rope attached to one of them. He tied the end around my neck then brought out a knife. I thought for a moment that my end was come. He cut the thongs tying my hands behind me and retied them round the front. He spoke again, quite gently, 'At least you can take a piss now. Someone will bring you food later.' He reached out and gripped my shoulder. 'You've had a hard day boy so get some rest, let's hope that Harold lets you live. I'd have torn out my dog teeth to see you kill that bastard Eardwulf.'

I slid down to the floor and looked around. Looking away from the setting sun I realised I could see the same hills I'd seen every day of my life. We were on Bradanreolice, "Island of the Graveyard". I shuddered, was I to be buried here? I preferred its other name, Fleet Holm. Either way, although it was not far from home, it was surrounded by treacherous waters. Even if I could escape there was no way off. Inland I could see guarded enclosures of mud and wattle. Inside people were shifting and wailing, crying out for food and water. Slave pens! I hoped Moira was still alive, in there somewhere and not raped and murdered in a ditch. I curled into a ball and wept with defeat and exhaustion until sleep drew me into the dark.

◆ ◆ ◆

I was kicked awake by a boy about my own age with a smiling round face and brown tousled hair, behind him stood a darker, older boy glowering down at me. He was the first to speak. 'I don't know why you aren't in the slave pens instead of us having to wait on you.'

As I avoided his eyes the younger boy said, 'I'm Gyric, Scalpi's son. He says to give you this.' He passed me a lump of bread and a bowl of water but I couldn't hold them both at once with my bound hands.

The older boy laughed at me, 'So what you going to do?' I took the bowl of water and drank some then putting the bowl down I reached for the bread. As I did the older boy kicked the bowl over and stepped back. He was obviously taunting me, 'Come on then killer, come and get me.'

'Shut up Jokul! It's easy to be brave when he's tied up.'

'You saying I'm a coward then?'

They stood and faced each other. Gyric dropped the bread and I grabbed it as they scuffled, pushing each other about with no real malice. I stayed mute and concentrated on getting as much of the stale hard bread in to me as I could manage without more water. Sitting back against the post I already felt a little better as I looked around through my good eye. My face was swollen, my skin tight and the cut along my jaw was sticky and sore. I felt bruised all over but I was alive, at least for now.

Scalpi strode over cuffed the two boys apart then untied me from the post. 'Your turn now,' he said, 'Follow me.'

Gyric smiled at me. 'Good luck Welsh boy.' Jokul just glowered sulkily. I guessed he glowered a lot.

I found myself walking into the centre of a great ring of men. A few men sat on large stones or logs at one end of the circle. My eye was instantly drawn to the central figure, the man who had saved my skin. He looked in his late twenties, handsome, very finely dressed and obviously in command of these rough troops. Although he was unarmed a small group of mailed, helmeted warriors stood around him carrying shields and all with swords as well as their spears. One of them, even more finely equipped, sat beside Harold on one side. On the other an older man, a monk, was also seated in a place of honour.

Scalpi stepped back. I was alone in the circle except for one man. It was Oslaf.

He spoke, 'Earl Harold, this slave killed my father, he cannot be allowed to live.'

'Your father had ignored my orders and got killed through his own stupidity,' Harold replied.

'My father has served your family for years.'

'He served my brother Sweyn and his own interests nothing more.'

'If Eardwulf had not been waiting in Bristou for your brother you would never have got away.'

'True, he got us to Ireland but I think it was for my riches not my family,' Harold replied. His voice was quiet and calm but I could sense an air of menace. 'I cannot swear to it but in that storm where I lost so many of my men I thought your father and his sailors could have done more to keep us safe.'

'That's not true, Lord. We did all we could in the face of the storm. Our men survived because they were more experienced sailors. We've always been loyal. My men and my ship are yours to command.'

'They're only your men now because of this boy you want to kill.'

Oslaf started to get angry. He was not used to being argued with. 'I don't even know why we are here. He is my slave and I want him dead. That's the law.'

'What if I buy his freedom from you?' said Harold, 'Here take these for him.' His companions laughed at Oslaf's discomfort as Harold disdainfully threw a couple of pennies at his feet. They were only a fraction of a slaves true worth.

Oslaf dared not refuse Harold directly. He picked up the coins, 'Then if he is free he must pay wergild or die, that's the law.'

'The law, we are all outside the law or have you forgotten that we rebel against our king.'

One of the other seated figures spoke, his voice guttural with Norse dialect. 'Why are we wasting time on this boy? If Oslaf wants him dead let him kill him. What do we care about the life of one slave? Aren't we all leaders of our own war-bands? Can we not do what we like with our own slaves?' There was a murmur of agreement from the other leaders.

Harold rose to his feet, 'I am paying you all well for your services, you have taken oath to me before Diarmait Mcmael-Na-Mbo, King of Leinster and on the mantle of St Brigid. It is true though, your slaves are yours to do with as you wish. We have spent enough time on this.'

'Ha! He's mine then,' Oslaf exclaimed, 'I'll deal with him now.' He started to draw his sword. There was a gasp from all around and Harold's men all tensed hands on sword hilts. Oslaf, I later learned, had made another mistake. While in meeting to touch hilt or raise shaft, let alone draw a weapon before the Earl, risked death.

My life hung on a thread and I shouted into the silence, 'My Lord, my Lord I am not his slave anymore, you just bought my freedom. I'll swear an oath to you. I'll be your man. I'll do anything for you.' I fell to my knees and begged, pleading not to be given back to Oslaf.

'By God you've got some front. You speak English, Welsh boy?'

'I do sir, and Irish, some Norse. I could translate for you and I'm not Welsh, I'm Saxon', I gabbled, 'my mother was Saxon.'

My mother had been determined that Moira and I learnt English and knew that we were Saxons. She'd press our hands on the knife. 'This is a seax,' she would say, 'the weapon our people were named after.' 'Saxon's, the people of the knife,' she'd hiss at us,' these people, the Welsh,' she would say, 'are foreigners, not proper people, you are not of the Cymri.' English was our secret family language that always set us apart and made us suspect to some. Really I felt Welsh, almost everyone around me was Welsh, the other children were Welsh but for Ma we were Saxons. Our Da taught me the Irish tongue and from those around us we learnt Welsh and the coastal language that had no name. A mixture of Norse, Irish, English and Welsh that everyone used to do business among the ships, merchants and fishermen that plied their trades around the Safearn Sea. I loved all these words and their different sounds and different names for the same things. Sometimes I would be given food or cloth for helping when men from inland talked with the sea traders.

'I have many men to do that but I've known few boys who had the courage to kill a warrior like Eardwulf the Fox.' Harold eyes sparkled. He seemed to find me funny. 'Will anyone speak for this boy?'

Oslaf screamed as he had the day before, 'He killed my father, you cannot let him live.' His manner was not approved of by those around. He was losing their sympathy.

'I will speak for the boy,' the voice came from the seated monk. 'I, Aethelric will speak for the boy. I could use his quick wits maybe he could learn to read.'

As he spoke I caught a movement out of the corner of my eye. I ducked as a stone flew past. Then another, I weaved to one side and that missed too. Then another, I could no longer keep balanced with my hands tied and slipped but that stone also missed. As I got back to my feet another voice shouted.

'I will speak for the boy.' It was the warrior behind Harold. He'd been throwing the stones. 'I was told when he attacked Eardwulf he struck as fast as a snake, see how he dodged those stones. I could make a fighter out of him, skinny though he is.'

'I can learn to read and I am quick.' I certainly was. I'd been ducking and weaving all my life. 'I'll learn anything just please don't give me to him.'

'So you can be a cleric and a warrior! I will keep you alive but you serve Aethelric every day before noon and Thurkill from then on and we'll see how you manage,' Harold pronounced. 'And you Oslaf will have to accept this until our business with King Edward is dealt with. If the boy survives we will talk again.'

Oslaf was furious at this turn of events, 'I could take my ship and leave that's nearly a tenth of your army!'

'You could, but where would you go? Edward won't take you back. The Irish are now my friends. The Welsh will kill you just for being English. My family has a very long reach, to Denmark and beyond. Just how sure are you that the men who followed your father will follow you?' Harold replied calmly. He didn't look much older than Oslaf but he commanded respect in a way Oslaf could not.

Oslaf backed down casting me a look of pure evil, 'I will accept your decision though you treat me unjustly.' Red patches burned bright in his white face as he pushed his way out through the circle of men. I was left alone.

'Well boy, you've stirred up the wasp's nest but there's something about the look of you I like.' Harold gave me a shrewd look. 'What was your father's name?'

'Oh, I had no father, I never had a father.'

'Ha, ha, ha what's that make you then, Jesus Christ born of a virgin,' shouted a voice came from the crowd.

Everyone laughed at the break of tension. This had all gone on too long.

'Do you have any kind of name or shall we just call you Welsh boy?'

Sar, my Lord, they call me Sar.'

'Sar, hmmm, well Sar no man's son will you swear to become my man.'

I fell to my knees, 'I will sir, I swear by Almighty God to serve you for the rest of my life. Thank you, thank you.' Then I remembered Moira, 'My sister, sir, what about my sister?'

'Sister?' he frowned, 'What about your sister?'

'She was captured when I was, sir. I think she might be in the pens.'

He cast a glance in their direction. 'Forget your sister boy, that's the price of your life. You will have no other family but mine and think on this. An oath is a serious thing.'

I would have protested but Scalpi cuffed me hard and pulled me out of the ring. 'Shut your mouth, boy, you are lucky to be alive, be grateful for that. Now get lost.'

So thats how it was. On that fateful day I became Harold's man, an Englishman, lost my sister forever and was given a name I carried with both pride and shame. That of Sar Nomansson.

CHAPTER 2

T he next few days passed quickly. The whole camp was in furious activity preparing for a raid. I reported every morning to Aethelric. He had me running errands for him all over the camp. I found that there were not only five ships on the one beach but four others drawn up on the western side of the island. They were large ships, and between them they carried five to six hundred people, mostly warriors. There were also some slave women, a few monks and priests and a small swarm of boys aged about 12 and up. I was excited and fearful of this huge crowd of fighting men and their hangers on. I'd never before seen so many people in one place.

The first afternoon I reported to Thurkill, the commander of Harold's house-carls, he told me to 'bugger off and find something useful to do'. He would see to me when he was ready. As both Aethelric and Thurkill were attached to Harold's ship, *Maeve's Lover*, a beautiful craft the king of Dublin had given him, so was I. Scalpi was also part of the crew so I hung around him at meals and somehow got food and drink. Bit by bit the men got used to me being around. There was no peace, someone always wanted something doing, getting this, moving that, fetching and carrying for anyone that asked. I'd no time to think and it kept me away from the slave pens. I was scared in case I was caught trying to see Moira. Shamefully I stayed away, then one day a fat-bellied knarr moored sideways onto the beach and all the slaves were herded up a ramp and into its belly. I may have caught a glimpse of my twin's dark red hair but I wasn't sure. I could see Oslaf chatting easily with the master of the slave ship. He came away with a smile on his face and a bag of silver in his hand as he sold my people, along with my sister, into slavery. I hid in a small cave that night and cried and as I cried all my pain went into a small dark hard place inside me. I swore I'd never cry again. The next day they beat me. I just stood and took it. I believed I deserved all the pain the world could heap upon me. I had failed to save my mother. I had failed to save my sister. Now no-one cared for me and I cared for no-one.

I became immersed in a sullen silence, doing as I was bid, that much and no more. Gyric, who was with our ship, tried to befriend me. Jokul continued to be hostile, shying the odd stone in my direction while giving me evil looks. I learnt why he was the way he was but I did not care. His father was a terrifying Norseman, Thord, who criticised everything he did. Scalpi was much less rough on his boy, or on me. All the boys, there were probably about fifteen or twenty in the whole camp, had to be hard to survive.

I learned more as the days went on. I found out that Harold was in rebellion against his king, King Edward, and that I was among a force of paid men, mostly Norse and Irish, bought from Dublin. They were hard landless men who practiced warfare as a way of life. One of Harold's brothers was here, Leofwine. That they'd heard from their father, Godwin, and that they were to raid lands now ruled by other Earls. We'd heard of the great Earl Godwin even in our lost corner of Wales. One of the mightiest Earls of England, he was now outlawed along with his sons. Except that is, for the youngest, Wulfnoth, who along with Harold's nephew, Hakon, were held hostage by Edward the King of all the English. Harold's sister, King Edward's wife, Eadgyth England's queen, had been put in a nunnery by the King. A Norman, Robert of Jumierges, had been made Archbishop of Canterbury instead of Aethelric. He, Robert, was being blamed for poisoning the King's ear and scraping open old wounds. I learnt a lot scurrying around after that monk while keeping my ears open and my mouth shut. What I never learned is why Harold had saved me. I wondered on this. What strange fate had kept me alive?

Then one night everything changed. The smiths put out their fires and the camp stayed awake waiting through the short night for the dawn. Men were armouring everywhere putting on coats of mail, checking fastenings and straps on shields and sheaths. Then all the bustle and activity slowed. The last of all sounds to stop was the whistling of whetstones up and down the blades of axes, swords and spears. Silence fell over the camp.

Then Harold gave the order, 'Board your ships, men!'

As the cry was repeated across the island we all embarked. Everyone seemed to know just where they were to go so I climbed in with the rest and crouched in the ship's belly.

We left just after the high tide turned, sweeping down on the ebb with the river's force behind us. The speed felt fantastic and I could not help jumping up and down with the sheer joy of the movement. I was shocked to hear myself laugh then someone knocked me to the deck. 'Get down you idiot'. The rowers bent to their oars and the ship leaped on, spray bursting up around the bows. At first we stayed centre stream and I could see ships before, behind and beside us. Some had magnificent carved monsters attached to their prows and banners flew from the masts. Oslaf's ship flew a fox's brush, his father's emblem, while on Thord's ship, the lean black *Sea Serpent,* flew a tubular banner that snaked in the breeze as we ourselves seemed to snake and fly. Harold's banner was a 'Fighting Man', embroidered with gold and jewelled, which flew belligerently over *Maeve's Lover*.

To our right the coast of my childhood grew small while before us and to the left the English coast grew more visible. The outlines of its hills getting more distinct as our ships bore towards them. As we got closer I could see up over the heads of the oarsmen and realised that as we moved along the coast fires were being lit on the tops of hills to our left, dark smoke curling into the sky.

'They know we are coming then,' said the steersman high on

his platform, above and behind me.

'Yes, but they don't know where, when or if we'll land.' It was Harold speaking. 'They'll have had the fyrd out for days now. We'll have been seen coming up the Channel. Hopefully they'll think I was planning to attack Bristou or further upriver. Meanwhile they'll have had time to argue amongst themselves. How many thegns do you think they'll have?

'Ten, maybe twenty,' said Leofwine. 'Many were Sweyn's men once. Some may refuse to fight.'

'I think Sweyn lost a lot of their support after that business with the nun. Remember too, all our thegns were sworn to the king when we were outlawed. On the bright side, the more thegns they have the more they'll argue. The more they argue the more time we have. Their new Earl, Odda, will be at court licking the King's arse, not here leading his men.'

We swept on past another bay then around a massive wooded hill, more smoke rising from its crest. Now we were in a proper sea swell. The water changed from muddy brown to blue-green and bottomless. I'd heard of this but to see it was new. I felt a bit sick but so, so excited I could barely stay still. 'Stop fidgeting you little bastard, this is serious business,' grunted an oarsman near me. Fully armed men knelt in the centre, hands tensing on their spear shafts, spitting for luck, as the ships turned into a bay cutting hard around the point. Somebody told the steersman to keep to the middle of the bay as further along the beach was made of huge stones that could break a vessel. As we swept towards the beach the rowers leant down on their oars, pushing the blades high up out of harm's way, as the ships grounded on a ridge of sand and gravel rising to a shingle crest. Men leapt to their feet, running forward, up and over the bow. After the first rush a ladder was dropped over the front and the rest of them climbed out. I picked myself up from between the rower's chests where I'd been shoved and looked around. On both sides of me men were running forward and pouring off the ships. A few men lightly armed and carrying bows ran to the sides, scouting, while heavily mailed men formed up before each ship.

We had landed unopposed on a long ridge backed by a salt marsh. The tension melted and the men drew the ships up onto the ridge above the tideline. It would be hard to attack us across the marsh and easy to defend at each end. Everyone had things to say but all seemed pleased with our landing and Harold's management of it.

A party of warriors were sent off to investigate a small village on the east side of the valley. 'You boys follow them and come back with fresh water.' We did as we were told, grabbing the leather pails from the ships then excitedly running inland. I even found myself grinning back at Gyric. The warriors spread out around the hamlet which lay by a broad stream. There was silence. 'They've all fled,' someone cried and the warriors moved in. There were only four or five huts and they were soon burning.

'Nothing here to steal boys. Go above the village for the water, we don't want to be drinking their shit.' We had to go to the edge of the forest to do this and men came with us. 'There may be people in the woods stupid enough to draw a bow on you lads.' Nothing happened though and no-one was to be seen. We filled our pails and trudged back to the camp strangely subdued.

'I thought there would be fighting,' said one, 'and here we are carrying bloody water again'.

'Not great is it?' another voice complained.

Gyric's voice came over cheerfully, 'But what a sight it was landing like that, all the men armed and leaping off the ships!'

We cheered up at that, competing as to who had seen what. I tried to join in though really I'd seen little crouched down on the deck. Jokul turned on me, 'Shut up goat boy, what do you know? You're just the monk's pet.'

Somehow it had got around that I'd been herding goats when my home was raided. To these sons of warriors that made me a peasant. Not only that, I had to run around after a monk which to some of them was even worse. Some of the other's started to chant, 'Goat boy, goat boy, baa, baa, baa!' and throw stones at me. I withdrew back into my shell and when Gyric touched my shoulder I shrugged his hand away.

We got back to the beach to find everything boringly normal. Fires were lit, men washed and cooked, the Norsemen combed their hair, the Saxons their moustaches while the Irish combed nothing at all. A couple of priests or monks went from fire to fire offering blessings and prayers. I found Aethelric and sat beside him at Harold's fire, where I felt safe from the other boys.

They were discussing war. Scouts had been sent out and we were waiting for their return. Listening in I realised things were not as good as they seemed. Our force needed provisions, badly, and men were openly questioning Harold's forethought. He seemed confident, 'We'll pillage until they face me, then we'll beat them, then we'll pillage some more'.

The scouts were followed by bands of men, twenty or so from every ship. First the village above us called Porloc was pillaged. There were a few houses, a small hall and a church obviously recently abandoned. A man called Toki took me along. He was small compared to Scalpi but like all the men his upper body was hugely muscular as a result of rowing. His gap-toothed face had humour but no mercy. He grinned at me and cuffed me round the head, 'What you called boy?'

'Sar, sir.'

'No need to call me sir, my names Toki, sworn to Harold. Housecarl. First thing you need to do is find a sack.'

I found a leather bag beneath a small almost empty granary. 'Hmmm not much here, but it's a start. We'll leave that to be collected later. Foodstuffs will be pooled. Aethelric will probably have you counting every grain tomorrow.' Toki obviously found this funny. I didn't. It wasn't so far from the truth.

We took everything, every nail, every scrap of leather, all clothing, even cutting the cloth from the looms in the small homes of these peasants. I mumbled something about meanness. Toki turned on me, 'Look lad, most loot is not stores of treasure and gold, it's the small things. Things we need to keep us fed and clothed and iron mind, any metal, but always iron.

Never enough iron.' He pulled me to him, 'Get this, gold, silver coins, anything of real value we have to give to our Earl, who pays us, he is the wealth giver.' 'But,' he grinned at me slyly, 'all the small stuff we get to keep so the iron we take to the armourer and he does things for us. Surprising how much you can make out of the small things. Now you carry the stuff for me and I'll teach you how to loot in return.'

'I don't get to keep anything then?'

'Cheeky sod,' he cuffed me again, 'bloody cheeky sod. Let's just get on with it.'

He did teach me how to loot, to look in the thatch, under the hearth stone, soft places at the bases of posts, smoked food in the roofs. We worked hard and fast as others were also stripping the village clean. A few of us gathered round the small church of St Dubricius, but some of Harold's Danish housecarls guarded it, cradling their massive axes in their arms.

'Shame about the church,' Toki commented. 'That would be the richest place in the whole valley. Harold's looking after his reputation. There's nothing for us here.'

We returned to the camp with some smoked pig, a dried fish, a leather jerkin, a small sack of bits of metal and cloth, a sickle, some iron pothooks, the pot, a bronze clasp and two silver pennies from under a hearthstone. Toki seemed quite happy with this. 'Hand it all over then lad,' he said, as we approached the camp. I did and true to his word, he kept it all.

Over the next day cattle and sheep started to come in to everyone's joy and with them a few horses. Things started to happen faster as troops of riders spread out, coming back with more and more livestock and horses laden with plunder. We boys were not allowed to go out with the raiders so we tended to hang around the slaughtering yards set up toward the eastern edge of the beach. The drama of slaughter drew us like the flies that pestered us all.

Unwilling to be friendly but wanting company I hung around the other boys after my tasks with Aethelric were done. They were larking about in two gangs throwing pieces of offal and cow-shit at each other. I joined in on the side of Gyric and Jokul and all seemed fine at first. We splashed in and out of the sea, laughing and dodging about. Then something thudded hard across my back.

'What do you think you are doing, Welsh boy?' It was Jokul. In his hand he held an ox-tail picked up from a pile left by the yard.

'Why do you hit me I was fighting on your side?'

'You should know your place, goatherd. We are the sons of warriors not scum like you,' he retorted, lashing out again.

Some of the other boys also picked up tails and started flicking them at me. Soon I was encircled by a mob of boys each trying to whip me. At first the blows stung, then bruised as I tried to avoid them. I did not know where to turn or who to turn to. I could hear Gyric protesting but he was brushed aside. I knew that if it weren't for Jokul this would not be happening. It was him I had to deal with.

'Fight me on your own, Jokul, you fucking coward!' I shouted.

At this direct challenge the other boys pulled back sniggering. Jokul was much bigger than me so to them the outcome was obvious. He wasn't so sure though. I saw a flicker of unease cross his face.

'Not so brave now are you coward?' I was pushing my luck but I had put Jokul's honour at stake. He could not lose face to a goatherd and I could not win against them all.

'I'll beat you to a pulp you little shit,' he said and lashed out at me again. I ducked but the tail caught me a rough blow across the top of my head. I could hear Gyric yelling that I was unarmed but Jokul took no notice lashing furiously out at me. The beach at this place was made of huge pebbles as big as a man's head and I danced from one to the other. He lumbered after me raining down blows. Most of them I avoided as the circle of boys spread out to give us room. He was breathing heavily as I eyed him warily. He struck again. I jumped back again, and then I jumped sideways. He was struggling to hit me while I could not get near to him. Suddenly I saw my moment. As his ox-tail whipped out towards me I grabbed it and pulled. He stumbled and I was on him, raging. All my pent up hurt and fear burst out as anger as I sat on him punching furiously at his face. I could not keep him down and he threw me off and stood up. He moved toward me menacingly, taking more care of his footing. I realised he was intent on my complete humiliation. Some-one pushed something into my hand. It was another ox-tail. I grabbed it behind the tufted end and lashed out with the bloody stump.

'Go on goat boy, try again,' someone shouted, 'You can do it.'

Someone was on my side! This felt better. I danced from side to side, flexing the tail back and forth. I could see blood above one of Jokul's eyes. I liked that. I wanted to see more.

I struck. He struck back and caught me across the hip. I grit-ted my teeth flicking the tail at him. I couldn't hit him as hard. He just seemed to shrug it off. The boys were all chanting now, mostly his name but some called mine. I skipped about hitting him lightly again and again. His frustration was plain. He was getting more and more furious while I felt almost calm

'I'm betting on the goat boy.' It was a man's voice with a strong Irish accent. Another replied that he was a fool and that Thord's son would thrash me. Now the circle was of both men and boys laughing and making bets. As the circle thickened I had less room to dodge. I tried to get some space but hands roughly pushed me back. I ducked another blow, jumped the next and then one hit me in the face. I staggered, tasting blood as my lip split. I could feel the scar on my jaw begin to open. I slipped. I fell. Jokul felt his chance had come. He rushed at me but could not keep his footing on the round boulders. As I fell I twisted, whipping the tail across the ground. It caught him round his ankle and he tripped, falling hard. He lay there, face down panting. Leaping to my feet I lost all sense of my surroundings and picked up one of the huge pebbles. I raised it above his head.

'No! Drop that stone!' I would have. I would have smashed it down on Jokul's fucking head. I was thrust aside hard. Now it was my turn to land painfully on the pebbles.

'That is enough, stay where you are boy or I'll kill you now.' It was Thord who grabbed his son and started slapping him around the face, 'You've let yourself be beaten by an untrained boy. You shame me. Get back to our ship I'll deal with you later.'

He stood over me and as I cringed he spat on me and stalked off. A gentle voice spoke from behind me, 'You went too far! If you'd not have been stopped you would have killed that boy, the son of a war leader. You will have to learn.' It was Aethelric, who then sent me to our ship's camp. 'You are in serious trouble, you ingrate.'

When the ships company ate I was left hungry while Aethelric pondered my fate. At last he beckoned me over. 'I had hoped to make you a novice monk when our affairs are settled with the King but your temper is outrageous. I'm not sure that I can use you though you are a skinny child and I can see little use for you elsewhere.'

I felt both annoyed and pleased at this. I'm not that skinny. I'd not been impressed carrying his papers around and listening to his endless prayers while I knelt daydreaming about being a great warrior beside him. 'I'm no monk,' I thought.

'However maybe, if you can learn some humility, perhaps you could still be of service to Our Lord. You will serve a penance for your crimes.' He continued, 'I have prayed for guidance and the Lord has seen fit to remind me of your peoples' greatest saint, David. I think you call him Diw.'

Of course I'd heard of him, my Da going on at great length about his pieties.

'Do you know how he tested his faith?'

'He stood in the water, Father, kept warm by his prayers,' I replied eager to please while wondering where this was going.

'And so shall you. Now follow me.'

I followed him along the shore until we came to the end of the beach where the fight had taken place. It was now quiet except for the lowing of a few cattle penned ready for the next day's butchery. As we stood on the shore heavy dark clouds shadowed the moon as the sun went down over the sea.

'What I am asking of you will sorely test you but once endured will return you to God's grace. If you fail in this task I will tell Harold that you are beyond redemption and have you sold into slavery.'

I was really nervous now. 'What are you going to do to me? They all picked on me, it wasn't my fault. This isn't fair.'

'You would have killed that boy, this is not justice. This is mercy. The tide is now high and about to turn. You must wade out to your neck and you must stay there until the tide retreats and returns again. I will come for you in the morning. I will pray for you and you must pray for God's blessing.'

I was close to tears now but was not going to show it. I glared at Aethelric who just gently gazed back at me. 'Go on boy, endure this ordeal and you will show me that I was right to speak out for you.'

I realised he meant to be kind and that I was only alive because of him. 'I'm sorry, Father, I will do your penance.' I waded slowly out into the cold sea and it embraced me in its chill.

Aethelric knelt on the shore until I turned to face him. Only my head was above the waves. As the darkness grew he became just a shadow praying on the beach. Shortly he stood and walked away. I was alone in the sea.

I grew colder while the sea rose and fell, rose and fell. I realised that sometimes now my shoulders were above the water. The wind chilled them more and I crouched slightly, shivering. My feet and legs got so cold they hurt and then slowly, very slowly, they grew numb. I hugged myself whimpering in misery. I felt so tired and as the numbness spread I started to feel drowsy. Was God taking me? My eyes blinked then suddenly shot open. There was a strange white shape moving on the shore. I trembled violently my teeth chattered uncontrollably. I could not move convinced the spirits had come for me.

'Do you not know me, Welsh scum?' It was Oslaf's voice. I was so relieved that the voice was human I almost shouted joyfully. Then I realised Oslaf's presence meant no good for me. I'd avoided him as much as I could since that first day and he pretended indifference to me. After his father's death his new role as leader had inspired him to declare himself as Oslaf the White, playing on his appearance. He sported a white cloak and had himself a new banner made, also plain white. Despite myself I could see he cut a fine figure amongst these rough warriors with his well-made clothes. He was also very skilled at arms and had a reputation as a winner in the training fights the army practised every day.

Now he was here, just him and me. 'I know you are there Welsh boy and when the tide goes out I will come and kill you.' I heard an ominous sound, tsssk tsssk, tssk. 'Do you know that sound, little turd, do you? These stones make marvellous whetstones. Are you saying your prayers? Do you think God is listening?'

He went on sharpening the blade. 'This is the knife that killed my father. This is the knife that will kill you.' Tssk, tssk....tssk tssk. 'Can you see me boy?'

I could but could he see me against the dark sea? I dared not move. I certainly wasn't going to answer.

'I know why Harold saved your life, I do. He didn't like my father so he's picked you up like a stray puppy. He's not here now, no-one to save you now, little pup.' His voice was strange, dreamlike. 'There was no-one to save Beorn was there? Sweyn was unsure, Beorn was family but my father put him straight. Beorn and Harold had betrayed him. Godwin would forgive him he always had, the fool. They didn't want Sweyn pardoned, they wanted his lands.' Tsssk Tssk went the knife. 'I'm going to skin you alive, boy. Take your skin off slice by painful slice.'

The sound made my stomach clench. I'd already felt that knife.

'Tied up he was no match for Sweyn and Eardwulf.' Oslaf's voice whispered eerily on. Whoever this Beorn was, his death meant a lot to Oslaf.

'They grabbed him. They held him against the side of the

boat. But who finished him? Who killed Beorn? It was me little turd. My first kill. I killed him just as surely as I am going to kill you.'

I could see his white shape upon the shore as he hissed as much to himself as to me. I was crouching harder to keep my body below the waves. The tide was going out. I had to do something. I was used to the sea as I'd grown up beside it and could swim well. I would have to move and risk not being here in the dawn. I slowly sank beneath the surface taking a deep breath then gripping the rocky floor. I moved under the water heading out from the shore. I couldn't stay under for long and rose gasping. Frightened he would hear me I frantically looked to the shore but there he was still muttering like some evil sprite.

'We got away too. Those fools from Hastings went after the wrong ships.' He laughed, 'My father wasn't called 'the Fox' for nothing.'

He was standing now. His arm's outstretched in the flickering moonlight. He seemed lost in his memories. His body swayed then suddenly went rigid. His voice rose sharply, 'Harold couldn't stop me then and he won't stop me now.'

He sat down again as a cloud covered the moon. His voice fell back to a whisper. I couldn't make out any words as he crooned to himself in the shadows. He began again to whet the knife. The sound cut clearly through the background ripple of the breaking waves, tssk, tsssk, tssk.

I could go no further out for fear of being swept away. I trod water watching him with just my eyes above the waves rising and falling with them. Feeling was painfully coming back into my legs. I wanted to scream and bit my arm instead. I sank again crawling under the water for as long as I could hold my breath and rose again. Strangely the sea floor felt like stone tree roots and I used them to pull myself along. As the tide fell I found myself surrounded by slowly emerging stone tree stumps.

A wind blew up and swept the clouds away. Suddenly I could see everything along the beach. Oslaf's white cloak stood out shining in the moon's silver glow. He leapt to his feet. He'd realised I'd moved. Could he see me? I sank lower lying in the shadows of these strange cold roots. He couldn't see me. He was furiously casting up and down that part of the beach. 'Where are you, you turd? You are not to drown before I gut you like a herring.'

I knew there was a good chance he would find me. I crept back into deeper water. I couldn't come ashore and he was between me and the camp. I drifted uncertainly then became aware of a current even colder than the sea. In the moonlight I could see little wavelets shining silver over the rocks being exposed by the falling tide. There was a dark patch of shadow where a small wharf had been built. The water beside it would have to be deep enough to conceal me. I thought I could see an even darker patch of shadow behind them and knew it must be where a river entered the sea. I decided to risk following the current in. The cattle were lowing loudly. Something must have disturbed them. I half crawled, half swam into the darkness below the wharf. I stopped again trying to control my heaving breath. The river curled round behind this small dock into a deep gully. I had little choice, either run into the gully or go back out to sea. I dashed into the gully running over the slippery, tumbled rocks.

I could now look back along the beach at Oslaf who was jumping at every sound. His ghostly form was striding up and down the beach. He was peering out to sea and then twisting back uncertainly to look toward the milling beasts. He knew I'd gone but could not work out where. I crept further into the shadows my heart thudding in my chest so loud I was certain he could hear every beat.

I crept out of the river, freezing. I could barely move as my legs began their own shaking dance. Pushing myself into a hollow in the bank I just lay there shuddering uncontrollably. Unable to see where Oslaf was I gave myself up to fate. I could do no more. Now I prayed knowing that God was now my only hope.

Time passed and the shaking slowed but the drowsiness returned. I think I even dozed. Then I froze. Something was touching me.

'Shush, Sar, it's only me.' It was Gyric's voice, whispering, 'No noise, now, Oslaf might come back.' He was rubbing me with a woollen cloak then pushed a leather flask into my mouth. 'Drink this.'

I tasted the warming sweetness. It was mead. Even in my distress I wondered how he's got hold of such precious drink. Gyric wrapped the cloak around me hugging me to him until his warmth spread into mine. 'I came to look for you,' he whispered. 'Aethelric's a fool sometimes and I knew you couldn't survive all night. Then I saw Oslaf.'

'Did you hear him?' I asked through juddering teeth. 'Did you hear what he said?'

'About killing Beorn? Yes, yes I did.'

'Who was Beorn?'

'I don't know, but I do know that Sweyn is Harold's older brother. My father says he's bad to the bone but never to say so out loud.'

'This is a big secret. Don't tell anyone what we heard or he'll try to kill you too.'

I could see Gyric's eyes widen in his round face at the thought. It was the light before dawn. I was warmer now and we crept up to the gully's edge. The beach was empty, the cattle quiet. 'Did you hear the noise they made in the night?' Gyric whispered. 'That was me. I thought I was bound to be caught.'

'I think that noise may have saved my life, my friend,' and then I knew it. I had a friend. Gyric was my friend. I was no longer quite so alone.

Before the sun rose Gyric went back to the camp. I went to where my ordeal had started and waded back into the sea.

When Aethelric arrived I was stood facing the morning sun up to my waist in the ocean with my hands clasped before me in prayer. He claimed that Saint David had looked after me and that I was now redeemed in his eyes. The camp as a whole decided that they'd had enough of us boys and that from now on we would be trained to fight every afternoon with the other warriors until we were too exhausted to cause trouble. Slaves would probably do our work better and with a lot less fuss and of course, you could kill them if they argued back.

I was told about this later. I had crept into a space under the steering deck of our ship and slept so deeply that even my nightmares couldn't wake me.

CHAPTER 3

Harold and Leofwine were always in the company of a small group of select warriors. Many of them were either Danish or of mixed English and Danish blood as was Harold himself. I was told that these were Harold's house-carls. Like him, many of them wore their hair longer than was the usual Saxon way. They habitually carried swords as well as training with both heavy and throwing spears. Six of the largest of them carried huge two-handed axes of the type Eardwulf had used to such horrific effect. They were all professional soldiers under the command of Thurkill. They trained every day and our company of boys had to train alongside them. Gyric and I had become inseparable while Jokul arrived at the first training session with many more bruises than I had given him. I don't know how it happened but we were enemies no more.

Under the harsh discipline of Thurkill and the other warriors we had no time to squabble amongst ourselves. Although we all came from different ships companies we became a small company of our own. Despite his loss of face Jokul was still our leader being bigger and fiercer than the rest of us and also the son of Thord. Paired up with Gyric, and having earned some respect, I was now treated almost as an equal by these sons of warriors. We were given heavy spear shafts and some of the smaller men's shields to practice with. For me it was hopeless. I was weighed down by the shield and however hard I practised I could not seem to cope with the heavy weapons as well as the other boys did. I lost every combat round. The shield dragged me to the floor and my spear arm trembled after every bout. When we practised the shield wall, shoving and pushing at each other, it always broke where I stood. The respect I'd earned quickly dwindled as who would want to risk their lives next to me? I began to withdraw again brooding over my losses.

One day after training I sloped off to gaze at the sea from behind one of the ships where I could not be seen when I heard the gravel crunch behind me. I leaped up grabbing a large pebble fearing it was Oslaf come for me. 'Hold up lad, I'm not going to eat you'.

It was one of the strange Irish warriors from the far west. 'May I sit?' he asked in a gentle tone.

I replied, 'If you must,' my tone surly.

He sat down his arms around his knees and said nothing. After a while I sat down too. 'Glad you could join me,' he said. His accent thick around the English sounds. I was strangely comforted by the familiar brogue.

'You're welcome,' I replied in Irish.

He looked startled and spoke rapidly to me in his own language. I asked him to slow down and he asked me how I spoke his tongue. I found myself telling him of my home and my Da who gave me what Irish I knew.

'We all have a story and the world is hard.' He gazed at me steadily. 'I'm Muirchu from Aileach,' he said, 'and your name is?'

'Sar.'

'Well Sar. I made a nice little pile betting on you the other day so I'm going to return the favour.'

I had no idea what he meant then he explained it to me. 'You're never going to fight the way those housecarls fight, never. You're too small and even if you grow some inches you're just a kind of wiry type.'

'I know. I'm only good for being a monk's servant. Aethelric says he'll make a novice out of me.'

'That's not a bad life you know but there's some things I would miss.' He leered at me with a sly grin and I knew he was talking about women.

I blushed and loudly agreed though I'd not so much as kissed a girl. I'd followed a couple around the village to their visible amusement.

'Look little man, how did you beat that boy the other day? Come on be serious now, how?'

'Lucky I guess, he slipped.'

'You were quicker than him, you moved quicker and you reacted quicker.'

'How does that help me be a warrior? I can't even hold up a shield.'

'There's more than one way to fight boy, war isn't just about pushing and hacking each other in the wall though you Norse types seem to think so.'

'I still don't understand.'

'A lot of us Irish fight light, drives you lot mad. True, unarmoured we can't win a stand up fight against a mailed wall but we can skip around and when the moment comes, in quick, stab and out again.'

I was still puzzled.

He pulled something out from under his cloak. It looked like a miniature shield, no bigger than from his wrist to his elbow, more boss than shield. 'We call this a targe,' he said, 'Here take it and stand there.'

I did as I was told. 'This isn't going to protect me from much,' I grumbled. He picked up a handful of pebbles and walked away from me.

Turning toward me he raised an arm. 'Now use your eyes and don't think.'

I held the targe in my left hand and he threw the pebbles straight at me, hard. None of them hit. I punched each aside quick as a flash. He threw one low. It hit my shin with a crack.

'Fuck, ouch, that hurt!'

'Why did that hit you?' he asked, turning another stone in his hand.

'I don't know,' I yelled. I saw the next one coming and jumped aside.

'Because you stood still, Sar, you stood still.'

His message started to sink in. I looked at him as understanding dawned. 'Keep moving, let your body do the thinking,' he said patting me on the shoulder. Then he turned his back and walked away.

'I've got your targe!' I yelled after him.

I just caught a reply in the sea breeze. 'Keep it. It's yours,' and with that he disappeared around the bow of the ship.

'That was odd,' I thought but I knew I'd been given a gift, not just his little shield but a way to fight. I looked at the shield. It had a protruding bronze boss incised with curling patterns and though old had been well made. Its wood curved slightly back from a thick centre to a fine rim. It had no shoulder strap but could be gripped in two ways. One so as I could hold a spear in my hand behind the shield. My arm went through a strap leaving the hand free. Inside the boss was a bar and when I clutched that the small shield was like an extension to my fist. I found a short length of rope and passed it through the hand grip and over my shoulder. By tying it across my front I could carry it on my back leaving both hands free. From then on, where I went, it went.

I still practised in the shield wall with the same effect though I learned that I did well enough when others were pushing me from behind. It wore us all out holding up the shield and trying to manage the long ash shaft. We grew visibly more muscly and hardened to blows. We could stand our ground for longer. We felt that we too could become men. We watched the other men train and there was much more to it than the wall. They had to practise opening the wall, forming wedges and always protecting each other. It's the spear you don't see that kills you, the spear from the side. Each ship's crew trained separately, each leader jealous of the loyalty of his men, but a shield wall could unite such disparate groups as each man's shield covered him and the man to his left. Most of the warriors had heavy padded mailed coats, byrnies, down to their thighs. A few were lighter troops, some with hunting bows. These did most of the scouting and foraging and weren't so highly regarded.

When I turned up for training with my targe I was subjected to more ridicule but in single bouts I tried out my new way. With my light little targe I could knock blows aside as long as I never took them front on. If I did I was rocked back on my heels and open to attack. I armed myself with a light throwing spear shaft and found that I could get in many blows and stabs against the slower heavily armed boys. Muirchu was right it did drive the others mad so if they did get close I got punished for it, hard. I spent long hours throwing the spear again and again. I could rarely equal the range of the other boys but I was far more accurate and could throw with some skill even while moving. I could not heave and hack so well but I could run, jump and climb better than them all.

Since my ordeal Aethelric now regarded me with great favour and gave me the task of bees-waxing the box containing St. Brigid's mantle, a holy relic that King Diarmait had given Harold for his help in capturing Dublin. The relic was a small dark red oblong of some cloth with greenish blue linen lining in a flat wooden box whose gilt and painted surface was wearing back to the wood.

'The Godwins will have that put in a jewelled reliquary when they return home. St. Brigid's own mantle,' his eyes grew wide as he whispered reverently.

We were sitting in Harold's tent avoiding a steady drizzle that chilled the spring air. 'Shouldn't it be white?' I asked.

He looked at me sharply. 'You are a strange boy. What makes you say that?'

'St Brigid's white cloak is famous. It magically stretched to cover acres of ground and some Irish king gave her it for a convent,' I pronounced.

I was frowned at. 'Not magically, Sar, miraculously. There is a difference.'

'Whatever, it should be white,' I replied.

'Where did you get this story from?' he quizzed me.

Once again I found myself telling of my Da.

'He wasn't your father then?'

'No, no my father was an evil man.'

'Your mother's husband?'

'Nooo, not exactly.'

'So they weren't married and you say he was a priest?'

'More a sort of wandering monk.'

'This just gets worse Sar,' he replied sternly. 'So your stepfather was some kind of Celtic heathen storyteller.'

I was shocked, 'He wasn't a heathen. He was a true Christian. He always said the English priests were out to destroy his church.'

'As the French seek to do ours,' Aethelric said, it seemed to himself. 'He doesn't sound like a Christian to me.'

I jumped to my feet defensively. 'We were Christians when you English were worshipping lumps of wood in bogs.' I was shouting at him waving the box in the air.

He grabbed it from my hands, 'We, Sar? Who are we?'

His question stunned me. Who are we? Who was I? Once again I felt lost. Was I a Saxon, therefore English, or was I Welsh where I was born? What made me, my birth place or my parents? I slumped miserably before him. He looked at me sadly and then he confided in me.

He too was in a world not his own. He'd spent his whole life in a monastery where he became an efficient and well liked administrator of church properties. 'They all voted for me,' he said sadly, 'the monks of Christchurch but the king overruled them.' When Robert became Archbishop instead, Aethelric fearful of the Norman, felt it safer to leave with Harold who was cousin to him. Now he administered the supplies of a war party surrounded by rough warriors instead of gentle chanting monks. For a moment I felt close. He talked of teaching me

Latin and singing. I told him I would be a warrior. 'Sar,' he said, 'be careful of your dreams. You have no real place.'

'What do you mean?'

'Harold freed you but you are a freedman who is attached to no land. All that protects you is Harold's whim.'

'I swore him an oath,' I said grandly.

'You are not some thegn, like Scalpi, with lands or arms and men of your own. You are a boy of no family. What can you do for Harold?'

'I serve him don't I?'

'Listen, Thurkill and I spoke up for you to save Harold's face in front of the other captains. It was foolish of him to confront Oslaf, just because he hated Eardwulf, but he could not be seen to back down.' He patted me on the shoulder, rising to his feet. 'The Church could give you a good home if we survive the next few months.'

'Fuck the Church and your stupid singing. You think you're like me. My mother was killed in front of me. I killed the man who did it,' I spat at him. 'I don't want to learn to sing I want to learn to kill!'

I pushed past him out of the tent. I knew he meant well but I did not want to be a monk. I rushed through the camp eastwards. Fording the shallow river I ran into the woods and started to climb. I felt angry, miserable and homesick, not only for Ma and Moira but I missed the little ones too. Those people were who I'd been, had defined me, now I felt as though I were nothing. I mattered to no-one and I believed no-one mattered to me.

The hill rose steeply, though thickly wooded there was little undergrowth and I climbed steadily and quietly. I paused as I heard someone struggling through the trees puffing and panting. It was Gyric. I wanted to hate him. I wanted to be left to my misery. I watched him sweating his way up the hill cursing me out loud as he came. Despite my black mood I had to laugh. 'Bloody Hell Gyric, what are you doing coming after me?'

His red face beamed at me, 'Couldn't have you going off without me, having all the fun.'

I jumped on him and we pummelled each other rolling down hill in the mould until we crashed into the bole of an old massive ash tree clinging to the steep hillside, too twisted for the carpenter. 'Let's climb to the top.'

We climbed up through the woods until the land flattened out into grazed pasture between circles of gorse. At the peak were the remains of a massive fire, the ashes now cold and deserted. 'This must have been where the beacon we saw was lit. A fire could be seen for miles from here.' The view was fantastic. We could see right out to sea and down to the bay where the ships were beached. We felt like God's looking down on a miniature world. 'Look you can see the whole army exactly where everyone is and what they're doing.' We exchanged comments excited by being so high.

Going back to the crest of the hill we looked around. To the north the land seemed to be full of lakes with flocks of birds rising in clouds above sparkling reflections. Looking east we could see ranges of steep hills, with clear tops and thickly wooded slopes. Here and there smudges of smoke rose from the villages and farmsteads our army had raided and burned. Different coloured patches marked different vegetation while around the settlements and in places on the hill-tops small collections of rectangular reddish brown patches showed where people had ploughed. Brighter green streaks revealed areas that had been heavily grazed until we came and stole their herds. Crossing the entire width of the valley in the far distance was a greyish stain across the green fields.

'Look at that. Looks a bit like a wood,' I pointed, 'but I swear it's moving.'

Gyric agreed, 'That's strange. That makes no sense. Could it be a herd? Too dark for sheep. Cattle maybe?'

I thought we'd pretty much cleared all the livestock for miles around. The 'herd' seemed to be gathering together and moving with purpose. Then the sun came out from behind the clouds. Suddenly the mass glittered with reflected light.

'It's an army,' he breathed, 'and it's not ours. Let's get back to the camp. Fast.'

By the time we got back it was late in the day. Our shouts alerted the whole camp as we found ourselves dragged before a council of all the leading men. We faced a barrage of questions from all sides. Harold's firm voice cut quietly through the hub-bub, 'Let the boys speak.'

The noise quieted as we tried to describe where the enemy were and how many of them. We told them what we could. Their army was bigger than our camp, we thought. We were listened to intently and praised for our effort.

Scalpi took us away, 'Well done boys, we've all got slack here. Our scouts should have known they were coming long before now. Now go eat, they won't attack tonight.'

He was right. There was no night attack. We woke to find a considerable force assembling across the valley. From first light our camp was in turmoil as the men armed themselves and had their positions explained to them.

'Their army will be squeezed as they come through Alrseford we could form up across the valley there where it is narrow,' said Thurkill to Harold. I was hanging around Aethelric and as no-one was noticing me I was listening in.

'Their army may be eight hundred men, maybe more. I cannot split our force nor leave the ships exposed to a flanking attack. So we meet them here then, with the marsh on one flank and the steep hillside on the other.' Harold was magnificently dressed for war. His helmet gleamed as did his mail. His sword was held in an enamelled sheath, its pommel inlaid with silver and gold. His belt passed through a large gold buckle. His shield was stained red around a large polished iron boss inlaid with silver. Behind him stood his standard bearer with Harold's richly embroidered and jewelled banner of the 'Fighting Man' displayed for us all to see.

'We'll have to leave some men on the other end of the beach. It would only take a few men to fire the ships and we're done for.'

'Yes, see to it, not Oslaf's crew. I want him where I can see him. There is no place for those Irishmen in a shield wall. Range them along the edge of the marsh and they can trouble the enemies flank with their throwing spears and slings.'

A group of warriors set off for the western end of the beach, straddling the ridge of tumbled stones between sea and marsh. I could see some of the other boys ordered by their fathers to stay by the ships. I waved at Jokul who was stood on *Sea Serpent's* bow, and Gyric who stood disconsolate by our ship. With no father to order me to safety I was determined to stay in the thick of things and have the best story to tell.

Our army began to spread out creating a thick narrow front. The leader's talked and the right flank spread to cover the edge of the marsh, the left to the stream at the base of the steep wooded hillside. To avoid the risk of panicking beasts between us and our ships the horses were herded out and stampeded up the valley toward the oncoming force.

'Shame to lose our horses,' grumbled a seasoned fighter from amongst the Norse.

'Not at all,' joked Harold, 'they're a gift to help them run away. We'll fight this fight. Strip the dead of all their wealth, then take to our ships tomorrow. There'll be more horses for you to fondle, Hrothgar, if that's what works for you.'

Men laughed, they liked Harold's easy going style and his joking eased the tension. It was obvious now that the force we faced was quite a bit larger than ours.

'How many banners can you see? Twenty? Maybe more? At least twenty then, more than I thought,' said Leofwine. 'Looks like they don't want us Godwinsons back in these lands.'

'They've no reason to like us, brother. Our father's quarrel with the king has split the country. We're here because a civil war would open our country to invasion. All our thegns are sworn to the king now,' replied Harold. 'If our men were all English they'd probably not fight for us. Why else would we need all these paid killers who fight for gold not land?'

Our army began to spread along the inland side of the marsh, slowly forming into a rough line alongside their war leaders. I expected everyone to run at each other and start fighting but I was to learn battles take a long time to begin while your belly crawls with tension and the shadows plague your mind. All around warriors were swinging their arms, flexing their bodies and stretching their jaws. Some joked and laughed, others were growing quiet drawing into themselves, all sought to lose their fear. I did not know this. To me this was all some hugely exciting game.

Slowly their army spread out across the valley while we stood watching. Their front was wider than ours. Their front ranks were only slightly above us but the steep slope meant their other ranks went up in tiers.

Leofwine spoke again. I hung around, I thought unnoticed. 'We cannot lose too many men, their line is long and we will have to attack uphill. This will be a hard fight.'

'There are a lot of them but many will be the local fyrd. Many will only have a helmet and a spear. That said the thegns and their retainers are all well-armed and some will be skilled but few are true veterans. All our men are seasoned warriors fresh from the Irish wars, well-practised and trained,' said Thurkill.

'Realise this, Leofwine, you and I are probably the least experienced fighters on our side,' said Harold. 'But note this. We are protected on our flanks, however deep their ranks, their wall can only be as wide as ours.'

He looked around and loudly observed, 'We can beat this rabble with ease.' Those who heard cheered him. 'But if we can win without a blow then why fight?'

Aethelric seemed to know what was expected of him. Seeing me stood there he shoved a cross headed staff into my hands. Aethelric in his monk's robes and with his tonsure gleaming, sweaty in the weak sunshine, walked out into the space between the two armies. 'Follow me boy,' he whispered nervously, 'and keep that cross high!'

I followed him as a loud murmuring came up from both sides. 'God preserve us Sar, pray that they respect my cloth.' About half way across he got slowly to his knees and loudly prayed. 'Our Father in heaven, protect us from the weapons of our enemies,' and more in the same vein. In both armies men began to lower weapons and bow their heads. Once it grew quiet Aethelric stood and spoke again, 'My Earl would avoid your deaths if he could, is there anyone who can speak for you all?'

'I am Sigeferth and I have called this force together on the orders of the true Earl of these lands, Odda of Deerhurst. I will speak.' The owner of the voice then turned and handed his shield and spear to a follower and walked out from the line. 'Will your traitorous pirate come and speak with me?'

Behind me I could hear Harold and Thurkill handing over their arms while another unarmed warrior stood by Sigeferth. Slowly they approached. I suddenly felt very small dressed in my rags, barefooted between these huge, armed and wealthy, men dressed in ferocious finery. I clutched the staff of the cross and prayed. I stood armed only with a cross between two armies of men readying to kill each other. Suddenly I understood Aethelric's fear.

Harold offered them a chance to leave in peace, that when his father was reinstated he would treat all the thegns with respect. We have brought back precious relics for the King he told them.

Sigeferth spat on the ground, 'You beg because you are weak. Who are you to make offers to us? You are a rebel against your rightful king.'

'We are rebels against the traitors who pour venom into the King's ear.'

'You over mighty arrogant Godwins have lost this time. Go crawl back into the Irish arsehole from whence you came.'

'I am here Sigeferth so where is your Earl, where is Odda? Holding Edward's piss-pot with his nose up some Norman skirt while you do his fighting for him?' Harold retorted coldly, slowly turning his helmet around in his hands.

Sigeferth reddened with fury, 'You insult both your King and my lord. We will wipe your heathen scum from the face of the earth and take back all that you have stolen. You and your brother we will enslave and mutilate as your father mutilated the King's brother.' He turned and shouted at his army. 'There will be no peace here. We will fight.'

Aethelric pushed me ahead of him panting heavily and tripping on his robes. I clung to his staff as we wriggled between the warriors as they began to form their shield wall. Leaning heavily on my shoulders Aethelric steered me to the space behind the ranks. 'Oh dear God, I thought I was to die there,' he panted falling to his knees. 'Please Lord, take me back to my cloister, I would ever be your humble monk.'

Behind me came a huge roar and a thunderous rumble as Harold's men shouted and thumped their shields. The English army did the same but with less conviction. I could not miss this. I shoved the butt of his staff into the ground and left Aethelric praying beneath its cross. I turned back to our army. They were all shouting and beating their shields but all I could see was their backs.

Shouts bellowed along the line and the army began a slow deliberate march forward. As they approached the enemy force a volley of throwing spears flew over from the rear ranks. I could hear screams as well as shouts as the volley hit home. Over the heads of our troops I could see the rear ranks of the foe shifting down the hill. Light spears and a few arrows started to drop into our side rattling between the shafts of the great war spears. Most were dodged or caught on shields. I could not see the front but knew that solid walls of shields bristling with spears would be facing each other across the gap. Another great shout rose and our army stopped marching. Above the din I could hear Harold's voice, 'Hold fast! Let them come.'

There was a deafening crash. I could imagine the warriors trying to push the spears up, trying to reach under the shields of their opponents. Desperate men were trying to close the gap to pull and hack shields, heads and legs. On each side men unable to reach the front were throwing back spears and even rocks over their front ranks. The armies heaved at each other. I wriggled into the fray and pushed my weight into the back of men in front. The walls heaved against each other. They could not break us with weight of numbers. The din of metal on metal, axe into wood and flesh screaming and grunting crashed over me like a storm. Suddenly the initial fury dropped and the fighting lulled as the two sides pulled back exhausted. A few heavily bleeding warriors reeled out from the ranks. As the press of men lightened I wriggled through to where I'd heard Harold's voice.

'There's more of their dead than ours.' It was Leofwine's voice, 'Our experience is showing.'

'It's not good enough, we cannot lose too many. Our force is already small, what use are we to our father if we are whittled down to a bunch of brigands,' Harold replied. 'I've been a fool here. We should have avoided this fight.'

'For all you stand for, do not lose heart now,' ordered Thurkill roughly. 'We are evenly matched despite their number. Think quickly. We need a ruse, some surprise.'

Harold visibly shook himself together as he became aware of his men sizing him up. If he failed they all failed. They all knew this was his first real test in war. Luckily the enemy too seemed hesitant, content to lick their wounds while the stalemate continued.

'How can we get behind them unseen? A small force attacking from an unexpected direction could save us many lives.' Harold paused, 'but how with our backs to the sea.'

Suddenly it struck me, 'Sir, sir I know a way.'

I pushed forward and started tugging at Harold's belt. 'Listen to me, Sir, I know a way round.'

Everyone seemed shocked at my temerity and hands started to pull me away. Harold checked them, 'No, listen to the boy. What do you know?'

I told him. 'I remember you. You're the boy that speaks Irish, Eardwulf's killer. Go tell the Irishman Faelan what you told me. He will know what to do.'

Another roar rose from the ranks of the foe. Harold turned away, 'Quickly boy, go, go now!'

I ran over to the Irish contingent puffed up with the importance of my mission. I drew up to them and faltered, they are a wild lot the Irish. Few wore mail or carried the large round war shields of the Norse or Saxon. Their hair was piled up in wild and extravagant styles, some putting lime in it making it white and stiff. Most had tattooed faces, gold or silver torques around their necks and many arm rings above their elbows. They carried small targes and bunches of throwing spears decorated with feathers. Behind each shield they carried a short broad bladed spear and clubs, swords or knives hung from their belts. They seemed impervious to weather wearing only light woven cloaks over their tunics. They were terrifying to look at and being lightly armed they could move fast and quietly.

Plucking up courage I ran up to the leader and tugged on his cloak, he turned and stared haughtily over my head. I almost looked behind me to see who he was talking to. I jumped up and down for his attention and realising I did not know a respectful way to address him, I shouted, 'Harold says!'

His eyes turned to mine, the irises so huge and black I felt that I could be swallowed up in them. He seemed mad and unreal, 'Harold says what? 'Who are you that speaks to me?' His voice was loud, deep and otherworldly.

'Be very polite,' it was Muirchu who spoke. 'The battle madness is already upon him. He is with his ancestors who walk with us into the valley of death.'

Bowing and stammering and maybe not speaking Irish as well as I thought I introduced myself. Then I gave him Harold's message. He smiled grimly and without replying he turned his men back down behind the shingle ridge pushing me along with them. Hidden by the ridge we ran westward to where the beach became piled with the huge pebbles over towards the wharf. The Irish seemed incredibly sure footed while my youth ensured my agility. There were about forty of us and we moved swiftly along the shore. 'This will do us well,' their leader said as I showed him the small river rushing from the wooded gully where Gyric and I had hidden from Oslaf. We turned into it slowing now as we carefully stepped into the forest, scouts running ahead to check that our way was clear. No-one spoke, Faelan seemed to control everything with small gestures and meaningful looks. The silence was eerie as we moved away from the screaming of gulls and the rough shouts of the opposing armies.

We followed the line of the hillside climbing up and along until Faelan was satisfied. We all crouched silently among the ferny undergrowth. I can still see the curling stems bright green on the forest floor as I crept beside a tree to look out over the farmed land. We could clearly see the two armies lining up against each other as we peered over the nettles at the wood's edge. The enemy force was almost double ours with an equal front but much greater depth. Our army already looked much tighter. Its line was firmer with far less milling about. Faelan held up his hand, the whole band, perhaps forty men, stopped with barely a sound. 'Sar Nomansson, you are not a fool. If you survive come to me tonight.'

I nodded, survive? God, I might not survive. Shuddering at cold reality I nodded, 'I will sir, I will.' We were now looking down across the battlefield behind the enemy left flank. I could see Thord's serpent beyond them, Oslaf's banner over on the far right while Harold's still flew in the centre. Enemy thegns could be seen struggling to dress their ranks for another attack as some men tried to leave while others, battle crazed, had to be restrained from attacking alone. Our men were jeering and yelling insults over the bodies of the dead and wounded. I guessed they had repelled another attack as we had been skirting the field.

We watched quietly as Harold's line changed shape. His force moved forward creating a bulge in his battle line under his banner. The move complete his army once again stood still calmly awaiting their fate. A strange hush descended on the field then the English army charged down hammering into Harold's shield wall. The crash of the impact was stunning as the more experienced fighters pushed up the spear points with their shields. It seemed as if the massive weight of men would have to force Harold's men back. The mass thudded into the line. It staggered then once again held. Forced together the dense seething mass of men made it hard to strike a blow. The air was filled with frustrated cursing and the odd scream as men started to fall. Once the attackers had passed the spear points it became a matter of shield against shield, knife and axe against knife and axe. Men were trying to reach over and hook their opponents shield down or hacking into the splintering boards. Others were looking for a face or leg to stab with their knives. At such close quarters there was no room for sword play.

Most of this was lost to me. All I could see was a struggling mass of men heaving backwards and forwards. Arm's rose and fell, hacking anything in reach, men began to go down and the screaming and cursing got louder and louder. The attacking force started to divide around the bulge of Harold's housecarls, each man trying to follow his leader's banner amongst the chaos. Then in a moment the battle changed. Suddenly Harold's men opened their shield wall and the two-handed axe men came out between the shields. The massive axes swung and helmets and shields split under the heavy blades. Limbs and heads left their bodies in brutal slaughter. At another shout these huge men stepped back and the wall closed again. There was havoc in the centre of the enemy line. Their line would have crumbled but for the men being pushed into the gap from behind. Harold's army stood still then slowly, ever so slowly, started to push the mass of men back up the hill. They must have been marching over the wounded and slain, hacking into the exposed parts of the enemies breaking wall. In the rear ranks men could be seen bending down stabbing into the bodies beneath them.

I could see the Irish leader watching the battle. What was he waiting for? Why weren't we attacking the enemy flank? I could sense the tension in the men around me. One of them snarled at me, 'Stay still whelp, see those numbers, there's not many of us if Faelan oi Airtre,' he nodded toward his leader, 'misjudges the moment we all will die.'

We could see men crawling out from the back of both armies, wounded or stunned. Many paused for a while then went back into the fray but from the back of the enemy army a trickle of deserters were starting to creep out through the village.

'See that. They're wavering, those peasants. Poor souls. May God have mercy on them,' said Faelan. Who then to my great surprise began to pray. His men joined him, heads bowed in plainly sincere worship, each carefully placing his weapons on the ground to make the sign of the cross. Strange people it seemed.

Then before I knew what was happening they jumped to their feet and ran, screaming blood curdling incomprehensible battle cries, bursting out from the woods into the flank of the enemy. At the sound Harold's wall opened again. The massive axes rose and fell and all along his line men stepped apart and started wielding axes and swords, hacking and hacking again and again, into the English line. Now their experience really began to show and the fyrd folk got more and more confused as their leaders shouted to rally them. As our small force of demonic madmen came charging out of the wood throwing volleys of spears they started to break. This was too much for them. They'd given their all and now they were being attacked from behind by screaming devils.

I came running after them screaming insanely, completely caught up in the madness, my arms flailing wildly as I charged downhill. Luckily the foe was also running as I came to the first bodies and realised that I had no weapon. I wasn't even carrying a stick. I dodged a crazed spear thrust from a wounded fyrd man too dazed to know what he was about. An Irishman stabbed him through the back with a spear. Blood spurted from his mouth and his soul left his eyes right before mine. The Irishman grinned at me, shook his bloody spear in my face, laughed, and choosing another victim stabbed again.

This brought me to my senses and I crawled back into the undergrowth as the enemy forces totally fell apart. The slaughter was merciless. No one commander meant there was no one man to surrender. Slowly the battle grouped around the few mailed men attached to each thegn's banner. I could hear Harold's voice above the din yelling, 'Yield for God's sake yield!' Then I could see him trying to stop his battle mad mercenaries from slaughtering the beaten Englishmen. 'We've won, we've won,' but there was despair rather than victory on his face. Whatever the need, his own countrymen were being murdered now, no fight left in them.

Gradually the killing stopped. Men were being rounded up and disarmed. Many were fleeing the field, the trickle turning into a flood as soon as the banners fell. Our exhausted army just stood and watched them run. We had done what was needed to be done. We had broken the local fyrd and killed or captured many thegns who had bravely fought for their King, their Earl or the lands we had so ruthlessly plundered.

That evening was horrific. Harold had stopped any torturing of prisoners saying they were his countrymen. The whole hillside was covered with horribly maimed corpses. The moaning of the wounded and dying rose and fell in strange waves of misery. Crows and magpies came as if from nowhere pecking at open flesh. Slowly the wounded were taken away or dispatched with a sharp thrust of a knife. I learned how to strip a corpse and that I could not just take what I found. Loot was to be gathered together and there was a lot of it. Men dressed in their finest for war. We would all receive our share according to our station in the days to come. I got new clothes though, too big for me but my old rags were falling away. I got shoes! I took a warm cloak to sleep in. I also found a small knife that I decided to keep to myself. It reminded me that Oslaf still had mine. As I stood shuddering in that field of corpses I remembered him and shivered, feeling certain his eyes were on me. I returned to the camp, to the firelight, to something like safety.

CHAPTER 4

I woke with a start, sweating. My mother's ruined face clear in my vision from yet another nightmare. I crawled out from my sleeping place under the steering platform. The men mostly slept ashore but I felt safer hidden on the ship. As I started down the ladder I could hear strange human sounds above the surf. It was Toki huddled up against the curved side of the ship in a deep sleep but sobbing his heart out. He lay there twitching and starting and crying like a baby.

'I'm not the only one who has nightmares,' I thought. I already knew that many of these strange fierce men whimpered in their sleep when lost in the world of dreams. Not Toki though, I'd never seen it as bad as this. I dared not wake him knowing it would shame us both. It felt bad to see Toki so exposed and I knew that I would never speak of this. I climbed back into the ship, got my cloak and lay it over him.

The camp was different tonight. I could hear the groans of wounded men while others were still drunkenly singing or brawling by the dwindling fires. I could see that most had dropped into exhausted sleep drunk on ale or victory or both. Many lay where they had fallen, on tents rather than in them, across paths and in the ashes of fires. Harold's tent was quiet and I knew that even Aethelric would not be up before dawn. Our ships main tent, made from its sail, had collapsed over the sleeping men. Heads poked out from all sides, snoring and mumbling. One shape was shorter and rounder than the rest. It had to be Gyric.

I gently shook him awake, 'Gyric, come on, get up. It's me Sar.'

His eyes opened slowly, he moaned and sat up, 'Leave me alone Sar, just leave me alone.'

'No, come on!'

He crawled out from under the sail, 'Alright, alright, don't wake my father.'

We walked carefully through the camp skirting, as always, Oslaf's tents. No voice challenged us. There seemed to be no guards on the ships or round the camp. It grew lighter as the sun rose out of sight behind the hills. We walked to the edge of the battlefield. As the sun began to rise ravens, seagulls, buzzards and kites as well as crows were flocking in, making the air hideous with their squabbling cries while crowds of flies buzzed and swarmed. Gyric and I stood gazing over the field of corpses appalled at the squalid sight.

Gyric puked. 'Ugh, that's too much after a belly full of ale and no food,' he said spitting and wiping his mouth. 'Where did you get to yesterday?'

I told him how I'd been with the Irish. How I'd led them round to the gully we'd hidden in. I remembered too that Faelan had wanted to see me.

Gyric wasn't happy with me, 'I saw you run by with them. You'd already left me by the ship then run off without a word.'

'Your father had told you to stay.'

'You could have stayed with me, or later taken me along. You only want to know me when it suits you. I knew the way as well as you. I saved your life that night and you just ignore me.'

'It's not true,' I said but I knew he was right.

'You're weird, Sar, you know that? You don't really bother with anyone. Nobody likes you Sar. You don't know when to stop. You don't fight like other boys. You would have killed Jokul.'

I mumbled something but Gyric just carried on, 'Did you ever thank me for passing you that ox-tail?'

The memory of it appearing in my hand came to me, 'I never

thought…..'

'You never bloody do, do you? It didn't get there by magic. You never thanked me for coming to you that night on the beach or chasing after you when you were upset.' He stood up suddenly startling some nearby crows.

He continued, 'Have you ever for a moment thought about me? I took a risk befriending you then you turn up at training with that stupid miniature shield. You don't tell me where you got it, you don't tell anyone. People ask me, he's your friend they say, and I can't tell them and all you do is throw your spear for hour after hour.'

'Why should I care? No-one gives a shit about me,' I shouted jumping up and facing him.

'You just pity yourself. People might care if you let them. My father was kind to you but you ignore him if you can. Aethelric dotes on you but you just abandon him when he's frightened. You're not the only one who's had a hard time!'

I could see that Gyric wasn't just angry, he was upset. I looked at him, perhaps only really seeing him for the first time. I tried to put a hand on his shoulder.

He pushed me away, 'I don't know where my family is either. We had to run with Harold. I never saw them to say goodbye.'

I was shocked. It had never occurred to me that Gyric had troubles. He had Scalpi and seemed always cheerful. He carried on, 'We were chased all the way to Bristou. God alone knows why we weren't caught. We sailed through a terrible storm and people I'd known all my life drowned in front of me. We get to Ireland somehow and then we're in a war. Fuck you Sar, I know it was bad but we all have our stories.'

I remembered Muirchu's gentle words, 'We all have our stories.' I started to understand what he meant. I felt really ashamed. We both abruptly sat down, staring in different directions over the crow ridden carnage.

I knew it was up to me, I tugged away at a tussock not knowing how to begin. I changed the subject, 'I got that shield from one of the Irishmen.'

'So?'

'He told me I could never be one of you. That I had to learn a different way to fight.'

Gyric grunted dismissively.

'Gyric,' I said desperately, 'I don't know what to say. I don't know who I am or where I belong. I don't know what to do.'

'More self-pity. You could try asking me how many siblings I have, or where did I live, you could even just try saying sorry.'

I hung my head while my insides felt pulled in all directions. 'I am sorry, Gyric. I am.'

I got the words out through clenched teeth as my throat tightened into a hard lump. This was too much for both of us. He jumped up, 'Didn't you say that Irish chief had wanted to see you. Come on, let's find him.'

We found Faelen and his men gathered around two holes in the ground. He recognised me, 'You did well yesterday. You showed courage.' He drew a thin arm ring of twisted silver wire from his upper arm. He looked at me and laughed dryly, 'My arm ring, your torque skinny boy.' As he placed it around my neck I glowed with pride.

'Do not be too joyful Sar. There has been a price.' He stood aside. 'I believe you knew Muirchu.'

In the bottom of one of the holes was Muirchu's body. Faelen spoke again, 'You would have done better to have come last night as I asked. He died of his wounds as the sun rose over the hills.'

I stood at the edge of his grave, sickened and shocked. As their priest began to chant the Irishmen circled the graves. I pushed my way out. 'You see Gyric,' I shouted as I ran from him, 'Everyone who is good to me dies. Be nice to me and you'll wind up dead!'

It took us three more days to bury our dead, pack up and leave.

I followed Aethelric around, immersed once again in sullen silence. He was writing down the names of hostages, apportioning provisions and much to everyone's delight dividing the loot between the crews in Harold's name. There was so much that we all got something from the embroidered hangings, mailed shirts, inlaid helmets and jewelled sword hilts for our leaders to the broken broach, a belt buckle, a bag of raw wool and one silver penny that came to me.

To my surprise any books that had been looted in our raids were kept by Harold. Some were finely bound their value clear, others looked rather dull.

'They are a learned family the Godwins. Queen Eadgyth, Harold's sister reads and speaks many languages. Harold will especially treasure this,' Aethelric said passing me a book bound between thin boards.

I looked sourly at the meaningless squiggles but marvelled at the glowing pictures. 'Hawks and dogs,' I said excitedly, entranced, forgetting my resolve not to speak.

'Yes,' he replied, 'Harold loves to hunt. This is a book on falconry.'

Up until now the only book I'd ever seen was Aethelric's psalter and the only writing Aethelric's scribbled lists. Despite myself I was a little fascinated but could see no obvious use for these things.

'Aethelric,' I said, 'I'm sorry for leaving you on the battlefield alone.'

'I was not alone Sar, God was with me.'

'Don't be kind to me, people who are kind to me die.'

He turned to me, his brown eyes in his kind, tired face looked at me with concern. 'Sar, you do not have that much power. You are not responsible for the evils of the world.'

I grunted, unconvinced.

'You'll see my boy, you'll see. We'll be off tomorrow really this time. Back to the sea and away.'

I knew he hated the sea but his message was clear. Tomorrow was a new day, a new chance to begin again. I fingered my torque. I had some wealth. I had survived my first battle and proved myself to Harold. Skinny and haunted I might be but I would become a man with a place in the world.

Aethelric was right, we embarked the next day. Our ships were crowded now with hostages from the better families and slaves with their newly cropped heads. Somehow I seemed to have got attached to Toki and my goods were stored with his. My bag of wool went into the belly of the ship while my smaller items went into the chest on which he sat to row. There were also piles of raw hides and half smoked meat as well as sacks of leathery loaves made from a mixture of the flours and grains we'd pillaged.

There was a lot of good tempered grumbling as everyone found their places. As the tide reached its height the last men were hauled aboard after pushing the ships off the beach. The oars began to catch and our flotilla was under way again. We rowed backwards from the shore. Then, once leeway had been gained, we turned around to row forward, turning the ships in the bay. Oars churned one side, then the other, to the shouts of the shipmasters stood by the steersmen at the rear of the ships. Slowly we all pulled around the headland to continue with the sun on our left, heading westward along the coast, our faces into the wind.

I was more aware of what was going on this time. There was great skill and method behind the working of these beautiful craft. As we got under way I could see that we would get no help from the wind and the sail was kept furled on the yard arm. This lay down the centre of the ship propped on crutches which kept it above the stacked cargo and the huddled people.

The journey continued onwards. Men swapped around taking turns on the oars while slaves were set to bailing using long handled scoops. Even Harold took a turn, good naturedly remarking on how rowing firmed the muscles and back. It did. It also blistered my hands and my arse until both were raw and bleeding. I have never worked so hard. Gyric and I were set to take the ends of an oar each, backing up the rower. I twinned with Toki while Gyric aided his father on the long oars. We rowed and rested, rowed and rested. As the sun reached its height food was handed round and then we rowed and rested some more.

After a back breaking first day we turned south west and spent the night on the ships anchored just beyond the surf in a wide bay. For the next three days we navigated in a series of steps down the coast. The sails went up, the greased cloth billowing in the wind as the steersmen made the best of a wind that seemed out to hinder us. More rowing, more nights spent cramped inside the ships. They began to stink of vomit and shit despite the sea and the wind. Poor Aethelric suffered dreadfully from sickness as did many of the slaves.

Oslaf's white banner led the fleet. His shipmaster knew this coast well. Eventually he led us to a small estuary at the end of a long sandy beach. We crept into the estuary two abreast and found an abandoned port and to our delight two equally abandoned merchant ships. The inhabitants must have seen us coming. One of the ships smelt of pine resin and was covered with sticky black rings. 'Pitch', said Toki, 'valuable stuff, probably came all the way from Sweden. Somebody was buying this and a lot of it.'

Scalpi agreed. 'The Cornwaelus have metals, copper and tin, lots of tin. They've been selling it for hundreds of years.'

'They've not been spending it on fine buildings and churches that's for sure,' said Toki looking around the squalid port. Here and there lay sledges, some loaded with ore, surrounded with filthy mud churned by the hoofs of oxen and human feet. Roughly thatched sheds covered what looked like slave pens. This was a miserable place.

While some of us were set to packing the merchant ships with the slaves from Porloc and the stinking hides. Others went out to scout the dunes and the hills beyond. The slaves were not willing and much brutality was used moving them from one place to another. They were set to swab down our dirty ships and move our goods persuaded by blows and spear points. If I hadn't killed Eardwulf I'd have been one of them. Killing worked for me.

There was a wide track leading inland from the port winding up, through the mud flats, to firmer, higher ground. A band of riders carrying bushes on spear shafts appeared on the brow of the hill. Forewarned a number of our men were already fully armed and forming a loose wall across the road.

One of the horsemen spurred forward, 'I speak for Conor, Lord of Cornubia. Who are you that invade our lands?' He spoke good English with a strong musical lilt. His tone was courteous. He carried no arms but had a small harp slung across his saddle bow. His dark hair hung in plaits decorated with coloured stones and small balls of gold.

Harold strode forward accompanied by the Dane Thurkill and Aethelric, 'Tell your master, Bard, that I am Earl Harold of the house of Godwin, Earl of Wessex.'

'My master has heard that you are no longer an Earl and your father is in exile,' replied the bard with a smile.

Harold met charm with charm and smiled back, 'It is true my father and the King, my brother-in law, have had a little falling out. Families have their difficulties do they not?'

The bard laughed, 'And then they drink together and sing to become friends once again.' He strummed a couple of dramatic chords into the wind. He walked his horse closer to Harold. Spear points were raised towards him.

He laughed again, 'Fear me not brave warriors, my master offers peace. He would support your cause Harold Godwinson but expects to be remembered. He would invite you to a feast with thirty of your chosen men. There will be song, and ale, some wine. We are not savages here, and women, well-bred courtly women.'

Harold was captivated, his delight in women was well known

to us and a ripple of laughter went through our ranks. 'Can we see your master who makes us such a generous offer?'

The bard called out in his own language and one of the horsemen on the hill rode forward. A gold circlet ran through his thick black hair, his horse's ornaments glowed in the sunlight. His shoulders were cloaked in sleek shiny fur above gleaming mail. He dismounted and walked forward, stocky and powerful, with his hand on a richly ornamented sword hilt. He stopped and stood still letting us take in his appearance. He raised an arm and beckoned to his men. Three well-dressed men rode out, unarmed, followed by their grooms on foot behind them.

The bard spoke again, 'We do not take you for a fool, Harold. You may suspect a trap. You can see my lord is a noble man and we follow noble ways. While we feast his brother, his son and a nephew will stay in your camp, as guests, until the revelry ceases.'

Harold bowed towards Conor, 'We appreciate the gesture. Perhaps your son would like to travel with us as part of my household when we leave?'

The bard smiled, 'Perhaps he will. Are we agreed, shall we feast tonight?'

'Yes, we are agreed,' replied Harold.

'Would some of your kin care to come and view our preparations?'

'Sadly, none of my close relatives travel with me,' Harold lied smoothly. 'However we have great men among our number. Oslaf, Scalpi, Aswald. Would you care to escort our musical friend?'

The three of them shrugged agreement. Then after removing their sword belts they mounted the vacated saddles of the tribesmen's shaggy ponies. Gyric started up but Scalpi ignored him and staring straight at me said, 'Sar, my son, you will come with me.'

I looked at Gyric startled. He nodded slowly whispering. 'My father will not risk his entire bloodline in an exchange of hostages.' I felt the bard's gaze shift towards me with a wry smile.

I suddenly understood what was going on. Our lives were being held as surety for our sides good faith Briefly I clasped Gyric's arm then ran to stand by the ponies as did two other youths.

Conor still up on the hill nodded his satisfaction. The men Harold had chosen were finely dressed and obviously of stature amongst us. As we joined Conor's party I ran alongside Scalpi as best I could acutely aware of Oslaf's presence behind me. I knew now that I was the object of a blood-feud and that being Harold's man would not protect me for long. Oslaf, or any of his family, had to kill me to avenge his father's death. One day he would try again but meanwhile he could bide his time and choose his moment. All I could do was avoid him as best I could. Or could I kill him? Ridiculous, I was only in my teens, I thought, with no weapons of my own and no family. He led a war-band and was an experienced and skilled fighter. Should I run? I was sworn to Harold and life had got better. I'd eaten more meat everyday than I'd eat in a month before. I had nowhere to go and would end enslaved by the first strong man to find me. I had to stick it out and take my chances.

These thoughts preoccupied me as I ran beside Scalpi. Before long we came to a rambling settlement centred on a finely built wooden hall with a long low thatched roof surrounded by a low palisade. Outside this fence there were a number of small huts and pens around a large barn. This was the biggest building I had ever seen that wasn't a Roman ruin like that of Caer Dydd. Its walls were of turf and logs, its roof again of thatched straw. Men and women were scurrying about herding out young animals and feedstuffs while others were carrying in green boughs and rough benches.

The bard explained, 'We are preparing a hall for the feast. All of our people are busy in honour of a Godwinson.'

'We are not feasting in your royal hall then,' asked Oslaf, 'Do you insult us?'

The bard laughed again, 'Forgive us, my lord Conor is mighty in these parts but his hall is not great enough to host so many in the style you deserve.'

Conor turned and smiled at us saying something in his own language which had a familiar lilt to it. 'He is welcoming you to his home until we feast later,' the bard interpreted.

Scalpi and Aswald dismounted smiling and bowing at Conor. Oslaf hesitated. I could sense he was unhappy about something but really he had no choice. We were all invited into the fine hall and were welcomed by young women with bowls of curds and honey. As the weather was fine the boards had been removed from window holes. In the beams of sunlight could be seen a sumptuous space with woven wall hangings and cushioned benches around a long hearth. The floor at the far end was raised. On this platform were comfortable chairs covered in furs. Conor threw himself into one and invited us to join him. 'Us' of course did not include myself and the other followers. We were left to sit at the edge of the hall as Scalpi and Aswald joined Conor, the bard and a couple more warriors. They were joined by some women dressed richly in brightly coloured gowns. They too had circlets of gold in their hair. Other young women scurried about, dressed in plainer clothes, serving drinks.

I could see that Scalpi was loving it. He liked rough humour and stories of fights but also we had seen few women and had little luxury for many weeks. Everyone laughed and joked enjoying the little misunderstandings of different languages while the bard translated. He took out his harp, played and sang gentle little tunes, and soon we were all transfixed by their beauty.

'More, more,' cried Aswald and Scalpi stamping their feet in pleasure.

'There will be much more tonight, many songs, much drinking and fine roast meats and oatcakes with wild honey for you all tonight! Be patient my friends and rest awhile while we go and prepare.' The bard exclaimed exuding charm and smiles. Everyone looked happy and relaxed. This was a fine welcome. The other lads and I also felt happy. We'd been given milk and oatmeal and been smiled at by girls. Relaxed as we all were, I even now kept an eye on Oslaf. I could see he was keeping himself slightly aloof but then he was always an odd man.

The afternoon passed pleasantly enough even though we were hostages. When one of us went out to relieve themselves armed men were never far away and we were gently but firmly made to understand we should stay in the hall. After some time shouts and cries of wonder and welcome were heard outside. Harold and his party had turned up. Neither Leofwine nor Aethelric were there but Thurkill was and so were Thord and Faelan. They were all dressed for a feast with fine clothes and jewelled ornaments. Harold wore a magnificent cloak as befitted his status. An English Earl outranked any Cornish lord however he may style himself. With his long hair combed and his arm rings and enamelled clasps and gilded buckles all highly polished. He looked like he'd stepped from a palace rather than one of our cramped longboats. Scalpi, Aswald and Oslaf were asked to join them. The first two were already staggering slightly, leaning on each other and giggling.

Oslaf stalked over to us, 'Fools, drinking without meat, they'll not last the night.' He turned his gaze to us as cold and snakelike as ever. I swallowed hard and resisted the impulse to pull away and reveal the fear he struck in me. His voice fell to a sibilant hiss, 'I don't like this, lads. I can see nothing wrong here but I sense treachery.' His eyes bored into mine. I cringed, I couldn't help it. 'You, Welsh scum, do you know these people are related to yours? Listen hard you might understand them. Keep your eyes and ears open. If any of you suspect anything come to me.' He turned and left with the others.

Oslaf's serving man, Wihtgar, a young bussecarle, a fighting sailor, spat into the sand strewn floor dismissively, 'That's Oslaf, always jumping at shadows.'

Ketil, Aswald's retainer, not much older than me said, 'But what if he's right?'

'Pah! He's nervous as a cat and twice as spiteful. Let's just rest up while we can. We won't be at the feast but at least we're not working.'

'Aswald says that Harold's got far too cocky far too quickly since Porloc. For Conor to make a feast this fast he must be slaughtering every animal around. You don't do that for nothing.'

Wihtgar shrugged, 'Nothing we can do anyhow.' He got up and walked over to flirt with a group of women who were polishing horn cups. An older woman scolded him and he came back to sit alongside us. We were ignored then, left to just sit and watch the comings and goings, in and out of the hall.

I thought about how sly Oslaf was. How he talked the night of my penance about some treacherous deed. Takes one to know one, the words unbidden came to mind. He could be right. I pondered this as I watched men lifting heavy barrels of drink. There was an altercation as the same bossy woman who had scolded Wihtgar lost her temper with one of the porters. As I listened I realised Oslaf was right, they were speaking a dialect of my home tongue. 'Not those barrels, not yet, save them for later when all are drunk. Listen well. These barrels are for the heathen not our men. Do you understand?'

The man cowered, a slave judging by his cropped head. 'Yes mistress, these are strong and make you sleepy. They are for the heathen. This for our men,' he slapped the top of another barrel.

'That's right you dolt,' she answered, cuffing him sharply about the head. 'Get that wrong and I'll make sure you drink enough from here that you'll never wake again, understand?'

He nodded meekly, tipping another barrel on its side and rolling it through the doorway. The woman gave us a sharp look and I grinned back at her hiding my suspicions. She looked at me as if I was an idiot and turned back to chiding the group of women who also ran out carrying cups and jugs.

I whispered to Ketil what I had heard. 'We've got to tell someone,' he said getting up and walking over to the woman and asking her if we could join the feast. It was obvious she didn't understand but she also made it clear that he should go back and sit down. Ketil then loudly complained that his friend was sick.

I caught on and started holding my belly and making retching noises. She looked disgusted and marching over grabbed me and pushed me out of the door scolding me for worthless heathen scum as she did so.

Suddenly I was outside and from the calm glow of the hearth I was now in a world of leaping flames and dancing shadows. I went to the side of the hall and pretended to puke trying to get a sense of what was happening. It appeared that the feast was going on all around as well as in the barn. It was well into the evening and with Scalpi and the others gone no-one was watching us closely. There were groups of men around many fires, lots of men, very few women, not so strange, but lots of men with weapons? Oslaf was right. Why would they be armed?

I dodged through the confusion making my way towards the barn which was set away from the main village. I walked boldly up to the guards outside. 'Message for my master,' I said pushing myself between them.

One of them grabbed me shoving me away with a slap. I tried again and without a word he punched me. He didn't need to speak his meaning was clear. I staggered back to my feet and ran away into the shadows and crouched in the dark wondering what to do next. I slunk into the darker shadow behind the barn. There were no doors and no guards. Following the wall round in the darkness I stumbled into something hard and round. I pulled back as my fingertips went into something sticky. Instinctively I brought my hand to my face and smelt it. Pitch! I found another barrel on its side. The contents had been poured along the base of the walls. I knew two things about pitch. It kept water out and it burned fiercely. Our men were in a trap and could be burned alive. I slunk around the third side of the barn. Now I was out of sight from the village.

On this side about twenty strides from the barn a latrine pit had been dug and railed. Men were coming in and out of the hall in ones or twos, to piss or vomit, gently steered in the right direction by sober Cornwaelians. Some were so drunk they had to lean on the rails to get their cocks out without falling in the pit. It was already obvious that few if any of our men could protect themselves if it came to a fight. Then I saw Oslaf come out. He stalked towards the pit. He was only staggering slightly, clearly less drunk than the others. I crawled through shadowed clumps of coarse grass until I could smell the reeking pit. As he came near I hissed his name. I knew people could hear their own name through any other sounds.

'Oslaf, Oslaf, stop but don't look towards me.' He faltered but quickly recovered. 'You were right,' I whispered, 'some of the barrels are stronger and will make men sleepy.'

He leant against a rail, retching at the smell and acting drunker than he was. 'Drugged ale, we've been stupid.'

'It's worse than that,' I said, 'there's barrels of pitch poured around the back walls of the barn.'

'We've been really stupid. We have our head in the wolf's jaws. You need to create a diversion,' he whispered.

'How?'

'I don't know. They want to burn us. Burn something of theirs. I'm going to try to leave and warn the others.' He casually pissed on the ground then walked away from the hall. Men quickly rose to stop him. He argued briefly. One man looked quickly around and seeing no-one was looking hit Oslaf hard over the head from behind. He collapsed to the ground then was dragged into one of the low huts.

What was I supposed to do now?

CHAPTER 5

I went back around the barn. Then I walked openly towards Conor's hall. No-one took any notice of me as I went back in. People were still going in and out with barrels and food. The old woman scowled at me so I hung my head and wiped my mouth trying to look as if I'd been sick. It was clear she had no time for oafish youths.

I told the others what I had seen, warning them not to show alarm. 'We're going to set this hall alight,' I said pretending a calm I did not feel.

'We're inside it, fool,' said Wihtgar.

'Yes, that's why you have to get near the door and make a row to draw people away from us and the hearth.'

'You're fucking mad,' he said.

'No, he's not,' said Ketil, 'If he's right we'll all be dead or slaves by tomorrow.'

'You know what we have to do then?' I asked.

I could see Wihtgar swallowing hard, 'God help me. I'm scared.'

'Don't be a coward.' said Ketil harshly, 'You'll be near the door. Make a big a noise as you can. They'll forget you once the fire starts.'

I nodded encouragement, 'You can do it! We'll all be heroes when it's all over.'

He looked at us ashen faced, then drawing a deep breath he got up and marched over to the old woman. He stuck his face in hers and yelled, 'What about us you fucking British vermin? Give us some ale and food and a feel of one of your women.' He pushed over a barrel and grabbed one of the serving girls breasts. Immediately there was uproar. Wihtgar threw himself about shouting and kicking in all directions. As everyone in the room turned, Ketil and I rushed towards the hearth.

We quickly grabbed the ends of two burning logs each and ran to the back of the hall. I thrust one of mine up and under the thatch and the other beneath the edge of a finely woven wall hanging. For a moment I regretted the loss of such valuable plunder. Ketil had done the same. Running back to the long central hearth I snatched another burning branch and used it to swipe fiery cinders across the hay strewn floor then pushed it too under the thatch.

I turned in time to see Wihtgar double over as he was stabbed in the belly. His screams rose horribly above the growing crackle of the burning thatch. It burned fiercely. The thatch inside, tinder dry, caught quickly and the room started to fill with smoke. Men and women torn between saving the hall and catching us milled about getting in each other's way. Girls started screeching as trestles overturned and barrels crashed down rolling about the floor. I pushed the end of another burning branch into someone's face and headed for the door. The man who had stabbed Wihtgar was standing over his writhing body staring madly about him as he tried to take in the scene. Blood was dribbling from his blade. He was between me and the door. I still had the smouldering branch in my hand. It glowed redly as I sliced it through the air. The man knocked it aside but as he did so Wihtgar grabbed his ankles and pulled his legs out from underneath him. I leapt as high and hard as I could and threw myself at the door and pushed it wide open. As I did I could hear the fire roar behind me as it sucked in the wind.

Outside I was stunned to find everything just as it was before with the same warriors around the fires and the same dancing shadows. I threw myself into the shadows desperate to mingle with the crowd. A hand touched my shoulder, I whirled snarling, but it was Ketil. He had escaped with me. We stopped panting heavily and turned to look behind us. The roof of the hall was just beginning to steam when all the people came pouring out from inside yelling of treachery and fire.

There was a pause before those outside could take in what was happening when abruptly a ribbon of flames burst through the roof flickering high up into the night sky. Ketil and I backed out from the gathering crowd who were turning to watch as the hall started to blaze. Everyone was so distracted that we were not noticed as we ran through the crowd to the barn. Men were staggering out in various states of drunkenness and excitement. We pushed our way in to find Harold. We found him slouched across the top table his arm draped over the shoulders of a young woman who seemed to have his whole attention. Around him other men lay over and beneath the tables, some still drunkenly boasting or drooling over women. Others were already snoring in the straw. I tried to get Harold's attention but did not want to arouse the suspicions of the women. Harold just waved me away, slurring some unrecognisable command.

I hissed to Ketil, 'There's nothing we can do here. We must try to get back to the camp and warn them.'

Outside Conor seemed to be creating some order from all the chaos as he shouted at men to pull the thatch off the roof. Ketil and I ran as fast as we could from out of the settlement over the hill towards our ships, desperately trying to get our bearings in the dark. Before we had got very far we ran into a body of fully armed men. It was Leofwine himself who recognised us. I quickly explained the treachery and that it was us who had fired the hall.

'I had feared the worst,' he said, 'you must guide us to Harold.'

We attacked the village. Conor's men stood no chance. Many of them were unarmed trying to fight the fire. Any guards that may have been posted were quickly killed as we rushed in from the darkness into the area lit by the furious blaze of the burning hall. Once again I was without a weapon in the middle of a fight. I was crouching behind Leofwine when I heard a familiar voice.

It was Gyric.

'Here have this,' he said pushing a throwing spear into my hand, 'I thought I might be seeing you.'

Savagely our men started killing anyone who came in the way of our formation, men, women and children. In ones and twos they started to fight back. Those who fought also died, brutally hacked to pieces. Eventually a number of them grouped together around Conor and stood in a body between us and the barn.

There was a pause as the two sides took stock of each other. There was no doubt our initial surprise attack had caused great damage but, in the darkness, neither side was sure who had the advantage.

Astoundingly in the pause rose the sound of harp music. The bard stepped out between the two sides. 'My master wants to know why you break our agreement and attack us in our own homes.'

Leofwine yelled out, 'You know why. You plan treachery against my brother.'

'Your brother?' replied the bard, 'and who would that be?'

'Don't play with me minstrel. My brother, Harold.'

'He lied to us then, you attack us and yet you accuse us of treachery?' The bard raised his voice. 'What evidence do you have of this so-called treachery?'

Leofwine was lost for words. Truth was he had no proof. He didn't trust Conor so had set Gyric and others to watch the hostages and had armed a large party anyway. When Gyric had seen one of the hostages servants order his supposed master to do something that had been enough to start Leofwine marching. The only other evidence he had was my word, the word of a renegade murderer of doubtful loyalty. On my word he had attacked the village and slaughtered Conor's people.

There was only one way to prove this! Oslaf! Oslaf was hidden nearby. My mind worked furiously trying to work out which hut he was in. Where was he? I had to move fast. I could hear Leofwine stalling for time, challenging the bard to deny his suspicions. Pulling Gyric by his tunic I pushed our way out into the space behind our men. 'Follow me,' I said to Gyric and ran in an arc to the side of our forces to where I had last seen Oslaf. I recognised the hut and as I did so became aware that it was guarded by a sole warrior. We drew up before him.

'We have to get into that hut,' I said, 'trust me we just have to.'

'By the good Christ, what do you want of me?'

'Your father's still in that barn, Gyric, probably drunk and drugged as well.'

Gyric was armed with a spear and shield but even under his helmet it was obvious he was not a fully-grown man. The guard snarled something in his own language about bitch's whelps. He seemed to take no notice of me at all, dressed as I was in just a tunic. It's possible that in the darkness he could not even see the spear I was holding. He spread his feet and dared Gyric to come on. Gyric squared up to him bravely, his shield held firm before him. He tried a quick underarm thrust. It was easily fended off by the guard's shield. He feinted towards Gyric's face. Then the guard quickly tried to stab under Gyric's shield as it rose to protect his eyes. Gyric jumped back in time and firmed himself for another blow in this unequal conflict. The guard raised his spear once again for a powerful overarm stab, twisting his weapon down and over Gyric's shield. If I didn't act now Gyric would be beaten to his knees and finished off.

I saw my moment as the guard was focused on killing Gyric. All those sulky hours throwing spears paid off. I ran in and threw it from close range into the exposed armpit under his right shoulder. He screamed with shock, surprise and pain and his spear dropped from his hand. He tried to grab the spear with his left hand but his shield hampered him. Gyric crashed against him and he fell writhing to the ground. I ran in, seized the butt end of my spear, and pushed. The shaft snapped as he twisted to get away from me, lashing out with his feet. Gyric stamped on his arm which held it steady for enough time for me to wrench the broken shaft out from his body. Blood gushed from his wound and I felt that same fierce exultation that I'd felt at the death of Eardwulf. Pure joy coursed through me as his life leaked out into the grass. My stomach clenched and the blood pounded through me. I felt stronger than I'd ever felt, dark and powerful.

Gyric shook me, 'What is with you, Sar? Come on, the hut, why are we here?'

I came back into myself and taking up the guard's spear poked it ahead of us into the hut. There was no-one inside but Oslaf. It was dark in the small hut and for a moment he did not know who I was. 'Ah! It is you Welsh boy, are you a traitor now, joining your vermin cousins? Are you come to kill me while I am bound?'

'Shut up Oslaf, I need you to prove their treachery against us. Leofwine has attacked the camp. Ketil and I set the hall on fire. Your man Wihtgar is dead.'

'You are here to free me are you boy? What a fool. You could kill me now and avoid my vengeance. We have a blood-feud, you and I. Whatever you do won't change the fact you killed my father.'

I looked into his eyes. There was no fear there at all. He was bound hand and foot on the floor yet was talking down to me. I could kill him now and be free of him forever. I had his life in my hands but I was afraid to take it. I could feel Gyric squirming impatiently behind me. I saw something colourful and familiar in the gloom. It was the handle of my family knife at Oslaf's belt. The knife I had used to take his father's life.

I pulled it from his belt, 'No!' I said, 'I'll let you live but I'll have this back.'

'Wise boy. If I died my men would kill you anyway. And if they don't get you my family will be told. Be sure, little turd, you will be skinned alive even if I have to come from beyond the grave.'

I shivered but braved it out, 'You're tied up on the floor.'

'Think I can't harm you?' Suddenly, somehow, he launched himself up and his head smashed into my face. Blood poured from my nose, its metal taste sickening. I fell back choking.

'For Christ's sake, you two, stop it!' Gyric was furious caught between our fight and looking out from the doorway. 'We need to get out of here.'

Oslaf laughed, 'Cut these bonds then if you dare.'

I wasn't completely stupid. I only cut the ropes around his feet spitting blood as I did so. Gyric and I dragged him from the hut. He wasn't in good shape despite his defiance. His fine white hair was matted with blood from the blow on his head. He staggered at first supported by Gyric.

I turned to the body of the guard and for reasons I don't really know knelt by his corpse and sawed his head off with the still sharp knife. It was harder than I'd thought it would be. I cut his helmet straps and then by gripping his hair could get the blade between the bones of his neck. At last it twisted off with a sickening crunch just like a goat's but with no horns to grip and wrench with. Rising, I ran with the others towards our men, my glistening knife in one hand and the head, dripping gore, dangling from the other.

When we got there the situation had changed. Harold supported by a couple of other drunken revellers was furiously yelling at Leofwine for attacking our friends. The number of Conor's men seemed to have diminished as their leaders plans had started to unravel. Conor himself was acting as a mild-mannered conciliator between the Godwinsons, protesting his own innocence.

Gyric and I pushed Oslaf towards the space between the quarrelling men. Our voices unheard I stalked into the space and threw the bloody head at Conor's feet. Looking insane with my smoke reddened eyes behind a sooty and blood smeared face I must have appeared like some strange demon lit up by the flames of the burning hall.

I pointed towards the head, 'You know that man, Conor, don't you?'

Conor nodded, 'One of many you people have treacherously slaughtered.'

I turned to Harold, 'That man was keeping Oslaf prisoner!'

Harold turned on me, 'What do you think you are doing? Are you the cause of this?' He was rapidly sobering up as he grabbed my hair and forced me to my knees.

'Sir, sir, look at Oslaf, sir. Look at him!' I pleaded. 'There are barrels of pitch opened around the barn. They meant to burn you all.'

A couple of Leofwine's men untied Oslaf's hands and he strode towards Conor. 'You had this done to me you traitorous dog!'

Harold stared aghast at Oslaf's bleeding scalp. Realisation of the true situation dawned on him. He dragged me into the ranks of Leofwine's armed supporters and ordered them to attack.

'I want Conor alive and that slippery songster too. The rest you can slaughter.'

Our men didn't hesitate. Very rapidly a number of Conor's men were hacked down overwhelmed by our practised ferocity. More men had arrived from our ships heavily armed and mailed, drawn to the sight of leaping flames. Now outnumbered and outsmarted Conor soon threw down his arms and ordered his men to surrender.

Taking their cue from Harold the fighting stopped and those Cornishmen who had not slipped away or been killed were herded into the barn. The women in the barn were herded out. Our men, some like Scalpi still sleeping, were slapped into consciousness and made aware of our situation.

Conor and the bard were separated out from the others. The bard began to try to charm Harold, still claiming there had been a misunderstanding. That Conor could make them all wealthy men from the profits of the tin mines. Conor agreed pleading for his life in his own language offering riches and lands.

Harold stared at them, 'Oslaf, make this bird sing.'

After beating him, Oslaf started breaking the bard's fingers one by one over the bridge of his harp. Oslaf knew how to hurt a man's soul as well as his body. Strangely the bard held out until every single finger was broken and twisted. Then he revealed Conor's plan. They had planned to capture Harold once all were drunk or slumbering then burn his leading men in the barn. Then they could buy off our leaderless troops and either seek favours from King Edward or a ransom from Godwin. They knew all about Godwin's quarrel with the King and reasoned that by capturing Harold they could win whatever the outcome.

His, and my, story was backed up by the discovery of barrels of pitch by the barn doors and along the walls. Drugged and drunk Harold's men would have stood no chance. Harold ordered that a barrel of pitch be poured over Conor who now regretted his surrender. He had changed from pleading for his life to angry defiance, vehemently cursing the English race.

Harold laughed at him, 'Look at you now,' he said, 'the last King of the Cornwaelas. From today your people will be ruled by Saxons, your wealth will be ours.' With that he ordered that Conor be set alight. As the pitch caught fire his flesh burnt and bubbled and screams came from the red gash in his face that was his mouth. Our men pushed his writhing, flaming body into the barn with their spears. The barn began to burn. The warriors inside raised a great shout and tried to break out through the back. They were met by armed men with long spears. The barn burned fiercely fuelled by the barrels of pitch that it made the now smouldering hall pale into insignificance.

We stood in a great circle around the blaze until the screaming stopped. It didn't take long. Then Harold let us loose.

There was no mercy. Stung by Conor's treachery our men killed every living thing they could find. Men, women children and animals were all slaughtered. At first I took no part in this. I sat with Gyric and his still befuddled father but as men started to queue up to rape the women I got excited by the idea of losing my virginity. Did I not deserve some reward? I had saved our leaders from a disgraceful death. I saw some men dragging a half-naked young woman, her pretty face distorted into ugliness by terror. I ran over, they laughed and offered to hold her down for me. 'Come on boy, make a man of yourself.'

I felt proud and powerful. I had killed a man and now I would take a woman. There were no rules now, I could do exactly as

I liked. I felt my prick harden and got it out. She looked up at me blue eyes pleading. There seemed something familiar about her face. I felt a strong sense of wrongness but by now the men were egging me on and I dared not back out. In my mind I knew what I wanted to do was wicked but my balls felt like they were bursting and I wanted to do it. As I was about to kneel on the ground, my prick in my hand, I was thrown violently sideways to the floor.

'What the fuck!' I found myself on the ground staring up at Toki. He grabbed one of my feet and pulled me out from the ring of men.

'What are you doing you bastard? Why is some fucking shit always pulling or pushing me around? Why can't people leave me alone?'

Toki calmly leant over and slapped me across the face hard, 'I'm returning a favour boy.'

I didn't understand. He explained, 'You put that cloak over me on the beach at Porloc. I woke up. I knew I'd been crying. You treated me with kindness and never said a word.' He paused weighing his words carefully, 'I'm not ridden by nightmares and wake crying because of what has been done to me. I have nightmares because of what I have done to others.'

I looked up at him and saw the monster inside of me. My exposed prick shrivelled and I felt like a small and pathetic child. Unable to cope, overwhelmed with shame, I got to my feet and ran off into the shadows, and kept running.

By dawn I was roaming among windswept sand dunes screaming at the sky, my head full of unwanted visions. The guard writhing on the ground, his head in my hands, a girl's pleading eyes, blood pumping from Eardwulf's neck, my mother's shattered face. Leaning against a sandbank bathed in the cleansing wind from the sea I sank into an uneasy sleep.

I sensed something. Somehow I knew I was not alone. I slowly opened my eyes. Someone was sat beside me, I reached for my knife. It had gone.

'Make no sound and I'll not hurt you.'

I got to my knees and looking round found I was looking into the eyes of the bard. His battered face was unrecognisable but the decorations in his hair told me who he was. He was cradling my knife in his broken fingers.

'I could not stab you if I wished, boy of many tongues,' he winced as he spoke.

'How did you get here?' I asked amazed to see him alive.

'They soon tired of kicking me around when the greater sight of a burning king was on offer.'

'A King,' I spat into the sand, 'What king?'

'Conor was king to us, the King of the West Britons, what few of us are left,' answered the bard. 'I crawled here on my elbows. Look what your friend has done to me.'

'Not my friend,' I said bitterly, 'not my friend at all. I could have killed him last night and been rid of him forever.'

Ignoring me he held up his broken hands. His fingers were bent horribly in all directions. 'I have played in many halls, sung before many lords in many lands before I came home to my own wild country to end like this.' Tears ran down his face. 'Music is our heart, the harp is my soul. You savages have broken my fingers and stole my soul.'

I was struck with sadness remembering the beauty of his playing in Conor's hall. I'd never heard anything like it. I was a stranger to music. 'Can't we fix them, your fingers I mean?'

He looked at me through hollow eyes, 'I'll never play again, but if we could splint these fingers I might be able to use my hands.' He explained to me what I needed to do.

'I'll need my knife.' I stood carefully looking around to check that we were alone.

He raised his cupped hands cradling my knife and looked directly into my eyes. I took it knowing I was going to help this man, our enemy, but not knowing why.

On the slope behind the dunes was a narrow belt of birch scrub. I walked along the top of the dunes signalling him to run, crouching, through the trough between. We reached the scrub and huddled amongst the small trees. Under the bards instruction I cut thin branches and using strips cut from my tunic I splinted his fingers. I had to pull them into something approaching normality but it was obvious that his hands would never be more than claws.

He masked his pain well by asking me questions. 'That knife,' he said, 'that knife. Where did you get it?'

'It was my mothers,' I said. 'She took it from my father before she escaped from him.'

'Do you know your father?'

'I've never known my father, never seen and never want to see him.'

'Well, if this was his it came from some old and wealthy family.'

'He probably stole it. My father was not a good man.'

This sort of work is old but fine. I told you I have travelled. This is the work of Angles but from long ago,' the bard rambled on. 'Clean it up with vinegar and water I think you'll be surprised. Your father's, you say?'

He whimpered briefly as I jerked another finger straight. 'I don't want to talk about my father,' I said. Compared to what I had done and seen over the last few weeks it was hard to see my father as the monster my mother portrayed. He seemed much the same as other men, mostly cruel.

'So that man with the white hair, not your friend then?'

'Oslaf? Christ. No! I hate that bastard and he hates me,' I retorted.

'So we share something then.'

I looked at him, a broken man with broken hands, 'So what if we do?'

'I will want revenge,' he said.

I laughed at him, 'You've nothing, not even a pair of hands.'

'Don't laugh, if I survive you'll have an ally somewhere in the world. Now tell me about Oslaf.'

I told him my story, about killing Eardwulf, about Harold saving me from Oslaf and Oslaf's strange mutterings on the beach at Porloc. I found it easy to talk to him as I cut strips and splints. With my hands occupied I didn't need to meet his eyes.

'He murdered someone then, this Beorn. Who was he?'

'I don't know and I'm afraid to ask, only my friend Gyric and I heard his ravings.' I stopped aware that I had revealed my friends name and stared at him. 'Why do you ask? What does it matter to you?'

He looked calmly back at me, 'Don't fear me lad, I can't hurt you and wouldn't. I owe you.'

'I wouldn't be too sure of that,' I retorted, 'last man I told my story to died soon after.'

He looked at me sadly, 'You're a strange young man to feel so cursed. My name is Candalo. Candalo Harp they call me or they did.' Once again he held up his ruined hands. 'Will you give me your name?'

'Sar!' I spat at him. 'My name is Sar.'

'Hmmm, in the Saxon tongue your name means pain, does it not?'

I didn't answer just stared gloomily across the dunes. We sat quietly together.

I got up. 'I'd better go. Someone may notice I'm gone.'

'I have a daughter, I hope still alive. Will you look for her?'

It suddenly hit me. The girl last night, she looked familiar. She looked like Candalo. My stomach sank and I flushed red.

'You know something, I can see it. You know where she is.' He entreated, 'Tell me, you must tell me.'

I spoke into the distance, 'It's not good. It is really not good.'

Horror crossed his face. We both knew what I meant. 'She was alive when I last saw her that's all I can say.'

'Her name is Morwid.'

I got up and ran towards the smouldering buildings now hissing and steaming in the light rain which preceded a thickening sea-mist.

By the time I reached the village the mist had thickened. Man shapes blundered around in the fog making it easy not to be seen. I didn't know why I'd helped the bard but I knew that I had to look for his daughter. I kept thinking of my twin who I felt I had abandoned. If I can help this girl maybe God would help my sister.

I did find her. It took a long time. I found other girls and women crying or their bodies, stripped and abused, dead amongst the wreckage of their homes. I left them there fixated on finding Morwid.

I found her in the corner of a sheep pen huddled behind a hurdle. Her ears and neck were torn where her jewellery had been ripped away. She tried to cover herself with the tattered remnants of her dress and cloak. She was filthy with ash, mud and tears but by her blue eyes and curling black hair I knew her for who she was.

She cowered away from me trying to bury herself deeper under the woven branches. As I went to touch her she flinched away from me making a quiet keening sound. I didn't know what to do.

I sat in the dung left by the sheep slaughtered for yesterday's feast and looked at her. She was clutching something close to her. I gently pulled the hurdle to one side. She closed her eyes tight and squeezed her body hard against the fence. I could see what she held. It was her father's harp.

I touched it and spoke to her in Welsh, 'Morwid I know where he is. Your father, I know where he is.'

Her eyes opened and she looked at me suspiciously.

'I can take you to him,' I continued, 'He's hidden in the birch break at the end of the dunes.'

'Why should I believe you?' Her voice was hoarse, not much above a whisper.

'I know your name.'

'Means nothing,' she buried her head against the wall her body shuddering.

'I know his name, Candalo Harp.'

'Means nothing.'

'What have you got to lose?'

She thought about that for a while. 'Don't look at me.'

I looked away but could sense her pain as she slowly got to her feet. I glanced around. She was stood hunched over. Holding the broken harp against her belly with one hand she was trying to hold her clothes together with the other.

'I said not to look at me! You go, I'll follow.'

We crept slowly through the village, through the fog and through the dunes. Crouching fearfully away from moving figures, from hiding place to hiding place, we reached where I had left her father. When she saw him she started sobbing and shuffling faster towards him. He held his arms out to her and wrapped her in them. I turned and headed for the ships alone.

I found the port already surrounded by tents and busy with the comings and goings of men and animals. The pens were slowly filling with miserable captives their heads roughly shaved denoting their new status as slaves. I pushed my way through the crowd to where *Maeve's Lover* was moored. I knew I would find at least some of our crew there.

Before I got there Gyric, Jokul and some other lads grouped round me excitedly. One of the captives had told us where Conor's treasure was kept. Like any peasant the bulk of it was kept under the floor of his house. Pulling away the smouldering remains of his hall that had been hissing and spluttering in the light rain revealed the raised stone platform. Buried under its heat cracked slabs were a number of coffers some filled with coin others with fine old silver and bronze bowls and chalices covered with whirling incised designs. There were a number of gold torques and circlets and a jewelled crown all slightly melted into each other. Beneath them, and finest of all, were some ancient golden crosses and croziers which Harold had immediately handed over to the care of Aethelric.

'Treasure!'

'We are like Vikings now!'

'Maybe we'll all be rich.'

'Where have you been, Sar?' asked Gyric, 'No-one has seen you since last night.'

'Around. How's Scalpi?'

'Nursing a very sore head and feeling very sorry. He comforts himself with the knowledge that many others are in the same boat.'

I pulled him out of the crowd. 'Did you, you know, do anything last night?'

He looked at me then flushed red, 'No, Sar, I couldn't do that. I've got sisters. I had to look after my Dad anyway.'

'I nearly did, Toki stopped me.'

'Good, it's wrong!'

'I've got a sister too Gyric. Where do you think she is?'

'I heard the ship that came to Fleet Holm was out of Bristou. Slaves go all over from there. She could be anywhere Sar, anywhere.'

'Someone must keep records, Aethelric writes everything down.'

'Sar, you can't chase after her. Even if you could track her down you made an oath to Harold.'

I felt desolate. He was right. It was hopeless to even think of it. 'Gyric,' I said, 'I've done something else.'

I told him about the girl and the bard. I told him that I'd talked about Oslaf and what he said that night.

'Christ Sar, are you mad. That man and Conor planned Harold's capture and the death of many of our best men. Don't let anyone else know. People aren't sure about you, you know.'

I was shocked, 'I saved everyone.'

'Maybe, but some say that you are always in the middle of trouble, that you are not natural, that you are a changeling, an elf child.'

I didn't know what to say. It was uncomfortably close to what I thought about myself.

'That business with the head didn't help. Oslaf's men spread rumours about you. How could you have killed the Fox so easily? Or your mother speak clear English in a Welsh shithole?

They say it was unnatural that you survived that penance. Some say that you were swept up in the night by a demon. Sometimes I'd wonder about you myself if it hadn't been me that saved you that night.' He sat on one of the wrecked sledges. 'So you told him that I heard what Oslaf said?'

'Yes, I think he got that.'

'Sar you are so fucking closed mouthed then you tell our secrets to some complete stranger.'

'He can't do any harm.'

'I hope you are right Sar, I really hope so. Oslaf scares me near to death. He's not right in the head.'

I changed the subject, 'So we're all going to be rich are we?'

Gyric snorted, 'Look how many of us there are. I saw that treasure. It wasn't so great. All the ships except ours and Oslaf's are mercenaries. They'll claim their share and still demand pay. We might get a penny or two if we are lucky, nice to have but a long way off rich.'

Over the next fortnight we laid waste to the whole region. As we scoured the area more wealth was found in the form of blocks of partly refined tin and copper in an old mine. We also found scores of emaciated worked out mine slaves who were just left to roam or starve, not worth the trouble of capture or feeding. Their wailing cries followed us around like spirits haunting the wind.

I visited the birch wood where I had left Candalo and Morwid but although I found their camp I found no sign of them. I left the food I had stolen for them hanging in a tree. As I returned I saw Oslaf and some of his men riding out. His cold stare followed me. I put my hand on my knife with a small thrill of triumph before my mind went back to Morwid. Her black hair, her blue eyes, her frailty possessed me. It was hard to get her out of my thoughts.

We soon discovered that the south coast was only a day's ride away so Harold decided that only the sailors, the wounded and a few extra hands would take the ships around Pentwithstart.

Aswald was to lead the land party across taking Aethelric with him. He feared the sea and the next stage was around fearsome rocks and ragged reefs. I was advised to walk but I asked to go on the ships and was allowed.

CHAPTER 6

Before we left I said goodbye to Faelan and his men who had decided to head home. They were taking one of the merchant ships with slaves and hides as part of their payment. 'Ireland is a great market for slaves,' they said and so they left.

As their boat crept out through the estuary I ran along the shore. 'God bless you, Faelan oi Airtre, Lord of War, fly safely across the waves, fly safely,' I yelled in Irish, waving the targe Muirchu had given me.

To my surprise the fierce Faelen called back from the retreating stern, 'Go well, child of strife, fear not the shadows.'

I stood and watched them disappear into the distance, those wild men who had given me courage, wealth and protection. I hefted the targe back over my shoulder and rubbing my torque for luck I trotted back to embark once again on *Maeve's Lover*.

Being back out at sea was exhilarating as was turning the end of the country. I bailed when I was told to bail, pulled ropes when I was told to pull and rowed when I was told to row. I felt so alive in the storm of the surf, watching the ragged-toothed rocks reach out for our ships through the crashing waves. With our skeleton crews and little baggage the lightened ships flew above the waves and we all rounded the points safely. Once around and sailing east a gentle west wind skimmed us along until we turned and sailed north into a small bay. Here we met Aswald who declared that he'd like to stay with some of his men and the worst of the wounded. 'I'm going to found my own settlement here,' he said, 'Aswaldton. I like the sound of that.'

We continued on westwards, around another frightening peninsular then into calmer seas carried as before by a westerly wind. Our ships were full again, though the losses at Porloc and our recent fight left gaps that weren't there before we had left Fleet Holm. We still had the nine longships with the merchant's knarr wallowing behind playing catch up every night. With Aethelric back aboard my role once again was to take care of him, to get his food down him, then to get rid of it when it came back up.

I found peace at sea, peace in the wind, peace in the sound of the waves and the cries of the sea-gulls that I had heard since birth. I dreamt I could be a sailor and master these ships and conquer the seas. Then I would remember that I was sworn to Harold. I was his man and could only go where he commanded. We had recently rounded a headland called Portlande when we saw a skute, a small light sailing ship, tacking towards us. We drew the ships into a half moon around the craft and as it came nearer could see it flew a banner of the White Dragon.

'Your father's banner, Sir,' called the steersman.

'Not my father, Wessex, loosen your swords men,' said Harold cautiously.

It turned out to be his father's banner and with it messages from Godwin impressed with his seal. There was no enemy fleet between us and the Isle of Wight. Harold and Leofwine could meet with their family there. Our mission too, it seemed, was changed and we were instructed not to pillage Wessex but to seek friends, provisions and hostages along the coast. We should only attack those we knew were directly opposing Godwin's return.

Harold was visibly relieved, joking and laughing with us on board. 'We will solve our quarrel with the king and regain our Earldoms,' he cried. We all cheered him as if the Earldoms were our own. He even spent some time to talk to me as I checked the stowing of the casket holding our holy mantle, my daily task.

Calling me to the edge of the steering platform where he was sat he threw an arm across my shoulders. 'Sar, isn't it? You are a strange boy but you have proved your loyalty in my eyes. I kept you alive because I hated Eardwulf. ' He looked at me. 'Really hated him. When I was a boy him and Sweyn, my elder brother, gave me and my sister, Eadgyth, now the Queen you know, a very hard time, taunting and bullying us.'

I didn't know what to say. Harold talking to me of being bullied! I mumbled something. He continued, 'My father always stuck up for them, still sticks by Sweyn even though he brings us nothing but trouble. And Eardwulf was always there, smirking in the background. Then you, a child from a dung-heap, kill him like the pig he always was.'

He laughed out loud enjoying the memory. 'Don't like that Oslaf much really either but he has served me well and he, his family and his following are a useful force to have onside. He probably won't kill you openly while we are on campaign but be sure he wants you dead. So stay away from him.'

'I'll try,' I said, 'and thank you Sir, for everything.'

'You don't need to thank me Sar, just serve me. You are nearly a man and I need men, loyal men. How old are you?'

I shook my head reddening with shame, 'I don't know, Sir, twelve, fourteen maybe, I don't know.'

'Old enough to kill and quick enough to learn. My housecarls are all men from known family or men who have proved themselves in my family's service over years. Your friend Gyric will probably join them soon but you, you come from nowhere and besides you are too skinny.' He poked me in the side tickling me roughly, laughing at his own good humour.

'I don't want to be a monk, please don't make me a monk.'

'No, I won't make you a monk, and I know you are a willing servant and you can stick in the knife if need be. You are to serve Aethelric until we get him back into Canterberie and have hung that bastard Robert by the heels. You're quick with languages aren't you? I heard you speaking something close to Danish with Thurkill. Learn as much as you can, especially of languages, but don't let people know what you hear. Let me know. Then you can serve me but only in the background as a servant. Meanwhile you can train with the fighting men when you've done your other duties.'

He clasped my hand, 'A deal Sar, a deal, as man to man?'

'A deal my lord, a deal,' I was overcome with embarrassment and completely taken in and charmed by his manner. I would happily serve him in any way I could.

'And, my man, carry a spear and that little shield of yours when you are in my escort.'

'I will, sir, I will.'

He turned away to talk to greater men but telling me I could bear arms made it clear that I was his servant not his slave. He'd given Oslaf money for me and just what my status was hadn't felt certain but I knew no slave was allowed to carry a weapon.

Some days later we arrived at the Isle of Wight. We were now a fleet of fifteen ships as other men joined our banners. We had done as asked and not only had our fleet grown but a small army had gathered and was following us along the shore. My eyes had been opened. I had seen towns and villages, wealthy ones with stone churches, large wooden halls and long quaysides with rich farmland behind them. My squalid home in the ruins of Caer Dydd seemed far away indeed.

Harold was proclaiming his family's greatness. 'All the wealthy towns and ports of Wessex owe their prosperity to my father and the protection of the fleet the heregeld paid for. Can Odda and Ralph protect them from me, Harold? No! No they can't.'

His men cheered him on. These fighting men loved a good boast and Harold had earned their acclaim.

I asked Aethelric what he was talking about. 'All men used to pay a tax, the Heregeld or Danegeld as people called it. It was the first tax a man had to pay and the heaviest. Once it had been used to pay off invaders then it was used to pay the Danes themselves to man a fleet for us as expert seamen and raiders. We set pirates to catch pirates and for many years it has worked.'

'What happened?'

'People hated the tax, it kept men poor and when they couldn't pay it wealthier people would and so small men lost their lands. The pirates were forgotten and no-one wanted to pay foreigners to do nothing. Edward, falling out with Godwin, who managed the fleet anyway, wanted to be popular.'

'So he stopped the tax?'

'He did, and the fleet disbanded. As we heard from Godwin, it hasn't gone well for the King else he would not be on the Isle of Wight.'

'And who are Odda and Ralph?'

'Well, let me see. Odda of Deerhurst is a great Earl and a benefactor to the Church and so is Ralph, who is French. Ralph of Mantes, the King's nephew. They are trying to manage the fleet now what remains of it.' He went on, 'but they are not seamen Sar, and the seas are a mystery to landsmen.'

'Good for us then?'

'Yes Sar, good for us, though it is sad that men must fight. I long for my cloister, for the peace and quiet. I just want to be home. I don't even want to be Archbishop any more, even if they were to vote me in again. I want to be unafraid, to not be sick and to see no more horrors.' Tears sprang from his eyes and started to roll down his face. I gently pulled his hood over his head. It would do our men no good to see him cry. Our monk, our lucky monk, was much loved for his care for us. Who else could love us whatever we did or were?

Keeping the Isle to our left we entered a wide bay on the eastern side with a long sandy beach. There were ships everywhere, many riding at anchor, sheltered from the winds that had brought us here. Many more were drawn up along the beach which was heaving with men. Our fleet just seemed to disappear as we merged into this much larger force. A small karve came out to meet us and to ferry Harold, Leofwine and Aethelric to the shore with their serving men which meant that I went too.

We beached beside a small stream coming from a village called Sencliz. Passing files of men rolling water barrels to and from the stream we walked to join a small group of well-dressed men sat beside some waterfalls.

A powerfully built man, quite stocky, and obviously in charge jumped to his feet with his arms held wide apart. 'My sons! Harold, Leofwine! How good it is to see you.'

As we got closer I could see that he was older than his vigour would suggest. In his early sixties perhaps, I had seen very few old men. His hair was grey but with a still russet beard. His stern face was now wreathed in smiles but as soon as it relaxed it became hard and calculating. After bowing before, then embracing, his father Harold turned and hugged another man. 'Tostig. I have missed your solemn looks.'

Despite his words they were clearly delighted to see each other. Hugging and playfully punching each other like boys rather than the lords they were. Tostig looked very like Harold, nearly as tall and also fair haired, but his looks were darker and he had none of Harold's easy going swagger. Gyrth, a slighter figure, perhaps two or three years older than Leofwine, stood a little awkwardly to one side. Harold winked at him and he shyly blushed with pleasure.

'And Sweyn, where is he?'

'Sweyn is on a pilgrimage, as a penance, walking barefoot, 'said Godwin, 'to Jerusalem.'

'Good riddance,' said Harold, 'His presence would make our task much harder.'

Godwin cast him a sharp look, 'My first born is atoning for his crimes.'

'Would be much better if he'd never committed them,' retorted Harold harshly.

Godwin looked angry, 'Let the past lie. Let it lie. What is important now is to get our positions restored and to get your youngest brother and your nephew back from the King.'

'Yes, come on,' said Tostig, 'It is bad enough we quarrel with our King. We must not be divided among ourselves. With our Earldoms taken from us and Wulfnoth and Hakon hostages in Edward's care we have better things to do than argue. Come Harold and you cousin Aethelric, join us, eat, drink and celebrate how well we've done so far.' There was a general murmur of agreement and as they all embraced again the tension lifted. Tostig it seemed could persuade where Harold, if he wanted, would have simply charmed.

'Tostig, you are right and how are things with your bride, the honeymoon bed still warm?' said Harold throwing his arm across his brother's shoulder.

Tostig looked pleased, 'It is brother, Judith of Flanders. I miss her every day.'

'And every night too, I'll bet.' Harold laughed out loud, 'Well brother I'm sure we can find you a consoling slave girl somewhere on this island.'

'I'm not like you Harold. She's my wife and I aim to be true, as God is my witness,' replied Tostig.

'No, you're not like me. If you're not with the one you love then love the one you're with is what I say.' Laughing together the brothers followed their father into a large space tented with sails where food and drink were laid out in abundance.

I was not invited so I scrounged some food and a bowl for water. I thought back to earlier and realised that when Harold and his family and other leading men talked together their accent changed somehow, more smooth and rounded. Aethelric later told me that the noble English all spoke that way. I recalled my mother's lordly tones as she berated Eardwulf. Pushing my memories aside I ate and slept in a sandy hollow content with my lot, safe and happy with the world and my dreams of

Morwid.

◆ ◆ ◆

It was way past the height of summer when we assembled to leave. Harvests were coming in while Godwin had the southern coast scoured for supplies for our fleets and the ever growing land army. He was paying out vast sums of money as well as calling in debts and occasionally forcing the recalcitrant to donate. I knew all this because once again I was trailing after Aethelric as he recorded, counted and distributed supplies among the leading men. It was a huge task and I had little time for friends or weapon training. Like it or not I was on the way to becoming a cleric. I learned to write some numbers and even a few common words, cattle, bread, spears and the like. I learned to write my name, Sar Nomansson.

'That's more than most men can do you know,' said Aethelric, 'Mind you only Danes have names like yours. The English sometimes say where they're from or occasionally what they do, or their father did, which for most people is the same thing.'

'Can Harold write?' I asked.

'His name, most of our Lords can write their name for charters and the like.'

'Does he write Godwinson?'

'Sometimes.'

'Then I shall write Nomansson. And what about reading?'

'Not many read, they use clerics for that, Harold can read some, English only, books on falconry like those I showed you. Most warriors think reading and writing are for those who are soft in the head.' He shook his head, bemused at man's stupidity.

I wasn't so sure I wanted to read and write. Mostly I counted up piles of stones representing different things and scratched tallies into bits of wood and argued with men who had to exchange them for loaves, bowls, boots, or sheep or arrows. I ran errands all through the host taking pride in being fast and accurately memorising messages. I became a familiar sight dodging around formations of soldiers and in and out of campsites with my little shield on my back and my precious throwing spear in my hand. Most seemed to welcome me but I'd catch the odd man muttering charms against the elves. I kept well clear of Oslaf and his crews who now blamed me for Wihtgar's death at Conor's hall.

Some mealtimes I would see Gyric and we would exchange a few words. The other boys I had known were now spread among the host and I saw little of them except to exchange the odd word in passing. Any free time I had I spent throwing my spear at a mark or slowly cleaning the hilt of my knife. Candalo was right, as I rubbed away the black greasy layers, accrued from years of handling, I discovered a gleaming metal pommel inset with a large blue stone surrounded by small red ones. The guard was made of heavy silver and once polished its battered surface revealed faint incised patterns. The grip was made of plaited wire twisted tightly over wood and leather. I'd never really looked at it closely it was so much a part of my life and childhood. It was just my mother's knife but it was obvious now that the blade had once been much longer and heavier. Like all saex it had only one edge and had a heavy blunt back. I showed it to Harold's armourer who told me that the hilt could be removed and the blade replaced. He named a price well out of my reach commenting that the fine hilt deserved a fine blade. I tucked it into the sheath I had made puzzled and pleased by my discovery. As he turned back to his work I took the opportunity to steal another throwing spear from under a hide covered rack.

I loved my weapons and looked after them well polishing and greasing the bronze and iron while I bees-waxed the shafts with the wax meant for St.Brigid's casket. I felt she wouldn't mind and the ash-wood shafts turned a rich dark butter colour. Despite my role as reluctant quartermaster's assistant it had been a happy month being part of this great army. I got to see our leading men who came to consult with Aethelric and the priests who helped him about their worldly goods as well as, more rarely, their souls.

By the time we left it felt as if all the streams on the island had been drunk dry, every morsel of food eaten and the whole land smelt of shit. Our now massive and varied fleet set sail comprising every different keel that could be imagined. Thurkill, being Danish, was entranced by the sight and took pleasure in naming the craft. He pointed to one ship larger than any I'd seen before, 'That's a true sea-going knarr, that ship could take you to Micklegard carrying your family friends and all their goods and livestock.'

'That there,' he went on, pointing at a long but still broad ship, 'that's a busse, holds many men and provisions, a proper warship. You can see it has many pairs of oars, some have as many as thirty-five.'

'So what are those?' I nodded towards a group of ships smaller than most of our original fleet but the most common among us now.

'They are karvs, usually about fifteen pairs of oars, respect them. Though they are small they do most of the work. When my ancestors took your country most of us braved the Northern Sea in just such craft.'

'What is our ship, and Thord's and Oslaf's?'

'Skeides, war ships for raiding, many oars and many men, you may have noticed we've been a little cramped and very close to the sea.'

I certainly had but until now had thought little of it, 'So that one looks the same but is broader and higher in the water.'

'That Sar, is a snekke, great ships good for both travelling and fighting, one day I will own one of my own,' he smiled at the thought, 'and raid your rich Saxon monasteries.'

I laughed, 'Just whose side are you on? So, what is Godwin's ship?'

'A drakkar. That ship is why Godwin took so much treasure to Count Baldwin. You might say that's a snekke and a half.' We both paused contemplating this magnificent ship. It had thirty-eight pairs of oars, a fearsome gold and red dragon head on its prow with another rearing up and facing forward on the stern post. Somehow Godwin had thought to procure fresh paints and it glowed with crimson and green stripes while the oars flashed white in the foam. From its mast flew a sinuous white dragon banner, tubular like Thords, its open mouth and its teeth gnashing as it gulped in the wind.

'That,' Thurkill continued, 'is a truly great ship, some call them dragon ships or serpents as they flex through the waves defying their size. Only a truly wealthy man can build and equip one of those, let alone crew it.'

'How many men?'

'I'd not be surprised if he could get more than two hundred aboard that vessel.' He turned to me, 'It's not the first he's owned.'

'It's not?'

'He's had two before, perhaps even greater, one manned with eighty fully equipped warriors the other even more. They were both gilded and painted with all the sails, oars and tackle complete and he gave them away!'

My jaw dropped, 'Why?'

'He gave one to the King Harthacanut to atone for handing Edward's brother to the King's enemies, and the other, the greater one to Edward.'

'Is that why they fight?'

'Not now, well, not openly, but I think that King Edward has never forgiven him Alfred's murder. He died horribly from being brutally blinded and left to wander.'

'Did Godwin do it?'

'It would mean death to say so, but no, I believe he handed him to Edward's half-brother, Harold, son of King Cnut.'

'So, that Harold was king?'

'You ask too many questions, it could get you killed.'

'The ships, though, what happened to the ships?'

'Who knows? Harthacanut did not live long and though Edward has commanded the fleet before he is no lover of the sea. He was reared by the Normans and they have turned their backs on their Viking past and pay no heed to seamanship. They do, though, harbour Flemish pirates who raid our coasts when the Norman lords let them off the leash. That said, some of those pirates are here with us,' he laughed wryly. At that Thurkill recollected himself and his position and ordered me off to do 'something useful.'

We moved along the coast travelling towards the rising sun. Various ships visited different ports as we travelled but ours stayed at sea. The weather got colder and the squalls more frequent. Rowing in wet clothes made our arses sore even though we sat on stolen fleeces. Eventually we assembled again and a large raiding party led by Godwin's great craft went into Sandwice hoping to surprise the King's fleet at its moorings. It turned out that they had left some time before for Lundunburh and never returned. We then turned into the Wantsum Channel between the Isle of Tanet and the land of Cantium. Shallow waters meant that the deeper ships were towed through by ships like our own. This was hard rowing and once again the muscles in my back burned with strain and my palms blistered despite the cloths thrown over the oars to protect them. While I grunted and sweated next to Toki, as we passed a wide reed bordered river mouth, Aethelric came to me.

'Up that river, the Stour, Sar is my home, Canterberie. There is a great church, a monastery and many holy places where God is praised and peace is honoured in song. We copy the gospels in gold and lapis and pilgrims come for healing at our shrines.'

I could see he was having another fit of homesickness. I was feeling that way myself, earlier that day we had passed some crumbling ruins that looked very like the ruins in which my family had hollowed out the home of my childhood. I'd found my little half-brother and sister had come to mind, Adaf and Elena, Welsh names as my Da had put his foot down. He said that they needed to fit in. What had become of them? Moira, I knew, was a slave somewhere but how would the two little ones have survived?

I had no time for his snivelling. 'Yes Aethelric,' I snapped. 'It's where all those fat, drunken monks feed and drink on the wealth of common people.' My Da's words really. 'I'll take you to your family of priests one day but now I could do with a drink of water more than your self-pity.'

He looked at me shocked by my vehemence, 'Careful, Sar, don't forget where you come from.'

That was the trouble. I couldn't. I didn't answer as he got up and staggered to the stern still unable to balance on a boat. I turned back to the oar. A little later I felt a tap on my shoulder and a beaker of water was held to my mouth. It was Aethelric, kind and humbling.

The next day our forces landed and burned the King's town of Middletone to demonstrate King Edward's inability to repel us. As part of Harold's fleet we had no part in this, we had already fought hard. Some felt that Godwin was over reaching himself and that Harold was wise to distance himself from acts against the King's property. As we rowed north of the Isle of Sheppey we could see the smoke rising. We met no opposition and saw no enemy vessels. Wherever the Earls Odda and Ralph were now they had failed to attack us.

The rowing continued for days and days as we pushed our way into the mouth of a mighty river, the Temese. We were headed to Lundunburh to join with our land force and confront the King, as we grew closer, so too grew the tension among the men. Tempers frayed and snapped, as some grew fearful or too serious, at the prospect of war against the King, while others got excited and bragged about the deeds they imagined they might do. The wide river was margined by reed beds and mudflats with no defined edge. We stayed to the middle fearing stranding or attack from the people of the marshes whose fires and squalid homes we saw from time to time.

The rowing got harder as we approached the city and settlements more frequent. We rowed south, we rowed east, we rowed north against the flow of the river and then against the falling tide. Then rowing east again we could see a massive bastion of stone and brick rising above the mist. Our ships were crammed together, strung along the river as it narrowed to where a huge wooden structure bridged the river. Already as the mist rose I could see innumerable houses and churches to our right below a cloud of smoke and mist but nothing prepared me for that bridge. I was astonished that men could build such a thing. It stood on massive pillars made of whole trees and the river rushed through, forced into a twisting maelstrom by their constraint. I could see towers at both ends and crowds of men leant against the railed sides staring and pointing at our fleet. Many, if not all of them, appeared armed. By land or water this bridge would cost many lives to take.

The falling tide had left us all confined to a narrowing channel bordered by stinking mud. Some of us were stuck fast but Godwin's ship had found a mooring at a long wharf beside the southern end of the bridge. We tied our ships to the dragon headed posts that reared up from the green chilly river. Harold and Aethelric and some followers clambered across Godwin's ship to join him. We were in a place called Sudwerca which marked the southern end of the bridge. This had been part of Godwin's Earldom and many of his thegns had come here to meet him in a large hall next to the church of St.Olaf.

Godwin addressed the thegns, acknowledging their support which they upheld by confirming their desire to have him back as Earl of Wessex. He thanked them with kind words and added, 'I have sent messengers ahead to consult with some of the merchants of Lundunburh. It is their great city which makes or breaks our Kings today however great Wincestre's past.'

As he spoke a runner came in and announced their arrival, he continued, 'Their representatives have been promised safe passage and must be treated with honour.'

Four finely equipped fighting men strode into the hall followed by two priests and two men like none I had ever seen before. The foremost was a huge man with layers of fat rolling over each other instead of a belly, above which rose pendulous chins surmounted by a globular head covered in thinning brown hair. Under the un-fastened jewelled clasps of his felted crimson cloak his bulk was wrapped in fine shiny embroidered silk.

I heard Harold whisper to Godwin, 'By God, his shirt alone is worth an army.'

Struggling for breath the bulk spoke, in strangely accented English, 'Find me something to sit on. I did not expect to be wading through the Temese mud to meet you Godwin.'

'What mud? You came by horse across your bridge,' answered Godwin lightly. 'Give my dramatic friend a seat.'

Fulk laughed, fatly, 'Horse, no horse can carry me. I came by cart. Now where's that seat.'

Harold waved at me and I dragged a bench from its place by the wall into the centre of the room. The bulk sat upon it. Waving bejewelled fingers at Godwin he declared, 'Thank you Sir, no need to apologise,' not that anyone had, 'Now I hear that you want our help.'

Godwin introduced the huge man, 'This, my thegns, is Fulk of Wissant.'

One of the thegns spoke, 'A foreigner, my Earl, I thought we came to speak with the men of Lundenburh.'

'Be respectful countryman, this man holds the keys to the

city in his hands,' the voice came from another of our visitors. A more normal sized man but almost as richly dressed he was fastidiously trying to wipe his boots in the straw on the floor. He wore the moustache of a fighting man but his soft hands and lack of weapons showed that his wealth was earned some other way. 'I, Stanmaer, alderman and port-reeve can speak for the city.'

'Men,' said Godwin, 'these two men command half the trade in Lundunburh. This city runs on trade and its trade pays many spearmen. We need their people and their spearmen on our side or, at least, not against us.'

A murmur of discontent ran around the room.

'I know you think we can win all by fighting but if we can win without it then we all can win.' Godwin spoke forcefully, 'West of the bridge the King has a fleet and an army to rival ours. Do we want to spill the blood of our countrymen and leave ourselves open to invasion? And as for foreigners, my wife is Danish, my sons have Danish blood many of our great lords are part French or Norman. It is not all foreigners we want gone it is the venomous churchmen who have so ill advised our King we want gone!'

There was a roar of consent, this was a popular view. Fulk sat completely unruffled by all the noise, as it quietened he spoke, 'Half the fleeces of the country pass through my hands, half the slaves, the Fuller's earths of Redehelde, and ingots of lead pass through my hands.' He paused, 'I take greasy wool, dirty unwanted people and lumps of dirt and grey metal and I bring you back silk for your embroideries, jewels for your sword hilts and lapis lazuli to illustrate your Gospels and, of course wine to cheer you through your cold wet winters.'

A stir went through the company. There were few men here, the leading men of their counties, who had not enjoyed the luxuries years of peace had brought. 'This is a wealthy country but if I close my hand many of you will go without. When I open my hands your people work, your estates grow rich and your children grow to inherit. If I take my trade away to another place they will profit while you will suffer. This is why I can deliver

Lundunburh.'

Stanmaer spoke next, 'Above the bridge our King has fifty ships and an army at Lundunwic almost equal to your own.' Godwin's face was a mask, its iron features revealing nothing of what he thought. Stanmaer continued, 'You have come so far now that you cannot retreat without Edward treating you as he has treated Godwin and his sons.'

Stanmaer paused and Godwin remained silent. The company talked among themselves. If they fought many would die. If they lost all would be lost and if they won many of England's fighting men would be lost. Many here could remember the civil wars of Cnut's sons followed by waves of piratical raids and years of invasions. Some could remember the Danish conquests, the lives lost and the terrible results of famines caused by untilled fields.

'But,' Godwin shouted, 'but I have my rights and if the King can trample them and my people be sent into exile then what can he do to you and yours. I have no wish to depose our King I merely wish to re-establish my family to its rightful place.'

'And Lundunburh is the finger on the scales that tips the balance,' Stanmaer calmly pointing to the nub of the matter. 'Our own men hold the city and we can close the gates and the bridge to whichever army we choose. Since King Alfred rebuilt the walls we can resist any army as we resisted the great Cnut.'

Everyone here had seen the massive walls and could not doubt his words. Those of us who would have to pass under those arches against a resolute foe knew our chances would be slim. No matter how great the ship, one boulder, dropped from above, could destroy it in an instant.

Fulk spoke again, 'Godwin has promised us trading concessions we would desire. His son, Tostig, has recently married a daughter of my Count, Baldwin of Flanders. Flanders is a great market and can make us all wealthy. Give us those concessions and the city is with you and you will hold the upper hand.'

A tall wiry man spoke out, 'I am Wistan, Thegn of Redehelde, and many other hundreds this side of the river. I have much to lose if I lose your trade Fulk but do we have the Church on our side? Can we succeed if we do not?'

'I think I can answer that,' said one of the priests throwing back his hood.

'By the Good Lord, Ealdred, are you still chasing me?' asked Harold visibly pleased.

Ealdred laughed, a deep rich laugh that seemed to set all at ease, 'By God Harold if I'd have chased you any more slowly I would have been going backwards.'

'I did wonder how I'd time to reach Bristou when Edward pronounced me outlaw.'

'Well now you know, I didn't want to catch you at all. I count us as friends and hope we can continue that way.'

Harold stepped forward and embraced the priest, 'You are still Bishop though are you not?'

'I am, of Worcester, and as such I have been talking to Bishop Stigand. He and I and many other churchmen are heartily sick of the imperious ways of these Norman priests, especially Ulf, Bishop of Dorchecestre and of course, Archbishop Robert who was so wrongfully given Aethelric's rightful See. They would tell us how to pray and what and when to sing. They have the ear of the King at our expense. We also want them gone.'

Stanmaer spoke, 'While on matters of the Church we want Spearhafoc back as Bishop of Lundunburh.'

Godwin replied, 'Now that I cannot promise, is it true he ran away with the King's crown? That appointment is in the King's hand only. What I can promise is to seek Bishop William's removal with great pleasure.'

The alderman nodded and Fulk too signalled assent to Godwin's words saying. 'It is well not to promise what you can in no way deliver. Now, to what you can deliver. You, Godwin, own Sudwerca that is joined to Lundunburh by our bridge. You also, should you retrieve your position,' Fulk gave Godwin a hard look, 'will be once again Earl of Wessex and your son, Earl of East Anglia.'

'That is the truth,' Godwin declared.

Fulk continued, 'For us to give you free passage up-river you must give free passage to all goods exempt from tolls or taxes to you, your sons or any of your thegns both across the bridge and throughout your Earldoms,' he paused, 'for all the Guildsmen of Lundunburh!'

There was a sharp intake of breath all round. Someone shouted, 'That will hit many of us hard, Godwin, very hard. Why should men carry goods and slaves across our lands and use our ports and we receive nothing?'

Godwin appeared to consider this question, 'You have a point my friend but note I stand to lose more than all of you.'

Another angry voice shouted, 'That Godwin is because you have so much more than us in the first place.'

'Have I not earned my lands, my father was unjustly banished and I have fought my whole life to regain our lands and increase my patrimony.' Godwin spoke forcefully, 'and many of you have prospered beside me.'

An older, grey bearded thegn spoke out, 'You certainly smelt the winds of change and knew when to change your allegiance.'

For a moment Godwin looked like he was going to lose his temper his face darkened with rust red patches on his cheeks. 'You do me a great injustice, search your memory old man, I am no traitor!'

The old man was not the slightest bit ruffled, 'Watch your pride Godwin, your temper and that of your monstrous eldest boy have got you into this mess. You need us more than we need you.'

Godwin visibly struggled to regain his composure, 'This is a useless diversion. Fulk, Stanmaer what if we keep the port duties and tax you no more than one twentieth of your goods.'

'One fortieth Godwin, any more and your army can whistle for our support but we will give you none,' Stanaer pronounced, 'and then you can all go home and wait for the King's vengeance.'

'Shire-reeves, Thegns and Aldermen I think we have heard their last word on this, what say you?' Godwin bellowed this out then paused for his words to take effect. 'If I accept these terms will any of you object and place us all in peril?'

There was much shifting and muttering but no-one spoke out. 'Fulk, Stanmaer we accept your terms.'

Fulk nodded his pendulous jowls quivering. 'That is good,' he said his guttural tones thick with greed and satisfaction.

Godwin spoke again, 'Now can all see that we are in agreement and that my cause, our cause is just. We must act as if we are going to fight, and perhaps we will, so see to your men and your arms. The merchants of Lundunburh have written the terms of our agreement.' At this the other priest stepped forward with a scroll and a small horn of ink and some short quills.

'We have our conditions written here, do you wish me to read them out or would you like your priest to read them for you?'

Wistan spoke again, 'You had it all arranged before we got here Godwin, would you have signed without our knowledge?'

'I needed and desired all of your consents. We will read out the terms and any of you who wish to do so can witness this agreement. I have nothing to hide,' Godwin answered amiably. Now he had got what he wanted he was all smiles. He continued, 'We must come to a decision and plan our strategy. The tide does not wait for us to finish talking. We need to go through the bridge on the rising tide or run with our tails between our legs.'

After the terms were read and plans were laid the leading men all went into the church of St.Olaf to swear their oaths before God. 'St.Olaf's church, what better omen' declared Godwin, 'did he not pull down the bridge to save the city? We will do better. The city will stand unharmed while we save our ancient rights.'

'It is an especially Holy day this day, the Feast of the Holy Cross, so while we pray for our success let us remember Our Saviour.' These were Ealdred's words, showing his blessing and acceptance of the terms.

Harold drew a deep slow breath, 'Let us hope that Our Lord is with us this day by reconciling us with our King tomorrow.' He spoke these words aloud to general applause but under his breath I heard him mutter to Ealdred, 'Because if not we're nothing better than pirates and nithings.'

Godwin's plan worked. We went through the bridge on the rising tide unopposed by the Lundenburh men who could have done our fleet great damage. We kept along the southern side of the river with our army beside us. By now the vast majority on both sides were English the mercenaries among us were relatively few as were the Frenchmen and Normans clustered around the standard of the King. As Godwin threatened to encircle the King's fleet the great men on either side called for truce. The King's fleet looked in poor condition but his army crowded the bank in both directions under many banners. If it came to a fight the slaughter would have been enormous and the outcome uncertain. Bushes, which must have been prepared in the night, were raised up the masts and an uneasy truce held until an impressively dressed churchman appeared on the prow of one of the King's ships.

'Your rightful Lord the King has sent me, Bishop Stigand, known for my impartiality to call on you, Godwin of Wessex and your sons to seek his pardon for your actions against him.' The Bishop shouted across the water and there was a great murmur as his words passed through the fleet. 'He asks, Godwin, that you send your rebels and your pirate allies away and then he will agree to meet you.'

As I watched Harold spoke to Leofwine, 'The King knows he's lost, he's sent Stigand because he was my father's friend. If Archbishop Robert had appeared it would have been war. My guess is Earl Leofric doesn't like seeing the King depose another Earl. Can you see his standard? A double-headed eagle. Earl Siward won't be here. He'll not send all his men south while the Scots are at his back.'

'So why were we hounded out of the country?'

'The King resents our father's power, when he found his excuse he took it. The Earls supported the King because they wanted us humbled not humiliated. Even Ralph and Odda were not our enemies. The sentence was so extreme because the Norman priests poisoned the King's ear.'

'I'm not so sure about Leofric, his son Aelfgar will lose his Earldom if you, Harold, are re-instated,' said Aethelric. 'You've heard the rumours that the King received the Norman bastard while we were away?'

'Yes, yes' replied Harold, 'If true why?' He looked thoughtful at this, 'He puts aside my sister and receives a visit from Normandy where he grew up. Why?'

As he spoke there was a mighty shout from Godwin's ship as he strode forward to stand by the great carved dragon's head. He stood solid, braced against the prow, as the ship was rowed towards Stigand's perch. The tumult died as his presence commanded quiet. Godwin's reputation was immense. Believed to be over sixty but still a strong man he had fought with Ironside and Cnut, had married a Danish princess and had founded the most powerful Anglo-Danish family in the kingdom. Two of his many sons had held Earldoms and the rest had been expected to follow. His eldest daughter had married the King. His rise to fame, fortune and power were known to all. He was a living legend.

The legend spoke, each word loud, clear and precise, 'Your Grace, Lord Bishop, it is good to see you. Tell the King I will not disperse my force until I have received justice. Neither will I seek his pardon until my daughter is returned to her rightful place at the King's side and those responsible for misguiding the King are themselves brought to justice.'

As these defiant words were passed from mouth to mouth, from ship to ship and from the ships to the shore, through the rival forces, men tensed and shouted. The armies roared at each other readying themselves for battle.

Godwin and Stigand both turned to the forces arrayed behind them and called for silence. As calm descended Stigand shouted again across the water, 'The King knows you are a proud man Godwin and has instructed me to suggest that you and he meet in Lundenwic at St.Clement's to discuss your future.'

'I am not some novice monk to have my future discussed!'

shouted Godwin. 'Tell the King that I have proved my power, that I have made it clear he can neither protect our coastlines nor command our southern counties. His Earls are unable or unwilling to defend him in sufficient numbers to defeat me.'

He paused as a great roar of approval rose from our excited ranks. Right now we would have fought every man alive for our leader. The return shout from the King's forces was far less confident. Without a blow being struck we could feel the advantage turning our way.

'I will meet the King, not in St.Clement's but within the walls of Lundenburh. I require hostages from the King and may I remind him he already holds members of my family.' Godwin paused to let his words sink in. To make us all aware of who was dictating the terms here.

The Bishop replied again. 'I will convey your demands to the King meanwhile as a leader of the Church I command that both your armies put down your arms. If any man should attack another I will see that they are put to death by their own commanders.'

Leaders of both armies made us sheath our weapons and lay our spears upon the decks or on the ground. Food was disbursed and we all settled down to eat and wait. Harold and Aethelric were rowed over to Godwin's ship. Being left behind I took this rare opportunity to sit with Gyric and chat for a while.

Gyric, who was now dressed in a mail byrnie and metal helmet, looked very sweaty so I told him so.

'You're only jealous,' he said gently smiling at the exciting scenes around us.

He was right. While I had been counting sacks and sheep he'd joined Harold's housecarls and been trained as part of an armoured force. He'd continued to grow and fill out, chubby boy fat turning to hard muscle, while I'd remained light and skinny and my small buckler and throwing spear seemed feeble compared with his sword and battle spear.

'Yes, Gyric, I am, but I accept it better now, Harold wants me for something and I am to enter his household once Aethelric is back in Canterberie.' I sighed, 'It could have been a lot worse, Gyric. I'll never forget those poor, crazy slaves from the mines.'

'You're right to think like that Sar, this year has changed our lives forever. We're men now.'

'And friends?'

'Yes, Sar, always friends.'

We sat together silently as each knew the other was thinking over the summer we'd spent together. The things we'd seen and done as part of Harold's fleet, whatever the outcome of Godwin's quarrel with the King, that part of our lives was over.

CHAPTER 7

There was much more arguing before hostages were exchanged. The King had resisted Godwin's demand for the return of his and his son's Earldoms. Sometimes great angry shouts arose from the opposing army but the Earl and his sons held their ground until even the King realised that he had not enough support to refuse Godwin. Every so often Aethelric explained some of what was happening to our crew. Apparently Edward hated Sweyn even more than he hated Godwin. When he was assured that Sweyn was on his way to Jerusalem he agreed to meet Godwin and his sons. Many of our thegns or their sons were rowed across the river in exchange for a similar number of Edward's followers. With this exchange of hostages Godwin felt it safe to cross the river.

The King had not entirely given into Godwin's demands and would not meet in Lundunburh. The actions of its burgesses in letting us through the bridge may have made him fearful for his safety. We were to meet the King at his palace at Thorney, further upstream. Many of our leaders and their followers joined us. I went as Aethelric's servant carrying a bag of parchments, ink and quills in my satchel but with my spears over my shoulder. Gyric, his father and many of Harold's housecarls came too, as did Oslaf and some of his crew. We joined Godwin's men to make a considerable, heavily armed force. Godwin, Harold and Tostig were dressed magnificently as if for war, helmeted, armed with swords and carrying their shields. They marched at our head surrounded by their bannermen, the banners waving and snapping in the wind.

As we approached the open ground before St.Clement's Church a procession of the greater men of Lundunburh converged upon us. Some of their soldiers rode on horses. As they approached two of them peeled away and sped towards Godwin. Our men quickly surrounded them as they reared to a halt. One of them cried out, 'Sire. Fulk had sent us to tell you that many Normans and Frenchmen are trying to run.'

'By Olaf's bones I want those poisonous bastards to answer to me, where have they gone?' Godwin was clearly furious.

'Sire, some have already fled west along Waecelinga Street. You'll never get past the King's army.'

'And the others?' demanded Godwin.

'The Bishops William and Ulf and Archbishop Robert are fighting their way across Lundunburh.'

'Robert is with them!' Godwin roared angrily. 'Then we have a chance, Harold organise a pursuit but you, you must stay here.'

'Thurkill, 'said Harold, 'Take my men, and those of Oslaf's that are here, and catch those churchmen. These soldiers will lead you.'

'My place is with you.'

'Not now Thurkill, I am well protected by my father's men. Now go!'

Thurkill gathered his men together as did Oslaf. Between them they numbered about fifty. 'Throw down your shields,' cried Thurkill.

'Yes,' said Oslaf, 'we need to move fast.'

They threw down their shields though it could be seen they weren't happy. I threw down the bag of parchments while my targe was firmly strapped to my back. As they started to run after the horsemen I quickly joined them before I would hear Aethelric's pleas to come back. Swapping one of my spears to my other hand I ran alongside the warriors as they stormed over a small bridge and through an open gateway. I passed between the two towers and suddenly found myself surrounded by tall houses and a monastery wall. We were in Lundunburh. Dark and smelling strangely rotten, the air was full of smoke. Despite the horsemen ahead and the fear of our weapons we were still pushing through a dense crowd. Very suddenly we erupted into an open space by a mighty church. I could not take it all in, the huge buildings, people everywhere, houses all crammed together, and overwhelming noise. Then shouts from the riders rose above the din, 'To the East, to the East. Follow us through the cheaps!'

Once more we pushed into a maze of streets. All I could do was keep my eyes on the horsemen's helmets above the crowd and keep running, trying to ignore the slime under my feet. Some of our men slipped to the floor as the effort of trying to run and push through the crowds carrying spears was too much. I was pushed into some man's chest, arms crushed to my side, my spears, thankfully, heads up. His red face spat at me as I pushed away and turned back to the race. Then we crashed through a market, stalls flying everywhere, but the crowds at last began to thin. I tripped over a crawling child. Dazed I picked myself up as it scurried away with wide frightened eyes. More shouts, 'They're heading for the East Gate, men are being killed.'

We turned left and then right again, then abruptly we all stopped. Instead of a crowd there were bodies of young men lightly armed, some writhing wounded, some dead, in an otherwise empty street.

'They're up ahead trying to force the gate, we were told to stop them but they are veteran warriors heavily armed.'

Scalpi knelt down to the wounded, sobbing youth, 'Calm now boy, you'll live. Did they have priests with them?'

'They did and packhorses. They're all mounted too, big horses, wealthy men.'

'You did well son, you did well.' Scalpi stood and turned towards us shaking his head.

I looked at the youth feeling strangely connected, despite all the death I'd seen, as he choked then spewed up a great gobbet of blood as his soul flew.

We pressed on more cautiously, now being directed from behind by the mounted men. We could hear the sounds of fighting
up ahead. At the end of the road was another gatehouse. Twin
towers supported an arch above the roadway. I glimpsed some
dismounted men struggling to lift the bar on the gate while
the last few young soldiers were being cut down. Dead and
dying people lay all around, some armed. Others obviously by-
standers caught between two forces in a fight not their own. A
half circle of maybe forty, fully armed and mounted men faced
us. Between them and the gate I could glimpse a group of richly
cloaked men. A few pack horses were pressed up against the
city wall defended by a couple of armed men with naked swords
from a small mob of townsmen seeking plunder.

'That's them. That's the Bishops!' someone shouted as we
spread out seeking a way to attack. The enemy were well
armed. All were helmeted with mail byrnies, all carried swords,
while a few had long lances. Some had strange long shields
which I'd never seen before which tapered to a point below
their knees.

Thurkill yelled, 'Hold men, hold, those with spears to the
front.'

Our men advanced forwards, a bristling hedge of spears
flanked by house walls. Their leader shouted a command and
the mounted soldiers tried to charge us but their horses baulked
at the points of our spears. As they retreated a couple of lances
flew in our direction and at least one man went down grunting
in pain. While in the street our flanks were protected. Once
past the row of houses we would be exposed on both sides.

'We must punch into them hard and fast,' said Thurkill. Then
he saw me, 'Sar, you should not be here. Stay well out of the

way.'

He looked around, 'Second thoughts; see that roof. Get someone to boost you up there and do what you can do distract them.'

'Toki, here mate, give me a shove.' I'd spied him in the throng.

He came over and shoved me up and over the edge of the steeply over-hanging eaves. I grabbed the thatching ties and pulled myself, hand over hand, onto the roof. Stamping into the thatch I steadied myself to regain by my spears as Toki passed them up. 'Pity you don't have a bow,' he said, 'Here, take these as well.'

Toki passed me up two bundles of barrel staves. I guessed I was on the roof of a cooper's shop. One by one I rolled the bundles to the peak of the roof steadying them by stabbing my spears through the packed straw. Soon I was seated astride the ridge looking down over the area in front of the gate. 'We don't have much time,' I shouted down, 'they'll have the gate open any moment.'

Then I noticed something else. On two of the horses young men were bound to their saddles. 'They have captives!' I yelled, 'Two men. Tied and gagged.'

One of the townsmen who had joined us shouted, 'The foreigners took them. It is the Godwin boys that were given to the King.'

Scalpi's roar rose above the din, 'By God men, they've taken Wulfnoth and Hakon. Fight them, fight them now!'

Our men roared the war-cry of the English, 'Out, out, out!'

As they shouted Thurkill formed them into a wedge, the 'Boar's Snout', with two of the great axe-men as the tusks, flanked by spear men on either side. As they prepared themselves to charge I cut open the first bundle of staves and grabbed one. A number of the foe dismounted in front of the bishops while some of the horsemen spread out to either side. It was obvious what would happen. As Thurkill's wedge punched forward and left the street the mounted men would surround them from each side.

With a roar Thurkill's men pushed forward. Shield-less their protection was the close knit wall of spears. They thrust them into the enemy line. They fended off the points with their shields. This opened them up to attack from the great axes. One of the enemies went down, his shield smashed by an axe blow which crushed the arm behind it. A horse reared up, kicking and screaming pierced by spears as its skull was split by another axe. Brains and gore flew as the horse collapsed and its rider went down to be hacked to death on the ground. Our men surged into the gap roaring incoherently. Then the inevitable happened. Our push forward weakened as our flanks were attacked. I could see Oslaf stabbing his spear fiercely at the horsemen who were using their mounts as platforms to try and cut down on our men. Mad with excitement I started spinning the barrel staves down through the air at their men. In themselves they did little damage but they distracted the riders as they tried to probe their lances over our spear-points. I saw Scalpi slide a spear over a saddle and into the rider's groin as a stave flew off his helmet. I saw Gyric stab upwards at a horse's head with his spear and I threw another stave in the rider's direction. I hoped it helped. I kept on flinging them down as the mass of our men lurched from side to side striving to reach the gate. The screaming of horses was terrible as the long spears drove them back. I'd not heard that sound before or seen them in a fight, all hooves and teeth and staring crazed eyes.

The chaos increased as the townsmen took advantage of the fighting to plunder the pack- horses and suddenly they, terrified by the mayhem, plunged into the seething mass of fighting men. All formation broke down and it was every man for himself as spear shafts shattered and axes and swords were drawn. I could see an enemy soldier heaving up the bar of the gate as the last of the defenders went down to be trampled underfoot. I pulled a spear from the thatch and threw it hard. It pierced his mail between his shoulders and the bar dropped back into place. I had bought some time. All the barrel staves were gone and I was left with one spear which I was loath to lose.

The seething maelstrom of grunting, screaming, blood-maddened warriors continued to hack away at each other. Slowly the mounted men forced us back as two more men heaved the bar up. A moment later the gates flew open with a crash. I saw the Bishop's great horses push aside their own men as they sought to force their way through to safety. Arching my back I threw my last spear high in the air and it curved up and over the mayhem. Plummeting down it stuck firmly upright in the haunch of one of the cleric's horses piercing through a thick saddle bag. The horse screamed and stampeded straight for the open gate with its rider grimly hanging on. The horses carrying the hostages were tugged along by other mounted warriors, their helpless riders swaying, ungainly, in their saddles.

I looked down and saw a little packhorse trembling against the wall beneath me. Launching myself off the roof I landed clumsily on its back. As it reared in surprise I clutched its mane for dear life. Once the first horses had burst through the gate, the others all tried to follow. Around me I could see men grabbing at horses, pushing off packs or pulling down wounded riders. By now a sizeable group of the foe had escaped ahead of us and their troop was piling down the road as the stragglers were finished off. My horse bolted after its friends. I clung on fiercely, never having been on a horse I had no idea what to do but stay on as best I could. Caught up in the excitement of the chase I followed them through the gate. I wanted my spear back.

At first I was hard on their heels as my unarmoured slight frame made me an easy burden for the little horse but soon its humble origins showed and it pace faltered. I could hear more riders coming up from behind. Ahead of us stretched a wide road going off into the distance in a dead straight line towards a forest. Soon I was at the head of a gang of us galloping up the road, yelling and beating our mounts remorselessly, trying to catch the Archbishop's party. As the tree line approached and the broad track narrowed I could see a dark line crossing the road. A dark line surmounted by spear heads and banners.

I heard Thurkill shout above the drumming hooves, 'I don't know who those men are but we need to catch those bastards before they reach their lines.'

As he spoke the horse with my spear still jutting from its buttock went down. Horsemen milled around as the dismounted Bishop struggled to mount up behind a mailed man.

'Now's our chance,' I screamed shrilly, goading my failing horse hard.

There were no more shouts now, just grunts and curses as we all concentrated on getting the most from our mounts. Trees flashed by on either side. I sensed another horse coming alongside mine. I looked to my left and there was Oslaf's malevolent face grinning at me. 'We're on them!' I shouted but as I did he pushed his mount into mine and I saw the sudden flash of a blade. He'd stabbed my horse in the shoulder, the knife flashing in, and as quickly, out.

Screaming wildly, the little horse skidded to one side barging into another rider. Suddenly horses and men were crashing into me cursing and whinnying in anger and panic. I was flung to one side, too stunned at first to realise what had happened. I staggered to my feet to feel a heavy hand clout me across the head. Falling back to the floor I heard Thorkill curse me, 'You stupid fucking cretin we've lost them now.' He spat at me and stalked off to remount.

I got up again just in time to see the Archbishop's men swallowed up by the line of armed men. Many more than we could attack with any hope of success. Out of the corner of my eye I spied Oslaf who'd stayed on his horse. He urged it toward me. 'Still alive you little shit,' he hissed, spitting down at me.

'You did this,' I waved at the chaos of injured men and horses, 'you stopped the chase.'

He hissed again, 'You think so? No-one will believe you.' He narrowed his eyes at me. A couple of his men moved closer. I quickly stumbled towards some of Harold's men fearful for my safety.

Scalpi walked towards me scowling, holding his awkwardly

bent left arm with his right hand. 'Oslaf made me fall, it wasn't my fault,' I pleaded.

He gave me a hard look. 'We'd have caught them Sar, what the fuck were you doing? Take the blame. Be the man you aren't. Look,' he said, suddenly blanching, 'I've broken my fucking arm because of you.'

Thorkill came back. 'They are Aelfgar's men. They won't give up the Archbishop or any of his men. Or, their leader says, the hostages without the King's permission.'

Scalpi, still angry, retorted, 'You told them that we are Harold's men?'

'I did, he says 'Who is Harold to him?'.' He says that Aelfgar holds the Earldom of East Anglia and that he will decide who has safe passage and who has not.'

We stood there breathing heavily, arguing amongst ourselves as more of our men caught up with us. Gyric was with them having run all the way. Behind him Toki ambled up on the back of a captured horse.

Gyric drew up panting, his face red, demanding to know what had happened. 'Ask your friend here!' said Scalpi, still angry. Nobody was in a hurry to return and face Harold with failure or worse face the wrath of Godwin.

'My horse went down in front of the others and the Archbishop and his men got away,' I explained. Oslaf stood to one side, grinning, all the men with him equally unconcerned. I didn't repeat my accusation, there was no point.

Gyric drew close to me but Scalpi wasn't finished. 'You should stay away from Sar, Gyric, you're a housecarl now. He's just human flotsam washed up by the tide of war.'

'Father, he is my friend.' As Gyric said this I thought Scalpi would burst. 'I am a housecarl and also a man. I will choose my own friends.'

Everyone fell silent. Gyric was close to defying his father, a great and respected thegn and warrior. As Scalpi breathed in heavily lost for words Toki's voice rang out.

'Perhaps we are all too quick to judge. I have been told that if their own horses had not stumbled they'd have got clean away whatever we did. Is that true?'

Somebody grunted assent. 'Then look here,' continued Toki as he trotted his horse back into the group leading a larger horse which stumbled along on three legs. 'Did any of you carry throwing spears to the King's council? Did you?'

There was no answer. 'So whose is this that I pulled out of this poor beast's arse?' He raised a spear, my spear.

'It's mine,' I shouted, 'it's mine! I carved an S into the shaft.'

'As I thought, you threw it from the roof. If it were not for this spear we'd never have got close. Don't blame the boy we should look to ourselves.' He threw the spear into the ground at my feet and pointing his horse back toward the city headed off with the Bishop's fine steed limping after him. Seeing him go off with his two captured beasts reminded me of the horse I'd arrived on.

It too looked sorry for itself, limping heavily on one foreleg. I grabbed my spear and stretching it out tried to herd the horse toward me. It skittered away but Gyric sharply turned it and grabbed its harness. He smiled at me, 'You know nothing of horses do you?'

'I don't,' I said, 'but I know that one has a wound in its left shoulder.' We were ignored now as other men tried to catch horses and dispatch those with broken limbs.

'See' I said to Gyric. 'See that's where Oslaf stuck it.'

'You can't prove anything with that Sar, nothing. Even if you could say why Oslaf would do that the horse was in a fight.'

'Oslaf would do that because he hates me.'

'Enough to lose an Archbishop?'

There was no answer to this but as I took the rein from Gyric I realised that a small fine leather satchel was still tied to the horse. The rest of its load had been cut away in the city.

'Look at this Gyric.' I pulled out a long band of finely woven cloth a hand-span wide. 'What is it? It's finely made but what is it for?'

'You could ask Aethelric, it's something to do with the church. See the crosses embroidered on.'

'Yes, maybe, but the horse is mine anyway. Do you think we can heal that leg?'

Gyric looked at the wound. 'It's not that deep. It's been more frightened than hurt. This is no fighting man's horse but a nice prize all the same.'

We trailed along behind the others exchanging views of the fight. He thought he'd killed a man in the fight at the gate and he'd not lost courage. His first real fight had worked out well for him. 'My father will be proud of me later,' he smiled, 'and when he's cooled down he will forgive me my words.'

We caught up with Thurkill and the rest arguing with the gate-keepers who wanted to deny us re-entry. They gave way but once inside we were shocked to discover our two dead and few wounded had been stripped of their weapons and clothes. The Norman dead had been treated the same way but if there had been any wounded there were none now.

One townsman shouted that they had killed their boys. Thurkill said that was so but why mistreat Englishmen? It came close to a fight, our mood was ugly following our fail-ure and the townsmen, it seemed, blamed us for the Bishops getting away. If it wasn't for Stanmaer's arrival with his own armed escort things may well have turned out badly. As it was we were escorted back through the town feeling more guarded than welcome. Our dead were tied across our captured horses before we sadly led them back into the streets. The town it-self had gone back to normal as if nothing had happened. The noisy crowds only grudgingly gave us way through the slippery, stinking, streets. I smelt bread baking and whiffs of boiling meat and my belly churned as I realised how hungry I was. As I pulled the leather strap I used for a belt tighter I became aware of how tatty I was compared with many of the crowd around. My clothes, stripped from the dead after the fight at Porloc, had grown threadbare and faded over the summers passing. I shivered at the thought of approaching winter lonely with no family hearth to huddle by. No brothers and sisters with cold sores and chilblains to treat and to share the long dark nights.

We paused for a while in one of the cheaps, a market, where Oslaf and Thurkill bought food for their respective men. They returned furiously complaining about daylight robbery from these thieving townsfolk. I didn't care. I wolfed down the lump of coarse bread and dried fish like it was a feast day. I was still bewitched by the town, by all the buildings and trades, by the storekeepers yelling their wares. To me the noise was deafening, I'd never heard anything like it other than the clamour of battle. In some places the sound echoed back from stone buildings and one massive church, the biggest building I had ever seen, soared up into the sky. I marvelled at it, at how it even stood.

Even so it was a relief to get out through the gates on the other side beyond the great walls. We found our men camped between St.Clement's and the river where some of our ships were beached. Handing the bodies over to one of the priests we then sought out our crew who were camped along the river bank.

It had been a long day, Harold and the rest had not yet returned from their council with the King. Thurkill set off to seek him out. Our wounded were treated by a local bonesetter while one of our priests muttered and sang the necessary words. Scalpi roared out once then fainted. I looked at Gyric feeling both grateful and guilty.

'I believe you Sar, it was Oslaf's doing again, but why?'

'Why would he want the Bishops to escape?'

'Yes.'

'He fought hard at the gate, maybe it was just to get me into trouble?'

Gyric looked at me and laughed, 'I think you are just a tool. He hates you of course, you killed his father but when Godwin's business with the King is over Oslaf may well seek a new Lord.

125

Harold and he are not great friends. Partly because of you it has to be said. If he leaves Harold, Sar, he's free to come after you.'

I shuddered remembering that night and the sound of iron against stone, tsssk, tsssk. 'He stabbed my horse when we saw those other men.'

'Aelfgar's men,' Gyric looked puzzled, 'Why would he do that?'

'To gain favour with his next Lord perhaps?'

It was only when we got to the ships that it dawned on me that I now had a horse. No way could I get it on *Maeve's Lover*. At least, I thought, we did not have to board tonight. While Gyric held the horse I boarded got my cloak and some spare rope. Then I tethered the animal where it could graze and rolling up in my cloak fell into a deep dreamless sleep.

The next morning we awoke to the sounds of loud cheering. The King and Godwin had made up their differences. Harold strode over to us.

'You failed to catch the Bishops.'

I jumped as Oslaf's voice spoke from behind me, 'We nearly caught them. If it wasn't for your pet we would have.'

Harold looked at me and then past me at Oslaf. His face was a mask, 'I heard all about it from Toki.'

His eyes turned to mine, cold and searching. 'And from Scalpi,' he added.

I knew I had done nothing wrong but thought it wiser to keep my mouth shut. I gazed boldly back at him. He nodded twice, slowly, and then looking away he addressed us all.

'Wulfnoth and Hakon were the King's hostages. Whether Aelfgar or Robert has them they will not be harmed.' Harold paused, 'None of you will lose because of this. You lost a small fight but the greater battle has been won.'

With a great sigh we all relaxed.

126

Harold smiled, 'and without a blow being struck.' Then he laughed out loud. 'You missed a fine sight. We got to the palace armed to the teeth and looking warlike as hell. The King, he's braver than he looks, met us outside with all his thegns. Leofric, Ralph, Odda and that lanky Norman Ralph the Staller were all there when Godwin threw down his weapons at the King's feet. Ha, ha, I swear he jumped back all of a yard.'

Harold paused for effect. It was Gyric who spoke first. 'Then what? Lord. What happened next?'

'My father dropped to his knees and swore his loyalty to the King, swore that he was innocent of all charges against him.'

'What did the King do?'

'Well he had little choice but to raise Godwin up and accept him back as Earl. We have everything back that we lost.'

We all cheered excitedly.

'And my sister will be restored to her proper station as Queen of the English.'

Thurkill shouted, 'Now lads. Cheer for your Queen, for Queen Eadgyth and Edward, your King.'

So we found ourselves cheering for the King and for Godwin who was, once again, Earl of Wessex and Harold, once again, Earl of East Anglia. Leofric of Mercia had stayed firmly on the fence only mildly protesting at his son Aelfgar's loss of his Earldom. He was content with the King's promise that his son would get it back when Harold succeeded to his father's estate.

Everything it seemed had been a misunderstanding which could be laid at the door of the scheming Robert. He had sealed his guilt by running. Everyone knew, at least those around Harold and the other Godwinsons, that the King was saving face by blaming the foreign churchmen. The reality was that his other Earls would not unite to crush another Earl in case, one day, the same could happen to them.

I wasn't too happy. I'd hoped to see the King and we were to leave our beautiful ship. At least I no longer had to worry about my pony. Even though it had a stiff leg and limped everybody wanted it now. I decided to keep it.

Harold did come to talk over the events of the day before. Oslaf did blame me. I kept the truth to myself and once again Harold covered for me. 'I'm told young Nomansson had never ridden a horse before in his life. Is that right Sar?'

'Yes, sir.'

'Hmmm and you landed on it from a roof and stayed on for the chase.'

'Yes, sir. Oh, and I also found this.'

I pulled out the strip of fine woven lamb's wool with its embroidered crosses. With a cry Aethelric rushed over and took it from my hands.

'Sar,' he breathed, 'do you know what you have here?'

I shook my head. Aethelric went on. 'This is a pallium, the Archbishop's pallium. The Pope himself has handled this. This boy has captured Robert's, soon not to be Archbishop of Canterberie, pallium.'

His face was rapturous, glowing with holy joy and some unholy glee at Robert's discomfiture. 'Sar, don't you get it. This is what the Pope gives an Archbishop to confirm his appointment. He hangs it around a new bishop's neck with his own hands and gives his blessings. This has been blessed by the Pope!'

'Well, that's all alright then. It should be yours now Aethelric. Surely you will be Archbishop now Robert has gone. You will be a great prince of the Church and get out of those hairy robes,' I replied laughing.

Suddenly his smile was gone. 'No, Sar the King aims to keep a firm hold on his ecclesiastical appointments. As a cousin to the Godwinsons I think that position is a step too far for him to stomach. Stigand, Bishop of Wincestre, will be getting Canterberie.'

'And you?'

'I shall be one of his monks, hairy robes and all.' His smile returned. 'I meant what I said before. I want no more part in the doings of great men.'

Harold spoke again. 'The pallium is quite a trophy. Robert will be most upset. I shall keep it to give to Stigand. He can use it until he gets his own from the Pope. Well, Sar, if you think you can learn to ride that pony of yours you can become one of my household messengers, though not dressed like that.' He grinned mischievously.

Oslaf who had been muttering in the background suddenly yelled, furious, 'You honour that Welsh boy again!' His voice rose to that strange shrill shriek that I remembered from that frightful day. 'Have you forgotten, Harold, that scum killed my father? You should give me his life.'

Harold turned on him, 'Oslaf, you do not tell me what to do. This man is sworn to me as are you. You have served me well and you will be well rewarded in due course.'

'But why do you deny me that boy who should have been a slave?'

Harold laughed his disarming laugh, 'Why? I think he brings me luck.'

'So my father lies un-avenged so as you can have a good-luck charm.'

'He does, Oslaf, he does. Enough of this I am still your Lord.'

'I can choose my own Lord, Sire. I can seek another.'

'That, Oslaf, is your right. Once we have disbanded our army and you have been rewarded with the estates I have for you, that you have honourably earned, then you are free to go. If you go now, you go with nothing.'

Oslaf's face whitened leaving two fiercely burning red patches, his knuckles white on his sword hilt as he fought to control his tongue. A strange suppressed keening sound was all that could be heard as he turned in a swirl of cloak and stalked away.

Thurkill spoke, 'You are making a dangerous enemy of that man Harold.'

'I don't trust him, I never trusted his father and I don't trust him. Perhaps it would be better if he went. I don't like him be-hind me.'

As midday approached discipline was starting to break down as the news spread through the armies. There was much to celebrate. We certainly saw ourselves as winners while the King's men could celebrate peace. Most of us were relieved not to have been involved in the huge battle that had been avoided.

At noon all of Harold's companies were drawn together by their ships. Each shipmaster produced a pile of our food bowls and placed them on the ground next to a fire in the centre of each ship's crew. We each took one of the wooden bowls leaving a small pile on the ground. Aethelric started to lead a prayer.

I nudged Toki, 'What is happening here?'

'Before we started our campaign each man was handed an eating bowl before he embarked. That pile represents those who have not made it home.'

For a moment I did not understand him then it hit me, each bowl stood for a dead man. As the shipmaster fed the bowls into the fire faces came to me. Faces of men I'd seen at the oars, most whose names I'd never known. I was reminded of Muirchu who'd died so soon after giving me hope. As Aethelric's prayer continued we all stood quietly in remembrance. I'd never seen our men so solemn. As they bowed their heads tears flowed down many cheeks left to run without shame. Try as I might I felt nothing, just cold, numb and uncaring. I hung my head copying the others but no tears came, just a slight hardening of the black, cold, hard stone inside of me. As the prayer ended we all said 'Amen' then returned to our tasks. No-one spoke of what had just occurred but a solemn cloud hung over us.

The mood changed dramatically later as the mercenary captains were paid off. For the crews in Harold's service meat, drink and music was provided and through the day we received our rewards. Mostly promises as it turned out. Men like Scalpi and Toki were to receive estates when Harold had sorted out the affairs of his Earldom which Aelfgar would now have to relinquish. My reward was formal acceptance into Harold's household which meant that I would be clothed, housed and fed at his expense in return for any service he should require of me. I could bear arms legally. I swore again to be his man.

Toki explained to me that I had done well for a bastard who

knew not his father's name. 'Some will envy you while others will see you as raised above your rightful place.'

I knew he was right. Harold had saved me from Oslaf's vengeance, either death at his cruel hands or the worst kinds of slavery, but I was still neither fish nor fowl. I was neither tied peasant, nor warrior free to choose his lord, neither was I a slave. I still depended on Harold's whim for my survival. That night I ate, drank, and boasted along with the others as I had learned to do. All along the river bank was noise, rough music, dancing and brawling as both forces feasted and put aside their differences. While they were looking forward to getting back to their homes, farms and families I was looking to an uncertain future without family and short of friends.

CHAPTER 8

The next morning all was manic activity as our goods were unloaded from the ships. Gyric and I bade farewell to Jokul who had also thickened and hardened over the year. It seems he had finally proved his worth to his father and he had lost his sullen bullying air. From somewhere he had looted a short thick fur cloak which he fastened with a piece of iron chain between two gaudy enamelled clasps. With his long black hair and his face darkening with the promise of a thick beard he was coming to look every inch the Irish Viking. The three of us swore eternal friendship and cutting our palms we mixed our blood.

'Will you be going back to Dyflin now?' I asked.

'No, the autumn gales make the journey too risky. We're to overwinter with Godwin's fleet at Boseham. It seems he likes the company of us wild Vikings.' Jokul laughed as he enjoyed this picture of himself. With that he turned and waded through the muddy shallows to his father's waiting ship without a backward glance.

Far sadder for me was that I was to part from Aethelric. He was to return to Canterberie with a group of wealthy pilgrims and their escort. 'Who will organise us now?' I demanded, 'and where will I go for advice?'

'Sar, my boy, it is not too late. I know you have seen and done things that few novices have but, after you were shriven, you would be welcome to train as a monk or, if the monastery doesn't appeal to you, for the priesthood. Even with your humble birth you could minister to a village.'

'You could stay with us. Harold would always care for you.'

'I made my choice, Sar, I am promised to God's service. I shall bow to Stigand and pray to be forgiven for leaving the cloister. I am at peace as a monk who works at administrating to the needs of Christchurch and serving God in Holy Orders.'

With that he climbed clumsily on a donkey while I fussed around him tightening his girth strap and tying on a small bundle of food. Then he laid a hand on my bowed head and quietly rode away leaving me staring after him with sore eyes and a lump in my throat.

There was one other parting I was most happy to see. Oslaf and his men also rowed off downstream. As they passed he saw me watching. He pointed at me, smiled wickedly, then drawing his finger across his throat he shouted, 'I'll come for you goat boy, and you will die in pain as I promised. One day I will skin you alive!'

I couldn't help but shudder as I ran my forefinger along the scar he had cut along my jaw-line. At last, at least for a while, I was free of him, free of the fear of sudden capture or a knife in my back. I could feel the tension drain out of me as the relief flooded in. I turned away to see to my pony. Burying my face in its warm side suddenly I was sobbing uncontrollably. Once again I saw my mother's ruined face as she lay on the ground and Eardwulf crashing down in his death spasms as hot blood spurted from between the fingers clutching his neck. My legs gave way and I frantically clung to the pony's withers so as not to collapse. I did not want to be seen like this. I was sweating furiously and sucking my breath in and out like a bellows. By the Saint's blessings I came round before anyone took notice of me. Shaking, I wiped my face in the pony's coat and after pulling its tether I led it away to escape for a while from the camp and the eyes of men. I'd seen these visions before and others, bloody and violent in my sleep. I often woke sweating with the memory of Oslaf carving my face as his ice blue eyes stared into mine.

But in daylight, awake, this was something new and it scared me.

Later when I'd pulled myself together I considered my pony. I didn't know much about horses but I knew I'd need a saddle and a bridle to ride her properly. I still had my silver penny and the other trinkets and thought that would be enough. Toki and Gyric laughed at my impatience. 'Harold will equip you when he's ready,' they told me.

'You just want my pony to carry your things,' I accused them. I was impatient to ride properly to prove to Harold that I could be his messenger. I was worried that he would forget his words now the campaign was over.

They agreed to come and help me. Outside the town's West Gate was a huge livestock market. Local people were coming from all over to take advantage of so many men wanting food and horses.

'Olaf's teeth! It's busy here,' cursed Toki. 'Hang on to that animal of yours in case it gets stolen.'

'Everyone wants to buy. You'd get a good price if you sold her,' said Gyric.

Stubbornly I insisted that I wanted to learn to ride. Pushing through the crowds we came upon a weasel-like man with broken blackened teeth and his slave boy standing over a pile of horse tack. They were keeping the crowd back with long sticks as they cried their wares. We told him what we needed while he looked us over. I think we confused him. Gyric spoke well and obviously knew about horses but was young, yet well dressed in fine but weathered clothes, with a good, though plain sword hanging from his belt. Then there was Toki, squat and broad, with a web of white scars on any skin not covered by his numerous arm rings while his hand lay gently on his sword hilt. Then me, the buyer, skinny, all knees and elbows with hanks of dark red hair flopping round my face. I was also oddly dressed with the stolen clothes of bigger men yet with a torque, an arm ring, and a fine knife. What he could see was that I was hopping from foot to foot desperate to spend my money.

As we tried to find saddle and harness to fit I realised how little I knew about horses. I had no idea how to even put a saddle on and properly tighten a girth. 'It'll rub here and here, you'll need some padding under that saddle, God knows what shape horse that thing was built for,' muttered Gyric as he pulled open its mouth. 'You've a little mare,' he saw my puzzled look, 'woman horse, get me?'

'Christ Gyric, give me a break, tell me something I don't know.'

'Well she's never had a bit in her mouth and she's younger than she looks.'

Not really understanding I just nodded while they forced the bit into her mouth and pushed the bridle up and over her head. She champed and foamed around the bit shaking her head unhappily.

'That'll do it,' said Toki. 'Come on, Sar, help me adjust all this.'

I fumbled around trying to copy him as Gyric searched out some serviceable reins. I'd seen the fancy harness on the Bishop's horses and this all seemed very plain. I said as much to the seller who told me that I had a lot of his property on my pony and that, though plain, it was all excellent quality. This started everyone arguing as we claimed it was all close to rotting with mould while he claimed everything was almost new. Meanwhile the dealer's boy was hovering around my unhappy animal. While she miserably chomped on the bit he was rubbing a greasy cloth on any bit of leather or iron he could reach in an effort to make it shine.

I looked at my pony with saddle, stirrups and harness and I flushed with pride. I just wanted it all now. I got out my money and my goods and said, 'Will this cover it all?'

Toki groaned. 'Sar, what are you doing?' I knew what he meant, I'd haggled and bargained since I was a small child, but I'd never before used money or owned clasps or broaches. I had no idea what they were worth.

'That will do fine,' said the dealer immediately, his face lighting up with greed.

As Toki and Gyric remonstrated with him he declared that, 'A deal is a deal'.

I handed it all over, I didn't care. He pushed my goods into a greasy leather bag at his waist then took a long hard look at the penny and said. 'Sorry boy. Can't take this.'

'What do you mean? It's money. Got a king on it,' I yelled, 'you got to take it.'

'No,' he said, 'can't do that. It's not current. Against the law for me to take that.'

Toki snatched the coin away, 'He's right lad, you're not meant to use this.' He turned to the dealer, 'Look mate, you're getting a lot more than that tack is worth and you know it. Take his money and take it to the mint yourself.'

The dealer looked slyly around. In the hubbub of the market no-one had noticed our exchange. 'You know it's against the law, my friend, but I can see the boy can't wait. You could sweeten the deal with one of your arm rings.'

Toki went red, his arm shot out and his strong hand gripped the man's face squeezing his nose between thumb and forefinger. Now it was the dealers turn to go red. As his mouth opened gasping for air Toki shoved the coin into it. 'You'll take this and you will shut up,' he hissed pushing the man's head to one side and punching him in the belly. 'My arm rings are my own and to sweeten the deal I will take these'.

While the dealer spat out the coin, gasping for breath on the ground, Toki calmly helped himself to a couple more worn sheepskin saddle cloths. Clapping me on the back he said. 'We're done here Sar, time to go.'

We walked away leaving the dealer viciously taking his anger out on his slave boy. Within moments we were once again pushing our way through the crowd.

'What did he mean about the money, Toki?'

'Ah yes, I'd forgotten that. Look every few years you have to take in your old money to a mint and change it for new.'

'You do? Why?'

'Don't know, King says, been like that for a long time.'

'So why didn't we change my coin, there must be a mint in Lundunburh?'

'They charge you, so you can't really change one coin you need lots. You might have to pay one in twenty, more or less.'

'So how can you change small amounts?'

'You can't, you have to give your money to someone who can.'

'And of course, they will want something for doing it,' put in Gyric.

I thought about this for a while, 'So people with a little money end up with less while people with more money end up with more.'

'You've got it,' said Toki, 'Way of the world.'

'And the King and his men get a piece of everything that way,' added Gyric.

I gave up at this point. It was all beyond me, changing money for money to make rich men richer.

'Let's get this horse back to camp so I can ride it,' I said pulling her away from a clump of grass she was struggling to eat unused as she was to the bit in her mouth.

Gyric and Toki smiled at each other. 'Alright then Sar, Harold wants to see this too.'

I puffed up a bit at this then felt a little uneasy. Why would he be interested and why were Toki and Gyric grinning like fiends?

We got back to the camp to find that *Maeve's Lover* had left her moorings. Our beautiful ship had gone with all the familiar faces of its crew. We were now down to a small company of about twenty men, all that were left of the party that had left for Ireland, and of course me. All the forces were now dispersing in different directions. Tostig had gone with the King to meet his sister while the other Godwinsons had gone with their father. Harold, having his own Earldom, was to head to East Anglia taking us with him.

That afternoon I got my chance to try to ride my little brown horse. Gyric helped me put on the bridle and check the saddle. He then showed me how to mount using the stirrups. 'You'll not be able to jump on it from a roof every time you want to ride,' he joked.

Laughing I agreed and after a couple of attempts with me hopping on one leg while the horse walked round in circles I successfully got on. Sitting up there I realised that I was sur-rounded by a loose circle of men all grinning at my efforts. Blushing to my roots I jigged the reins and stuck my heels in as I'd seen others do. 'Get on,' I shouted, 'Get on.'

The bloody animal went nowhere. It just stood there trying to crop the trampled grass. By now everyone was laughing at my efforts, even Harold. I pulled on the reins and her head came up and she started to go backwards. I dug in my heels harder and she leapt forward then stopped dead and I found myself half way over its head. I felt more and more stupid. When I'd jumped on her before all I'd had to do was cling on to her mane while she galloped on after the others.

Gyric was practically hysterical but he pulled himself to-gether long enough to show me how to hold the reins. I calmed down and made clucking noises as I'd heard horsemen make and she lifted up her head and began to walk. I was riding, grinning myself now I pulled on the reins to try and turn her. She stopped instantly shaking her head and fighting me. I got her moving again but she just went where she wanted heading for some bet-ter looking grass. The men all got out of her way punching each other in their amusement. 'Come on now, Toki,' shouted Har-old.

Toki came ambling across my front on his own horse. Mine pricked up her ears and ran after him. I nearly fell off again. I pulled on the reins and once again the horse took no notice. Toki turned his horse round and cantered off. My horse turned and followed, completely ignoring my efforts. This time I did come off, flying over the horse's arse to land on the ground with a solid thump. Winded and red faced with embarrassment I lay on the floor in a circle of laughing men. Then Toki came riding back with my little horse briskly trotting along behind him.

Harold strode up and pulled me to my feet chuckling as he brushed me off. 'Don't be angry boy. We've all had a good laugh. It was a packhorse, Sar, all its ever done is follow the horse in front. We all knew what would happen.'

I shuffled my feet awkwardly as the men crowded round thumping me on the back and sharing their pleasure. At first I was angry and then I saw the funny side. As we all laughed together I realised how much I felt a part of this battle-scarred band of weather beaten warriors. Gyric led my horse back to me and as I got back on they all cheered. I sat up there highly pleased despite my fall and more devoted to Harold than ever.

After a day's marching from Lundunburh, along the same road we'd galloped along after the escaping bishop's, we came to Waltham which was a manor of Harold's gifted him by the King on receiving his Earldom. On our arrival we all had to squash into the church which was small but well-built in stone. Inside was a strange black stone cross on which was attached a figure of Our Lord Christ. The figure was crowned in gold and jewels and upon the altar below lay a naked sword. Its pommel was ornate but the hilt was worn. This was the sword of a wealthy fighting thegn.

A priest called us to kneel and give thanks to God for Harold's return to his Earldom. After the prayers were over we got back on our feet and Harold turned to face us. Familiar to us all as he was he still remained a commanding figure with his fair shoulder length hair, his tallness, broad shoulders and quiet authority. He held up a hand and we all fell silent, eager to hear what he had to say.

He began by saying, 'The sword behind me belonged to Tovi

the Proud, King Cnut's bannerman. The crown was gifted by his wife, Gytha, as devout a Christian as her husband was a warrior. Tovi brought this cross here from an estate of his in Sumersaeton many years ago after a dream. We too have come from Sumersaeton to here, from Fleetholme to Waltham. Tovi had this cross loaded on to an ox-cart and by a miracle the oxen could only move in this direction.'

Someone shouted, 'Convenient that. They would only go to another of his estates.'

We all laughed while the priest looked shocked. Harold grinned, 'Probably took them a while too but remember, lads, we're back in civilisation now.'

He resumed his serious air and we all hushed to listen.

'Tovi served Cnut as my father served him. I knew Tovi before he died and was taught to respect the old warrior. When he died his estate reverted to the King who presented it to me. It seems that the Holy Cross has brought me good fortune. I came to Sudwerca with my father on the Feast of the Exultation of the Holy Cross and we are now in Tovi's Church of the Holy Cross. From now on alongside my banner of 'The Fighting Man',' he paused for us to cheer, 'will fly a banner of the 'Holy Cross'.'

We cheered again. He went on, 'from today the battle cry of my men will be 'Holy Cross'.' Drawing his sword and thrusting it into the air he cried, 'I give you the 'Holy Cross!''

Cheering again we chanted. 'Holy Cross! Holy Cross!'

As I shouted along with the others I felt that same sense of being part of something now, a new family, a new sense of belonging.

Harold lowered his sword and his voice. 'Now, my men, last of the band that has fought, feasted and prayed alongside me. I must return to my duties as Earl and we will no longer be that band. Some of you will return to your lands and families, others will become the core of my housecarls under Thurkill here, and you Sar, will become part of my household.'

Pleased at being singled out I reddened, bowed my head and shuffled my feet. 'But', his voice rose above our chattering, 'but you, and the crew of my ship, will always be dear to me. Should you ever need my help, remind me of this day, and I will be there for you. This I promise. Now go, get on with your lives, seek peace but be ready for war. Go now my friends and find your loved ones as I am off to find mine.'

Something troubled me and puzzled I cast my mind back over the events in the church. It was the name Gytha. I shuddered remembering when I last heard that name. It came from Eardwulf's mouth, 'Gytha will give a good price for you.' Not this Gytha. I asked. She'd been dead for years.

So more partings, only now did I learn that Scalpi was already a thegn with estates of his own, now greatly increased in reward for his services. All of the veteran housecarls who had been with us in our campaign gained large enough estates to regard themselves as Harold's thegns. Some ended their service while a few, like Toki, elected to remain. Gyric and the younger men all stayed on as did Thurkill and four other Danes who served for more portable wealth and a reputation to take to their homes.

Scalpi embraced his son before climbing awkwardly onto his horse, his arm splinted and bound. 'Gyric, Harold will give you leave to visit your family for Christ's Mass.' He glanced towards me, 'You might like to bring your friend.'

Gyric's face lit up as he turned to me, 'Told you he'd come round.'

After Scalpi left, everything quickly began to change. As Harold resumed his duty as Earl his retinue just grew and grew. I was no longer one of a select group but merely one messenger boy among many. Our work was usually to warn shire-reeves, thegns or the managers of Harold's numerous estates that the Earl was coming to hold court or administer justice. This meant many tired, cold and wet, journeys criss-crossing the Earldom then returning to Harold's court to wherever it may have moved.

There was much to be done as Aelfgar had been more concerned with collecting revenue than enforcing the law. There had been a lot of unrest as squabbles over taxes and land turned into fights and feuds. Meanwhile the simple people suffered and some turned to robbery. 'No wonder,' people said, 'if our lords can rebel against the King why should ordinary men work their lives away so their Earls can rest on pillows of feather and silk?'

PART 2

CHAPTER 9

T he rain seemed to find its way through even our birch tarred and hooded leather cloaks, only the best for the Earl's men. It trickled clammily into our greasy woollen tunics which were meant to keep us warm. I was supposed to blow a horn every so often along the road to let people know we were not robbers. Not a chance, in this foul sleet all I could produce was a wet farting sound that even Toki could no longer find funny. We were late, we should have reached Gipeswic long before but the sticky sucking mud had slowed us to a crawl. We were picking our way along the edge of the road by the trees of a small wood to avoid the deepest sloughs. I shivered miserably cursing Harold because we were only here to order crockery for his mistress. Well, that and to pass Harold's messages to the port-reeve. Beautiful Edith might be but surely this could have waited until the roads froze hard.

Gyric and I had fallen into sullen silence while Toki spat and cursed, 'By Cuthbert's holy fucking onions surely it can't be far now. It's getting dark. We'll be shut outside the town if we aren't there soon.' His horse lurched as one hoof slipped into yet another quagmire in the road.

I turned to look and as I did caught a movement from the corner of my eye. Without even thinking my arm shot up and my targe deflected a spear heading straight for my face.

'Ambush!' cried Gyric. 'Gallop for it!'

I jabbed Maeve with the butt of my javelin and she lurched

forward gamely trying to pick up speed. Two more spears flew by as I drew ahead of the heavier horses who were struggling against the sucking mud. Fearing that we would founder I looked ahead for a way off the track. Then through the deepening gloom I saw something strung across the road.

'There's a rope across the road,' I shouted quickly kicking my feet from the stirrups. As my pony went under the rope I managed to slide off her back and thumped down on my back into a slurry of liquid mud. I had no time to see where my spear had fallen before I was twisting away to avoid the trampling hooves of the other horses as Gyric and Toki pulled their beasts to a rearing, snorting halt. I stayed face down. I realised that covered in mud I was as good as invisible. Down the road through the sheeting rain I could see two figures running out and grabbing my horse. 'Bastards!' I thought as another hoof came down just in front of my face slopping more mud over my prone form. Four more figures came out pointing long spears at Gyric and Toki. Six of them and only three of us and I was no true warrior. Gyric was fighting hard with his panicked horse. Toki had lost hold of his spear but had somehow managed to draw his sword.

'Give us your horses and we will spare your lives,' shouted one of them his voice rough with tension.

Toki bought time as he twisted his shield to his front to hold its grip, 'Do you know who we are? Who we serve?'

The same man spoke again, his eyes shifting nervously to his companions. 'What do we care who you are? Your horses and your weapons. Now!' He pushed the point of his spear against Toki's shield. Toki let his horse sidle from the pressure. Gyric had got his horse under control and was warily eyeing two spear points close to his face. By now I was a few yards away from the action still prone in the mud.

From my vantage point I could see that they were a rough looking lot. The speaker, older than the rest, wore a boiled leather cap over greying unkempt hair. The man next to him wore the rusting remains of a mailed shirt. The two threatening

Gyric were helmeted, one with a bow across his back, useless in this rain, the other had a sword in his belt.

From behind me I could hear the other two slushing towards me leading my horse. I felt terribly exposed. I could be cut down from behind before I ever got to my feet. I lay absolutely still with my nostrils just above the watery muck. One of them cried out.

'Where's the other one?'

'I thought you had him, Hutha.'

'Nah, he flew off when he hit the rope.'

'Well he can't be far, find him!'

The rain gusted heavily, drenching us all and making it even harder to see. I could hear Toki arguing. I could not make out his words but I knew he would not give in without a fight. These men must be outlaws. There's no way they could let us live.

As they came up beside me I slid my right hand under my belly to where the hilt of my knife was digging into my flesh. Slowly, I eased it from its sheath. Their slushing feet passed by to my right. It was now or never. I wrenched myself out of the sucking mud and slashed hard across the back of the nearest man's knee hamstringing him. He collapsed to the floor screaming, clutching his leg, thrashing around in agony. My little horse, squealing with fright at the sight of me rising from the earth dressed in mud, reared up, dragging the man holding her bridle under her hooves.

Everyone was startled but Toki reacted first. Pushing his shield on to the point of one of the spears he turned the other with his sword. Then he lunged forward and hacked down hard on the older man's head. It split sickeningly, the leather cap as good as useless. Whetted iron cleaved his skull. Greyish pink slush flew into his friend's face. In that distracted moment Toki spurred his horse over him. Losing his footing the outlaw went down heavily, thudding into a protruding tree root. I saw Gyric take a spear point across his cheek as his other adversary turned and stabbed his spear towards Toki's back. Toki arched violently as the spear caught in the layers of leather and cloth. I fought hard to get to my feet. The crippled man thrashed beside me in the mud. Gyric, with no time to reverse his spear, shoved the butt hard into the other helmeted man's face. He stumbled back but stayed on his feet spitting gobbets of blood from a split mouth.

My horse had been brought back under control by her thief, Hutha. Seeing their reversal of fortunes, he leapt on her back and took off into the woods. Gyric's horse, panicked again at the mayhem, neighed frantically as it lost its footing. Going down on its haunches it began to founder. Gyric, who'd been riding since he could walk, letting go his long spear jumped off onto the mud of the road. Planting his feet firmly he pulled his sword out from under his cloak and swung his shield from his back to face his enemy. With one wounded, one dead and one running we and our attackers were now evenly matched.

The man in the rusty mail was pulling himself to his feet still holding his spear in one hand while he tried to rub the mud off his other hand to get some grip. I slushed my way to Gyric's side. The three outlaws lurched towards each other to form a group. The screams of the man on the ground behind me descended into sobs and curses. Apart from Toki, who was still on his horse, we were all soaked in mud and dripping heavily. It would have been funny if death had not been so close.

We faced each other, long spears against shields and hand weapons. Gyric and his adversary both had blood dripping from their chins. It was a stand-off.

Toki was the first to speak, 'Bitten off more than you can chew, haven't you scum. You're not even real fighters are you?'

The mailed one answered, 'What would you know?'

'One run, one dead, one squealing in the mud and you ambushed us? Any fool can tell.' Toki's voice sounded taut to me but I daren't take my eyes away from their spear points.

Toki spoke again, 'So attack us then, come take our arms and our horses.'

One of the helmeted men thrust his spear at me. I was the least well-armed and looked an easy target with my little shield and only armed with a knife. I swayed quickly to one side, the spear point passing by my ear. Gyric lashed out with his sword and all but severed the spear-shaft. Seeing his spearhead hanging uselessly towards the ground the man's courage fled and so did he. As he turned to run his companions retreated slowly into the trees with their spear-points firmly in our direction.

'Shall we attack?' asked Gyric, his voice whistling eerily.

'No lads. Let them go,' said Toki, tiredly.

Once they realised this they quickly disappeared into the gathering darkness under the trees. The whirling, falling leaves hid their passing as if they'd never existed.

One of them remained alive. 'We should take him for justice,' said Gyric, who was gentling his horse up and out of the mud. As he spoke I saw his teeth through his cheek, bubbles of blood and spit oozing out. The spear had cut his face wide open.

'And how we going to do that, Gyric? You need your face sewn up and I've lost my horse.' I turned to the man in the mud whose curses had turned to pleading.

'Have mercy, please. Don't kill me, don't kill me. I have a family.'

I squatted on my haunches and watched him, fascinated by his fear. 'Not much good to them as a cripple are you? Eh?'

He continued to plead. I smacked him in the head with my targe. Stunned, his words died but his eyes continued to beg. I watched for a few moments more then punched my knife into the side of his neck and bled him out like a pig. His blood ran black against the mud in the fading light. His body juddered with the spasms of death.

Suddenly my bowels griped and quickly pulling down my breeches I squirted liquid shit into the mud of the road. 'Holy Christ, I thought we were all to die in this mud,' I yelled at the sky.

I was shaking as I stood and pulled my breeches up to see Gyric staggering under Toki's weight as he slid semi-conscious form his horse.

'I think he's hurt, Sar. I think he may be badly hurt.'

Insanely I wanted to giggle at the strange sound of Gyric's speech wheezing and bubbling through his open cheek. Then I saw Toki's face was ashen even in the gloom. Gyric pulled his arm out from under Toki's back and it was soaked in blood. Toki passed out.

'Is he dead?' I asked, really frightened now as the battle rush died away and weariness overcame me.

'I don't think so. We need help.'

There was no way we could look at Toki's wounds through layers of wool and leather in this foul rain. 'We passed a side track some while back.'

'We'll have to find it,' said Gyric, 'and hope it leads to some settlement. Help me get Toki over his horse.'

We pushed and hauled his unconscious body up on to his big French horse, knowing all the time that we were tearing at his wounds. We realised we couldn't move as well as keep him on his horse. I remembered the rope across the road. I stumbled and sloshed my way to it and cut it down while Gyric took Toki's weight. We tied him to his horse with a leg each side of the saddle and with his hands tied under his horse's neck. I led Toki's horse while Gyric led his own, one hand on the bridle, the other holding Toki's body steady.

We trudged miserably and slowly back the way we had come. The rain finally eased off and a thin moon appeared. By its light we eventually discerned a side path between the coppiced trees.

'This wood is worked and the path clear, this must lead somewhere,' I said hopefully trying to encourage Gyric whose face was swelling fast. He hadn't even tried to speak for some time. I too had no more to say.

The wood opened up and I knew we had reached a cultivated field or pasture. As the clouds passed across the moon I could make out a ring fence surrounding a small church with a round bell tower and a long hall, animal pens and sheds. Beside the hall grew a mighty black poplar, its furrowed trunk leant over, shading another sturdy building, a weaving shed, judging by the open panels. As relief surged through us we found the strength to bash our fists against the firmly closed gatehouse.

No-one came. I looked at Gyric who was hanging on his horse's neck. He tried to speak but only strange grunts came out through his now terribly swollen face, 'orn, oor shlorn!' He nodded his head at me urgently. Letting go of Toki he pointed at my chest, 'orn, orn!'

I got it, the horn, I'd forgotten it and pulling it out from under my cloak I put it to my lips. I found my mouth was dry, had been dry with fear since I'd shat so forcefully in the road. I rolled my tongue around my mouth desperately trying to make enough spit to blow. I blew and the horn sounded weakly. I blew again and this time sheep bleated in reply and cattle lowed from a shed behind the gate.

I peered through a gap in the planking which had twisted with age, grey and silvered in the weak moonlight. I found myself staring at the fine flecked grain of the timber, lost for a moment in its beauty, as in a state of dazed tiredness my forehead rested against the boards. Gyric shoved me in the back. I came to my senses and blew again.

Something clattered. I looked again through the gap. One of the great hall doors creaked slowly open and a sturdy man limped out. He carried a sword, its blade bare. Walking to the cow shed he hammered on the wall and two more men appeared carrying spears followed by another carrying a wooden hay fork.

'Who wakes us in the night?' demanded the sword bearer.

'We are wounded travellers seeking help,' I pleaded, 'Let us in, we are the Earl's men.'

'How do I know that?' he retorted, 'In the last two years we've heard many stories of fighting and robbery.'

'Two of us are hurt. We can do no harm.'

A head showed above the timber wall. 'He seems to be telling the truth,' it said. 'One is hanging over a horse while the other has a bloody face.'

Gyric grimaced as he stuck his tongue out through his cheek.

The head retched, 'They are telling the truth.'

The man with the sword demanded we throw our weapons over the gate. Only then did I remember that my spear had been lost before the fight. I took off my targe and threw that over. Then Gyric's shield and sheathed sword followed. Toki's shield had been left behind but he'd sheathed his sword before he fell. That we unbuckled and threw it over, sheath and all.

'Knives, you'll all have knives, I want them too.'

Gyric threw his over, I untied my sheath slowly. I was reluctant to give my one connection to my past to anyone.

Gyric mumbled again, 'oo mushed, 'oki 'eeds 'elp.'

I threw it over, 'I want that back.'

'If you are who you say you are you will get them all back.'

The gate slowly opened and we walked the horses in. My legs gave way and I fell to the floor. A man came to help me but I waved him away, 'I'm not hurt, just knackered, see to my friends.'

The boy with the fork dropped it to hold the horses. He murmured comforting noises to them while the other two men lowered Toki to the ground. 'Carry him into the hall and lay him on his front,' the swordsman ordered.

As he walked haltingly toward Gyric we could see he was no longer in his prime but his air was that of a warrior. 'That wound will need sewing together or you'll live with two mouths,' he said, not unkindly, 'Go into the hall, there's nothing we can do in the dark.'

We went in to find Toki stretched out on a board with a woman each side of him visible in the dim, red glow of newly stirred embers. One, a plump older woman, was roughly cutting his clothes from his back. The other, much more finely dressed, pressed raw wool into a long wound, dark against his pale skin, going from low on his back across to his opposite shoulder.

'This man is badly hurt. We can staunch the bleeding but can do no more until daybreak,' she said without a glance our way. 'Lie by the hearth and warm yourselves, you'll be fed in the morning.' She turned and, followed by the other woman, went through a door at the back of the hall.

'You heard our Lady,' said the old warrior dragging a heavy bench across the door, 'I will sleep here and you will stay there.'

Toki began to moan. 'Quiet now my friend. Be quiet for we are safe,' I whispered, 'be still.'

Relief flooded through me as I heard the truth of my own words. Toki, weak through loss of blood, drifted away again. I slept fitfully, still hooded and cloaked, lying by the dying embers. Each time I woke Gyric was groaning quietly, holding his swollen face in trembling hands.

I woke with a start at the sound of a woman blowing hard, to coax flame from the piled ashes before placing morning twigs upon the hearth. Toki lay face down on the board grunting through clenched teeth. 'Sar, I'm stiff as the board I'm lying on. What's with my back? I can tell it's bad.'

It did look bad. There was a long dark gash, deep in places and still weeping blood, visible in the weak sunlight filtering through the smoke hole. 'Not easy to tell,' I said, 'the lady of the house will tend you soon.' I didn't know what to say or do. Toki was invincible to me. It was hard to see him incapable like this.

My bladder urged me out of the door. 'Where are you going, boy?' barked the old warrior from the back of the hall.

'I need to piss,' I answered, 'Sir!'

'Well piss on the dung heap, disturber of our peace,' he retorted.

I stepped out into the brightness of the early morning. The storm of yesterday had passed. I walked to a dung heap beside the byre and let go a warm stream of relief. The most satisfying thing since I bled out the thieving bastard who tried to take my horse. 'Fuck,' I thought, 'I've lost Maeve and my best spear.'

The gate was open as two roughly dressed boys herded out

the sheep. A number of small homes surrounded the hall, smoke beginning to thicken from their roof holes. The thought of warm food and more rest enticed me back indoors but the shame of losing both my mount and my weapon drove me out. I crossed the field and headed for the coppice. The morning was alive with small birds flitting, silenced briefly by the shriek and blue flash of a hunting jay. How could all be so different from yesterday morning when my friends were unhurt and the rain ceaseless? Loping through the trees I soon came upon the road. What had seemed an eternity last night, staggering through the dark, was now a brisk short run in the daylight.

Coming to the road I slowed. Would anyone be about this early? It seemed not. Good. I didn't want to be seen hunting around a dead man's body with no-one to explain my part. I headed to where we had been attacked. The corpse with the cloven skull was already attended by squabbling crows that were picking out the remains of his brains. The other body lay stiff and curled in the road coloured in its grey clayey mud. I spat on it as I sought out my spear trying to think back to the events of yesterday. I found the cut off rope and casting back and forth from that place I found my spear. A man should not lose his weapon before he's even used it. It was good to have it back comforting in my hand, my defence, my flying death dealer. I vowed on its muddy staff that I would revenge myself on the men who had harmed my friends. And I would get my little horse back.

Though sunny the morning was cold so pulling my hood back up and starting to shiver in my damp clothes I ran back to the settlement. As I came through the gate I saw that Toki had been brought out into the daylight, his board placed on a pair of sturdy trestles. He was moaning feverishly. Sweat was pouring from his face, from his back, diluting the scabby clinging blood clots across the gaping gash of his wound.

I stopped, shocked, taking in the scene. The lady was there dressed in fine but threadbare clothes. Behind her two young-sters, a boy and a girl, ten and eight perhaps, stared wide-eyed at

Gyric whose teeth could now be clearly seen through the hole in his cheek. He too looked sickly, a greasy sheen on his face, sat, leaning weakly against the bole of the tree.

'Can you help them?' I asked.

'Perhaps a better question is should we help them?' The lady replied gazing at me steadily. 'There have been many stories of thieves after Harold left his Earldom.'

'He's back now and we are his men,' I cried. 'We are his men. We are the robbed not the robbers!'

'Prove it, I want no leaderless soldiers in my home, wounded or not.'

I thought franticly. 'My friend is Gyric, he is well-born. Toki there, he was one of Harold's housecarls. We faced the King and expelled the foreign Bishops.'

'And you? You with the barbarous accent. You are no well-born Englishman.' She spoke with all the authority of the nobility. Christ. she spoke like my own dead fucking mother!

I shrank back, crestfallen, I believed that I could face any man but I'd had no dealings with women. 'Me, me, I'm nothing, no-one. I'm just human flotsam picked up in Harold's wake and just as easily thrown away.' My own words hit me like fists and tears sprang to my eyes.

She stared at me hard, 'Hmmm, can you do no better than to whine? Your 'well-born' friend cannot speak a clear word. This Toki has more scars than that chopping block. A fighter covered in the barbaric arm rings of a killer.'

'I know, I know, I know what we look like. Can you read?' I fumbled under my cloak. Thank the good Lord I still had my letter pouch. I pulled out two small parchment rolls. 'I shouldn't show you these. My duty is to only pass them on to the port-reeve and a Gipeswic thegn.'

She turned to the boy beside her, 'Godric, go fetch the priest. Tell him to come now. No excuses. Go!'

The boy went. Turning back to me she asked, 'Well, flotsam. Do you have a name?'

'Sar, my name is Sar.'

'Sar! Another word for pain. Your mother must have loved you.'

'Not a lot,' I replied thinking, 'you haughty fucking bitch' but knowing we needed her. I was struggling to hold my temper when Godric came back followed by a portly puffing priest.

'Look at these rolls for me, Father Eoppa. This boy says he is a messenger of Earl Harold's.'

I gave them to the priest who looked at the seals, and nodding at her said, 'Lady Ealhild, they are the Earl's seals.'

'So you can see they are meant to be private,' I put in.

'Open them, he could have stolen them. See who they are to.'

I winced as he broke the seals. My duty was to deliver messages intact. 'This one is to Baeldaeg, the port-reeve of Gipeswic and this to Thegn Holman concerning setting up a court. Hmmmm, and also to arrange a shipping of crockery.'

Lady Ealhild turned to me again. 'It seems you speak the truth, young man.' She shouted to her serving woman, 'Jofrid bring a large bowl of water and a bundle of dry moss. Now Godric I want you to run and ask Freana to come with his leather working tools.' Her voice softened so much when she spoke to the boy that I guessed that he must her own child.

Once the moss and water arrived she began to clean out the wound across Toki's back while Jofrid eased down his stinking breeches. Poor Toki had pissed himself, either in the fight or during the night. He grimaced in shame and humiliation but kept quiet. I looked at Gyric. We'd seen many wounded men but an exchange of glances was all we needed to know that we would never speak of this.

Another, younger, woman appeared. Her head was well wrapped in rough cloths while her chapped hands and bare feet defined her status, most likely that of a slave. Taking no notice of me she placed wet cloths over Gyric's face. He was acting tough and though I could see his eyes flinch, his face stayed still as stone. I dropped to my haunches leaning on my spear, pleased that at last my friends were getting help.

All was going well until I heard the clop, stomp, clop, stomp of the old man's limping gait coming up behind me. He pushed past and then slammed my knife down on the board making everyone jump.

He turned on me, glaring, holding his sword point in my face, 'Where did you get this? Tell me or I'll gut you.'

Despite his age the point of the sword stayed steady at my throat.

I gulped, were our troubles never to end? 'We've always had it, always.'

'Who did you say you were?'

'They call me Sar, Sar Nomansson.'

'No man's son! What are you then? Devil's spawn! Mistress have you seen that hilt before? Think back, think hard.'

She picked up the knife, the blue stone and the inlaid glass gleamed in the sunlight. She shuddered and dropped it back on the board. As she turned toward me I could see that her face had turned white. Sweeping towards me she tore off my hood. 'May Saint Mildred preserve us all. You! You came from the dead and stole our hope. And here you are back again, younger even than when you left!'

Everyone was staring at me. Jofrid was crossing herself over and over again, fervently mumbling prayers.

'Drop that spear or I'll cut your throat,' shouted the limping man. I dropped it and he pushed me to the floor.

'Are you all fucking mad?' I shouted, 'I've never been here in all my born days.'

'Look at him, Lady, look at him. He can be no other. He is the devil come back to crow over our ruin. I should kill him now.'

'No. No! No, stay your hand, Hjor, I need to think. Tie him up,' she replied, staggering back to lean against the board.

Two more cottars came from behind me and tied my hands and feet. I lay there, back in the dirt once again, certain that the whole world was going mad.

Toki spoke, his words coming in gasps, 'Leave him alone, he's a boy just a boy. Like he says an orphan picked up in the whirl-wind of war.'

'Very poetic, especially for Toki,' I thought wryly, 'but would it help with these crazed people?'

Lady Ealhild turned and crouched, her face inches from Toki's. 'We have seen him before. He came here and took my sister. He took my sister,' she hissed.

'When was this? When?' asked Toki.

'Nigh on sixteen years ago. He came here with that dark red hair and that rich blade from the ground. He came here and my sister left with him. Left with him and with his whelp in her belly bringing shame on us all.' She was almost sobbing now. 'After she went my father was elf-struck and our ruin followed soon after.'

She turned and screeched at me. 'You did that! You! You came out from the mounds of the Kings and destroyed my family. You! You and your dark ship and your even darker crew of ghosts.'

The sweat was pouring from Toki's face. 'He's a boy, taken in Wales. If he's a demon how can you have him tied?'

The Lady took in a long breath, 'He's the spitting image of the man who took my sister. I can see it now, that knife on the board, as he sat there with her on his lap. They were taunting my father. He claiming he'd come from the dead and would take her back to the underworld. She stood up and turned sideways in the light from the door showing the first swelling of her belly. I stood there unnoticed while she displayed her shame to my father.'

Toki grunted again, 'So who was this man, this demon?'

'We never knew, he said he'd come from the dead and we'd heard that one of the great mounds by the River Deben had opened in the night and ghosts had walked. His knife, that knife!' she pointed at my knife, 'was made like one of the rare heirlooms of the older Saxon nobility from long before the Danes came. No-one makes them that way now. My father was struck down, struck down without a blow!'

'What do you mean?'

'He collapsed to the ground and never took another step. It

was as if he'd been cut down. He was alive for another five years but he never spoke, and could only move one hand. His other limbs were made useless. We had him bled on the waning moon and under the physician's costly care but to no avail. He grunted and swallowed the mush we gave him while shedding endless tears through one great, sad eye.'

She stopped then, her own tears streaming down her face, drawing breath in great shuddering gasps. I could have felt sorry for her if I'd not been tied up on the floor.

'Well, whatever, I'm not him. I'm a man who's never been dead. Never been anywhere near here before and won't be again I hope. Untie me, help my friends.' I spoke harshly, angry now, what had all this history got to do with me?

She turned and leaning down grabbed my face in a surprisingly strong hand. 'You look just like him, red hair, not the bright red we often see but dark, bloody red, and the same white skin.' She turned my head so my left cheek was to the sky, my right in the dirt. 'I see you are scarred, nasty, from your ear to your chin. Someone else didn't like you eh?'

'Nothing the fuck to do with you,' I retorted.

'Don't curse round me, cur,' she hissed back grinding my face in the dirt. 'Whoever you are, I command here.'

There was a loud crash. Gyric had fallen to the floor fainting. Suddenly the Lady was all matter of fact. 'What are you all staring at? Help this young man,' she ordered the cottars.

A couple of them laid Gyric out while the slave girl went back to washing the scabs off his face. He came to, blinking in surprise. 'Been better if you'd stayed out cold,' said Jofrid who'd pulled a roll of silk thread out from her apron.

A man had turned up with a soft leather roll which he opened to reveal bright tools. 'Freana, you took your time,' said the Lady, 'use this thread and sew up this young man's face.'

'I'll try, Lady. It's not a new cut. I'll have to make it bleed again if you want it to join.'

'Do what you need to do.'

Gyric's fortitude deserted him at this point. Somehow it was easier to face a line of armed men than one man with a needle and scraper. The cottars had to hold him down while Freana worked.

'Jofrid, carry on cleaning that man's back. Father Eoppa I think God's help would be useful here.'

The priest made a prayer in Latin then went off to his church for some Holy Water and some blessed herbs.

The Lady turned back to me. 'I can see now you're not him, but so alike. How can that be? Two strange creatures like you here. Your voice is different, his was guttural yours lilts. His eyes too, I remember now seeing his eyes in the light, eyes like dark amber. Yours, almost familiar, light brown, green speckles, like...'

Hjor spoke, 'Like yours, mistress, like Inga's.'

'That was my mother's name, Inga, that was her name,' I gasped.

Her hands flew to cover her mouth as her eyes widened in shock. 'It can't be, not after all this time. It can't be! Inga's child but then you are that Devil's spawn.' She turned and, almost running, went back into the hall leaving us all stunned, staring wildly at each other as each of us made sense of what had just happened. It seems I had found my mother's family. They didn't seem too pleased to see me.

Hjor untied my bonds. 'Go and help your friends,' he said to me. To the little girl he said, 'Aebbe, I think you should find your mother and stay with her.'

The little girl ran inside, her shiny brown hair bobbing as she ran. My cousin. My mother's sister's daughter. I felt eyes on me. Looking round I found Godric staring at me. 'Hello cousin,' I said trying to smile.

He stared back at me, face cold, 'I'm going for the priest.'

'You do that, cousin, you do that.'

I moved to Toki's side. Jofrid and Freana looked like they knew what they were about. He sewed Toki's angry wounds together. 'I'm leaving some parts open to let out the pus that's sure to come. He has a fever, so does your other friend. It could kill them both yet. When that fat priest comes back with the herbs Jofrid here will make a poultice. I'd pray for them if I was you as the rest is in God's hands.'

For the next few days I tended my friends. Thank God the fever quickly left Gyric, his swollen face changing through shades of black, blue and yellow, while the wound leaked clear fluid which the slave girl wiped away. She smiled shyly but never spoke. Lady Ealhild stayed in the room behind the hall while the priest visited her often and spent as much time in there as in the church.

Toki got worse, his body got hotter and hotter and his mind wandered and he rambled madly, cursing foully, sobbing and calling for his mother. His mother, Toki had a mother, had been a boy, somehow that idea made no sense. But then it made no sense that I should be looking after him, cleaning up the mess that he voided from both ends. I washed his body to keep him cool when he sweated. I wrapped him in blankets and skins when he shivered. I hardly slept or ate only leaving him to piss or get a breath of clean air. On the fourth night he convulsed wildly then went completely cold and insensible. I knelt beside him praying as tears streamed down my face. I could not lose Toki, I could not.

Gyric and I stared at each other. Not knowing what else to do we knelt and prayed for we thought Toki's soul was leaving. As I knelt there, more helpless than I'd ever been, lost in my misery I felt a hand lie softly on my shoulder. 'It won't be long now, before morning he will either recover or die.' It was Lady Ealhild. She'd brought in some sweet-smelling waters and began washing Toki's pallid skin.

After we'd spent some time, sitting quietly and breathing in the scent as it rose above the sour smells of the sick room, she began to speak. 'Sar, it is hard for me to see you, to accept you as one of my kin. Your looks, it's hard to even look at you.'

'It was hard for my mother to look at me too. For the same reasons,' my voice quaked. Too many memories and Toki there, close to death.

'Please Sar, listen, the priest says I must forgive my sister. God is testing me, testing me again. Our mother died when we were young. My father was everything to me but to Inga he was the cause of our mother's death. One too many babies, after she'd lost so many, to leave only two daughters when her life finally bled away from between her legs.' She paused, breathing steadily calming herself, 'Inga went wild, while I tried to make everyone happy she'd be off riding, hunting even, like she was a boy. Not a boy though, a boy can do those things, but she was a girl, a woman, and her wildness and beauty were spellbinding. Men were drawn to her like moths to the firelight. My father pleaded, ordered, even beat her, and he was not a hard man, but always she would escape and always the stories followed her.'

She wrung the cloth out onto the reeds on the floor while I took in this picture of my mother. She continued. 'Then the stories stopped, the young men stopped coming and Inga no longer railed at my father. She no longer stormed in and out instead she just came and went quietly like a shadow. We were pleased at the peace and no longer asked questions.'

She looked at me, haunted by her memories, 'But we should have Sar, we should have.'

Dampening the cloth, she washed Toki's face. 'Go on,' I said, 'go on.'

She drew another deep breath. 'About that time there was talk of a visiting snekke rowing up the creeks, up the Belstede brook, buying beasts, ale and women with hack-silver. Talk too, of hit and run raids, of people stolen and farms burnt, of a red-headed demon and a godless crew. Before all that started we'd heard a terrible tale of the broken mounds of the Kings of old and ghostly lights moving in the dark. How could we connect those tales with Inga's quietness?'

'You talk of my father?'

'It would seem so. One day my father got up to find your father sat in our hall, my sister on his lap. I saw it all, I saw Hjor beaten to the ground and a hard-faced warrior bringing the back of an axe down on his leg. I saw my sister leave the hall like some wild queen as she ordered those bastards to loot our home. I saw my father, rigid and speechless with shame, crash to the floor never to speak again.'

Christ but this was a lot to take in. Toki lay there still as death. Ealhild held a polished piece of bronze over his mouth. It misted slightly. 'Your friend still lives.'

I looked at Gyric. 'I need to get outside, come and get me if anything changes.'

Ealhild reached up to grab my sleeve. I shook her hand off. I couldn't look at her. I pushed open the door and stepped out to find a world turned white with newly fallen snow. The sky was clear and the stars glistened. How could the world look so pure when I felt so filthy? With parents like mine what hope was there for me?

I breathed the cold clear air, shuddering as my lungs filled. It took a while but I knew what I had to do. I had to put it all in that dark hard place where all the painful things went. I remembered some stones that a trader from the north had sold Harold. Polished they were as black as soot and as shiny as a newly oiled blade, they called it jet. I put it all into my jet-black, hard heart.

I went back in and found Gyric and Ealhild talking quietly together. She turned to me and began to speak but I stopped her. 'Enough,' I said, 'that's enough for one night. Go and get that priest. He should be here. If my friend dies tonight I will want to know why he wasn't here praying for God's help.'

She looked at me sharply but didn't argue as grabbing a warm cloak she left. Gyric turned to me, 'You can't talk to her like that.'

'I know Gyric, I just couldn't take any more right now.'

As I spoke a terrible groaning noise came from Toki. 'Grrroar-haaah, huh, uh,' his chest heaved, 'GrrrrroooaaarrrhefuckamI.'

'You're alive, Toki, you're alive, what's that saint round here, Edmund, by Saint Edmund you're back,' I shouted with glee.

'I haven't been anywhere, you dolt. Get me up.' He started to heave himself up trying to turn over.

'No, no,' said Gyric pushing him back down, 'you are badly wounded. Your back is ripped right open and still oozing stinking filth.'

Sweat burst out from him and he lay back down. 'Ale then. Get me some ale.'

We turned him gently on his side. He tried to help but was weaker than a new born kid though he sucked on the ale horn as willingly as they sucked their dam's teats.

The priest and Ealhild came in. She knelt by Toki and felt his forehead. 'You are much cooler now. You have been very ill. Your friends here have been by your side for days.'

Toki looked confused, 'And you, have you been here?' He blushed, the rabid bastard blushed!

'Not so much, it's your friends you need to thank.'

He looked at us. I was waiting for the curses. He smiled a wry smile, bit his tongue then lay back exhausted.

'He's going to live, boys, come to my house,' said the priest, 'eat, drink, sleep.'

Gyric and I left with the priest leaving Ealhild wiping her scented cloth over Toki's smiling face. Neither of them noticed our leaving.

CHAPTER 10

T he priest fed us well with bread, broth and ale then left us to sleep on thick piles of rushes alongside his raised central hearth. We slept for hours and ate some more. I looked in on Toki who was sleeping peacefully with herbal poultices on his wounds. While we slept Father Eoppa had spoken more charms and chanted more prayers both in the church and by Toki's side.

Back at Eoppa's he sat us down. 'Your friend will have to stay here for some days or longer. We cannot take out his stitches until his wounds have drawn together and no more pus oozes from them. He seems a lot better but there is still a chance that his flesh may start to rot or his fever return. Only God can decide his fate.'

Gyric and I looked at each other. We'd both seen men die of wounds and knew the stink of rotten flesh. Gyric's face was not too bad but his wound was still seeping through the stitches and the scar was still red and angry.

'You're not so pretty now Gyric,' I said.

He grimaced, stiffly, 'I'll be alright.' He laughed and then he winced as it hurt. 'My mother won't be pleased, though.'

Eoppa spoke again. 'Gyric here, I think I can safely say, will recover and can stay here to help with his friend. Another thing is that you left two bodies on the road. They have been reported and someone has to see the shire-reeve. He will visit here soon which will cost us a sheep and stores to feed him and his men.'

'Will we be held to account?' asked Gyric.

'You have little to worry about. I can vouch for you and there have been thefts only recently,' said the priest. 'We have been bringing in all our livestock at night for weeks since two ewes disappeared from the outtake. Gyric can tell your story. You Sar had better continue your errands for your Earl. Tomorrow morning you must leave.'

'Is this because of who I am?' I demanded, though I well knew that my whole purpose was to deliver Harold's messages.

'It is not easy for us to have you here. Hjor is Jofrid's husband you know. Your father destroyed more than just his leg. His master's, your grandfather's, illness meant the taxes weren't paid and most of the families lands were lost. You can see with your own eyes the run down state of our hall. Your mother's shame meant Ealhild's betrothed left her. The children's father came later. He was a good man but no thegn. He had fevers and his spleen swelled. We had little coin left so we took care of him without a physician's help. He was given water from a blacksmith's forge which helped for a while but before long his fevers came again. He wasted away soon after Aebbe's birth.'

I cringed under his words, as if what I'd heard already wasn't bad enough.

The priest knelt before me and held my hands in his. 'I'm not being cruel, Sar. Go to Gipeswic, do your duties and when you return things may have changed.'

I went, on foot, neither Toki nor Gyric would let me on their horse. It turned out that we were less than half a day's walk from our destination when we were ambushed. I left under the clear skies of a frosty morning. The oxen rutted mud of the road was frozen hard. There were people everywhere on the road and working the great open fields, rooting up turnips mostly. It seemed we were ambushed in the only wood left in Sudfulc.

I jogged quickly along the road until coming to a footbridge alongside a ford. Grateful that I didn't have to walk through the freezing water I made my way over the bridge, then through an open gateway at the end of an earthen wall. I'd seen the port from the bridge and turning right, I was soon amongst the busy wharfs. I started to ask around about Baeldeag, the port-reeve. Soon I was found by a couple of his men who'd been watching the ships loads to make sure the right tariffs were handed over.

I was taken to him. I handed over my messages and told him of the ambush. He knew the Earl and gave me a friendly ear, promising to send one of his own messengers to reply to Harold and let him know where we were. I was fed and then told to head into the centre of the town to seek Thegn Holman's house. With the wind in the east the upper town was smothered by choking smoke from the kilns outside the town. I was welcomed once again although I'd turned up alone and on foot. I was given a packet to take back to Harold. The thegn said there was no urgency. Harold would be told as soon as his goods arrived in Grontabricc, close to Lady Edith's main estate. So after our meeting I was to stay and to eat. As a person of little value that meant being placed near the lowest end of the hall.

'You were with Harold when he met the King then?' asked a skinny young man who stank of horse shit and was covered in spots.

'Not quite, I was busy somewhere else.'

'Too busy to see the King?'

'I was on an errand,' I answered.

'Humm, just an errand boy then?'

'Yea, don't get to know much. How about you?'

'Me, why, I'm Ordwig, one of Holman's grooms. We get to know everything,' he boasted.

'Oh, right,' I nodded, knowing there would be more.

'Course Harold was our Earl before.'

'I'd heard that.'

He paused while a slave girl filled our horns.

'A lot of people weren't too happy when Harold went against

the King.'

We both drank, 'I thought it was the King that turned against Harold.'

'Well, whatever. When Harold left things got worse. Aelfgar took over collecting the taxes and the fines.'

'Nobody likes taxes,' said I, knowingly.

'True, but he was always in a hurry for them. Often angry and hard to read, people soon became wary of him.'

'They did?'

'Yes, and with the rebellion thieves grew bold and he did little about that too.'

'Huh, so I found out. My friends and I were set upon and robbed.' As soon as I spoke I wished the words back. His mouth opened for a question when there was a flurry of activity at the top of the hall.

The head of the hall was lit by candles so we looked from the shadows towards the great and the good. Up there in the light were the thegn and his lady, his family, his priests and his guests. They were all standing to welcome two people, a middle aged lady, tall and elegant, accompanied by a burly young man.

As they took their seats Ordwig commented, 'Now there's someone who's not so happy with Harold.'

'Oh', I went back to my bread and the fish broth.

'No, that's Lady Katla of Suthwalsham, Katla the Cold they call her. Though not to her face. She'll be wanting Godwin dead and that Aelfgar regains this Earldom.'

I pretended to concentrate on my food, this was exactly the sort of news Harold would want to hear.

'Yes, she hates Harold. Can't bear to see him, let alone give him her money. She's loaded, wealthy in her own right and her husband owned many ships, some for raiding and some for trading. Some of them bring peat from Nordfolc for Holman's potteries. That is why she's so honoured here.'

'Hates Harold?'

His voice dropped to an excited whisper. 'Yes, hates him. Her husband was meant to get Sweyn, his friend, from Bristou, but he rescued Harold instead.'

I dropped my voice too. 'He did?'

'Yes, without him Harold would never have got away.'

'And?'

'Well, he was killed.'

'Many men were killed.'

'Yes, but he was killed and Harold denied his son his revenge.' Ordwig's eyes rounded as he made his point.

An icy feeling ran down my spine. 'So who was her husband?'

'Eardwulf the Fox.'

I choked, coughing and spluttering, 'Oh God, fish bone... my throat.'

Ordwig started slapping me on the back. 'Come on now. Cough it up.'

'Get off me!' I pulled myself together as Ordwig jumped back startled, 'Oh sorry mate, look I think I'd better get outside.'

As I pulled my hood over my head and got up to leave I stole a glance at the top table. That was Oslaf's mother staring down the hall to see where the commotion was coming from. For a moment my eyes crossed hers. Pale, cold, blue eyes and from under her head-cloth a white blonde plait. Briefly I felt she knew who I was, but that was fear. Fear caused by seeing the same blue eyes that had stared into mine as Oslaf had carved my face with my mother's knife. The man next to her, powerfully built, brutish and bearded, was a younger version of Eardwulf. The apples in this family did not fall far from the tree.

Luckily I was not far from the door so it was easy to get out. The cold smoky air of the Gipeswic night provoked another bout of coughing. I whirled round as someone started to pound on my back.

'Woah up there, mate, it's only me,' Ordwig jumped back from me surprised. 'You're a nervy one, aren't you?'

'Sorry, sorry, you caught me unaware.'

He offered me a horn with some ale in. 'Just brought you this for your throat,' he said.

'Thanks, you're a good man, Ordwig, thanks.' I drank it down while getting my wits together. I'd not been seen even if she did know what I looked like. I didn't want to go back in though. Just in case someone mentioned a red-haired messenger from Earl Harold. There was a good chance Oslaf had seen his mother since we parted.

Ordwig and I stood there in the cold starting to shiver. 'How about we go back in?' he said through chattering teeth.

'How about we find an ale-house where we can get properly pissed,' I replied. 'Somewhere that'll take this.' I showed him a cheap ring I'd been gifted as a tip on one of my trips.

His face lit up, 'Yea, lets. I know a place.'

I'd left my spear, targe and leather cloak inside the hall but Ordwig was so keen for a night out that he happily went back in for me thinking I was just being lazy.

We went back down through the town to a rough looking tavern. The landlord took my ring, 'Alright, boys, ale for the night, it is.'

'And to bed in the straw? Don't want to be out in this.'

He looked us up and down. 'Alright, but if you puke you're out on your arses, get me?'

We agreed to his terms. The ale was strong but I'd practised with some hard drinkers. Ordwig though was a bit of a lightweight and was soon bragging away again about all he knew. 'Knows everyone in this town, I does. Everyone.'

I kept my tongue and drank slow. It wasn't really that I could handle my drink it was that I drank less of it. Ordwig might be a gossip but he was a good laugh too and soon we were happily chatting. Then I had a thought, 'You said you was a groom, didn't you?'

'I is. I mean am, a groom. I'm one of the thegns grooms. That's how I gets all the gossip.' He was wagging his fingers at me and dribbling slightly.

'So, you'd know all who buys and sells horses, right?'

'Ev'ry last one of 'em. There's a big horse market here every month. Tomorrow as it 'appens.'

Maybe my luck was about to change, 'You ever met someone

called Hutha there?'

He looked at me squinty eyed with ale, 'Hutha, yes I have. Got a bit of a reputation, him. No-one's ever proved anything but they say he ain't quite on the square, know what I mean?'

His attempts to wink were so comical that we both burst out laughing. Soon after that I had to bundle him out the door before he lost us our chance to bed indoors.

While he was puking I pissed into one of the barrels left out for the purpose. The piss would all be taken for the tanners or the fullers in the morning and welcome to it they were.

'Here, Ordwig, would you be able to point him out for me?'

'Sure,' he retched, 'but why? There's better men than him.'

'Never you mind,' I said. 'Let's get you back inside.'

We went back in where the innkeeper told us we'd had enough. After I'd stopped Ordwig from trying to fight him he slumped to the floor and started snoring loudly. I rolled myself up in my cloak and joined him in the cleanest patch of straw I could find.

We woke early, both parched and the worse for wear. The innkeeper was already up. He offered us more ale but I'd nothing else I wanted to part with. We were ejected without ceremony.

'I have to get back to the hall,' groaned Ordwig, 'If Holman needs horses I'll be in trouble.'

I grabbed him, 'You owe me remember?'

'Why? Thought we were having fun.'

'I paid, didn't I,' I waved my ring-less fingers in his face, 'Surely you're not the only groom in the stable.' I pushed my face aggressively into his.

'God's Truth, keep your hair on mate. What do want of me?'

'Drank yourself stupid, did you? Take me to the horse-fair.' I pushed him hard. 'Remember!'

He stumbled back, shaken, 'To see Hutha? Why? He's a rough one him. Him and his friends.'

'Let's just say we have some unfinished business.'

Poor Ordwig looked close to tears, 'You seemed like such a nice bloke last night.'

'Do what I say and I'll be nice again.' I started to feel a bit of a shit. He'd not asked for this.

As we walked to the horse-fair I started to wonder what I was doing. I guessed Hutha would not have as many friends with him now. Toki, Gyric and I had seen to that. Would he even dare to come? And would the friends he had deserted be standing by him?

The horse-fair was bustling. Boys were running the livelier beasts up and down showing off their paces in front of the buyers. Everywhere men of every station were making bids, haggling noisily, bigging up their beasts or scoffing loudly at the seller's claims. I found myself absorbed watching as a beautiful black stallion was put through his paces in front of an admiring crowd.

Ordwig pulled me away, 'Hutha won't be selling prime animals like these. He's generally at the lower end of the market. Come on mate, hurry I need to get back.'

'Aye, well it's only a small horse I'm after, anyway.'

'You can afford to buy your own?'

'I'm an Earl's man, aren't I?' I replied slyly. It was easier than lying outright.

Ordwig looked at me with more respect and seeming to shrug off his regrets perked up. 'I can help you choose a pony. Bit of an expert me. But leave Hutha out of it.'

'No, he was recommended to me. If he has what I need I'm confident of a good price.'

'If that's the case he's usually at the port end of the market.'

As we walked through the crowd I saw that the bottom of the market backed on to some mean looking dwellings with narrow alleys running between them down to the docks. 'Good for a quick getaway,' I thought, 'maybe good for some dirty deeds of my own.'

'There he is.' Ordwig pointed to a man dressed in a roughly woven tunic under a worn leather jerkin. He was standing by a couple of beasts. One was an obviously old gelding covered in harness sores and looking like he'd been worked too hard for too long. The other was a mare about the same size as Maeve but its dark mane and tail, glossy coat and hooves and sprightly air showed it to be a much livelier beast. If I couldn't get back my own horse I was going to have this one, but how?

Hutha could have been anyone. There was no way of recognising him from the dusk and mud of the ambush. Two Hutha's concerned with horses a couple of miles apart? 'Unlikely,' I thought.

'Hey you! You Hutha?' I hailed him. I strode up to him leaving Ordwig tailing behind carrying my targe and spear.

The mare perked her ears up and whinnied. 'Who's asking?' grunted the man.

'The names Gifel,' I said loudly for the benefit of those around. Ordwig gasped but said nothing. 'Your horse seems friendlier than you are.' She did, she was snuffling me and skipping around in her hobbles. 'Friend of mine, Toki, told me to see you for a good deal on horseflesh.'

'Don't know any Toki,' the man grunted back.

'Well he said he knew you. Said you were a bit shorthanded lately on account of losing a couple of friends.'

A shadow crossed his face, 'Who told you that?'

My words had hit home, I could see it in his face. He had to be the right man.

'Toki like I said.' He looked around shiftily. I had made him nervous. 'No matter, my friend,' I said reassuringly, 'whatever your losses I've an eye for this little beast.'

'Let me look her over,' said Ordwig, 'I know about horses.'

'Well, Hutha, Toki told me that could trust you so perhaps we could discuss price.' For a brief moment Hutha looked truly amazed. I doubt he'd heard that very often before. A leer of greed appeared on his face as I stroked my torque and shrugged back my cloak to reveal my arm ring.

'Toki's a good man. You can believe what he says.' Hutha's face was now wreathed in smiles and he good naturedly lay his arm over my shoulders.

'Look, my silver's in my pouch,' I said, 'I'd rather go into the alley so the whole market doesn't know.'

'Wise man. Careful beyond your years.'

I was amused at his flattery, enjoying the deceit, but still unsure how to achieve my aim. As we walked into the alley I could hear Ordwig's voice crying, 'Whoa up there, little horse, hold steady.'

I looked back and there was the mare hopping into the alley with Ordwig struggling to get round her. 'Funny beast,' I thought but pleased that she'd blocked the alley from the eyes of the market.

Hutha turned and lashed out at the mare with a short leather strap, 'Get back you stupid animal.'

'Oh, leave her be,' I called, 'I'll only be a moment.' I felt a small thrill of excitement run through me, now was the time.

As I reached for my knife he turned again and whipped me hard across my face with the leather strap. I gasped and flinched in pain as he pushed his forearm into my throat and threw me back against the wall. I thudded against it so hard that I could feel the wattle in the wall crack as I hit it.

'Stupid fucking kid, do you think I was born yesterday,' he hissed through clenched teeth. 'Knew who you were soon as I saw you. I come from around here you twat. People talk. Skinny little jumped up red heads aren't that common. Well your fighting men aren't with you now.'

I was gasping to get my wind back. 'I don't know what you mean,' I wheezed through my squashed wind-pipe.

'Yes you fucking do. Now give me your money.'

'I haven't any.'

'I told you I'm not stupid. Not like you, too stupid to know your own horse.'

'What! That's Maeve?' I said, genuinely surprised.

As I said her name she whinnied again and tried once more to force herself into the narrow alley bumping into Hutha's back. He fell against me and as he did so the wall behind me gave way and we fell through it in a tangle of limbs. Suddenly I felt icily calm and as his arm left my throat I quickly pulled my knife from its sheath and stuck it up under his rib cage. It caught against the layer of leather and the hilt jammed into my stomach. Sharply it punched through the leather as his own weight pressed his body onto the blade. Then it was in. In his guts.

'So who's stupid now?' I grunted as the wall continued to collapse under us.

His eyes, right next to mine, widened in shock, then they glazed and he coughed a gobbet of blood into my face and died. As we stopped falling blood and spit dribbled sickeningly from his mouth to run over my chin and neck. Bizarrely Maeve's head was framed in the broken wall while I could hear Ordwig's voice prattling on behind her.

'There's something not right about this horse, look I've got black stuff on my hands.' Then Maeve's head was pulled backwards and Ordwig's filled the gap.

'What are you two doing? You've broken this house.'

I fought an insane urge to fall apart laughing. I was wedged in the wall with Hutha's body literally pinned to me by my knife. I knew the moment my knife came out I would be drenched in his hot blood.

'For fuck's sake Ordwig. Get him off me.'

'What's wrong with him,' he gasped then as realisation dawned, his eyes and his mouth flew open. 'What have you done? I'm going for the market reeve.'

'No don't, don't, please, wait, get him off me first. Calm down Ordwig, we need to think.'

As Ordwig pulled I shoved with my left arm while holding the knife in the wound with my right hand until I could slide out from under his body. I was a bit blood-stained but thankfully not covered in gore. As we rolled him off me the wall cracked and groaned and a large chunk of it fell into the space behind.

'Thank the blessed saints no-one was at home,' I said, only now pulling my knife from his body. 'Quick help me shove him through this hole, we need to cover this up.'

'No, I'm not doing that. You've done a murder. We must tell someone.'

I was kneeling in the filth of the alley trying to twist the corpse so as to get it through the hole. I couldn't do this alone. The calm had left me and now I was scared. I had both the corpse and Ordwig to deal with. I flew to my feet and holding the bloody knife to Ordwig's throat I hissed at him. 'You will do as I tell you or I'll kill you like I killed him.' I knew that I sounded like Oslaf and all Ordwig had done was try to help.

The poor man was terrified, went lime white and my spear and targe fell from his nerveless fingers. Meanwhile Maeve was snuffling against my neck as firmly wedged in the alley as a bung in a barrel. This time I did start giggling. This was madness. I took the knife away from Ordwig's throat and gathered my senses as best I could. If someone should come up the alley I was done for.

Calmness returned. I climbed through the hole over Hutha's body and grabbing him under the armpits set about dragging him into the house. Ordwig helped, straightening the legs and pushing from behind. I pulled a small leather purse from the corpse's belt. By the light from the hole I could see that I was in a little used back room of some kind. Tearing a strip from his tunic I wiped my spattered face as best I could. Then I piled up some old rushes from the floor and tipped them and a broken weaving frame over the body. That was all I could do. Climbing back out through the hole in the wall I put some of the broken pieces back into the hole. The wattle was brittle with age and rot. No wonder it had collapsed. I guessed we were in an old, almost derelict, part of the town. Maybe a broken wall would attract little attention here.

Ordwig was puking weakly. Patting him on the back I told him that I was sorry. He replied that he was sorry too. Sorry that he had ever met me. I pulled open the purse and inside it were 13 and a half, silver pennies.

Ordwig spluttered, 'By Saint Edgar's crown, Hutha didn't look like a man with money.'

'You can have it if you keep quiet,' I said.

Some colour returned to Ordwig's cheeks and he snatched the

purse from me. 'Alright,' he said, 'it's a deal.'

He then came over very practical. 'Look put your leather cloak on and the hood up. No-one will be surprised in this cold and you can't go about covered in blood.'

I did as he said and then we pushed Maeve back out of the alley. As I picked up my arms Ordwig showed me how colour and oil had been rubbed into her coat. 'And worse,' he said, carefully standing to one side, 'that's why she seemed so lively.'

He lifted up her tail and under it Hutha had stuck a thistle head. 'Christ, I'd be lively too with that in my arse,' I said leaning forward to pull it out. She tried to kick me but I leapt back in time. Back by the old gelding we found my mare's saddle, bridle and bit under an old hide. Taking off the frayed rope headstall she'd been wearing I put the bit in her mouth and the bridle on over her head. Feeling her soft nose as she snuffled my face I realised how much I had missed my little beast. As I breathed in her musky smell my heart stopped hammering in my chest and I began to feel more normal.

No-one took much notice of us. One man called out and Ordwig laughed and answered, 'Hutha's run off. He's been caught out with a dose of the shits.

The man laughed back. 'You'd think he'd know better than to drink the ale they sell in this market.'

As we left we were stopped by a market official, 'Who'd you buy that off, young man.'

Ordwig, who seemed quite back to his old self, replied. 'From Hutha, sir.'

'And you paid?'

'10 pennies and a fourth part.'

'Ha ha ha, for that nag? You were robbed. Never fear though, the fourth we will dun him for tax.'

'Not likely,' I thought and with that he let us go.

Now Ordwig could not get away from me quickly enough but before he did, I did my Oslaf act again. I didn't want his loose mouth causing me trouble. To be honest I thought the money would keep him quiet where my threats would do little. He'd not want to explain that he robbed a murdered man.

As I splashed through the ford I was glad to leave Gipeswic behind me but I was proud to have got my horse back. I realised that before I went back to join the others I needed to clean the dye off Maeve and the blood from my clothes. I found the head of the Belestede brook and, thankful that the cold weather would keep people away, stripped off and scrubbed the front of my tunic in the stream. Having no way to make a fire I had to put them back on in the freezing cold then set about the horse with bunches of rough grass and reeds. Some of the colour came out but she was much darker than she should be. At least only Toki and Gyric knew what she should really look like.

We both left steaming in the clear cold air and I decided to tell Ealhild and her people that I had found my horse wandering in a field beside the road. Toki and Gyric would have to be told the truth.

Later that day I returned to Belestede. Arriving during daylight I entered unchallenged and turned the horse out with Gyric's. A couple of the cottars stared at me. I stared back and they returned to their work without a word. I opened the hall door behind which I could hear happy chattering. As I walked in the room fell silent. The women concentrated on their spindles waiting for Ealhild's lead. Toki's voice fell silent as she rose and greeted me.

'We had not expected you back so soon,' she said, to my mind coldly, 'but as you are here there is broth in the pot by the hearth.'

I didn't answer instead I stalked over to the pot and ladled some broth into a clay bowl. 'From Gipeswic right.'

'Yes, Sar the bowl is made in Gipeswic.'

I fumbled out my horn spoon and went to sit in the darkest corner of the room without thanking her or greeting anyone else.

'You're being rude, boy, you know better than this.' Toki's voice was harsh, as he tried to sit a sharp intake of breath revealing that he was still in pain. 'Apologise, Sar, now!'

'Why should I Toki? No-one wants me here, do they? I find the nearest thing I have left to a family. Am I welcomed? No, I am cursed as a demon's son.' I spat the last words out at Ealhild. 'Perhaps I should just go, or do you want to hear your sister's story?'

Ealhild turned to Toki. 'Lie back, maybe we all need some time.'

I ate sitting in the corner staring balefully at the women and children. The next few days passed like this. Toki and Gyric were angry with me, I wouldn't speak to them. It was Aebbe who broke the ice.

She came up to me in my shadowy corner where I sulked the evenings away. 'You are my cousin, aren't you, my mother's sister's son.

I looked at her and she looked back at me through great brown eyes in a round smiling face. I could not help but smile back.

'I like having a cousin. I've never had one before,' she continued.

'Well, you've four now.' I was quickly warming to her straightforward way.

'Four!' Her eyes opened wide with wonder.

I told her of my twin sister, Moira, and of my half-brother and sister, Adaf and Elena. I told her what they looked like and how we lived in a cave hollowed out of a giant ancient wall looking over a great river that went up and down like the chest of a breathing giant. As I spoke her brother joined her and they both sat in the rushes and I knew how my stepfather felt when he told us his tales. I pretended to myself that I was him and I told them the tale of the Children of Lyr.

'Swans don't sing,' huffed Godric. Aebbe though cried out joyfully that she would love to be a swan and fly to Tir Na Nog.

I looked up to find the women had stopped their spinning and all of them were staring at me. 'What, what,' I said, 'can I not tell a story to children now?'

Lady Ealhild stood up and came over to me. 'I have misjudged you Sar, I have blamed you for the sins of your parents. Can you forgive me?'

I didn't know how to answer. She seemed sincere. Speaking again she asked me to walk with her outside alone.

We went out into a deep blue evening scattered with an eddying of light snow. She shivered. 'They say it will be a hard winter.'

'We're not here about the weather are we, milady?'

'That's the first time you've addressed me politely, Sar, yet Toki tells me you learnt the manners of the Earl's court quick enough.'

'It's not been easy coming here.'

'Nor for me, and neither is what I want to know now. I want to hear of my sister. Where is she? What has happened to her? Toki says it is your story to tell.'

I felt the coldness inside. 'You need not worry. She is dead.'

Drawing a deep shuddering breath she drew her head cloth more tightly across her face. 'That is what I feared. Is that why you are here?'

'I am here by chance, strange chance, only the unseen workings of my fate. I knew nothing of my mother's family. Only that we were Saxons. She was very strong on that.' I was a little bitter about this as it had always set us apart.

'We descend from a once great family that was brought down in the days of Cnut's invasion but we were still proud to hold up our heads. That is until that fateful day of Inga's disgrace,' said Ealhild

'Well, she and we paid hard for that,' I said. Ealhild's dilapidated hall was far grander than anything I had seen in my homeland. 'I come from a village of fishy-smelling hovels.'

'Why did she stay there? Why could she not come home?'

I felt angry now. 'What! With bastard twins from one man

and two infants from another? That, and the scorn of all your so-called good people, with your airs and graces.' I spat on the ground folded my arms and stared furiously into the wind.

'You are right Sar, she was always proud.'

'She was proud, and hard. But even though to look at me made her shudder she worked heart and soul to raise and feed us.' As I spoke my voice trembled.

'Don't break now, boy!' Ealhild spoke sternly. Her voice whipped out in the way my mother's had. 'I need to know how she died.'

I told her, bluntly, I spared her no detail and she stood staring into my face and heard it all. 'Thank you, Sar,' was all she said and then she tried to embrace me.

I stood solid and cold I did not stop her but I did not respond. 'I see it is too soon,' she said drawing back.

'My sister is sold into slavery. My other siblings may have starved for all I know. You did not ask.'

'I could not take more tonight.' I saw now there were tears streaming down her face. Her hard words belied her true feelings.

I carried on, remorseless. 'I killed him. I killed the man that destroyed my family.'

'You have family now Sar, we are family.'

'No, I have no family but the Earl's. That was the price of my life.'

Ealhild touched me gently on the arm then went back into the hall. I stayed out breathing in the cold clear air until I thought all would be asleep then I crept in. That night the nightmares returned as I slept, restlessly, in my corner of the hall.

From then on things began to change and I joined in the workings of the village as well as helping with Toki's care. We decided that one of us should return to Harold and as Gyric was fit enough to ride and also a housecarl it was me that should stay. This would be the first time we had been apart since I had been snatched from my home. Toki told Gyric to tell Harold that his wounds prevented him returning before Christ's Mass and that he would keep me with him. Before he left we discussed my killing of Hutha.

Gyric was unhappy, 'You can't just go around killing people. We have laws and restitution. We have shire-reeves and courts to deal with these things. Wergild can be paid when men are found guilty, or they hang if they are slaves, or are enslaved if they have no money.'

Toki was more pragmatic, 'I would have liked to question him. To have found the men who have wounded me so badly. I want vengeance. To me it was Hutha's fate to steal from the son of a demon.'

He looked at me straight faced. Then one corner of his mouth lifted just enough for me to be uncertain if he was joking. 'I think you will get away with this killing, Sar. Ports are known for their violence as rootless men come and go. No-one will care enough about a dodgy horse dealer to seek out his killer.'

'That man Ordwig knows and the market official saw them leave and Ordwig told him they'd bought a horse from Hutha.' Gyric looked me straight in the eye with his honest troubled gaze, 'and no-one Sar, no-one believes you just found that pony wandering about saddled and bridled days after we were attacked.'

'I didn't know what else to say. How could I tell the truth?'

Gyric shook his head. 'It was a stupid lie. Everyone knows you lie and that I am friends with a man who lies. I am glad to be leaving to spend time with more honest straightforward men.'

I had no answer to this. When Gyric rode away I hung back and merely grunted a farewell, he half raised his hand then let it fall to his saddle bow. Then he turned and rode away. I would not be with Gyric's family for Christ's Mass. Had I lost my one true friend?

As the days passed without Gyric I told more tales to the children and learned to enjoy Toki's rough banter with Hjor. Their having no father made me feel close to the children. I could not feel so for Ealhild but I was no longer rude and she no longer harsh. While the people of the hall accepted me the cottars would cross themselves or mutter charms as I passed. This was not new to me but now it was not because I had killed a great warrior in a fluke attack but because my father was a demon. More and more I found I was choosing the company of the other outcast in the village, the slave girl, Ymma.

Ymma rarely spoke and kept no company. Up before everyone each morning, she had to draw water, set up the settles and bowls and blow the embers into flames. She seemed almost invisible, shrouded in cast off garments and shuffling along in worn clogs.

I'd awake to see her thin face lit up by the glow as she blew the hearth into life. She had little puff and would struggle to rekindle the fire so one morning I crept out into the chill and crouching beside her joined my breath with hers. As a small flame appeared we fed the kindling in enjoying the brightness of the flame. We smiled at each other then I picked up the heavy wooden bucket and carried it to the well. This became our morning ritual and while she would only whisper thanks and smile shyly at me I felt easy in her company.

Toki healed slowly, in the relief of him surviving the fever I believed that he would soon be back to his old self. One day he called me to him. 'I won't be re-joining Harold, Sar. My days as a warrior are done. Once I can reach the privy and hold myself upright to piss you will have to leave me here.'

'I don't understand. You are one of Harold's senior housecarls.'

'Sar, these wounds are too severe. I have survived wars in Flanders, Wales and Godwin's conflicts with the King only to be brought down by Saxon thieves. It is bitter but while my back may heal it will not mend true. I am no longer fit to campaign.'

I found tears in my eyes, to hide them I leant on my knees. To me Toki was indestructible.

'I am going to stay here Sar. With Ealhild.'

I looked up to see he was blushing. 'Your aunt and I have grown fond of each other,' he said awkwardly. 'With the income from the estate Harold gave me I intend to restore this hall and the Lady's fortunes. Her children will become mine. We will marry and I will become your uncle.'

I smiled at that.

A few days later one of Harold's messengers passed through, escorted by two housecarls. Neither of them was Gyric. One message was for me. I could stay until Christ's Mass then I was to return to Harold's train. The other was for all those who owed Harold service. News had come that his brother Sweyn had died on his way back from Jerusalem. Harold was now Godwin's most senior son.

Toki explained to me what this meant. 'Now Harold will definitely become Earl of Wessex when Godwin dies making him one of the three most powerful men under the King.'

'Who are the others?'

'The Earl of Northumbria is Earl Siward the Stout, a mighty and powerful lord. His Earldom is vast and he rules with an iron hand like the Norseman he is. He, like Godwin, came to power under Cnut.'

'And the other two?'

The rich heartland of the country, Mercia, is ruled by Earl Leofric and his Lady Godgifu. Aelfgar is his son. The third is Godwin as you know. When Harold gets Wessex, Aelfgar will get East Anglia. As Godwin's sons and the Queen's brothers Tostig, Leofwine and Gyrth will also demand part of the pie.'

'Will they fight?'

'It is unlikely but possible. Leofric is content to hold his own but he has a son and grandsons. Siward always has the Scots at his back but he rules a fierce and proud people and also has sons of his own. The rise of the Godwinsons threatens all their ambitions. Much depends on who can keep the King's ear when the balance of power shifts.'

'So the King decides?'

'The King holds the country together. If we fight each other England will fall. There are always wolves waiting to attack when the great stags fight.'

'There are?'

'Many. Your Irish friends for a start, as well as the Scots, the Danes, the Norwegians and the Flemish. The Normans grow strong again and whenever the Welsh stop fighting each other they raid our western lands. They raided us while Godwin was at odds with the King.'

'That's a lot of enemies.'

'It is, Sar, that's why we need a strong King and strong Earls who respect each other.'

I nodded sagely to cover my ignorance.

CHAPTER 11

Everyone was working hard to preserve food for the winter. The last of the animals to die were being slaughtered to be smoked or salted. The rest were herded into the byres where they would stay until the spring grass grew green after the snow. Anything that could not be preserved would be eaten at a great feast for all the people attached to Lady Ealhild's household and land.

In the week approaching Yule, when the nights were at their longest and darkest, preparations for the feasting at Christ's Mass reached fever pitch. Everyone wanted to look their best which for Ymma meant washing Ealhild's and Jofrid's clothes in the stream. The weather had warmed slightly as a persistent westerly wind blew in sleety drizzle. I came upon her, shivering and soaked through, beating the clothes on a wooden board.

'Let me help,' I offered.

'You can't do this, it is woman's work,' she replied smiling.

'I can beat clothes against a board as good as anyone,' I said, nudging her aside. Then I dragged a surprisingly heavy gown from the water onto the board.

She went to pull out more clothes from an open wicker basket where they were soaking. As she leant over the basket her head-cloth came unwound. I'd never seen her bare headed before and before I could stop myself I smiled at the sight of her roughly cropped hair.

She was furious. 'Don't laugh at me. Don't laugh at my

shame.'

All free young women wore their hair long until they covered it when they married.

'I'm sorry,' I said, 'I was surprised. I meant no harm.' I rose and gently placed the cloth back over her head. 'They make you keep it cropped.'

'Jofrid does it. It is my mark of slavery and it makes it hard for us to run.'

I found my hand stroking the softness of her cheek. 'Cropped hair doesn't hide your beauty,' I murmured. Then, gently tipping her head back, I touched my lips to hers.

She didn't pull away nor did she respond. 'Careful, Sar, neither my beauty nor my kisses are mine to give.'

'My sister is like you. She too is a slave somewhere unknown to me.'

'Then she too is property.'

'Sold to a Gytha, I think in Bristou.'

'Common enough name, certainly among the Danes. Even here we know Bristou is a great slave port. Your sister could be anywhere.'

I pushed the gaping ache of my twin's absence back into my deep dark heart. 'Let's get these clothes done.'

We pounded and wrung the sodden clothes. Then I carried them to the drying sheds. I helped her hang them over the ropes strung under the open sided roof. This led to more muttering and dark looks from the cottars. 'Fuck them all,' I said, 'I'll help a slave if I want. I'll do a woman's job if I want.'

I had grown up under the crumbling mass that the Romans had built at Caer Dydd. Their century's old ghosts had looked over our settlement of drifters, renegades, fugitives from marriage laws or escaped slaves. While we were no-one's people, eking out a poor living in the shadows between forest and shore, we had all been equal in our poverty. There was a lot I didn't like about this world where people looked down on some and fawned up to others.

It was Saint Thomas's Day, the shortest day of the year, and the weather began to change. It warmed and a steadily rising wind blew heavy gusts of rain in from the west. As Christ's Mass was only a few days away and many hours would be spent at church services we were rushing to get prepared in the few day-light hours.

I and some other men were carrying the flensed carcass of an ox into the hall. Freana was one of them. 'I don't like the look of those clouds,' he said, nodding towards an ominously dark sky. We hurried into the hall to set about bracing the ox's rib cage apart with stout iron stakes. Then we built tripods to support each end of the massive iron rod that would be skewered through the whole length of the beast.

We finally got it up over the hearth. For the next two days the hall would fill with acrid smoke and tantalising aromas as the animal slowly roasted. By the time we got back outside the sky had completely darkened and the wind was rising to a scream-ing howl. Hjor was stomping about shouting orders at anyone passing to secure roofs and haystacks. From the corner of my eye, as I struggled to pound hazel pegs into the reed thatch of the hall roof, I saw Ymma pulling clothes from the lines in the drying shed.

As the long night fell many of the cottars joined us in the hall. They prayed and recited charms as the wind's roar rose to a terrifying crescendo. The hours passed slowly while the smoke whipped out through the hole in the roof, dragged by the mighty gale. I watched it writhe and twist as the hole was lit up by furious flashes of lightning and then, in one flash, the hole doubled in size. 'The roof is going!' I shouted pointing at the now gaping, ragged, gap. Lady Ealhild took charge, 'Douse the fire. If the roof comes in the hall will burn.'

With regretful looks at the browning carcass we threw all the water we could find on the hearth. As some of the cottar men left to do the same to their own hearths Father Eoppa came struggling in. 'The byres have lost their roofs already.'

Hjor sent us out to release the animals. 'Set them free to give them a chance. Then go to the church. It's the only stone building around.'

I went straight to the stables. The horses were hysterical. The rain was pouring in and the thunder and lightning tore up the sky above their tossing, crazed heads. As I pulled open the door the wind caught it wrenching my arms painfully. It broke free from its leather hinges and whirled off into the night. The horses bolted for the door, desperate to escape, and once out they joined the stampede of cattle and sheep all running from the wind. They were causing mayhem, careering around in the dark like a whirlpool of maddened flesh, wild eyes and bared teeth. Their horns and hooves made them dangerous so someone opened the palisade gates. Seeing a way out, they pushed through the gap and disappeared into the wild night led by our precious horses. God alone knew if we would get any of them back.

Next I helped get the women and children down to the church. Its bell was ringing out above the din. In the flashes we could see that some of the dwellings had collapsed. The great black poplar that stood in the centre of the village groaned ominously, swinging violently back and forth, black against the darkness. Twigs and small branches flew stinging into our faces. The frightened children could not stay on their feet and had to be carried down to the church. Once inside the harbour of its stone walls and its strong wooden roof we regained some calm. Father Eoppa started calling the names of his congregation as Freana and I went back for Toki.

We wove our way back to the church staggering like drunken fools against the wind. Toki, laying his arms across our shoulders, gritted his teeth, as the pain of his stretched, barely healed, wounds tore into him. As we entered the church the groaning of the poplar growled into loud, tearing, cracks and bangs. Despite our desire for shelter we stopped and turned to watch as the mighty giant crashed over, slamming down onto the weaving shed roof.

Toki grunted through his pain. 'See Sar, all things come to fall, great trees, good soldiers, Earls and slaves. Live for the moment son, as good things, like life, pass quickly.'

I looked at him sharply. I'd have expected curses, oaths and bravado but he was passing me his wisdom. I held his gaze for a moment then nodded my understanding and, hefting his weight, supported him the last few yards to shelter.

By now the dawn was breaking, the thunder and lightning had ceased but the wind ploughed on tearing the last shreds of dark clouds from the sky. The inside of the church was still dark, filled wall to wall with huddled frightened people believing that God had deserted us. Everyone was sat with someone close to them. Toki with Ealhild and her children, Jofrid with Hjor, families grouped together with the priest circulating around in the gloom reassuring the anxious. I called out, 'Ymma, where are you?' No answer. I started moving around the room asking after her, shaking the sleepers and calling her name.

'Leave us in peace, boy.'

'Who cares?'

'Has anyone seen her?' I was shouting loudly now.

'She's in God's hands, Sar,' said Father Eoppa, 'Others may be missing too. Wait until the storm subsides and we will search.'

I remembered seeing her as the storm grew. 'No, I must go and find her.'

I pulled open the door showered by curses as the wind blew in waves of fallen leaves and shredded thatch. I struggled up to where I'd last seen her but where the drying shed was, it wasn't. Just some stark poles in the sodden ground were all that was left. I looked wildly about as the sky darkened again and more rain began to fall.

The sturdiest building after the hall was the weaving shed but part of it was crushed by the fallen tree. She'd not been in the hall, she must be in there. Spurred on by a huge crash of thunder I ran, slipping and sliding my way across the muddy ground. Grabbing the door frame I pulled myself in through where the doors should have been. Lightning flashed but all I could see was a tangled mass of branches and roof trusses.

'Ymma, are you here, Ymma?'

I caught a glimpse of a white face against the wall. The great tree's fall had been stopped by the sturdy wooden walls, leaving a space under which Ymma lay. I crawled in with her shivering and delighted.

'So glad I found you.' It was exciting to be this close to her warm body. I could feel her breathing quicken as she made room for me. The thunder crashed again, quickly followed by a violent flash. The space flickered with stark bands of black and fierce white.

'Good to see you too,' she said circling her arms around me. My hands ran up her sides, felt her warm small breasts through the woven stuff of her damp dress. Her nipples grew hard in the palms of my hands. I could feel her heart racing, pounding in her chest. My breath caught in my throat as I searched for her lips with my own. Lightning flashed and I caught her bright smile in the fierce light. She pushed me away from her. I faltered.

'No, don't pull back. Help me with my dress.' As the thunder followed I helped her hitch her dress up above her waist. I knelt up as best I could under the gnarly trunk of the old tree, pulling my breeches down fumbling feverishly and snapping the wet leather straps that held them up. The lightning flashed again and I could see her long white thighs and the dark promise of her sex. I groaned helplessly in lust and ecstasy as she drew her knees up and I slid between her thighs. Another crash of thunder and we were joined, bucking and grinding with all the vigour of our youth under the dripping ceiling of the great fallen tree. The thunder and lightning roared and flashed as we heaved and panted our way to climax.

'Pull out, pull out,' she gasped but it was too late.

'Oh God,' I shuddered, 'Sorry, I've never done that before.'

'I was your first?' she said, surprised and pleased. 'Look,' she said, 'and you mine.' She pushed her hand down between her legs and brought it up. 'See? Blood.'

I hugged her hard against my chest and as I did so Morwid's face came into my mind. Her brutal rape and how close I was to being part of that. In that moment I knew that I still yearned after her dark beauty. Puzzled that I should feel this now I hid my face in Ymma's shoulder both elated and also close to tears.

'We should go,' I said.

'No, lie with me a moment,' she replied. She turned my face to hers, 'Sar, you cannot speak of this. Ealhild is my owner, my body belongs to her.'

'I know, my sweetheart, I know.'

The wind died down and as it did the rain began to fall vertically. The remains of the wall had protected us from most of the slanting rain but now we were getting soaked. We crawled out from under the tree and out of the remains of the shed. The village was barely recognisable. Some of the cottages were flattened completely, all were damaged. Half the hall roof had completely disappeared. People were already searching for their possessions among the ruins. Women were sobbing quietly in shock while the men tore angrily at the remains of their homes. Children were staring wide eyed at their now unrecognisable houses and at the great ragged stump of the fallen poplar.

'Generations have played and grown old under that tree. This was a Saint Thomas' Day we will never forget.' It was Hjor, leaning on a staff to brace himself against the slippery ground. 'Ymma, go find your mistress.'

After she went he looked at me sternly, 'Sar, you're too close to that girl. Watch yourself. Now go find a metal pot and search all the ruins for some embers to get a fire going.'

'Where?'

'It will have to be in the church. Eoppa won't mind as things are.'

I clambered through the broken doors of the hall and hunting through the wreckage found an iron cooking pot. The spitted ox had fallen across the hearth. Its ash covered carcass was a sad reminder of the fate of tomorrows feast. I pushed my hand deep into the ashes but not even a glimmer of warmth remained in the sodden mush.

I searched the village but all the fires had been doused, soaked or smothered under fallen roofs. Hjor sent me off to a neighbouring village where they had a forge. He reckoned that if anyone could keep a fire in a storm it would be a blacksmith. I was glad to get away from the wailing of the women, the curses of men and the crying of children. The rain was easing as I ran along the track. Everywhere the country was devastated. Small flocks of sheep and herds of cattle wandered in the open fields, bleating and lowing miserably. As I ran along I realised how good I felt. I'd known a woman. I was no longer a virgin. Whatever the church thought, I was happy to no longer be pure. I laughed aloud at the thought of Aethelric's disapproving face.

◆ ◆ ◆

I came to the next village and found it in no better state than our own. The blacksmith's shed was a wreck but thankfully he had managed to keep the forge alight. As I got there his boy was working the bellows to bring up the flames.

I asked the blacksmith for enough embers to fill the pot. 'You'll have to wait until the people here have what they need.'

I helped stoke the fire with the shattered timbers of nearby dwellings. My pot was soon filled with embers and carrying it by its chains I took them to any villagers who had managed to make enough of a shelter to build a fire. Their gratitude was heartfelt. The wet and the cold was reducing people to shivering misery.

I pleaded with the blacksmith for my own people and eventually he let me go with my pot well filled with embers and fuel. It was heavy as well as hot now and I seemed to take an age getting back to Belestede holding the pot away from myself. I got there to find many of the people had returned to the church where they were huddling together for warmth. We built a fire in the middle of the church floor while men brought in the cut up remains of the ox. Soon bits of it were roasting by the fire, sodden loaves drying out and other bits of rescued food being passed around. Someone had retrieved a pot of honey and the children were given a spoonful each. They quickly cheered up and the adults began to follow.

'Some ale would be good,' cried a voice from the crowd.

'Haven't found an unbroken cask,' replied another.

I could hear Father Eoppa mutter under his breath, 'Probably just as well.'

Ale wasn't needed as the fire began to blaze and as the food was passed around the mood grew more cheerful.

A woman spoke, 'No-one died. That is good.'

Many had suffered small hurts but it was true no-one had died and no-one was seriously injured. The priest led us in a prayer of thanks for God's mercy. As the fire blazed hotter those nearest to it moved out to the walls to let others in. I found Ymma and we snuggled together ignoring Hjor's stern looks and Ealhild's cold gaze. I saw Toki, now propped up on a pile of damp steaming straw, smothering a knowing grin. With a half-cooked rib of ox in my hand and a warm woman at my side I felt deeply contented as I lay back against the stone wall.

This contentment only lasted into the next day. As men went out to try and retrieve lost livestock our only relief was that our horses had found their way back to the remains of their stable by picking their way through the shattered fences.

Toki sent for me. 'This great storm cannot be just a local event. Your Earl will need all the men he can get. It is your duty to return to your Lord.'

'But it's Christ's Mass the day after tomorrow.'

'There will be no feast. The grain in the granary has been spoiled as have many other stores. Any extra mouths are a burden.'

'Everyone needs help here.'

Toki ignored me. 'There may be desperate men out there so I want you to take my horse. It is bigger than any likely to chase you. It also eats as befits its size. We'd be better off without it here.'

I spent the rest of the day searching for my targe, spear and horn as I helped the men pull away the wreckage of the hall roof. Laid against the base of the wall they had survived undamaged. I attended a service in the church and slept there the night. In the morning I left at first light. I couldn't face saying goodbye.

I should have known. There was only one other person up so early, Ymma. I was just tightening the big gelding's girth when I felt a gentle touch on my shoulder.

'Where are you off to so early?'

I put my knee into the horse's side to check he wasn't holding his breath in. As I pulled in his girth strap an extra hole I drew in my own breath and turned to face her. 'I'm leaving, Ymma. It's time for me to go.'

Tears sprung into her eyes. 'You've taken what you wanted and now you'll just leave me here.'

I held her shoulders. 'It's not like that, it's not. Toki ordered me. I have to go.'

She twisted from my grip, 'Without even saying goodbye!'

'I haven't said goodbye to anyone.'

'And that's supposed to make me feel better? You're a cowardly shit, Sar, a cowardly shit.'

I climbed up onto Toki's big beast and looked down on her. 'I'll come back to see you. I promise. I'll come back.' I spoke angrily to cover my shame.

'Of course you will say that. Well, I don't think I believe you.'

'Ymma, please.'

'Let me help you leave.'

I'd forgotten that I'd have to pull open the gates. I watched dumbly as she strode up to them, lifted out the bar and hauled with all her slim strength. As the gate opened I rode through and as I ducked under the lintel she spat on the ground. 'I thought you cared, Sar. I thought I mattered to you.'

I caught a last sight of her face streaming with tears as she turned to run back into the settlement.

It took a while to get Toki's gelding to accept my control but I fought him hard and eventually got my way. After plodding along on Maeve this was a very different ride. We kept up a good pace. My plan, or rather Toki's, was that I should ride to Waltham for news then up to Grontabricc to find Harold. Everywhere I went I found the same devastation. Everywhere the same cry. 'Tell the Earl we need help. Tell him we need food.'

When I got to Waltham I learned that huge swathes of the country had been affected by the storm. I stayed with the priests for a few days as news came in. Then I was sent off with a head full of messages for Harold. There were no men free for an escort or one to be a guide. I had to rely on Toki's horse's speed and strength to stay out of trouble. As for the route, all I had to do was stay on the old Roman road that passed close by and head north.

I rode hard the first day and before dark found a priory set back from the road. I was welcomed there as the Earl's man and again I heard similar stories of widespread destruction. I was given directions to Grontabricc from where I could get directions to Lady Edith's home estate where Harold had planned to spend Christ's Mass.

I arrived there well before dark to find a fine hall in the centre of a large, well-kept estate. Here too there were many damaged buildings but parties of men were already at work repairing them. The hall itself, built in the lee of a mature wood, had suffered little damage. There were great gaps in the tree line and fallen branches everywhere. Again, men were at work clearing them up. A boy took my horse and told me to go inside.

As my eyes adjusted to the dim light I could see Harold stood at a table with Thurkill. Various housecarls stood around receiving orders. I guessed that it was due to all the soldiers in Harold's train that so much work was already being undertaken.

Harold looked up, 'Ah, Sar, run and find Liofa', a housecarl I knew by sight. 'He's dealing with the fallen trees.' I related my messages. He then gave me a list of instructions. I repeated them back to him. He nodded once and turned again to Thurkill. That was it. I was back in the Earl's household.

We all stayed around that estate for the following fortnight. I finally got to see the beautiful Edith the Fair, Harold's hand-fast wife. They had married 'Danish style' but had not been blessed by the church. This meant that either of them could marry again should they wish. She was a tall stunning blonde and always dressed in sumptuous finery to rival Harold himself. Her and her ladies, often veiled in gauzy fabrics, passed by in clouds of scent, silks and furs, followed by some or all of her children. Harold loved to hunt and hawk. Sometimes I got to go, usually to be sent back before we got started with some message or other. Otherwise my days were spent running or riding, carrying messages and returning hungry and exhausted. I'd retrieved my goods and now never went anywhere without both of my light throwing spears.

I kept myself to myself. Rumours about me, my birth and my killings had somehow got around. There were no secrets in this huge and much travelled company. The more important people didn't care but the serving folk were riven by little factions whose main currency was gossip. I was viewed with a mixture of superstition and fear. I didn't mind, they could all go to hell for all I cared. I served my Earl and was received with respect at the halls I had to visit as his messenger.

Harold's retinue was preparing to leave for the next wealthy manor whose supplies we would consume. No one place could support us for long so the Earl's court, like the King's, was always on the move. I was saddling Toki's horse when I felt a sharp nudge in my back. 'Alright, Sar, how's it going?'

It was Gyric's voice, cheerful and friendly. I whirled round and hugged him.

'Whoa, steady there,' he said, 'missed me then?'

I remembered the terms we'd parted on and pulled back sharply, warily, but he was smiling at me with that familiar, slightly chubby, laughing face.

'Are we friends?' I asked unsure.

'We are Sar. I went home for Christ's Mass and talked it through with my father. Well, you know you're not his favourite person, but he saw no reason to give robbing scum the benefit of a trial.'

'He didn't?'

'No. In fact he thought that what you did went some way to avenging Toki's injuries. Men like that could never have compensated him. Death was all they deserved.'

'What about my lying?'

'He said you need to get more cunning.'

'What!'

'Yes,' Gyric pulled a wry smile, crooked now because of the scar on his face, 'and he said that I'd better wise up or join a monastery.'

I was laughing now, so relieved that Gyric and I were still friends, 'You! A monk? Ha ha.'

Gyric looked serious. 'Well I do think the world could be a more peaceful and orderly place and what's the point in laws if we ignore them?'

'Oh God, Gyric, I don't know, things just happen. Anyway that's what you do isn't it? Enforce the Earl's laws.'

He lightened up again. 'I suppose I do. Come let's see if we can scrounge a drink before we go.'

'Great, I know a purser's assistant who's a little scared of me.'

'Hmmm, there's one more thing my father said.'

'Yea.'

'He said he's seen your type before.'

'He did?'

'He said you are a cold-blooded killer. Most men need to be fired up to kill. Be angry, scared or in a battle or drunk of course. But you, he said, don't. Like Oslaf.'

'Like Oslaf?' I wasn't sure how I felt about this. We'd found some strong ale and by the time we left we were swaying on our horses giggling like fools. Guiltily I stayed away from Harold but at one point on the journey the crowd parted and I'm sure he saw us. I can't be certain but I thought he was grinning.

CHAPTER 12

A t Easter we joined the King at Wincestre for the holiest time of the year. It was almost as big as Lundunburh but was a city of churches. There were two huge minsters built so close together that you could stand between them with one hand on the New Minster and one on the Old. The old one was full of crutches, stools, trusses and carved plaster hands, arms, legs and even heads from all the people who'd been cured by Saint Swithin who was buried outside. The New Minster was incredible, full of gold and silver ornaments and newly painted with greens, reds, blues and glittering gold paints. There was coloured glass in the windows and scented smoke drifted through the air. It was like heaven. At the front of the church was a great processional cross, always guarded, of solid gold and silver that King Cnut and his Queen, Emma, had donated. Always monks were singing. Their voices were like those of angels. Then other monks would chase me out. During services there was no room for anyone but the great and the good while the King and all his courtiers were in town.

Harold kept me quite close at this time. My quickness and memory meant that I was useful carrying his wishes and requests through the crowded streets and this was how I overheard things that maybe it would have been best not to have heard. The Godwinsons who were here, Harold, Tostig, and Gyrth were staying with their father in a large town house. When returning from an errand I ran in from the street full of my own importance. After handing my weapons over to the doorkeeper I pushed between the guards, two housecarls who knew me, into the crowded hallway. There were always people seeking the Earl's ear. I did notice there were more women and priests around than usual but just the same I wriggled my way through the press to squeeze into the private rooms at the back. A hand grabbed my tunic. 'Steady boy, the Queen is here.'

I shrugged off the restraining hand. Queen Eadgyth was Harold's sister and I had heard much about her. She spoke many languages, could read and write and besides was Harold's older sister. I wanted to see her. I could hear voices and headed towards them. I slid through the door meaning to announce my arrival and get to see the Queen. I found myself hidden behind a heavy tapestry that hung across the doorway and peering round the edge realised that only family members were in the room. Unusually there were no serving people or even dogs hanging around.

Godwin was speaking, his voice heavy and stern, 'So, Eadgyth, you remain childless. If you had done your duty none of the events of last year would have happened.'

I knew immediately that I should not be hearing this but the door had shut behind me and to turn to open it would have given my presence away. I froze behind the thick material with one eye peering through the tasselled fringe of the tapestry.

I could just see Queen Eadgyth standing in front of Godwin who was seated beside an older, richly dressed, woman. The Queen was very, very, richly dressed with a jewelled headdress and a pearl studded robe but her voice was trembling, 'It is not my doing father. I have always been available for the King.'

'He put you aside to all our shame. If you had given him a son that shit Robert could never have had you sent away.'

There were tears on the Queen's face when the other woman spoke, her voice thick with an accent I knew to be Danish. 'My brother's son is King of Denmark. I had hoped for my grandson to be King of England.'

'Mother, it is not my fault.' She was shaking visibly and crying. 'The King, he... well... he does, doesn't...'

'Doesn't what?' snapped her mother.

Eadgyth was flushing bright red, 'It is hard to say, mother.'

'Don't be silly girl, we are all family here.'

'You shouldn't speak to me like that. I am the Queen.'

'You are first and foremost our daughter. Now answer me.'

From out of sight I heard Tostig's voice. 'Don't be so hard on her, Mother. She has always done all that you wanted. She is the most accomplished noblewoman anywhere between here and Micklegard.'

'All that learning is wasted if she can't produce an heir.'

Eadgyth was sobbing loudly. Harold walked into sight between me and her. 'Eadgyth, you need to talk to us. What doesn't the King do?' His voice was gentle as he quietened her sobs.

'He does not make love to me.'

'What never! You must learn to please him,' said Godwin roughly.

'I used to, we used to, properly, but soon after our marriage. He... well umm he..'

Tostig stood and held his sister while Harold sucked his teeth impatiently. 'Come, sister, tell us what happens between you and the King.'

'Nothing happens now..... He just comes to my bed to sleep. At first he was hard like a man but before he got to me would spill his seed and shrivel.' Her voice went shrill then broke as she fell back to sobbing, 'Is it my fault? What could I have done?'

'He comes too soon!' It was Harold speaking. 'Well, he's hardly going to admit to that!'

'I think it's why he flies into such rages. He used to with me but now he does it anywhere. Look what happened before Christ's Mass. After that Welsh raid Edward ordered Rhys ap Grydderich to be slaughtered and he had his head brought to the table at our Yule tide feast!'

'He certainly has a temper, look how he was before our exile. Screaming with rage, demanding that I bring his dead brother back to life,' said Godwin. 'It wasn't pretty. I thought he was going to fall down in a fit. His spittle flew in my face. If he'd had not been my King I would have struck him down.'

'But he can also be so loving and gentle to me, like a father to a much loved daughter.' Eadgyth was weeping steadily.

'I'm your Father. He should be your husband.'

'You've never been very loving to me. You sent me to the convent. The abbess at Wilton was father and mother to me while all you cared about was power and schooling me to further your aims.'

Her mother shouted, 'What do you think daughters are for? Do you think I had a choice to marry your father? Do you?' Suddenly she laughed, 'Though I have to say it worked out alright for us. We've had some good times making babies, eh, Godwin?'

Godwin ignored her while Harold chuckled, 'You certainly made a lot of us.'

Tostig was comforting Eadgyth while Godwin looked shattered, slumped in his chair. His wife took to striding noisily round the room. 'You never thought to tell us of this, Eadgyth, of the end of all our hopes.'

'Look how you react!'

'I should slap you girl, Queen or no Queen.'

'Stop it you two, stop it! By all the Saints I need to get out, to think.' Harold strode towards the door and before I could move pulled the curtain aside leaving me standing there exposed.

His hand shot out and he grabbed me and threw me across the room. He was a very strong man and I flew through the air, crashing hard against the opposite wall. He was on me before I could recover, kneeling over me with his knife against my throat.

The noise had attracted attention and an armed man was pulling back the curtain. Tostig leapt up and pushed him back out. 'Stay out of here if you know what's best for you.'

The guard backed quickly out as Tostig firmly pushed the door back. 'You should kill that boy, Harold, for spying on us.'

'I might just do that. What did you hear, Sar? What were you doing there anyway?'

My thoughts were racing. I tried the second question first. 'I was bringing a reply from the Archbishop, sir. I didn't mean to hear anything. I'm sorry, truly sorry. I'll go now if you want.'

He swapped hands, choking me with his left while pointing the knife at my face. 'I asked you what you heard.'

I knew Harold would see straight through me if I lied. 'I heard about the King and the Queen.'

'Kill him Harold, you can't let him live,' said Tostig.

Harold touched the knife to the scar that Oslaf had carved in my face. 'I can't kill him. He saved my life in Conor's Dun. At Porloc his quick thinking shortened a hard fight we may have lost.'

I could hear guttural Danish curses before their Mother cried. 'If he's a threat to us kill him, if you can't do it Harold, give him to someone who can.'

Harold ignored her and turned to Tostig. 'This is the boy who killed Eardwulf.'

Tostig's face softened, 'This stripling. This killed Eardwulf? God, how I hated that bastard.'

Eadgyth spoke shakily. 'Me too, he was always creeping round me when I was a girl. Saying creepy things and trying to touch me, threatening me with Sweyn's anger.'

Godwin was suddenly standing over me, 'Eardwulf the Fox! My dead son's friend?'

'I didn't know he was your son's friend. He killed my mother. He smashed her face into a doorpost until she was dead. I killed my mother's killer.' I was pleading, not understanding what was happening.

'Hmmm. A mighty deed for one so young. Truthfully I blame Eardwulf for Sweyn's misdeeds.'

'For God's sake, Father! Sweyn needed no encouragement,' shouted Harold.

'Do not start all that again. Godwin, your eldest son was cursed. He even denied you were his father claiming that I had slept with Cnut. I! His own mother!' the elder woman exclaimed

Godwin grunted. 'Without Eardwulf, Sweyn would never have killed your nephew.'

Somehow the argument had moved away from me. Harold left them to it and while they argued he spoke to me. 'I can't kill you Sar but for the rest of Easter you must stay near me. You breathe a word to anyone and I will have you killed. And seeing the only person you seem to talk to is Gyric I will have him killed too. Understand me?'

And so it was that through the Easter ceremonies I was rarely from Harold's side. I slept on the floor at the foot of his bed. I passed him his clothes, helped him get dressed, I gave his lackeys the pot he pissed and shat in and I served him at the table. I spent hours beside him in endless church services and processions. No monks were evicting me now. His servants saw this as me being favoured while I knew differently. He didn't give much away, did Harold, and I knew that one corner of his mind was pondering my fate.

I made myself useful, rarely spoke and if I saw Gyric on duty I would nod and smile but quickly move on. I set my mind to anticipating Harold's needs. I wanted him to see me as devoted to his service as I truly was. He never used my name and ordered me around with gestures or single words. I had been around an Earl's household long enough to know that these powerful men had many enemies. His suspicious looks and blunt manner made me believe he thought me a spy.

And so that was how I came to be serving at Harold's right shoulder as Godwin, Harold, Tostig and Gyrth joined the King and other great Lords for a meal on Easter Monday. Earl Siward, a hugely powerful man, with a scarred face and many arm rings, looked like the warrior Norse Lord he was. Earl's Odda and Leofric both carried their power as easily as they carried the weight around their middles. They looked like prosperous farmers dressed as princes though each arrived with a priest and had large gold crosses hanging on their chests. Leofric's son, Aelfgar, glowered round the room from under dark sullen brows. Earl Ralph was a tall, gaunt, refined looking man, dressed with dark elegance. His accented English, softly distinct from the Saxon and Danish voices in the room, displayed his French origins. There were also a number of other leading men present, King's Thegns and Stallers, who were part of the King's household. Archbishop Stigand was there too, his sticklike figure and eccentric winged eyebrows marking him out from the other churchmen. He'd been in his element lately, preaching in the Minsters as Wincestre's Bishop as well as being head of the English Church as Archbishop of Canterberie. Easter was, above all, the greatest festival of the Church's year.

There was a buzz as King Edward entered. This was my first view of the King which wasn't past the backs of crowds of worshippers. He looked in his late forties, well-built and fit through hunting, his greying hair, shoulder length, under a gold jewelled circlet. Unlike the other Lords, who sported shaven chins under long moustaches, the King grew a pointed beard which he stroked as he watched each of his great men through calculating, narrowed, eyes as they seated themselves.

I stood behind Harold, shifting occasionally from one foot to the other, quickly bored. Like the other young men who stood behind our Lords we had no real purpose here beyond appearances. All the drink was served by young women and the food brought in by the male cooks. They all used the space in the centre of the tables leaving us stood between the seating and the walls. My stomach was driven to grumbling loudly knowing that I wouldn't get to eat until much later in the day.

As I stood behind Harold's left shoulder, behind and between him and his father, I became aware that Godwin and the King appeared to be arguing with each other in fierce whispers. The King had a truly malevolent look on his face as he hissed at Godwin. My ears picked out the phrase, 'no grandson of yours will ever rule my realm.'

I couldn't see Godwin's face as he replied. 'You still hate me for Alfred's death don't you?'

'You know I do.'

'Yes, better it were the other way round, maybe if you'd have died blinded at Ely we'd have had a King who could give his wife a son.'

The King's face reddened.

Godwin continued, 'Yes, we spoke to Eadgyth about her expulsion from your court and why.'

'No doubt you and that battle-axe of a wife of yours browbeat her into some admission of her barrenness.'

'Not hers, yours.' Godwin was struggling to keep his voice down.

The King voice grew spiteful. 'Remember I still have Wulnoth's and Hakon's lives in my hands,' he hissed.

'While my other sons serve you well,' snarled Godwin.

'They do, Godwin. I like your sons, especially Tostig. They are all far more loyal and far less devious than the serpents that bore them.'

'At least I don't spill my seed on the bed-sheets,' spat back Godwin.

I missed the King's reply because at this point Harold became aware of the tension between his father and the King. He beckoned to me. As I leant over him he asked. 'What are your sharp ears picking up now?'

'Sire, they speak of the Queen and Alfred has been mentioned.'

'Oh Christ!' He pulled on his father's shoulder.

Godwin shrugged Harold's hand off and half standing over the King he was demanding, 'and where are my dead son's child and my youngest boy. Where are they?'

Harold was desperately trying to make Godwin sit down. By now other faces were turning toward us.

The King's face looked darkly malevolent as he replied. 'They are in safe hands, very safe hands.'

Godwin, sensing a hidden message, was taken aback. 'What are you saying? Are you saying they are in God's hands? That they are dead already?'

'They are in Normandy. They are in the hands of the Duke,' replied the King, clearly enjoying Godwin's dismay

Harold was now stood behind the pair of them whispering urgently that this was not the time.

Godwin wouldn't stop but lowering his voice he went on. 'That poisoner. Why there? Why Normandy?'

'Because that's where I told Robert to take them.'

Godwin sat back down looking pale still asking, 'Why?', when the King leant in for the killing thrust. 'Why Normandy? Why? Because I promised my crown to Duke William when I die.'

Harold looked shocked. 'You promised the crown to the Bastard?'

The King was grinning now, but pale, when suddenly Godwin made a strange strangulated noise from deep in his throat. Harold whispered quickly to the King, 'We'll talk of this later.'

Godwin was shuddering and his face turned a ghastly, blotchy purple. His hands clasped at his chest and he tried to rise. Then he collapsed between the chairs, his legs sliding under the trestle. The King stared at him with a cold gleam of triumph in his eyes. Tostig, Harold and Gyrth ran to support their father. The King recollected himself and his audience who had all jumped to their feet at the noise of Godwin's fall. 'Take him to my private rooms and send for my physician.'

'Take a leg, Sar,' ordered Harold.

I did as I was told while Gyrth lifted his father's other leg. Tostig, who looked shocked and frightened, helped Harold support Godwin's torso. Carefully we carried the now unconscious man into the King's chamber.

'Fetch the Lady Gytha!' Harold shouted at me.

'Gytha. Who is the Lady Gytha?' I stammered. My mind was racing as I heard that name again.

'My mother, you damned fool, my mother.'

I ran to the town house and banging hard upon the doors was

soon let in. 'Earl Godwin has been taken ill. I'm to fetch Lady Gytha.'

She appeared, almost instantly. Imperiously sweeping me along in her wake, we returned to the stricken Earl. Immediately she took charge of the sick room, ordering the King's physician and his servants around as if they were her own. Harold and his brothers were sharply told they should leave her to deal with their father and stop getting in the way.

Trying hard to hide a smirk at seeing these warrior Lords ordered around like small boys, I followed them out of the room and out of the King's palace. After collecting our arms we found ourselves back in the over-crowded streets. Someone barged into us pushing me against Tostig's back. He turned on me with a snarl. 'God boy, wherever I look there you are.' He pushed his fist into my face. 'Stay out of my way, you hear or I'll put your fucking eyes out.'

I was still recoiling when Harold, after giving me a sharp look through narrowed eyes, declared, 'I need some space to think before the world knows about our father. Let's get out of this stinking town.' He set off, striding through the crowds who parted before him like the waves before the bow of a ship. We followed him as he headed out through the town gates to the meadows where our horses had been set to graze.

Thurkill was there with a few housecarls, one of which was Gyric, who were battle training under a gentle spring sky. I felt like a burden had been lifted just from having space around me after the closeness of the King's palace, the seething streets and the days of close attendance on Harold. Seeing the Godwinsons more men started to gather, some Godwin's, some Tostig's and some retainers of other Lord's and thegns. The brothers and Thurkill ignored the gathering crowd and huddled together whispering. I stayed close to Harold as ordered while trying to keep away from Tostig.

I heard Thurkill in shocked surprise, 'He's promised the throne to William, to the Bastard of Normandy.'

'Hush,' said Harold, 'not so loud. I don't think many people know. Stigand would never have approved it. This was more of Robert's work.'

'I am fond of Edward, my sister's husband, but even he must know that an English King can only recommend his successor not appoint him,' said Tostig in an undertone.

'He does, but does William?' Harold raised his hand, 'Enough of this for now. The King does not look likely to die soon, but our father may be dying already. We must prepare ourselves.'

They drew closer together all visibly shaken by Godwin's sudden illness and the nature of his quarrel with the King. Now I could hear little but I did hear my name mentioned with the words, 'he heard what the King said' and 'he knows too much, that boy'. By now news of Godwin's seizure had spread from the town and the men gathered together talking quietly in sober groups across the meadows.

From behind me I heard men cursing and the jangling of harness. I turned to see a large group of fully armed men nudging their horses through the crowd. With them was a man, being dragged, bound, gagged and stumbling along on hobbled feet, by a rope tied around his neck. He fell to his knees as the leading horseman reigned in his steed. The bound man had long hair, in that hair were coloured stones, fewer now than when I'd last seen him, and there were no longer any balls of gold. There was no mistaking who he was. It was Candalo Harp.

I looked at him then followed the rope up to the man who was holding it. He sat there leaning calmly on one arm draped over the bow of his saddle. My eyes moved up to his. Gazing out at me from under each side of the nose-piece of his helmet were a pair of pale blue eyes, cold like ice, above the bared teeth of a smiling mouth.

'Earl Harold,' Oslaf's hated voice rang out. 'Earl Harold, I would speak with you.' He took off his helmet shaking out his blond, almost white, hair.

The crowd too seemed to shake itself until there was a large circle of assembled warriors and grooms with Oslaf and his horsemen on one side with Harold, his brothers and I opposite them.

'Oslaf, son of Eardwulf, what brings you here on this fateful day?' answered Harold. 'Whose man are you now?'

'I serve Aelfgar of Mercia, son of Leofric,' answered Oslaf as he dismounted. Then he kicked Candalo to his feet. 'Sire, you have a traitor by your side.'

'You'd better not be meaning my brothers or Thurkill here.'

'I mean Earl Harold, that red-haired Welsh boy,' he pointed squarely at me.

'You bring your feud to me again, at Easter, with my father sick in the King's chamber?' Harold was offended.

'Your father is ill? I knew not of that. I and my men will pray for him when we leave this field,' answered Oslaf. 'Do you recognise this man before me?'

Harold looked at Candalo and replied, 'There is something familiar about him. Perhaps you should remind me.'

'This is the Bard of the Cornwealas. This is the man who tried to lure you to your death.'

'We killed them all.' Harold went to turn away.

'Not this one. This one was helped to escape by one of your men. By someone who swore an oath to you in exchange for his life. This one was hidden by your loyal pet.' Oslaf stood quiet to let his words sink in.

I felt like a hare put up by the dogs as many eyes turned to me but unlike a hare I had no place to run. Tostig's hand whipped out and grabbed my tunic and putting his face in mine he hissed at me, 'You again. Harold, you need to deal with this boy.' He drew closer to Harold and whispered, 'This also solves our need for his silence. Kill him now.'

Oddly it was Gyrth who spoke for me, 'Harold, you are an Earl, you can't just murder a boy with no trial.' He lowered his voice, 'We are also surrounded by witnesses.'

'You can let me fight him to avenge my father and let God decide.' Oslaf had given everyone a way out. 'At least we can give the traitor a warrior's death.' At this there was a murmur of agreement from the surrounding men. He made it sound like he was doing me a favour.

Harold drew me to him, 'I find this hard to believe, Sar, that all those months ago you betrayed me. You gave shelter to my enemy. Is that true?'

Gyric cried out, 'Sire, he meant no harm.'

Harold didn't even look at him, 'Gyric, if you knew of this say no more for I would not dishonour your father by hanging you above the town gates.'

I shook my head at Gyric who shrank back. 'It was nothing to do with him. I hid the Bard and gave him food until he could escape,' I said.

Harold looked at me with sad eyes. I looked back tearful and ashamed and could not hold his gaze. I was tempted to go for my knife knowing I would be hacked down before it left the sheath. I felt death would be easier than facing Harold's reproach.

His voice was soft as he spoke to me as if we were the only people in the world, 'I saved you from Oslaf's revenge on that Welsh shore and you swore to be loyal to me in return.'

I nodded too choked to speak.

'I'm going to give you to Oslaf now. To fight him. Not for him to flay you alive. This is my last favour to you Sar Nomansson.'

Then he walked to the edge of the circle. I stood in the centre of the now widening circle of men as more of them sought a place in the front row. I had betrayed my oath to my lord and now my whole world was falling apart. There was something familiar about all this. I had been here before. I had faced Jokul on the beach at Porloc in a circle of jeering men. And I had beaten him.

Oslaf strode out into the circle, helmetless but carrying a shield passed to him by one of his men. He also wore a mailed byrnie and carried a sword. I stood opposite him in my light tunic carrying my little targe, my two throwing spears and my family's knife in my belt.

There were cries of disgust from some in the crowd. 'This is man against boy and he isn't even properly armed.'

Oslaf laughed and lifting his shield shouted, 'Would you take your boots off to tread on a rat?'

That gave me an idea so I sat on the ground and unlacing my boots took them off and threw them to one side. As I did so one of Harold's men stepped out and offered me his sword while another gestured at me with his shield. Knowing them from our campaign I stood and thanked them politely by name while refusing their offers.

I crossed myself and as I waited for the calm that came when my soul drew into the cold, black jet, heart of myself I felt Muirchu's spirit looking down on me. I would fight as he taught me to fight. I knew I couldn't beat Oslaf, there was no doubt in him as there had been in Jokul, but I would hurt him before he killed me. I had not been able to live as a warrior but I could die like one. As I accepted that I was going to die I felt strangely at peace. The shouts of the crowd seemed to disappear and my senses heightened. It was as if I could see every blade of grass, feel the gentle breeze on my skin and every breath ease in and out of my body.

Oslaf's voice broke my reverie, 'Look at you, boy, barefoot as we found you among the goats.'

I returned his baleful glare, 'Yes, where your father showed his bravery by murdering unarmed peasants. His name will go down in legend.' I paused, watching Oslaf's eyes narrow, 'I heard he was killed by a goatherd with a cooking knife.'

There was some laughter from the crowd. There were men there who knew how I had sent Eardwulf to meet his maker.

Oslaf flushed then turned and addressed the crowd. 'That traitorous Welsh rat,' he pointed at me, 'is like all of his people. He will smile at your face then stab you from behind.'

Many in the crowd agreed with this. The Welsh had hit hard and often in recent years. To see me slaughtered would make up for some humiliating defeats.

'Look at him, barefoot, with a targe, spear and knife. Does he look English to you?'

Oslaf, with his white blond hair, his great shield and mailed byrnie looked every inch a true Saxon warrior. I didn't. There were cries from the crowd, 'Get on with it, Oslaf. Kill the traitorous savage.'

He raised his sword high, 'And I will avenge my father!'

He turned to face me as the crowd roared its approval. The time for talk was over. As Oslaf stalked towards me I untied the rope from my targe and threw it after my boots. Passing my left arm through the targe's leather strap I held one spear with my left hand and hefted the other with my right. Oslaf stopped and banging his sword hilt on the back of his shield dared me to attack. I'd seen Oslaf fight and knew how fast he was with a sword. I had to hurt him without getting close.

I ran straight at him fast, my bare toes getting a good grip on the short, heavily grazed, turf of the meadow. The crowd roared. At the last moment just out of the reach of his sword I veered to his right. Twisting to face him I jumped and threw my spear at his exposed right side.

He was not fooled. He turned just as fast and deflected the spear with his shield as easily as swatting away a fly. It flew weakly into the crowd. As I swivelled to face Oslaf again he took his stance and dared me to attack.

I moved my second spear into my right hand and shifted my left to grip the metal bar inside the targe's boss. I could not throw this spear. Its reach was my only advantage.

'You want me, you come to me,' I shouted. He walked towards me, sword point up, his shield covering his mouth, his cold eyes glaring at me above the rim. I saw them flicker. Then he rushed me. His sword flashed. I was quick and easily moved aside only for him to rush me again. This time his downward blow switched sideways in mid stroke. I only just escaped the end of his blade. I ran backwards from him suddenly sick with fear.

He walked towards me, goading me with his words, 'Why run, boy? I'm going to kill you, why drag it out?'

I turned and ran again. As I ran around the edge of the circle he walked across it. The crowd got restless. I could hear shouts, somehow distant and far away. 'Fight him, boy, at least try,' and worse, 'Don't die a coward'.

I stopped running, my head throbbed and my heart pounded in my chest. I sucked in huge breaths and tried to calm myself. There was no time, Oslaf was striding towards me. He raised his sword and I feebly lifted my targe but too late. He deftly leant over it and lightly slashed my left shoulder.

Somehow the pain and blood brought me to my senses. He was playing with me. He could easily have killed me in that moment. He grinned as anger surged through me and with it power. I jumped back and feinted at him with my spear. I had more reach than his sword but only a hand-spans sized leaf of shining metal on a thin wooden shaft against an arms-length of tempered, sharpened iron.

He leant back, avoiding the feint, and cut at the shaft with his sword. I whipped it out of harm's way and swirled it round. As his eyes followed the point I punched at his shield with my targe. Instinctively he pushed back. I pulled back my left arm and for a swift moment he was off-balance and I caught his head with the spear's ferrule.

There was no real force in the blow but it shocked him. I was pleased to see some long white hairs caught round the end of the shaft. He came at me again and I jabbed at his face but each time he ducked or raised his shield and kept coming. I kept stepping backwards and jabbing until the point of my spear stuck in his shield. I tugged hard and he struck. My left arm shot out and pushed the sword away with my small shield. Some of its rim, hacked away, spun off. I ducked under his arm and punched the boss into the side of his face and pulled hard on the spear-shaft. Leaping backwards in triumph I regained my spear. Then a searing sickening pain slashed across my left side as Oslaf saw his moment to strike.

I staggered back pressing my arm into my side. Bile filled my mouth and I spat its bitterness into the torn grass. He got in close and smashed his shield into me. The taste of bile was quickly followed by the iron tang of fresh blood as the blow forced my teeth through the side of my tongue.

I fell backwards on the grass scrabbling for my spear. I felt the shaft and gripping it hard thrust blindly up at the shape above me. I'd no idea where the blow landed but I heard a surprised grunt and Oslaf pulled back. Dizzily I got back to my feet to see Oslaf panting hard with blood staining his right thigh.

He rushed at me again and remembering Muirchu's words I just kept moving, avoiding Oslaf's slashes and thrusts. He paused again, panting hard. I felt blood steadily oozing from the cut in my side and the tear in my tunic was catching painfully at the edges of the wound.

'You can't dodge me forever, boy. I will kill you.'

He was right. I shouted my defiance, 'I can make you work for it though. I hope that wound in your leg poisons and you die slowly from gangrene, babbling for your mother.'

'Empty words, you little shit, that was just a lucky scratch.'

I didn't answer, struggling to get my breath. The crowd was roaring but it seemed no more significant than waves on a distant shore. I watched him warily. His face was swelling where my targe-boss had caught him and he limped slightly. He came at me again, shield firmly in front of him. He raised his sword straight armed above his head, aiming for a killing down-stroke. I twisted away from the expected blow and stabbed my spear frantically towards him but instead of hacking down he forced his shield onto my spear. This time the head stuck firmly. Now he slashed down on the shaft cutting it in two like a useless twig. I felt the wind of its passing as I snatched my hand away from the lethal blade.

I jumped back to put some space between us. I flung the now useless stick I held in my hand at Oslaf who laughed again as he flicked it away with his sword. He stopped to savour the moment as I drew my knife and adopted, as best I could, a fighting stance. The end of my spear, stuck in his shield, was too light to unbalance him but still he threw his shield to the ground. Nimbler now he danced towards me, balanced, his sword outstretched.

I watched his eyes knowing I was moments away from meeting my end. The whole world was made of Oslaf's cold eyes and his flickering blood-stained blade.

I talked frantically in a last futile attempt to unsettle him, 'Know this Oslaf, I am no man's son. I am a Demon's spawn. My shade will haunt you.'

'Maybe you are, the luck you've had,' he answered, completely unconcerned, 'but now the thread of your life is cut. The only thing you need to know that once I have killed you, your family will follow.'

'What family? I have no family.' My mind went back to the children in Caer Dydd. He could not know of them, I knew he could not.

Suddenly he raised his sword high and ran at me shouting, 'My mother knows your family!'

'Katla! Oh, by Christ. Ealhild and the children!'

As his sword came down I threw my left arm up to meet it and my targe took the blow straight on. It stopped his stroke but I felt my forearm crack and I fell, stunned, backwards onto the ground.

With my senses reeling I knew I was gone on my way into the next world. I could hear harp music and saw Morwid gliding above the grass framed by the pale blue of an early summer sky. There were great shouts and a distant drumming of many hooves. I waited for the death blow but mercifully I never felt it as the world disappeared and all went black.

CHAPTER 13

I was not burning. I was not in Hell. Weird sounds echoed in my ears. Maybe this was purgatory but my tongue felt so sore. I became aware of more pain in my left side where my clothes were stuck to me. This certainly wasn't heaven and my left arm was throbbing agony. Suddenly I was drenched in cold water.

'Help me! I'm dead and drowning!' I shouted as my eyes flew open and I found myself staring into the open mouth of a leather bucket.

The bucket was replaced by Harold's face staring down at me. He crouched down and slapped me hard on each cheek. 'What do you know of Beorn's death? What do you know of my cousin's end?'

'Beorn? What do you mean?'

Then Candalo's face was pushed into mine. 'This man says you know who killed Beorn,' continued Harold.

My mouth filled with blood as I tried to speak and I pushed myself up with my right arm and spat it out on the grass. The cut in my side opened painfully and the bleeding quickened. My shoulder felt sore. All the left side of me was in agony. I couldn't think.

'Oslaf killed Beorn.'

'How do you know that?' Harold leant over and grabbed my face, 'How?'

'He told me.' I mumbled the words out then I fainted.

I came round to find myself in a room in Godwin's town house. Someone was cutting my tunic away with a pair of shears while someone else was splinting my arm.

'This wound is still bleeding heavily,' said a voice I did not know. Rough hands pushed something against my side.

A cup was put to my lips and I drank, wine, warming wine, as it coursed through me some spirit returned.

'Can you talk Sar, can you talk?' It was Harold again and with him, Candalo still trailing a rope from his neck.

Candalo spoke, gently, 'Tell him what you told me in the dunes Sar. It is time to tell your Lord what you know.'

'I saw your daughter, Candalo, I saw Morwid.'

'I know that boy. She saved you but no questions now. Tell the Earl what you know.'

'It was at Porloc.'

'What was?' demanded Harold.

'I was in the sea.'

'The sea? What about the sea?'

'Sir,' said Candalo, 'with respect, I think you would get your story sooner if you let the boy tell his tale in his own way.'

Harold looked at him sharply then drew up a stool and sat down. I looked to my left to see that it was two monks who were tending to my wounds. I felt weak, sad and scared. 'Aethelric, is that Aethelric?'

'No, Sar,' said Harold more gently, 'Aethelric is not here. Tell your story.'

'I was in the sea. I was being a saint, no a penance that's right, there were cattle. I'd had a fight.'

I tried to sit, panicked, 'Jokul, I didn't kill him, I didn't.'

One of the monks pushed me gently back down. 'He may be a little delirious, my Lord.'

'No, I have some knowledge of what he says,' said Harold. 'Jokul lived Sar. Now go on. You were in the sea.'

'I was cold, it was dark, a ghost came but it wasn't a ghost. I was so cold. A white shape hissed and talked. He sharpened the knife on a stone. It made a noise, tssk, tssk.'

A thought came to me. 'My knife, where is my knife. My mother's seax, she'll kill me if I've lost it,' I pleaded desperately, like a small child.

Harold showed me the hilt, 'Your knife is here Sar, see?'

'My mother isn't though. I see her sometimes. I see her, her face all smashed in and bloody.' I started to sob. 'It's all gone, sir, everything's gone. I didn't mean to betray you. I've never told anyone anything I've heard.'

'Give the boy some more wine.' As I drank he said, 'Sar, you need to tell me what you heard on that beach. Now what was the white shape?'

'It was Oslaf, his cloak. Yes, he was threatening me. He was going to kill me when the tide went out.'

'Go on.'

'He told me he would kill me like he'd killed Beorn. He said you'd picked me up like a stray puppy because you didn't like his father.'

'There's truth in that. He said he killed Beorn?'

'He did, he said that he was no match for Eardwulf and Sweyn. I didn't know who Beorn was. I thought I should say nothing because Sweyn was your brother.'

Harold was getting angry, 'How did Oslaf kill my cousin? He wasn't that much older than you are now.'

'They held him while Oslaf stabbed him.'

'Be clear, who held him?'

'Sweyn and Eardwulf held him against the side of the boat and Oslaf killed him.'

Harold was breathing heavily, 'And you didn't tell me because you knew Sweyn was my brother?'

'Yes, Gyric said...'

'Gyric! Gyric knew of this?'

'He was there.'

Harold leaped up and shouted at someone outside the room, 'Get Gyric! Get him here. Now!'

Harold took to striding angrily around the room. I slumped

back, worn out and trembling, while a monk wiped my tear stained face. Candalo stood miserably in the middle of the room, his hands still tied behind him.

There was a knock on the door. 'In,' shouted Harold.

Gyric entered looking flushed and sweaty. He glanced nervously, fearfully even, towards me. I smiled at him weakly. 'I'm sorry, Gyric, it's all come out.'

I could see he didn't know what I meant and he was not at all reassured.

He stood straight and looked directly at Harold as one of his housecarls should. 'Sir, you called for me?'

'Gyric. What do you know of Beorn's death?'

'I've heard rumours Sire, that your brother was involved but I dared ask no more because of my father's warning.'

'Do you know who Beorn was?'

'No sir.'

'And what did Scalpi tell you about my brother?'

Gyric blushed and stammered, 'He, er, he said,' Gyric coughed, 'He said that Sweyn was bad, bad to the bone, and that it was better never to even speak of him, sir. What happened in the past was best left in the past, sir. Sorry, your brother, I mean, I never have sir.'

'Never have what? Gyric.'

'Never have spoken of him, sir.'

'Because of your father?'

'Yes, my father taught me to never question the doings of great men and to never listen to gossip. My duties are to serve my Lord before all else, to fight his enemies and to support my kinfolk.'

'You didn't know that Beorn was my cousin?'

'No.'

'And you knew nothing about what went on at Dartmouth?'

'Dartmouth? I know my father went there with you a few years ago but I don't know why.'

Harold looked thoughtful for a moment then left the room. Next thing I'm being put on a table and being carried up through the town by four puzzled housecarls. Each jolting step sent shards of pain through my arm. Gyric and Candalo were in front of us while Harold was striding on ahead yelling at people to clear the way.

We arrived at the Old Minster and Harold proceeded to push our way through the crowds of penitents and pilgrims up to the head of the church where a choir of monks were singing. Ignoring them he turned to a group of richly adorned tombs. He pointed at one of them.

'Do you know whose tomb that is, Sar?'

'No, sir,' I said from my table. The wound in my side was bleeding again from being lifted from the pallet but I decided to keep that to myself.

'You, Gyric?'

'Yes, sir. That is the tomb of King Cnut.'

'Right Gyric, and this tomb is the tomb of his nephew.' Harold pointed at an adjacent tomb. 'His nephew. My cousin. Beorn.'

Harold went on, his anger rising along with his voice, 'And this space here, is where my father's tomb will be if he dies. Which he may well do at any moment!'

None of us knew how to respond. Harold continued to shout, 'You will all three swear on Beorn's tomb that all that you have said to me is true.' He turned and shouted at the monks, 'I want a priest, get me a priest now!'

I had never seen Harold like this. Even when he was angry he kept his temper and showed little of what he felt. A priest appeared as if he'd been conjured from the air.

Harold shouted at him and he visibly quailed, 'I need you to witness the oaths these three make.'

Each of us in turn placed our hands, or in my case, hand, on Beorn's tomb and swore that all we had said was the truth or may the vengeance Beorn's ghost's haunt us for eternity.

The priest protested feebly that this was not Christian. Harold told him to shut up, to record our names and our oaths, then to empty the Minster of all except those who were praying for his father.

Harold then turned and kneeling at Beorn's tomb prayed for his forgiveness. Then leaning his head against the cold stone he wept. We all stayed silent, embarrassed, while behind us the great Minster quieted as some left and others knelt.

Harold stood up. 'Gyric, Sar and you, bard or whatever you are, I believe you. Oslaf will pay for this crime.' He then told the housecarls to take us back to the townhouse and to keep us there.

He gave us all one last hard look, 'I need to tend to my father now. Speak of this to no-one.'

Once back in the room the monks reappeared and dressed my wounds again, smearing them with honey. They did not speak and they quickly left taking the wine with them. After talking between themselves the housecarls decided to guard us from outside the room. I think they didn't want us to hear them as much as we didn't want them to hear us.

'So what happened, Gyric, why am I still alive?'

'Oh, Sar, you should have seen her.'

'Seen who?'

'Seen my daughter,' said Candalo, tears running down his face.

'I did see her, in a dream as I thought I was dying.'

'That was no dream, Sar, she was there,' said Gyric, 'as your fight was nearing its end she must have pushed through the crowd playing her harp. We could hear music then her beautiful voice singing out clear and loud above the shouting crowd. Everyone was spellbound.'

'How do you mean, spellbound?'

'Well first, of course, it was her voice, but once in the circle we could all see how striking she was. She wore a long, blue gown, the colour of the sky, and her hair, uncovered, fell in black lustrous curls all down her back. She seemed to glide across the grass and to care nothing for all the fierce men baying for your death.'

'Oh, and that stopped Oslaf?'

'Well she was also singing in a language nobody could understand so I think many feared that she really was enchanting us. I mean what normal woman would step into the middle of a ring of armed men watching a fight to the death?'

'But Oslaf?'

'It was Harold that stopped Oslaf. Oslaf had turned to see what was distracting everyone from witnessing the moment of his triumph. Then Harold told Thurkill to make Oslaf wait. To be honest most of us thought it was already too late. You looked like you'd already died.'

'I thought I had too. I just couldn't work out where I'd gone.'

'Anyway, Thurkill strode towards Oslaf calling on him to hold, his axe upraised and ready to strike. He then stood over you while Morwid spoke to Harold. Next thing suddenly men are rushing over to Candalo here, dragging him over to Harold and untying his gag.'

'What!'

'Yes, then Oslaf was shouting and cursing at his men for letting Candalo go.'

'And then?'

'Then he takes one step towards you, shouting that he needs to finish you off, realises he can't then runs to his horse and jumps on.'

'Seems like I missed all the excitement.'

Gyric laughed at me, 'I think you'd already had your moment of drama, don't you?'

'So what happened then?'

'Next moment our housecarls are drawing swords and running after Oslaf's men who are all spurring their horses and galloping off as quick as they can.'

'They got away.'

'Three or four didn't, either their horses stumbled or quick-thinking men had grabbed at harness as they passed and slowed them down. The men that fell were hacked to pieces before they could ask for mercy.'

'And the rest?'

'There were no saddled horses here and by the time they were chased they were long gone. Their horses were found wandering free along the banks of the River Itchen.'

'They escaped in ships.'

I turned my face to the wall. I should have felt grateful to be alive but all I could think of was that so was my enemy. Still alive and out there somewhere still intent on killing me. I stared at the stones for a while then fell into a deep sleep so exhausted that even the pain of my wounds could not disturb me.

Blood! Blood spouting from Eardwulf's neck. Blood! Dribbling from my chin as the blade split my face. Blood! Spurting from the mouth of a panicked man at Porloc. Blood! On Wihtgar's belly as the knife goes in and comes out with his screams. Blood! Warm and sticky on my hands as I sawed at the dead guard's neck at Conor's Dun. Blood! Oozing from a young soldier's belly as he died in an empty street. Blood. So much blood. Dark blood; gushing onto the evening road. Blood! Belching out of Hutha's mouth onto my upturned face. Oh God, blood, everywhere blood.

I shuddered awake. As I heard my screams fade in my ears I saw my mother standing at the foot of my bed. Her face was as broken and shattered as when I had last seen it. She pointed at me and from her ruined mouth cried, 'All is not well, Sar, all is not well.'

'You can't be here, mother, you died last year, remember? Leave me, I cannot see you like this,' I wept then pleaded, 'I avenged you, why do you haunt me?'

'All is not well. Sister and children. All is not well.'

'I know I abandoned them. I'm sorry mother I did not mean to. Oh, God, mother, I left Moira in the slave pens.' I was sobbing, now, consumed by my shame.

'Not your sister, Sar, not your sister, mine!'

Then I felt arms around me and mulled, bitter tasting wine

was poured into my mouth. I swallowed thirstily and then drifted back into the comfort of sleep.

When next I woke I was alone and the world was silent. I tried to sit but the pain in my side pulled me flat to the bed. I gave up though hunger and worse, thirst, plagued me. I lay there while a sunbeam worked its way slowly across the room. As the sun lowered the beam rose and then, in the late afternoon the house seemed to come alive with the slamming of doors and footsteps rushing to and fro.

The door opened and Candalo came in, 'You're awake, boy.'

'Where is everyone? I'm dying of thirst. Your hands are untied.'

'First things first,' he said, pouring water from a jug behind me. He pushed a cushion behind my head and I was able to hold the cup and bring it to my lips.

'Slowly, boy, slowly, don't gulp. You've only drunk what we've been able to dribble into you.'

I looked at him questioningly. 'It's Thursday now, you've been unconscious for three days,' he explained.

'Why has everything been so quiet?'

'Godwin died in the night, the town is in mourning. He was much loved in Wincestre, it would seem.'

'I've been out of my mind?'

'As if in a deep sleep. Though one ridden by the night hag I would guess.'

I remembered visions of blood and shuddered, 'That is true, my mother....' I snatched at some shifting sense of her words but they escaped me. I came back to the present. 'How is it that you are free, and Morwid? Was she a dream also?'

'It seems that my daughter has persuaded Harold that a Bard such as myself would grace his court.'

I looked at his twisted fingers as they struggled to grip my cup, 'You cannot play the harp.'

'I know the songs and many tales, I can play Irish poet, British singer or Danish skald and my daughter plays the harp. Between the two of us we make one great Bard.'

'And Harold agreed to this?'

'He did.'

I grimaced ruefully, 'I suppose she warms his bed to bend him to her will.'

Candalo angrily replied, 'I think not boy, she will bed no man. She has no love of men.'

'She saved me from Oslaf's revenge. She must care for me.'

'Don't fool yourself, boy, she saved me, her father and furthered our revenge.'

I didn't want to believe him. I'd whiled away many hours with Morwid in my fantasies. A thought struck me, 'You were with Oslaf. How?'

'Bad luck, an ill-chosen tavern, a chance meeting, maybe God was sporting with me. We'd been travelling, earning shelter and food by using our arts. I'd discovered who Beorn was and his end on the elder Godwinson's ship. Now I had found some weapons with which to avenge my broken hands.'

'And?'

'And we were making our way to Wincestre knowing the King and many of his Lords would be here for Easter. Here, too, where Beorn is buried.' He paused, looking down at his distorted fingers, 'Strange how things work out. I was recognised by one of Oslaf's men in Hamptun and seized. Some painful days later I was produced to prove your guilt whereas I was hoping to find you to prove his.'

I fell back to the pillow, 'As in the end I did.'

'You did, Sar,' he smiled at me with his candid blue eyes, 'We almost had him, boy. If we catch him we can kill him. He's been declared nithing.'

'He's outlawed!'

'He is.'

It was like my whole body eased in one great sigh. I felt safe from Oslaf, but was I safe from Harold?

'Harold, what does he say of me?'

'Nothing, Sar, not in my hearing.'

My worries returned as I remembered the events before

Easter. I shifted restlessly. Candalo placed my knife on my chest.

'The same seax I saw all thick with grime when we sat in the dunes,' he said.

I let him change the subject, 'Yes, you were right, it is old and wonderful. I would never have guessed the grime covered bright metal and glass.'

'Not just any bright metal, that is gold, and the glass is not glass, it is cut garnets. This has been the weapon of a truly wealthy man. Even though it is not the fashion today you could buy a small farm with this.'

'By all the Saints, Candalo, how can that be?' I gasped smiling inside. I was a wealthy man and I'd never known it.

I held it up before me, 'They said my father came out of a Kings burial mound with a crew of ghostly bussecarls carrying this very blade.'

'Do you believe you are the child of a ghost?'

'Some say demon.'

'Do you?'

'No, if I was I wouldn't get knocked about so much, but I think I may be cursed. People close to me do not fare well.'

'Well,' he said, laughing, 'I seem to be doing alright against all the odds.'

I laughed too but it rang hollow. In my mind shadows clamoured to be heard, their whisperings loud and insistent.

'Candalo, I know what it is that troubles my soul. My mother came to me.'

'Are you feverish again, boy?'

'No, no, she spoke to "not your sister, mine" she said! Ealhild and the children they are in danger!'

'I don't know what you are talking about.'

'My family, my English family, Oslaf's mother knows who they are. He told me so before he hacked me down!'

I found myself sitting up, the stiches in my side pulled painfully but they did not tear. I broke into a sweat. 'I can't explain it all now. Find Gyric for me, please, hurry.'

He asked no more questions but pushed me gently back onto the pillows and left. Before long one of the monks returned and tried to spoon broth into me. I got him to prop me up and found that I was able to hold a bowl in the crook of my left arm, though the shoulder was stiff and painful. I could feed myself. The patch of sunlight dissolved into darkness and I drifted back into sleep.

◆ ◆ ◆

I awoke to find my small room crowded with people. Morwid was stood beside my bed. I pulled the covers up embarrassed to be unclothed before her.

She laughed, a harsh short laugh, 'You've no need to hide from me, Sar. Remember how you saw me last.' She spoke in her own tongue, so close to the language of my home.

'I've not forgotten you Morwid. I've held you in my heart ever since.'

'I came to tell you we are even. I owe you nothing now. We need never speak again.'

'But I want us to, I want to know you.'

'Sar, you stood in line, you may not have raped me but you stood in line.'

'I took you to your father.'

'You stood in the line and you knelt to rape me.' Her voice was fierce and trembling, 'If that man had not stopped you, you would have.'

'Toki, stopped me. That man is in danger.'

'The only man I care for is my father,' she replied and turning abruptly left the room taking her father with her.

Gyric came forward, 'What about Toki? What were you saying?'

'I think Toki's in danger, and Lady Ealhild.' I explained to Gyric what Oslaf had said and how my mother had come to me in my darkness. 'We must get help.'

Gyric answered, 'Help from where? If it's true it's probably too late and our Earl is burying his father tomorrow. What makes you think he'll believe you anyway?'

I sank back, weak and defeated at the truth of Gyric's words while the monks fussed at my wounds and gave me food and drink. 'Gyric, has Harold forgiven me?'

'I don't know Sar. He's been a different man since Godwin collapsed. Then the news about Beorn hit him hard. I don't know if he's forgiven me, let alone you. I half expected that he would send me home disgraced but nothing happened.'

'He's let Candalo live.'

'Candalo was loyal to his Lord, Harold respects that and, don't forget, God has let him escape death twice.'

'With a little help from me.'

'Say no more about that Sar. I must go, I'm due on watch.'

'Gyric! I need to get to Sudfolc.'

For the rest of the day only the monks came in and out. They never spoke merely putting a finger to their mouths in answer to my questions. I ate and drank wolfishly and asked for more. When they were out of the room I sat up and by the evening had managed to stand wobbling by my bed. Only then did I see that my broken spear and damaged targe were propped in the corner of the room. For a moment I felt angry at the absence of my second spear then it dawned on me that to have any of my weapons surely must mean that I was no longer seen as a traitor

The next day no one came. Some footsteps passed my door then all went quiet. The town too was almost silent and through the quiet air I could hear a mingling of singing choirs from the two minsters. The services went on all day and into the evening. Every now and again the house would be filled with a flurry of activity and shouted orders then again fall quiet. All throughout the day I had tried standing and shuffling a few steps, stooping with the pain in my side and with my shoulder held stiffly at an angle. Driven by hunger and thirst I managed to hobble through the unguarded door using the broken spear shaft as a crutch. In the kitchen I found a single cook's help who gave me scraps of meat and stale bread.

'There's no fresh today, everyone has fasted in Godwin's honour until the funeral feasts tonight.'

I sat on a bench, slurping and gobbling gratefully, 'So how come you're not all here cooking.'

'They're all helping out at the Bishop's palace.'

'Not you though?'

'Nah, I'm meant to be feeding some bloody kid that got hurt in a fight.'

'Oh,' I said, 'that would be me, then. So when were you going to do that?'

He sat down across from me and poured some ale from a jug and pushed it over to me, 'I've done it now.'

I smiled at him as I held the bowl to my lips, 'You fucking cunt.'

He tipped the jug over his forearm, looked at me sideways, and then he took a long swallow. After putting the jug back on the table, he belched and said, 'Fucking cunt yourself.'

A couple of drunken hours later and after many toasts to the departed Godwin he helped me piss in a bucket then put me back to bed.

CHAPTER 14

'**C**ome on Sar, wake up, Harold would see you before the day's business starts.'

'Gyric, what?'

'It was my watch again this morning and I spoke to Harold at first light.'

'About what?'

'About Ealhild and Toki of course. I told him what Oslaf had said in the fight and about your dream. He crossed himself when I told him what your mother had said and demanded to see you.'

I pushed my slight hangover aside and with Gyric's strong arm to help I hobbled my way to meet Harold. Gyric led me to the room where I had overheard the family arguing. Lowering me onto a settle he bowed to Harold and left. Harold was seated in front of me with Thurkill stood at his right hand. To his left sat his mother, the Lady Gytha, dressed in dark clothes with a psalter on her lap.

Harold spoke first, 'Gyric tells me that the dead speak to you?'

'My mother came to me and told me that all was not well with her sister.'

'Your aunt, who my housecarl, Toki, chose to marry?'

'Yes, and Oslaf said something during the fight.'

Harold ignored that, 'So how did she speak to you?'

I described how I'd woken and seen her at the foot of my bed and that she spoke somehow from her ruined and bleeding face.'

'So it was not a dream?'

'I thought I was awake, maybe a dream in a dream, Sire.'

'Hmmm, do you have these 'dreams' often?'

'I've had many terrible dreams though they stopped when I found my family until the day I fought Oslaf.'

Lady Gytha spoke, 'Have you ever dreamt of my sons? Did you dream of my husband?'

'No, Lady, no never.'

'They say your father was a Demon.'

'Some do.'

'He came from the ground with a crew of ghosts?'

'I don't think it's true, Lady.'

'Why not?'

'Because I lose fights and I bleed, I am no demon.'

Gytha made a strange sign with her fingers that I didn't understand then Thurkill made the same gesture.

Harold signed the cross, 'Please, there's no need for Thor in these Christian days. Sar, you believe your aunt has come to harm?'

'I do, it is almost a week since my mother came to me.'

Gytha interrupted, 'You think you know it all Harold. My grandmother knew the old ways and her grandmother rode in Frejya's wagon and could see the past, the present and the things to come.'

'Mother, I don't see...'

'Of course you don't see. In the old days they talked of barrow-wights, men who came from the ground and walked between the dead and the living. This boy may be the son of one of those.'

'Nonsense, he's just the son of a grave robber.'

'Whatever he is, he survives and has visions.' Gytha turned to me, 'So if you were to visit your kinfolk you believe that you'd find that Oslaf's family has taken vengeance on them for Eardwulf's death?'

As she spoke my heart sank. I knew it to be true, 'Yes Lady, I am certain of it.'

She leant back in her chair, tapping her fingers on its ornately carved arm, 'Have you spoken of the things you heard in this house and at the King's feast?'

'No Lady, not a word.'

'The boy has shown he can keep his mouth shut, he's said nothing about Beorn,' said Thurkill, his voice quiet compared with Gytha's forceful tones.

'He told the Bard,' retorted Gytha.

I could not make her out. She frightened me. At one moment I thought she supported me, at another I feared she would order me killed.

As if she had read my mind she turned to me and said, 'If we wanted to, boy, we could kill you now and make it seem as if you had never been.'

I shifted uncomfortably trying to meet her gaze but not to stare.

Harold broke the silence, 'He did tell the Bard but God has used him to reveal our cousin's true killer.'

'So, you can avenge him Harold?' Gytha barked a laugh, 'Hah, you seem confused about your Christian beliefs. And you are right to be, the call of blood was old long before Christ was nailed to the Cross.'

She leant forward in her chair and turned to me again, 'Is that not true boy?'

'Yes, Lady, beyond doubt.'

'Hah, you seek to save your skin. You'd say anything now to gain some time.'

I took a deep breath and gambled, 'You are right my Lady, I would.'

She leant back laughing. Then, after taking a moment to re-arrange her gleaming furs, said, 'You have a sister, do you not?'

My mind raced furiously at this change of direction. What could she know of Moira? Then I remembered my last day at Caer Dydd and Eardwulf's words.

'You! You are the Gytha that likes young women. Where is my sister? What do you know of her?' I demanded, shouting, completely forgetting my place.

Thurkill took a step forward but Gytha checked him with a gesture, 'So boy, not so cool now. It seems you are loyal.'

'Yes I am, Lady. I'm sorry, please forgive me.'

'That's better. Yes, I am that Gytha. I trade in girls and young women of great beauty and distinctive looks to sell to Lords and Kings for fine prices.'

She turned to Harold, 'Why is it, son that you men go stupid for a woman who looks different from those you know? Does red hair or a white skin change a woman's cleverness, her ability to bear sons or how soft or tight her cunt is?'

Harold blushed, 'Do you need to be so coarse Mother?'

'Well, you son, are more foolish than most where women are concerned.'

'We are here about this man, Mother,' said Harold waving at me.

'I have a girl with red hair, dark red like yours who also dreams, or so she says. Could she be your sister?'

'She could.'

'Is her life worth your silence?'

'You have my silence already, Lady, as Harold is my Lord.'

'A clever answer. Harold your pet has wit.' She turned again to me, 'Tell me the colour of her eyes.'

I couldn't help myself. I turned to the Earl, 'My Lord Harold, do you have Moira, do you have her? Are you using my sister?'

'Quiet, Sar, be quiet, remember your place, your life hangs on a thread,' ordered Thurkill. Obedience to my commander was so instilled in me by now that I reacted instantly.

'Yes, sir!' I stood at attention, pleading with Harold through my eyes.

'I have no idea where your sister is. This is all news to me. I told you when I saved you that you should forget your family. It seems now that your relatives spring up everywhere. Answer my mother.'

'Lady, her eyes are not like mine. They are the colour of amber, dark amber flecked with gold in the sunlight,' I replied my voice choking a little with loving memories.

Gytha looked at me levelly, 'You love your sister I can see. Good, I can tell you she is safe but not beyond my reach.'

'Can I see her?'

In answer Gytha called me to her. 'You see this fur,' she held out a rich gleaming fur, 'this fur is from a wolverine. Wolverines live in the far north in a land of dark forests and deep snows. That is where your sister is heading.'

'You have sold her to some man's bed?'

'Yes, and your saving of her virginity made me a tidy sum.'

I flushed angrily and kept my tongue.

'Do you think her life so different from any woman's? So different from mine?'

'What do I know of a woman's life?'

'What you need to know is that her life depends on your loyalty. I am of royal blood and my word carries weight. One short message from me and, however treasured she is, she dies.'

Harold spoke, more gently now, 'Sar, she lives, you know she lives and not in drudgery on a peasant's farm or on her back in some soldier's brothel.'

He was right, at least I knew she was alive.

'Enough of this,' she nodded at Thurkill who opening the door beckoned someone in.

The man that walked in was of middling height, broad and muscled, his arms scarred beneath many arm rings. His brown deep-set eyes, each side of a flattened nose, looked fiercely out from under bushy untrimmed eyebrows. His chin was roughly shaven under a large warrior's moustache. His hands seemed to wander looking for the sword belt in which to push his thumbs. He ignored Harold and Thurkill and did not bow to Gytha.

'Lady, Earl Siward said you have business with me.'

'This Sar, is Grim, a fitting name don't you think,' said Gytha, amused by her own wit, 'Grim Haldorson fresh from fighting the Scots under Siward. He is, or was, Toki's brother. You are to ride with him and his companion to Belestede and find the truth of your dream. You will go from there to Waltham where further orders will await you.'

I looked at Harold who nodded, 'Go to the armourer, mend or replace your weapons. You leave tomorrow.'

Once outside the door I looked at Grim, 'I didn't know Toki had a brother.'

He looked back at me, 'I didn't know Toki had a wife.'

We made our way to what had been Godwin's armoury where I was given two replacement throwing spears. The armourer took most of the afternoon to repair my targe though he could do nothing for the gouge Oslaf's sword had taken out of the swirling patterns on its bronze boss.

'You were lucky to survive that blow. If you'd not have taken it on your shield he would have cut right through your arm and into your skull,' said Grim.

'Were you there?' I said, gratefully sitting down and tugging my tunic away from my stitched wound. My left arm ached like hell and itched dreadfully under the tightly bound splints.

'At the fight, yes I was. Earl Siward's horse lines were close by. Tell me, why no mail, not even a helmet?'

'They're too heavy. An Irishman told me I was not stocky enough to stand toe to toe wearing mail and carrying a heavy shield. It was he who gave me that targe,' I nodded towards the armourer. 'I knew that the only way I could beat Oslaf was to be faster than him. Stab in, jump back, quick.'

'You thought you could beat him?' Grim looked at me disbelievingly.

'Well, no.' l looked straight at him, 'but I did kill his father.'

'What we saw was a blood-feud?'

'Yes,' I tried to change the subject, 'and your scars. Where did you get them?'

'Fighting the Scots in the north.'

'A land of snow where there are wolverines?'

'No, you can walk to Scotland if you have the time. Wolverine furs come from overseas. Why?'

My heart sank Moira was further from reach than ever. 'Doesn't matter.'

Grim grunted, 'Hmmm keep your secrets. Gytha told Siward that you had some dream concerning Toki's wife and now I'm to go with you to Sudfolc.'

'It wasn't just a dream,' I said and told him what Oslaf had called out before he hacked me down.

'Whatever it was I need to know if my brother is alive. Are you going to be able to ride with that broken arm and stitched wounds?'

'I've been told the stitches are of silk and will rot away as the skin heals. As for riding I'll have to use my right arm. I'll tie my spears to the saddle and my targe to my back.'

I had one more night in comfort where the monks dressed my wounds for the last time and in the morning tied my arm up into a sling. While Harold's quartermaster found us provisions and me another leather cloak I sought out Gyric to say goodbye.

'East Anglia is Aelfgar's once again. Go carefully Sar, you do not have Harold's protection there.'

'I'm not sure I have it anywhere,' I replied.

Gyric looked puzzled.

'No matter,' I said, 'better you don't know.'

'Pay my respects to the Lady Ealhild.'

'If she's alive I will.'

When it came to mounting my horse, I couldn't do it unaided. Throughout the journey I relied on Grim's help and I returned his kindness with stories of Toki's deeds over the last year including his capture of the horse I rode. We could not ride fast because of the soreness of my wounds and it took us six days to get to Waltham. I went to the church of the Holy Cross and prayed for my aunt and the children. That night I could not sleep. By the following night I would know the truth of my mother's words.

We turned from the Gipeswic road into the small, wind wrecked wood soon after noon. I'd not long finished describing to Grim the story of our ambush and his brother's terrible wounds when I caught the first sight of Ealhild's hall. It was all too obvious that the village had been all but destroyed. The surrounding cottages were all deserted and crows were picking over the skeletal remains of at least two sheep and what may have been a dog.

The palisade was completely gone in places and the wooden gatehouse's ancient timbers were now burnt stumps. Our horses picked their way through the charred remains of the gates to the pile of sodden ashes and half burnt reeds that was all that was left of the hall.

I dismounted from the big gelding and passed his reins to Grim. Although little of the walls remained I still felt good manners compelled me to enter through where the doors should have been. Memories assailed me of Toki's struggle with the fever, of the rapt faces of the children and Lady Ealdhild's eventual acceptance of me as her nephew. Where were they now I wondered as I gazed at the bleak, grey black piles that surrounded me. Little gusts of wind blew eddies in the silt fine ash. It began to rain, large drops falling from an almost cloudless sky. Each drop crated pock marks, small craters in the ash. In the bottom of one I glimpsed something glimmer. I stooped to find that I was holding the now heat twisted silver spoon that Ealhild had used at every meal.

I turned it in my hands and walking away from the ashes cleaned it off in the long grass that was already growing lush where constant treading had once worn paths. Grim sat wordless, watching me, as I tore off one of the leather thongs that fastened my jerkin and passed it through a loop I bent in the spoon's handle. I strung it around my neck and tucked the spoon against my chest.

Grim dismounted and we sat together on the stump of the great black poplar. I remembered Gyric sat against it with blood and spit bubbling through his speared cheek. Many of its branches had been hacked away but the massive broken trunk still lay across the smashed remains of the weaving shed.

'I had my first woman under that trunk while lightning flashed and thunder roared,' I said to Grim, steering away from the painful subject of what must have happened here.

'Happier times.'

'Not for long, it was during the great storm. Shortly afterwards I left.'

'Leaving Toki here?'

'He ordered me to go.'

'This place could have been abandoned.'

'No look,' I pointed to a corner of the ruin that was not completely burnt, 'See those reeds, they are not old. The roof had been re-thatched.'

Grim stood, 'I see the remains of a stone walled church over there. Smoke rises, someone is there.'

He was right. As we led the horses down to the church a haggard looking Father Eoppa came out. 'Whoever you are, stay away from here. There is nothing left to steal.'

We stopped, 'Do not fear us Father, we mean no harm,' said Grim holding out his open palms.

I realised I was not recognised so I took off my leather cap, 'Eoppa, do you not know me?'

His eyes widened with a shock of recognition and taking his wooden cross from around his neck he held it towards me, his arm rigid and shaking. His voice rose to a scream, 'You Devil, get away from here, you bring ruin and devastation from Hell.' He then fell to his knees and began a fervent prayer in Latin.

Grim turned to me, 'What's he on about?'

'Too much to explain now.' I was angry. I'd had enough of all this crap about my looks. I crouched down and grabbed Eoppa's face and made him look at me. 'Father, I'm here to find out what has happened to my aunt.' I pointed at Grim, 'This man is Toki's brother. Now pull your pathetic self together before I forget your past kindness and beat some sense into you.'

His eyes wandered wildly before coming to rest on mine. I looked at him steadily. I owed this man a lot for his care of me and my companions. I spoke more gently, 'Father, I am no devil, I am Ealhild's nephew come to visit.'

He burst out sobbing, 'There is no one left to visit!' Tears ran down his cheeks as his face distorted with grief, 'They're all gone, they've all gone.'

I put my good arm round him and with Grim's help got him back to his feet. As soon as he was on them he started running, his sandals slipping on the wet grass. We followed his stumbling run to the other side of the church to see a row of new mounds in the graveyard.

My heart sank. This was everything I had feared. 'This is our village now Sar, so many dead and the rest have gone,' said the priest, dejection all over his drooping form.

'Whose graves are these?' asked Grim. 'Is my brother here?'

Eoppa seemed incapable of a straight answer. He wandered, pointing at the mounds. 'Some are cottars,' he named them then continued, 'and that one is Freana's. A picture flashed into my mind of Gyric's stony face as his cheek was stitched. 'That is Jofrid's, that Hjor's, that,' he faltered, 'that is Toki's.'

Grim stood wordless, his face seemed to harden as he clenched his teeth and his brows drew together. A few moments passed with the silence only broken by the pattering of raindrops on the wooden grave markers.

I opened my mouth. 'Leave me!' barked Grim.

I was not going to argue and I led Eoppa back around the church whispering to him, 'Eoppa, the Lady is not there, nor the children. Have they escaped? Are they taken?'

He didn't look at me but pulling on my arm drew me through the ruined doors of his church and gestured toward the altar. Set in the floor lay a long stone slab and beside that, two much smaller ones.

The world spun, I could not believe what I saw, 'The children too! Why the children?'

'Why any of them, Sar? Why were they killed?' answered the priest.

I felt accused, 'Because I killed Eardwulf.'

'Yes, this is the result of your murder. These people, all these people have died because of you, Sar.' Eoppa pointed a shaking finger at me. 'You, you are a Demon. Where you go you bring death.'

'Eardwulf killed my mother. He deserved to die.'

Grim's voice cut through our argument, 'You did not kill these people as you did not kill my brother. If someone killed my mother I would kill him if I could, Priest. Whatever you and your kind may preach.'

'But this is what it leads to, more killing, endless killing,' cried Eoppa crumpling back into tearful helplessness.

'So who did kill them, Priest? Who killed my brother?'

'I wasn't here, I don't know.'

Grim grabbed hold of Eoppa cassock, 'You weren't even here and you've turned into a blubbering wreck. Pull yourself together you spineless turd.'

'Leave him alone! Leave him! He has had the courage to stay and bury the dead and care for the survivors. He has barely slept in days.'

It was Ymma. She pushed me aside and started hitting and tugging at Grim.

'Ymma!' I shouted, 'Ymma, leave him.'

Grim held Ymma's struggling body away from him to avoid her attempts to kick his shins, 'You know this madwoman?'

He turned her to face me and as he did so I could see her swollen belly. 'Grim, let her be. She is with child.' I looked into her eyes my mind reeling, 'My child?'

Tears ran from her eyes as she nodded at me and ceased to fight Grim's grip. 'I saw the killing, I saw it all.'

Grim turned her again shaking her by her shoulders. 'How did you see this and survive?' he shouted into her face.

She turned her face to me, 'Tell him to let me go or I'll not say another word.'

'Grim, let her go,' I said quietly. I was trying to calm Grim down as he seemed to be getting angrier as each moment passed.

He let her go and glared at me. His right hand grasped the hilt of his sword and his left the sheath. I feared that if he drew his sword I would be dead before I could speak.

I backed away towards the door way with my hands held out open in front of me. I held his gaze, 'Grim, I am not your enemy.' The sword began to leave the sheath. 'Toki,' I shouted, 'We are here to avenge Toki.'

His eyes seemed to fill mine and in their huge darkness something flickered. He let out a long breath and slammed his sword back into the sheath. Only then did I realise I was holding my own breath in. I let it out and for a moment we stood panting as the rushing blood in our veins stopped pounding.

Ymma spoke, 'I was sleeping in the ruins of the weaving shed under the trunk of the fallen tree.'

Grim threw me a quick knowing look. 'Go on child, go on.'

Ymma moved over to Eoppa and embracing him took him to a rough hearth set up at one end of the church. 'Come Father, feed the fire and I will cook barley and beans.'

She moved a pot of steeping beans and grains onto the fire while Eoppa meekly blew the small fire into life. Grim got the message, 'Girl, have you water?'

She tossed her head towards a wooden bucket behind a small stack of broken branches. 'Sar knows the way to the spring.'

Grim and I got up together and left. As I led him to the spring he asked me, 'What is this about you being a Demon?'

'It is a long story. I will tell you but another time.' I paused and faced him, 'Toki died because of my feud with Oslaf the White.'

'Toki died because that was his fate.' He walked on, 'It cannot have been Oslaf who killed him or your aunt and little cousins. The timing is wrong. He was in Wincestre when this happened.'

'Ymma will tell us more.'

We went to the spring. After drinking deeply we filled the bucket and returned to the church. From somewhere Ymma produced a couple of bannocks each of which she halved. We sat quietly on the floor with our backs to the new graves while Ymma added herbs to the stew. She was still slim from behind but from the side I could see her rounded belly full of child. 'My child,' I thought in wonder, 'my child.'

Father Eoppa read my mind or perhaps I had spoken aloud. He patted my arm, 'The Lord takes away but he also gives.' He looked at Ymma and a small weak smile drifted across his face, 'She has taken care of me you know. Without her I could not have managed.'

Ymma put the pot away from the fire and we squatted around it dipping our bannock into the liquid. Grim smacked his lips, 'Hmmm, its good. Your woman is a cook Sar,'

I knew Grim was trying to be pleasant but Ymma snarled at him, 'I'm not his woman, I'm his slave.'

'Whoa, I'm sorry. I meant no harm,' said Grim.

'What are you saying, Ymma, what do you mean?'

She just glared at me, 'Eat your food.'

Stunned I got out my spoon and set to eating. Grim was right, from beans and barley Ymma had made a tasty meal. We ate in silence.

As we wiped the pot Grim declared, 'Right, enough is enough, by Saint Oswald's head you will tell us what you saw.'

Ymma seemed to shrink and started to shiver. At this the priest placed a hand upon her back, 'Tell your story Ymma, no harm will come to you now.'

She looked at him gratefully and taking his hand started to speak. 'The first thing I heard was the noise of the gates being dragged open. Men must have climbed over unseen. Why would we keep a watch? We have been at peace since I was a small child.'

'Go on, my child, go on,' said Eoppa gently.

'Through the gate came horsemen, some carrying torches. A

couple of cottars came out and were cut down on the spot. At this horror I drew back under the trunk and watched through a crack in the broken wall.'

'How many horsemen? How were they armed?' questioned Grim.

'Lots, maybe twenty, they seemed to be everywhere.' She paused remembering, 'Spears, they had spears and wore byrnies. Some had shields. They were frightening, but none so frightening as the woman that came with them.'

'Woman? What woman?' asked Grim.

'She was, oh maybe Jofrid's age, maybe younger, not a girl but her hair was uncovered and streaming out behind her, long white hair.'

'Katla,' I breathed out the name, 'Katla, Oslaf's mother. Go on, Ymma.'

'By now Toki and Hjor had come out from the hall door demanding to know why these men were here.'

'My brother, how did he look?'

'Fearsome, armed with sword and shield. He and Hjor stood firm and challenged them to fight one on one or leave. Then the white haired woman screamed, 'There will be no mercy for anyone who gets in my way, put down your arms or die.' Neither Toki nor Hjor deigned to answer. Then that terrible woman ordered her men to burn the hall.'

Ymma paused again, breathing deeply and shuddering. I passed her a cup of water which she nursed and sipped steadying herself to continue. 'While some of the men held Toki and Hjor back at spear point the others threw their torches onto the hall roof. Hjor grew furious and, limping, tried to attack the horsemen. They just laughed at him, taunting him while making their beast's rear and strike out with their hooves. Toki roared a challenge, 'Leave him alone. Fight me, get off your horses and fight me.' Then a man riding beside the woman got down off his horse and taking a large battle-axe from his horse's saddle bow strode towards Toki. 'I am Osric, brother to Oslaf, I will fight you,' he yelled.

'What did my brother do then?' said Grim his hand flexing on his sword hilt.

'He yelled back, 'Come on then, bastard scum, but tell me why we fight.' The woman, what did you call her? Katla? 'You are to die because your wife's nephew killed my husband,' she shouted, 'and that is why we will burn her hall and kill her and all those with her.' Toki laughed harshly, 'I see your other son has all of Oslaf's courage, coming here to kill women and children.'

Ymma stopped and turned to me, 'There was nothing to laugh at Sar, the hall roof was starting to burn but, being green, burned slowly making choking clouds of smoke. Then Toki struck out at Osric shouting, 'Hey woman watch me kill your son.' Even from where I was hidden trying to see what was happening through the shifting horsemen I could tell how stiff he was. His terrible wounds had healed into ropes of scarred flesh. Osric stepped back and two of his spearmen pushed their spears into Toki's sides from beyond the reach of his sword. As they did so Osric stepped in and hacked down again and again at Toki's writhing body. He stood no chance.'

Grim went silent and still, only the muscles tensing in his cheeks and the whiteness of his knuckles on his sword-hilt showed his feelings at hearing of his brother's end.

'And then, it was hard to see, a group of them surrounded Hjor and soon he too was a bloody heap on the ground. Then Jofrid ran from the hall, smoke billowing behind her, 'My man, my man! May you all be cursed forever and rot in hell.' Katla nodded and a spear was thrust into Jofrid's belly. Oh Sar,' Ymma was crying hard, 'she had driven me hard but she did not deserve to die like that. She died slowly, screaming, clutching at the spear shaft while its bearer twisted the blade.'

'What then?'

'Ealhild came out coughing hard, her eyes streaming from the smoke, 'Take me but let my people and my children live.' Katla looked down on her, 'I know who you are Ealhild, it is you I have come for. Your people and your children can go free.' Ealhild went back into the burning hall and a couple of cottars and their children came out. They'd been living in the hall since the storm. Then Godric and Aebbe came out with their mother behind them. 'Are these your children,' demanded Katla once the cottar's families had been held to one side. 'Yes, these are my darlings, free them and I will pray for you in heaven.' Katla answered, 'I am a mother and know a mother's love so send them over here and we will take care of them. You, though, must die for my unavenged husband.'

Ymma was overcome for a moment her face distorted in grief. 'Ealhild knelt and hugged and kissed them before handing them over to two of Katla's men. By now with the draught from the open hall door it had started to blaze, lighting up the whole area. Then Osric walked over to the cottars and their children and hacked them all down. It was horrible, as they put up arms to defend themselves or shelter their children the great axe just cut through their limbs. Other men finished them, stabbing down into the screaming mass of wide-eyed, flailing flesh and bone.'

Ymma was sobbing now, choking as her nose ran and the tears flowed, 'Ealhild shouted at Katla but I could not make out the words. Then, most horrible of all, they cut the children's throats. Ealdhild let out a wail so long and strange that it still echoes in my mind. Then she tried to run to their bleeding bodies. They turned her back with their spears. She held herself upright took one last defiant look at Katla and cried, 'You will burn for eternity as I will burn before I join my children in heaven.' With that she turned and ran into the now blazing hall.'

Ymma stopped speaking and sat quietly weeping. Eoppa tried to comfort Ymma and Grim stared into the embers of the fire. I could not sit still. I jumped to my feet and blundered my way out through the broken doors and was surprised to find that darkness had fallen. I wanted to cry and scream and rage at the skies but nothing would come but a dry shuddering, breathless, heaving. I set about un-saddling the horses still clumsy with my splinted arm. I welcomed the pain. As I tethered them by some grazing I wondered about my own horse's whereabouts. I'd imagined Aebbe and Godric riding her round the yard as Toki taught them how to manage a horse. Perhaps he did, perhaps he made them laugh by telling them about my first rides. They all came vividly into my mind as I pictured events that now could never happen. I felt a vast emptiness overwhelm me and I fell into it.

CHAPTER 15

I came round to find Eoppa pouring foul tasting liquid into my mouth while he chanted strange rhythmic words. Choking I tried to push the flask away from my lips only to find my hands were tied together. I struggled furiously until Grim firmly held me down. 'Drink it, you mad fool, drink!' He shouted into my face. Then he grasped my nose so tightly that my I had no choice but to swallow the evil mixture down.

No sooner did it hit my stomach than it came heaving back up. 'Oh my God, are you trying to poison me?' I gasped between violent retches.

'You are fiendsick, my son. You have been possessed like some madman for two days past,' said Eoppa. 'Grim had to hit you over the head and tie you up before you hurt one of us or killed yourself.'

This made no sense to me as my mouth filled again with the foul taste of bile. My stomach kept heaving as Eoppa started praying and chanting some more. Suddenly I felt movement deep in my bowels and frantically tried to rise. My feet were also tied.

'For God's sake help me before I shit myself!'

'Ugh, disgusting,' said Grim retching slightly, as he cut the ropes round my ankles and pulled me to my feet. I staggered towards a nearby bush pleading for my hands to be untied. Grim ignored me and pulling my breeches down forced me into a crouch. I was still puking watery phlegm as my bowels turned to slush and poured their contents onto the ground. Unable to prevent myself from falling over I clung, humiliatingly, to Grim's arms in absolute misery.

The priest came after us still chanting and walking around me in circles waving his cross. In my misery I felt convinced that he was having a good time.

'By Saint Oswald's talking head can you stop that moaning,' I yelled at him.

Grim, almost vomiting himself by now, told me to, 'Shut up! You were running around like a mad thing throwing your spears and arguing with the trees. When you threatened Ymma with your knife that was when I knocked you out.'

'I know nothing of this,' I cried but looking down at my clothes I could see that I was covered in dried mud and dead leaves. My arms were scratched all over and the wound in my side burned like it may have reopened. My left arm had been re-bandaged and throbbed almost as badly as it had in Wincestre.

Grim pulled me away from the pools of liquid shit and tugging handfuls of grass wiped me down like a woman does a baby.

'Do you have to do that? Untie me! Let me clean my own arse.'

Grim let me go and I fell to the ground. Eoppa bent over me and, lifting my eyelids one at a time, stared in into each eye in turn, 'Hmmm, I think he may be sufficiently purged. Carry him into the church and lay him by the altar.'

Surprisingly gently, Grim carried me in saying, 'Sar, I've seen this happen to men before, men who've seen too much in too short a time.' He laid me down on a bed of reed straw and untied my legs and arms. I tried to rise but fell back too weak to move. I could hear Ymma's voice behind me.

'Father Eoppa made you herbal drinks and knew the charms and prayers to sing. He says you may recover your senses, should God will it.' She leant over me and started to wash my face with warm water.

I pointed to my side. She gently raised my tunic and said, 'Your wound did open some but it seems to be free from pus and bad smells.'

I remembered something, 'What did you mean, not my woman but my slave?'

She covered my wound again and while looking at the cut in my shoulder said, 'When Ealhild and her children were killed you were the only remaining relative. Father Eoppa swore to the shire reeve that she had recognised you as her nephew.'

'So?'

'So you inherit what was hers.'

'You mean all this is mine?' I waved an arm which was meant to include all outside the church.

'No, unpaid taxes meant there was nothing to pass on but me.'

'You?'

'Yes Sar, I am your slave.'

'You can come with me then, with your child.'

'As my master orders me.'

'Not because you want to?'

'I am a slave. What I want doesn't come into it.'

'I want you to.'

'Then I will have to,' said Ymma getting up and walking away.

Something wasn't right here but I was so tired and weak that before I could work out what it was I fell into a deep and dream-less sleep.

When I awoke my nose was filled with my own stench. I care-fully sat up and could see in the faint glow of the fire that the others were all asleep. Feeling better in myself I got up and tot-tered my way outside. In the glimmer of the false dawn I made my way to the stream. Taking off my clothes I sank them under the rippling water and left them to rinse held down by stones. Finding a deeper pool, I stepped into the chill waters and let them flow over and around me.

Soon I was numb but I felt much, much cleaner in both my

body and my soul. As I listened to the twittering of the dawn chorus I felt calm, Toki, my aunt and my cousins were gone. Nothing I could do would bring them back. I hauled my wet clothes from the stream and wrung them out, twisting my anger into the fabric and letting its heat pour out. Now my revenge could lie cold and in wait for an opportunity that one day I was sure would come.

As the sun began to warm my goose pimpled skin I heard a noise behind me. I turned to find Ymma behind me, heading for the spring, bucket in hand. She covered her mouth with her hand in mock dismay at my nakedness. 'You gave me a child with that shrivelled worm?'

I looked down at my shrivelled penis while my balls clenched tight to my shivering body and for a moment was about to explain about cold water then I saw the joke. Suddenly we were laughing together until it hurt. Breathless, at last we hugged and kissed. I started to get aroused.

Ymma pulled back still laughing, 'Oh no, I think you should put that away until we have talked.'

I drew back and gently placed my hand on her rounded belly, 'Talked about our child?'

'No, not about that, about my slavery.'

I pulled on my wet clothes unsure where this was going. Then it came to me, the thing I knew was wrong. I ran my fingers through my hair, wringing out its wet, thick clumps and then looked her full in the face.

'Ymma,' I said, 'I can't have a slave. My mother risked her life so as not to be sold and my sister now is a slave in some stranger's house. How can someone be owned like a pot or a pig?'

Ymma picked up her bucket all laughter gone, 'But I am owned, just like a pot or pig.'

'I could free you, could I? Do you know how?'

Showing no emotion I could see, Ymma went to fill the bucket. 'Ask Father Eoppa,' she said over her shoulder, 'Ask him, he's a priest. He will know.'

I gazed after as she walked off, my hopes and my prick shrinking. The moment of warmth between us disappeared as fast as it had grown.

He did know and he drew up a deed which needed to be witnessed. The next day Grim, Eoppa and I went into Gipeswic to meet the shire-reeve. To my surprise the priest turned up riding Maeve who must have been stabled nearby.

'I'll keep this beast for my services to you, Sar,' proclaimed Eoppa with the first glimmer of a smile on his face that I had seen since I had returned.

'I owe you a great deal more than that Father. You are more than welcome to her,' I replied smiling. I was pleased to give this gentle man something for his care of us, especially me.

As we approached the town where Maeve had so comically saved my life I began to fear that I might be arrested for Hutha's murder. I didn't want to tell Father Eoppa the truth so I decided to take the risk and rely on Ordwig's silence. As it turned out the shire-reeve was only concerned with adding to his coffers in return for not making difficulties about my inheritance. Eoppa had anticipated this and slipped a couple of coins to the shire-reeves cleric. Ymma was now a free woman and we had a parchment to prove it.

When Grim asked about the murders of the Lady Ealhild and his brother the shire-reeve could not meet his gaze. 'There was no evidence as to who the raiders were,' he said. 'On what law could I act?'

We were told we could try taking the matter to Earl Aelfgar's court if we liked. No doubt the Earl would give us the justice we deserved. 'Are you here representing Harold or Siward officially?' we were politely asked, 'Or just private men, journeying fully armed in Aelfgar's Earldom?' I tried to protest but Grim, recognising the threat behind the words, bowed us out. We left Gipeswic knowing that there would be no lawful justice for the brutal murders of our kinfolk.

On our return I had imagined that Ymma would be filled with gratitude and willingly leave with me but it was not to be. 'I am a free woman now. I shall stay here to care for Father Eoppa who will shelter me and my child in return,' she said.

'My child too,' I said, 'my child. And how will you survive as an unmarried woman with a bastard child?'

She grew angry with me, 'I survived as a slave. Do you think that was easy? You survived as a bastard did you not?'

Ymma's freedom, or was it her pregnancy, had given her a strength I could not argue with. I promised her that I would return to see the child later in the year. She smiled her quiet smile and said, 'You might, Sar, you might.'

As we rode back towards Waltham it was Grim who pointed out an uncomfortable truth, 'You cannot promise the girl you'll see your child. She is now freer than you are. You are the Earl's man and are bound to him by oath. You have had too much freedom, you forget your place.'

As I spurred my horse into a canter I smiled to myself. I did feel free, free of a woman and a child I was not ready for. Truth was, I was both pleased and relieved at Ymma's decision. As for my place, I could not wait to get back into the hustle and bustle of my Earl's world. It wasn't to be. When we got to Waltham we were told to head for Lundunburh and to seek out Fulk of Wissant.

◆ ◆ ◆

Fulk's house was not hard to find. Standing tall between city and wharf, it was something of a landmark. After handing over all our weapons, except our knives, we were escorted by two hard faced soldiers to meet Fulk on an upper floor above a bustling warehouse. We passed through a sumptuous hall as lavishly decorated as the King's own palace to find the huge man, sat alone on a balcony, watching ships unload at the wharfs below.

He waved bejewelled fingers at some stools set around a small table. At another flick from those fingers four glass beakers of a dark red wine were placed before us by a prettily dressed youth. Grim looked at Fulk's silken shirt and back to the servant and winked at me with a wry smile. I knew he meant something but I didn't get the message. I gave him a puzzled look and he just looked at me, smiled, and shook his head.

'I never tire of this view, of my ships, and sometimes a few others, but mostly my ships, loading and unloading at the wharfs of this great English town. You English can't see it. You still see Mercia, Wessex, Northumbria and the others as little states of their own. This town and these wharfs are in the middle of the web that ties England together. And I, Fulk, am the spider that sits in the centre of that web.' He paused and raising a glass looked at me over the rim. 'Do you remember me, boy?'

I raised a glass to him, 'You are a hard man to forget, Fulk of Wissant, being so shiny and so large.'

'You have grown bold, and rude, for one who is so skinny and so insignificant.'

I thought for a moment, 'I beg your pardon for my rudeness, Sir. Perhaps you could tell us why we are here, and whose is the fourth glass?'

'You are here by Earl Harold's orders.'

Grim put in, 'I serve Earl Siward, not Harold.'

'Yet you are here because Gytha asked that you seek the truth of a boy's dream. A dream that might have concerned your brother.'

'Yes. And my brother has been murdered.'

'And you would seek vengeance.'

'I would,' answered Grim.

'I may be able to help with that.'

I was suspicious, 'Why should you help us?'

'You ask the right questions. Harold was wise to trust you.'

I was pleased at this but asked again, 'So why?'

'You know I helped Godwin regain his Earldom, now your

Lord's Earldom. You know my ruler, Baldwin of Flanders, aided Godwin and Tostig married into his family.' He laughed, his massive jowls wobbling, 'and you know I love wealth and have power.'

'I know all those things.'

'What you don't know is that my family and that of Gytha's have been allied since before Cnut's invasions. Godwin and his sons represented the greatest power in the land after the House of Leofric and his son Aelfgar.'

I nodded understanding but wondering where this was leading.

Fulk continued, 'One of Harold's housecarls has been murdered by the family of the man who killed his cousin. We know who by but we have no proof. The murderers live in Aelfgar's Earldom. Harold, as an Earl, cannot be seen to be involved in blood-feuds but he will lose the respect of his warriors if Toki's death is unavenged.'

'So Harold needs to strike in Aelfgar's Earldom,' I said excitedly.

'But in a way that doesn't point directly back to him,' said Grim.

'But why would you help with this?' I asked Fulk.

'Your master is becoming hugely rich and powerful. His sister is the Queen. We are friends and allies. I scratch his back he scratches mine. That is all you need to know.'

'No, it's not! I need to know that Harold is really arranging all this. I am his man, not yours.'

Fulk's whole body started wobbling and he made an odd wheezing noise. I realised that he was laughing again. 'And now,' he said, 'know who the fourth glass is for.'

He waved again, beckoning someone from the shadows behind him.

I leapt to my feet, 'Gyric, my God, Gyric!'

We hugged, 'Oh my friend, it is good to see you.'

'And you, Sar.'

As he stepped back I saw once again how the last year had

changed us. Where there was once a chubby lad there was now a muscle hardened warrior.

'But no ready smile for me, Gyric?'

'Toki, Ealhild and the children, Sar, I've no room in my heart for smiles.' His eyes filled and he quickly blinked away the coming tears. 'Harold sent me to Fulk. If what you feared was true we were to use his help. He would know what to do.'

'So you believe now that I act for your Earl,' said Fulk. 'Come look at this.'

Fulk heaved his massive bulk out of his throne-like seat to lean on the balcony rail. We joined him as he pointed to one of the ships below. 'See that knarr on the end with all those idling bastards hanging around.'

We looked over to see a tattered looking wide-bellied boat with a cargo of barrels and hides untidily scattered on its deck. Also on its deck was a group of about forty-five rough looking men engaged in eating, drinking and lying in the sun.

Grim sucked his teeth loudly and spat over the rail, 'What is that? I was expecting a longship or two, crewed by well-armed bussecarls.'

'Don't let their looks deceive you, those men are skilled hit and run raiders. Frisians,' said Fulk.

'Fucking pirate scum,' Grim declared glowering at Fulk, 'we'll be murdered as soon as we are off the wharf.'

'Pirates, true, but my pirates,' replied Fulk calmly as he manoeuvred his puffing bulk back to his seat. 'They do as I say. Grim, you will lead them, Toki was your brother. Their captain, whose name you don't need to know, will follow your orders.'

I felt excited by all this and quickly swallowing down my glass of wine I exclaimed, 'We are to attack Eardwulf's estate at Suthwalsham.' I caught the aftertaste of his wine, 'Hmmmm, fine wine, as good as any I've pinched from Harold's table.'

'True,' said Fulk, 'you have it.'

'True about what,' asked Gyric, 'the wine or the attack?'

''Ha, ha, ha,' wheezed Fulk, 'well, both, my wine is the best your country imports, though the vineyards Harold has inherited produce some of the finest wine in England.'

Grim slammed his hand down on the table, 'Sod your fucking wine, are we planning a raid or not? The nights only grow shorter.'

Fulk waved again his bejewelled hand, 'Another glass won't do any harm.' He leant forward and his tone changed, 'Now let me tell you what I've found out about Suthwalsham.

EPILOGUE

We sailed upriver, deep inland, as the sun set over this strange flat landscape with its huge sky dwarfing us. All around were massive heaps of draining peat, each higher than a man and longer than a great ship. Many other ships, as equally tatty and dirty as our own, were moored along the riverbanks or in water-logged ditches fringed with tasselled reeds, dug deep into the peat beds. Smudges of peat smoke were rising from the faintly glowing cooking fires each ship had set along the banks. Ahead of us on a sand and shingle bank was a large hall. It was strongly fenced, with a gate house on the riverside above a wide clearing which gently sloped down to a broad floating wharf. Other-wise empty of shipping there was one sleek fast looking snekke moored at the wharf. As we glided closer, our sail lowered and with only our four long sweeps giving us headway, I could see that the gates were closing for the night.

'See the snekke, do you recognise it,' asked the Frisian captain lisping slightly through broken teeth.

'No,' I answered, 'it is not one of Oslaf's, at least that I know of. It's like Fulk said, they keep one here to inspect the traders.'

'Oslaf's or not,' said Grim, spitting into the water, 'it means there are many warriors here.'

'Can we take them,' I asked.

'If these Frisians are what that boy lover says they are,' said Grim, his hands once again wandering, restlessly seeking his absent sword belt.

The Captain, a swarthy man, gap toothed and dressed like us in a rough tunic and with bare feet, answered, 'My men are the best that Fulk can pay for. Do you doubt his riches?' He hissed for quiet in his own language as a muffled curse came from the hollow pile of barrels roofed with hides.

'Oy, you there, you can't moor here,' shouted a man from the wharf.

Grim shouted, 'We have barrels of wine to be delivered to Lady Katla's steward.'

'Well, you are too late, as you can see the gates are all but shut.'

'Early really, we had an easy crossing. We'll moor against your wharf then until sunrise.'

'No one moors at this wharf, except to unload, and this late, no one at all.'

'It is as we were told,' I muttered, 'everything here is as Fulk told us it would be.'

The Captain gestured to the oarsmen to back water until our boat slowed almost to immobility, rocking gently on the swell.

'What are we to do then?' shouted Grim, his hands trumpeted around his mouth.

The man on the wharf pointed his spear to another wharf nearby, 'That's where you moor for the one night only. You will unload in the morning. If you need to stay longer find another mooring well away from the hall.'

'As you wish, cocksucker,' Grim replied.

'Cocksucker your fucking self,' the man shouted back over his shoulder, laughing, as he ran to squeeze through the closing gates.

We steered to an adjoining wharf where two other small trading vessels were moored. Their small crews rested on the bank by their fires. Our four oarsmen shipped their oars as I tied the mooring ropes. Then jumping onto the wharf they ambled over to the nearest crew waving their hands in friendly greeting. There was a sudden scuffle, a short cut-off cry and then there were four new figures sat at the fire each with a shapeless bundle at its feet. A man at the next fire rose at the commotion. Bowstrings thrummed as arrows flew from our ship. The man fell wordless while the seated crewmen never got to rise.

The arrows were quickly followed by knife wielding men and all whimpering cries of pain were rapidly stilled. More men left our ship, now each fire was once again attended by a group of men resting quietly on the bank.

Then Gyric came out from under the hides with a bundle of twigs and we built a small fire of our own under lumps of peat as the dusk settled into darkness. No one had raised an alarm, all had gone to plan.

'That was effective, those Frisians don't look much like warriors but they know how to kill,' I commented dryly.

Gyric shook his head, 'Innocent traders have been killed. This was not their fight.'

'Needs must when the Devil drives,' said Grim, looking happier as he joined us with a drawn sword, its blade smoke blackened to reflect no light.

As the darkness thickened the rest of the Frisians disembarked their movement shrouded in the gloom. All of us were dressed in dark clothes and either hooded or wearing boiled leather helmets. They smeared their faces in ashes and mud so Grim, Gyric and I followed suit.

Gyric looked uneasy as we returned to the boat to collect our weapons.

'What's up?'

'I've grown used to shields and banners and shining mail not this skulking about in dirty clothes.'

'They won't be mailed, nor will they be expecting us.' I whispered back.

'There's no glory in this creeping around like thieves. No one will remember us in songs.'

'That's rather the point isn't it?' I was impatient now. 'We are here for secret vengeance not glory.'

He nodded and gripped my arm, 'It is harder to face a fight without a man you know on either side.'

I saw then the fear in his eyes that comes before a fight and felt the first fluttering of my own. 'We have each other Gyric, you are the only man I need by my side.'

As we shook hands on this Grim hissed at us, 'Now come on ladies, this is not the time for gossiping at the loom.'

He sounded so like Toki that I smiled. Gyric did too, then speaking gruffly in Toki's voice said, 'By Cuthbert's holy fucking onions Grim. You are right in what you say.'

We all laughed quietly as I put my arm through my targe strap and gathered up my spears. By now all the Frisians were gathered on the wharf. Many of them carried bows and some bundles of rope tied to strange three-pronged hooks, grapnels I'd been told they were. The captain passed a long cord around the company and across his chest. Each of us held it in one hand as we followed him in two files into the creek that passed between our wharf and the one outside the hall. We slowly waded through the cold water, each step carefully taken in the slippery mud. The bowmen held their bows high above their heads while one man carefully floated a small raft ahead of him. In the dark I could see the faint red glow of a shuttered fire pot quickly shielded by a wet hide.

We came up alongside the wharf. One man crept over and peered into the snekke. He flashed his fingers up twice. At least twenty oars, our escape was assured. Slowly one by one the Frisians crept across to the shadow of the palisade, slinking invisibly through the darkness. A movement above the gatehouse and we all froze. I felt as if the thudding of my heart and the rushing in my ears were as loud as church bells. A face looked out over the tidal flow of the river then disappeared. We waited then as the Captain raised two fingers a man nudged my back. It was my turn to creep across the gap. I was sure my targe would reflect the starlight or the last shining strip of the waning moon though I knew it was smothered in mud. My spears felt about twenty feet long and sure to catch on something as I ran, half crouched, into the shadows.

Gyric soon joined me and I saw Grim cross into the darkness on the other side of the gate. His shape was faintly outlined against the flickering waters beyond the wharf. I jumped, startled, as the Captain made a loud cry something between the boom of a bittern and the screech of a night-owl. It was enough. I could hear voices above me as the guards came to peer over the parapet. Arrows flew and one body toppled over to land with a thud not far from where I crouched. Above our heads a strange, strangled, scream rang out and then suddenly all was mayhem.

From each side of the gate men threw grapnels over, their hooks gripping the trunks of the palisade. One hard tug to check they were secure then our men swarmed up the ropes and over the parapet. Above a rising chorus of men shouting and the hysterical barking of woken dogs I could hear a dull clunking as the gate bar was lifted. As the gate opened more of us rushed in unsure of what we would meet.

Inside there was a large empty space in front of a splendid hall. Its long side with its central door was opposite the gate we had entered. Two men and a dog lay dead on the ground. The door was opening as I turned to face it. We had gained almost total surprise. As a man looked around the opening door an arrow slammed into his face with a sickening crunch. He disappeared, pulled back into the hall by unseen hands, and the door thudded back into place.

As other men pushed in behind me I stared wildly around in the gloom my spear raised to throw. There was no attack. We spread in a rough line across the space. Flaming trails arced across the sky as fire arrows, lit from our fire-pot, sliced into the thatched hall roof.

I yelled some formless cry as I exulted in the beginnings of justice being done. This hall did not smoulder as Ealhild's was said to have done. This, dried by early summer sun, blazed quickly and fiercely. We could hear the screams of women and the cries of children as they realised the peril they were facing.

Suddenly we were attacked as men came running out from behind each end of the hall. Some were barely dressed, a couple had spears, few wore shoes, none had shields or mail but all of them carried swords.

'There must be a door on the other side,' shouted Grim, 'where are the rest of your men?'

'They'll be scaling the wall now. None who leave the hall will escape,' said the Captain settling into a fighting stance, a wicked looking long knife in one hand and an oddly rounded short handled axe in the other.

I felt wildly alive aware of Gyric shouting at my side as arrows flew towards the attacking men. I saw the Captains axe whirl through the air to gash into a man's chest stopping him instantly and throwing him onto his back. I just had time to be impressed as the mass of men attacking our flank turned from a mass into individual men yelling guttural war cries.

I threw my first spear. It caught a man in his thigh and he whirled round in an odd capering one-legged dance. I yelled again at the sky as arrows flew into the unshielded men. It was brutal. We were shadows in the dark whereas they were white skinned and lit by the rising flames. Slaughter this rapid was something I'd not seen before. They crumpled one after the other into whimpering bleeding cripples or bloody corpses as the arrows sought out their lives. Not one of them reached us to fight man to man.

Then the hall doors flew open and another group of men appeared. There were six of them, all helmeted, carrying shields and long war spears. Somehow they had armed themselves in the smoke and panic of their burning home. This would be a different fight. While they stepped forward from the heat of the burning hall I ran to retrieve my throwing spear. A few arrows flew to be caught on the warrior's shields. The Captain raised his hand and all went still as the cracking of burning timbers filled the air. Smoke streamed up into the night sky.

Grim nodded towards the flames, 'We have sent up a beacon that will draw men from leagues in all directions. We need to finish this.'

One of the hall's warriors called out, 'What cowards are you that burn our home in the night?'

I felt certain that the man was Osric, murderer of my cousins, brother to my mother's killer. I screamed at him, almost incoherent with rage, 'You are the coward, you who murder children.'

I was ignored as Grim answered, 'I am Grim Haldorson, and I am here to avenge my brother Toki, who you and your men slaughtered.'

The Captain muttered loudly, 'I thought we had no time to exchange Saxon pleasantries. A dead man doesn't need to know your name.'

There was a commotion as some of our men appeared around one end of the hall pushing before them a group of women and children. With a surge of malevolent excitement I recognised Katla. Her white hair was revealed when a man tore the shawl from her shoulders. The men around Osric faltered and as they did so, with no signal I could see, the Frisians threw themselves upon the six men. The only shield among us was my little targe so although the fight was short it was bloody.

I remember gore flooding over me as a Frisian died clinging onto the shield of a wide-eyed warrior shocked by the ferocity of a man forcing his way up his spear shaft to certain death. I remember Gyric's sword reaching past me to hack into that wide-eyed warriors face. I remember my spear driving under my targe into the side of a man on my left as I pushed him away with my aching shield arm. He went down under the stabbing and hacking of ferocious Frisian daggers and axes. Then all went calm again as the fighters drew back panting heavily.

Only Osric and one other man still stood. They were both bleeding heavily. I looked to my friends. Gyric had a long cut along his forearm and his nose was bleeding while Grim sat on the ground tying his sword belt around a badly gashed thigh. I realised that I had come through unscathed. By some miracle the only wounds I had were still those scarred on my face and body that Oslaf had inflicted.

The fate of Osric and his man was certain but I knew what I had to do. I pointed at Osric and shouted, 'That man is mine! I will fight him alone.'

Even as I shouted the man beside Osric slowly collapsed to the floor, either dead or nearly so. Somehow my voice had carried above the roaring of the burning hall. In the heat, of the burning and of battle, sweat was running through the muddy ash on my face. My eyes were stinging and I wiped them on the sleeve of my upper arm after throwing aside my leather battle cap. It felt good to have my hair flowing free.

Katla screamed from behind me, 'I know who you are! You are the bloody haired Demon child that killed my husband.'

Osric's eyes hardened as he realised who I was. 'It will be a fitting end that my last act on earth will be to avenge my father,' he said spitting into the dirt.

'You don't have to do this,' shouted Gyric.

'Oh, yes I do,' I shouted gleefully. I was seeking death or revenge for all that Oslaf had done to me and mine. I took a moment to raise Ealhild's silver spoon to my lips and kiss it in her memory.

As Osric raised his shield and readied his sword that quietness came down upon me again. This time though it wasn't cold, it was as if fire ran through my veins. This fight for me was like a dance. I felt Muirchu's spirit come down into my body and I breathed in, welcoming his presence.

Osric closed fast, slashing his sword across at waist height. I danced back, sucking in my belly and lifting my arms. As the point passed my guts, just grazing my jerkin, I raised myself up, high on my toes and jabbed my spear point under his helmet's rim.

'First blood to me,' I yelled as I saw blood well over his eye. He was half blind now.

Osric didn't bother to reply but charged at me with sword arm raised high as if to chop down hard. In a flash I remembered Oslaf's attack and knew they'd practiced this together. The threat from the sword was a feint. This time instead of the shield smashing into me I danced away and whirling round jabbed my spear into the meat of his right shoulder. It stuck slightly as I jerked it out. His raised arm slumped as the muscle tore. We were now in the centre of the yard as we both, unthinkingly, moved away from the heat of the blazing hall.

'Get on with it boy, we need to leave,' shouted Grim now propping himself up on a broken spear shaft.

I ducked as Osric's sword swiped over my head. He was off balance and as he turned I stabbed my spear hard into his left buttock. And there it stuck, sunk deep into his flesh. The shaft was pulled from my hand as he staggered back. Osric stood, obviously in agony, almost unable to move as I pulled my knife from its sheath. I kissed the blade in my mother's memory. I whispered to her that now I would avenge her sister's death. For me this would be another stab to Oslaf's bloody heart.

It was a short while longer before I finally killed him. Not once did he cut me with his wavering sword which he now struggled to lift. As I danced around him stabbing and slashing he began wearily cursing and moaning. He knew that his death was close. I danced in and out punching him with my targe and stabbing with my tomb born knife. I drove Osric crazy in memory of Muirchu's words, 'jump in, stab, jump out, jump in then stab' and I stabbed and stabbed and I stabbed again. Then finally the sword fell from his hand and he knelt leaning on his shield breathing heavily with blood seeping and flowing from his many wounds. He stared at me through his one good eye, all fight gone. I stepped round behind him and pulling his head back by his helmet drew my knife, hard, once, across his throat. As he fell to the ground I became aware of the silent crowd around me staring at my gore covered, triumphant self. I had fought man to man and I had won. I held my bloody knife in the air and screamed my victory to the sky. Then I heard a shrill keening wail of a woman's voice and turned to see Katla hurling herself towards me. A rough hand grabbed her long hair and twisting it round its forearm pulled her sharply backwards. She screamed briefly as a bloody blade point appeared through the centre of her chest. Pulling his sword out as she crumpled to the floor Grim spoke, 'She knew who you were, woman or not she had to die.'

I nodded looking at her dying, twitching body, 'The only fate she deserved was death.'

From out of a group of wailing children a boy of about twelve ran forward, knelt and kissed Katla's dying face. Grim pulled him to his feet, 'Stay away child, stay away.'

The boy turned a defiant face to me and shouted, 'You have killed my uncle and my grandmother. Either kill me now or fear my revenge.'

I returned the fierce glare of those pale blue eyes under a white blond fringe and I had no doubt at all about whose son this was. I remembered kneeling by my own dying mother as he knelt now. I remembered too his father cutting my face on the beach at Caer Dydd and again I knew exactly what I had to do. Then I didn't.

'I will not kill children as your grandmother and uncle did. Killer I may be, but not that sort of killer.'

The Frisian captain grunted behind me, 'You're a fool, man, if you leave that one alive. Come we must go.'

With that he turned and his men followed, carrying their dead and wounded. The children stood in a small wailing group. The boy, so obviously Oslaf's son, now back on his feet confronted me.

'This is my fate,' I said to the captain and as I ignored his reply, the boy, his face bone-white except for two red patches high on his cheeks, demanded, 'I am Eardmund, son of Oslaf, son of Eardwulf. Tell me who you are.'

'Who am I? You can tell your outlawed father who I am.' Leaning towards him I took one of his shaking hands and ran its palm along the puckered line of my scarred jaw. 'Tell him of this mark,' I said, 'and he will know.'

Quickly Gyric and I got each side of Grim and we dashed out to the waiting snekke with him slung between our shoulders. All the Frisians were on board either setting the oars or casting off the mooring ropes. We piled in as the ship got under way. Armed men were now appearing on the jetty attracted by the mayhem but unable to pursue us. A few spears flew uselessly into the water astern of the fast, sleek ship we had stolen. In front of the crowd stood the same small, defiant, white-blonde boy child determined still to get something from me.

He screamed across the water, 'Who are you? Your name, your family, whose son are you?'

I thought for a moment and then yelled back over the stern as we sped into the dawn. 'I am no-one. I have no family. I am No Man's Son.

HISTORICAL NOTE

The events of 1052 and the fighting return of the exiled Godwin clan were crucial to the pre-conquest history of Britain. The ascendency of the Godwinsons during the second half of King Edwards reign and Harold's eventually becoming King himself all stemmed from these events.

I have hung my story mainly on the framework of the Anglo-Saxon Chronicle while inter-weaving some of the more controversial arguments of the many fine scholars who have written on the period.

Harold's return from Ireland and the Battle of Porlock happened, though possibly further inland. Oslaf's raid on Cardiff is my own invention. One version of the chronicle has Harold laying waste to Land's End and Penzance was founded as Aswaldton though my Aswald is fictional. The last King of Cornwall is my invention but Kernow had held out against the English until the end of the 10th Century, not that long before their conquerors were themselves conquered.

Harold's mother, Gytha, did own Flat Holm Island in the Severn Estuary and is reputed to have dealt in attractive female slaves. Harold's brother, Sweyn, did murder their cousin, Beorn, a crime that shocked even in those violent times. William of Normandy's visit to England is controversial. He certainly was very busy in Normandy at the time but it is also striking how frequently major figures of the time would embark on voyages at very short notice. Wulfnoth and Hakon were hostages in Normandy, probably taken there with William (if he visited) or when the Bishop's escaped from London. Archbishop Richard's pallium was left behind to be used by Stigand. He never did get his own from the Pope in Rome. There was a fight at the East Gate in which young men from London were killed. Other French and Norman forces did escape to the West and eventually ended up fighting alongside MacBeth for the Kingdom of Alba. The pursuit by Harold's men and the intervention of Aelfgar's forces are my idea. The Bishop's finally escaped the Kingdom on a 'broken down ship' from the Naze in Essex. There was also a 'great wind' that year.

There seems little doubt that Godwin and Edward had a tense relationship, probably due to resentments around their interdependence. Although later to be revered as a saint, Edward was prone to violent outbursts, the demand for Rhys' head was made and obeyed. Why he and the Queen were childless is anyone's guess. He did repudiate her briefly as described but later they appeared to become close though possibly more in a father/daughter way than husband and wife. My explanation is complete supposition but is intended to demonstrate the frustrations of both Edward and Godwin in their ambitions for their dynasties. Godwin did die after collapsing at the King's Easter feast in Winchester. I couldn't resist giving Edward a small triumph at Godwin's end.

The two stone cathedrals also existed only to be destroyed along with all the large stone buildings of Saxon England by triumphant Normans. The church at Waltham and the stone cross Tofi the Proud, according to folk legend, brought there from Montacute in Somerset are based in reality. Harold was eventually to found Waltham Abbey in this area and his attachment to his idea of the Holy Cross and his banner of The Fighting Man is as historical as any record of this time can be. Throughout the book I have tried to interweave things we know and things we can guess. There were potteries near Ipswich and it seems that most of the forests of East Anglia had long been felled. So how were the kilns fuelled? One theory of the creation of the Norfolk Broads is that they were created by peat digging Saxons so I've put the two together. Apparently, there were no pine woods in England at this time so pitch for shipbuilding must have been a valuable import.

Another area I wanted to address is the idea that we were one 'English' nation at the time of the Norman Conquest. Not only was there the obvious fact that most of the country was heavily influenced by Danish culture as most of the English upper class had been wiped out by Cnut. The Godwinsons themselves were half Danish. The 'British' cultures of the Welsh, Cornish and Strathclyde continued. The entire West of Britain and the East of Ireland was heavily influenced by, and in areas like modern day Cumbria and the Isle of Man, dominated by Norse-Irish culture. 'English' trade and 'English' diplomacy interacted with most of Europe. Even in the 11th Century the British Isles were multi-cultural. It was also highly stratified with a fantastically wealthy ruling class whose opulence is hard to believe down to the many slaves who did not even own their own bodies.

That leaves warfare and warships. I've tried to keep things believable but the more I looked at this the less I felt I knew. Ships, ship building and the fighting seamen they carried were vital parts of any power play as Godwin's return clearly demonstrates. The re-enactment societies give us wonderful insights into the reality of fighting with the weapons of the time. But, no-one really knows what a shield wall actually looked like, or what did a warrior's shield bearer do exactly. Mail and swords were expensive and glamorous but no one sings songs about the lightly armed youths I believe must have existed. What is not in doubt is that warfare was bloody, close up and brutal. People don't change that much and many fighting men must have been severely psychologically traumatised. On a lighter note; my characters swear. Despite their reputation we know of no Anglo-Saxon swear words nor if they swore at all. If we were to judge Victorian society by the writings of its historians, novelists and clerics we wouldn't find any swearing there either but swear I'm sure they did. My characters swear because swearing is prevalent among modern English people, especially fighting men, and I want my characters to feel real to a modern reader.

I have always been fascinated by history and for me one of the most compelling ways to explore it is the historical novel. 'No Man's Son' is the first book of a series which will cover the greatest triumphs of the Anglo-Saxon kingdom, its greatest disaster and the rebellions and diaspora that followed. Sar will serve Harold and his family, pursue his own blood-feud and hope to reunite with his sister through many more years to come. Hopefully you will join me in following his exciting story while I continue to explore this controversial, often confusing, but crucial era in our history.

SIMON PHELPS

Now read the first chapter of

BLOOD IN THE WATER

the sequal to No Man's Son

CHAPTER 1

The tanner, you could tell he was a tanner by his slimy clothes and the stench that went with them, slowly got to his feet. He swore at us then spat, sloppily, through blackened teeth as he pulled out a short, plaited leather whip from his belt.

'Here we go,' I thought, 'another drunken twat who doesn't know when he's beaten.'

He flicked the whip back and forth in front of him, swaying slightly and burbling some crap about boys who think they're men. Then he lurched forward, straight at Gyric as I knew he would. No-one ever saw skinny me as a threat. I quickly side-stepped, then, as he passed, thwacked him across the back of his skull with my blackjack. He went down like a stone.

I grinned at Gyric then saw the flicker in his eye. Before he could speak I whipped round to find the tanner's mate coming at me. I saw a glint of silver in the moonlight. A knife. Now this was serious. To his obvious shock I stepped in, grabbed his arm, pulled him into me and swung him round. His mouth opened, screaming, as Gyric struck him hard across his back with his axe-handle. As his foul breath filled my nostrils I pushed him down on to the muddy, cobbled road. Gyric struck him again across his back while I gave him a couple of hard kicks between the legs. As he writhed onto his side to clutch at his crotch the knife fell from his fingers.

I picked it up and, after shoving it into my belt, knelt and spoke to the groaning man, 'If Earl Siward knew you'd used a blade on the streets of Jorvik you'd greet the dawn with your neck in a noose.'

I kicked him again in the head then stamped on him. Gyric pulled me away, 'Back off, Sar, he's out cold, done, alright? You kill him and you'll be the one hanging. Harold's man or not.'

We rummaged through their clothes but, as usual, by the time they were this drunk they never had anything of value left on them. I looked up at Gyric, 'What the fuck are we doing Gy? He we are, Earl Harold's men, trained warriors. Well, you are anyway, throwing out drunks from a tavern.'

'We're getting by 'til Siward lets us leave,' he replied with his usual easy-going grin. He winked, 'and life with Hilda isn't so bad.'

I grinned back. We both shared Hilda's bed from time to time as well as looking after her inn while her husband traded over the sea. Exciting stuff for Gyric and me. I might be sixteen and Gyric seventeen but we'd become killers before we'd been lovers. Hilda was fun and warm and we had much to forget.

We turned the drunk's faces out from the sticky mud so they'd not suffocate or drown in their own vomit and left them where they lay. We wanted no corpses here. Siward's justice was hard and its products hung by their necks, legs dangling, above the Mykla Gata Bar.

Jorvik was a hard city under harsh law. The winter had been long and followed by a stormy spring which had kept the fishermen on the shore. The hungry gap had come early this year. There was no grain, no wheat, no barley, to be found in this forlorn city while the crops were still green in the fields. Harsh law meant that robbers were hung, so when they robbed, they killed, it left no witnesses. I had long dirtied up the hilt of the honed down seax that had become my mother's knife. The richly decorated weapon that the father I'd never known had looted from the grave of an ancient king. I'd used it to kill my mother's murderer. His son, Oslaf, had used it to carve me from my ear to my chin. The scar still itched. I'd killed Oslaf's brother, Osric, to avenge the murders of my aunt Ealhid, my sweet young cousins and my warrior friend, Toki. I wasn't done yet. Oslaf still lived. I hunted him while he, he hunted me.

Back in the inn we asked Lodin about the takings for the night. His huge forearms opened to reveal the usual mixed bag of glass beads, leatherwork, combs and cheap jewellery and the odd cut penny. It never ceased to amaze me what men would trade in for the privilege of getting drunk on stale beer and sour wine. Hilda would string the beads into necklaces and bracelets to sell to the guilty or love-struck, to placate unhappy wives or to seduce easy women.

Lodin dragged himself out from behind his table heaving his way across the floor on crutches.

'Got a couple of smokies here as well, Saint Stephen in his church might know how old they are. I can tell you there's little mould and no maggots,' he said nodding towards a couple of withered looking wind dried and smoked fish.

I squinted at them in the firelight but could not really see them, maybe that was just as well. I took the skillet and placed it on the embers. Old fat sizzled as I flaked the fish into it. Gyric dropped some eggs into a pail of water. Then after throwing the floaters into the fire he cracked the others into the pan. Attracted by the smell of frying Hilda came down the ladder from above.

'Do you need salt, my lovely lads?' she asked, 'Eggs without salt make a poor supper.'

Lodin pulled out a fish flake and tasted it, 'No ta, the fish is a little salty as well as smoked. You joining us?'

'After I've put away the takings,' she answered as she rooted through the bits and pieces. After picking out anything of real value she climbed back up to hide it away.

Gyric cracked another couple of eggs into the pan and I stirred it all around. Hilda came back down and we sat around the pan each taking turns to dip our horn spoons into the scrambled mess. I swore in Welsh as I did when I was particularly pissed off.

'Speak English, Sar,' said Gyric.

'Or better still Dansk,' added Hilda.

I wiped my spoon off on my once fine tunic and spat into the dusty straw, 'I'm fed up with all this, no offence Hilda, but last year I was eating meats from an Earl's table. Siward won't give us leave to go or service at his court. Even Grim don't come and see us anymore.'

'Northumbria is a vast Earldom and Grim is away on the Earl's bidding as trusted housecarls often are. You know this Sar, he will come for us when the time is right,' answered Gyric, 'It is as God wills.'

Grim Haldorson was Toki's brother. He, with a Frisian pirate captain, had led the raid on Oslaf's mother's hall which we had burned to the ground. Once we had escaped from the hostile ships of Earl Aelfgar's East Anglian navy into the endless maze of the Fens it was decided, to Grim's delight, that we had no choice but to come north. After an arse blistering row, we had finally found our way to the Humber and up the Ouse to Jorvik. Earl Siward had welcomed Grim back with open arms, literally bear hugging him with arms so powerful as to make Grim look small.

I'd seen Earl Siward before and instinctively liked the old rough Viking warlord with his grizzled beard and blunt speech. He didn't feel the same about us. He stared down on us from his high seat of black ancient wood, carved with polished entwined, writhing wyverns and declared.

'Hmmm, Harold's men eh? Never cared much for Godwin's silver tongue. Slipped far too easily into Cnut's trusted circle,' he chuckled at his word play while Gyric and I exchanged startled looks. 'Not sure I care much for his over-dressed and over-mighty children either,' he continued sniffing and glaring at us while spitting into the rushes on his mead-hall floor.

I had shuffled uneasily curbing my tongue. Gyric politely asked for horses to allow us to return home.

'Thegn Scalpi's son, aren't you? Now there's a man I respect. Proper Dane, but no, you can't have a horse. You and that red-haired streak of piss next to you will stay in Jorvik until I decide otherwise.'

At first it hadn't been so bad. Jorvik was a big town with lots going on. We ran and wrestled every day outside the town walls to keep fit. Gyric would practise with his sword while I threw my remaining throwing spear over and over again. I also learned how to throw the wickedly sharp little axe the Frisian captain had given me before they rowed away.

'Fulk will pay my family well and you fought like a man,' he had said, 'though I won't tell you my name, I will give you this.' He brought out the little axe. As he did so a memory flashed into my mind. Now I knew how he had stopped a charging man in his tracks against the flickering background of a burning hall.

'That's how you did it!' I breathed excitedly.

'Aye, my ancestors fought with these. Though they have long ceased to be the fashion my grandfather taught me their use. You have this, I can get others made.'

I liked throwing weapons. I struggled to fight in a mailed byrnie while carrying a heavy shield like the Saxon housecarls who'd been meat-fed from childhood. I had to rely on quickness, agility and my cold killer's heart when I fought, or killed.

The winter had dragged, we'd traded away anything of value we were willing to let go of. Neither of us would sell our weapons. For Gyric that was his sword and a knife. We'd not taken mail or war shields on the raid. Me, I had my knife of course, my little wood and bronze targe and the throwing spear I liked to fight with, as well as the axe. We'd both had arm rings which we'd traded away while Gyric had sold his fine metal cloak clasps. I kept my silver wire torque that Faelan oi Airtre, an Irish warlord, had given me after the battle at Porloc, and the silver spoon I had found in the ashes of Ealhild's hall. Gyric had a ring of his father's he had sworn to keep. With nothing else left, we wound up working for our lodgings in the tavern Grim had found for us. Hilda's warm bed was a welcome comfort though Gyric's Christian principles had worried him.

'She's not a real wife though, not church wed,' he'd fretted, 'not really adultery.'

'Oh yea, so you'd shag Earl Harold's Edith and say, sorry sir, but she's only wed Danish style,' I laughed at him.

He blushed at the thought. Who didn't fancy the beautiful Edith? Then he shook his head as he imagined Harold's vengeance.

'Look at it this way Gyric, she's the one good thing that's happened in this stinking town and you'll know how to keep your wife happy when your father finds you one.'

He had smiled at that and we pushed to the back of our minds the thought of what would happen when fine weather brought the traders back from over the sea.

Coming back into the present I returned to my grumbling, 'We must go to Siward again, ask him to give us some real work and some proper food or let us go home.'

Lodin said, 'There'll be work on the docks soon enough for willing hands.'

'I meant work for the Earl, not labouring for merchants.'

Lodin was offended at this. His legs had been smashed when he'd slipped under the keel of a newly built longboat as it launched down the slips. 'Get over yourself you poncey little runt,' he growled, and dragging himself to the bundle of blankets and old furs, he bedded down for the night.

Hilda laughed and with a swing of her yellow hair and a flounce of her ample skirts she headed for the back door. 'Now, you boys stay in here while I go and do what even a lady such as me must do from time to time.'

She had a laugh like silver bells and always seemed cheerful so despite my sour mood I grinned back at her as she left.

No sooner had I put the skillet into the fire to burn it clean when the street door banged open. Without looking I could tell they came from the docks and had recently been at sea. I could smell the salt. 'Fuck off,' I said, 'We're closed.'

Gyric spoke, 'Excuse my friend, but we are shut.'

A gruff voice said, 'Sit down boy, I'll decide if we're shut.'

I turned to see five burly seamen. Two of them carried a large sea-chest while their leader shook off his dripping fur cloak. As he turned into the glow of the firelight I could see that he had a huge nose that at some time had been badly broken. If his eyes were looking to the prow of a ship then his nose was pointing firmly off to the steerboard.

'I don't know who you young men are but I am Einvar Crook-Nose and I am the owner of this tavern.' He stared round the room strode to the nearest bench and sat. 'So where is my wife?'

Gyric jumped to his feet, even in the firelight I could see that he was blushing violently, 'You mean Hilda. You're Hilda's husband?'

Einvar stared at him, hard, 'Yes, what of it?'

Gyric started to blush and stammer. I didn't like the way this was going. 'Oy,' I said, 'Crook-nose! Why they call you that then?'

Einvar leaped to his feet, if Gyric's face was red, Einvar's had gone deeply purple. He was furious. Swinging a fist as big as a badger ham at my face he charged at me. I ducked under his arm and dove straight into the boot of one of his men. Grabbing the boot hard I tipped the sailor on his back and jumped up onto a table daring Einvar to come at me.

'Want me to straighten that for you, eh?' I shouted, lashing out at his nose with my foot. As my right foot smashed into his nose, my left was wrenched out from under me. I crashed down between the benches to find Lodin's powerful shoulders holding me down to the floor, his forearm pressed against my windpipe.

'Get off me you fucking cripple. What are you doing?' I said, choking my words into his hairy face.

'Saving your stupid life, now stay down.'

Behind the noise of the benches being dragged aside I could hear Hilda pleading for Gyric's life. Then one of Einvar's boots thudded into my side, another kick deadened my thigh. Lodin grunted as a third kick slammed into him as we thrashed about on the floor.

'Stay still, you skinny git.'

I wriggled sideways and got my lower half out from under only for Einvar to stamp on my belly. Vomiting chunks of fish into the straw, badly winded, I gasped for breath. Lodin rolled off me as Einvar landed another kick to my ribs.

From the corner of my eye I could see Gyric held up against the wall with a knife to his throat while Hilda was pulling at Einvar's clothes and pleading with him.

'Let them go husband, they have been helping here this winter. One of Siward's men lodged them here.'

Einvar drew back, 'Siward's man eh?' He paused, thinking slowly, as Hilda tried to dab at his bleeding nose with the end of her shawl.

'Yes husband, Grim Haldorson, he left them here in the autumn.'

His eyes narrowed, 'Grim eh?'

As he pondered I began to breathe again, sucking the air in shuddering gasps. 'Yes, Grim,' I said, 'he brought us to Jorvik.'

Einvar made his mind up. 'Throw them out,' he said. Then turning to his wife he kissed her, 'you glad to see me darling?'

I missed her reply as Gyric was given the bum's rush then I too was dragged along the floor and thrown out into the mud and rain of Guthrums Gate.

'Christ, Sar, what was that about?' asked Gyric as the door slammed shut behind us.

I lifted my hand out of a fresh pig turd and sat up, 'You were blushing like a little girl. I thought next thing you'd be defending Hilda's honour.'

'Oh what? You were saving me? Were you worried that we might get a beating and get thrown out into the street,' retorted Gyric ruefully. He was standing now, vainly trying to rub clinging street slime off his clothes.

'Would have been worse if he'd have guessed the truth.' I became aware of strange snuffling grunts. 'Ha, ha Gyric, would you look at that!'

Just up the street the tanner was struggling to get to his feet under the weight of an enormous sow. Her frantic litter of piglets squealing excitedly all around. Gyric and I waded in, laughing helplessly as we kicked the sow away. The tanner rose to his feet and looked around for his mate. Seeing he was gone the filth covered tanner scuttled off into the darkness of the alleys.

Gyric and I looked at each other, breathing heavily and giggling gently.

Suddenly Gyric stopped giggling, 'Sar, our weapons and our cloaks, they are all in the inn.'

I shook my head, suddenly despondent. Without good clothes, with no weapons and no lodgings, we were nothing but vagrants.

ABOUT THE AUTHOR

Simon Phelps has had an interesting life so far. After his education was interrupted by an accident leaving him in a wheel-chair he co-founded a commune, then went on to work on a City Farm. After marrying for the first time he helped run a market stall then a smallholding. After the appeal of living similarly to a medieval peasant wore off, he finally caught up with his education studying up to Master's level in the history of science, technology and medicine. He then changed tack and trained to become a counsellor, the profession he still pursues. He lives happily with his second wife in a full life interrupted by children, step-children and now their progeny.

He has always been deeply interested in, even obsessed by, history after being inspired in his childhood by adventurous historical novels and a good story. Now he wants to use his own cast of fictional characters and their journeys to illustrate the real histories of our past, while creating a good, entertaining read. Above all he would like to inspire more people to share his love of history. If you'd like to get in touch with Simon about his book or the sequels to come or just to chat about early English history you can contact him through the following details:

Email address:
simonphelpsauthor@gmail.com

Facebook page:
www.facebook.com/simonphelpsauthor

Printed in Poland
by Amazon Fulfillment
Poland Sp. z o.o., Wrocław

62222300R00171